THE

FEAR
of
INTIMACY

KENADEE BRYANT

First paperback edition March 27, 2025

Book design by Booksnmoods
Edited by: Sara Tallary and Simply Write

ISBN: 979-8-9913333-2-0 (paperback)
ISBN: 979-8-9913333-3-7 (ebook)

PLAYLIST

The Bolter by Taylor Swift

I Dare You- Rascal Flatts/ Jonas Brothers

Hands On by Austin Giorgio

Guilty As Sin by Taylor Swift

Ordinary by Alex Warren

Cost Me Time by Austin Giorgio

Kiss Me Again by We Are The In Crowd

Love You A Little Bit by Tanner Adell

Butterflies by Abe Parker

Baby I Am by Dalton Dover

DEDICATION

For those who have been strong enough to realize they deserve more.

And for those who have always wanted a kinky hockey player.

WARNING

Slight trigger warning:

Mention of past sexual abuse.
Explicit Sex Scenes

TASHA

"**Y**ou do realize something will go wrong on this vacation, right?" I said through the phone as I moved around my office.

"Don't say that. You'll jinx us!" my best friend Josie Scott scolded with a laugh, but I was right. Something always went wrong on vacations, whether you forgot to pack underwear, got the wrong hotel room, or worse, missed your flight, thanks to delays.

"Are you excited to go?" I asked, although I already knew the answer. This vacation was the only thing Josie could talk about for the last few weeks. Literally every single day, my phone had at least two to three messages from Josie talking about this trip.

When her boyfriend, Wyatt Boone, the captain of the Toronto Knights hockey team, won the Cup Championship game a few months ago, Josie threw a small party to celebrate. But with the hockey season about to start again, Jo thought why not take a trip with our entire group of friends to celebrate?

After aligning everyone's schedules, all eight of us were

set to go to *Whitsunday Island*. A beautiful island off the coast of Australia that looked beyond beautiful in the photos Josie sent to the group chat. Bright blue waters and gorgeous, sandy beaches. A cute little town.

"Of course! Are you packed yet?"

"Jo, we leave in four days."

"So? You don't want to forget anything."

I'd known Josie since University and knew how she could get. She was the type to pack days ahead and then stress that she forgot something. It wouldn't surprise me if she already had her bags packed and sitting by the door, ready to go. She was the "airport dad" who got there hours early and made sure everyone had their tickets and waited at the terminal way earlier than needed.

"I promise I'll start packing when I get home from work," I said as I went over to my desk to grab my notepad. My next patient was set to come any moment.

"Remember, we'll be there for five days," she reminded me.

"Thanks, Mom," I teased, knowing she meant well. "I better go, babe. I have a patient coming. I'll text you later."

I barely ended the call when a knock sounded on my office door.

"Come in," I called out, snatching up a pen as soon as the door opened. I smiled at the sight of my next patient, a young seventeen-year-old girl who I'd been seeing for the past three months.

"How have you been, Lily?" I asked as I took a seat in my chair across from hers.

"I've been good."

Inwardly, I cheered at the fact she didn't stutter and was actually looking at my face. When Lily first came to me, she couldn't sit still for longer than a minute, always messing with her hands, clothing, or hair. She wouldn't even look up at me the first week. The poor girl had such bad social anxiety, along with a few other things, that brought her here.

I was pleased with the progress we had made these last few months. In just a short amount of time, I'd seen Lily slowly come out of her shell more and more. She held conversations now and even cracked some jokes.

It was people, or kids, like Lily, that made me love my job as a counselor. A lot of people assumed I was a psychiatrist, and I guess in a way I was, but I didn't prescribe medication. I was here to listen to anyone who needed someone to talk to. To be the soundboard for whatever they were going through.

While I loved my job, it was also very draining. It could be incredibly hard hearing things from patients. Some days were more emotionally draining than others, but knowing I'd made a little difference in someone's life made it all worth it.

I hadn't always known I wanted to be a counselor. Ever since I could remember, it was an unwritten rule that I would follow in my parent's footsteps. Be a part of the family business, but it was the last thing I wanted. I wanted to pave my own path and do something that gave me a purpose of my own.

It wasn't until the end of my freshman year in university when I took a psychology class that I knew what I wanted to do. Growing up, I may not have had someone who listened to me, but I could be that for someone else.

"How has school been?" I asked as I settled back in my chair.

"It's been good."

With that, Lily launched into how her week went. The once shy girl talked animatedly while I gladly sat back and let her talk. "I-I think I'm going to go hang out with some girls from school on Friday," Lily said, her words surprising me.

3

"Oh really?" That was the first time she'd ever mentioned hanging out with anyone from school. One of the main reasons her parents brought her to me was because she wasn't making friends. She was shutting herself off from talking or meeting people. So, hearing her say this brought a smile to my face.

"A girl from my history class asked me," Lily said shyly. She played with her fingers as she spoke, but I could tell from her body language that she was suppressing her excitement.

"That's great, Lily. What are you guys going to do?"

"Maybe go to the mall and see a movie."

"I'm proud of you, Lily. This is a big step for you. Going out and making friends is exciting."

"Yeah," she whispered. I knew she was nervous, and I had a feeling she might try to talk herself out of going. Setting my notepad aside, I sat forward a bit.

"I promise it will be fun. Just be yourself and don't over-think it. Be in the here and now, okay?" My voice was gentle as I spoke. I didn't want to push her, but I also wanted her to know she didn't need to be in her head and worry. Which I knew she tended to do.

"O-Okay, I can do that." She nodded.

"But always remember, if you don't like something or don't want to do anything, say something or call your parents, okay?" Again, she nodded. Seeing the clock above her hit an hour, I slowly stood up. "When I get back, you can tell me all about it." Definitely going to be one appointment I was looking forward to having.

"Thank you, Ms. Davis." When Lily stood her shoulders were less by her ears and her head was held a bit higher.

"Anytime, Lily." I gave her an encouraging smile as I led her out of my office with the promise to see her soon. I made a quick note in my notepad to call her parents and see about cutting her appointments down.

Once Lily was gone, I closed my office door and sat back in my chair with a sigh. It was always a good day when you saw the self-growth of a patient firsthand, especially someone as young as Lily. With no one else scheduled for today, I let myself sit there a bit longer, rolling my neck at the stress building in my shoulders.

With it already being four thirty, I tapped my intercom, telling the girl at the front desk she could go home early. No point in keeping her here when it was just me. The building I worked in had multiple counselors, along with medical offices. All five of us had our own offices but shared two assistants.

With everyone gone, I welcomed the peace and quiet as I twirled in my office chair. I had some paperwork I needed to get done and sorted before our trip, but I took a moment for myself. With back-to-back patients, I was drained.

Knowing that the sooner I got my work done, the sooner I could go home to a glass of wine, I groaned inwardly. I sat up and got to work on finishing up some things, the desire to go home urging me to get it done faster.

No sooner had I picked up my pen, my phone rang. I didn't bother looking at the name flashing across the screen, figuring it was Josie or one of our other girlfriends.

"Hello?"

"Tasha." The voice belonged to neither of those options. I sat up straight and gripped my pen.

"Mother." I couldn't remember the last time I talked to my mom. It wasn't often she or my father reached out.

"How have you been?" Normally, that kind of question would come with actual curiosity from people but not my mother. No, it was more of a courtesy to ask but came with an underlying meaning of 'I don't really care.'

"Good, I—" I started to answer when she cut me off.

"You won't believe who your father and I ran into the other day.

5

Ryan..." My mother went off about some son of a wealthy businessman that I had the displeasure of meeting a few times.

Back in the day, my parents would drag me to socialite events, forcing me to interact with people my age who had rich parents like my own. Something I despised. I hated being paraded around by my parents like I was some prized toy.

My parents cared more about how people saw them on the outside than anything else. Didn't care that their only daughter was miserable. Didn't care that she only wanted their attention, not their money.

Not wanting to go down that rabbit hole right now, I pinched the bridge of my nose and interrupted my mom.

"Why did you call, Mom?"

"I can't call and talk to my daughter?" We both knew that was a lie. She didn't call just to talk to me. She wouldn't listen even if I did speak. *"I wanted to see if you would be attending our yearly gala in a few weeks."*

Ah, there it was. I knew there was a reason behind this phone call, seeing as it's been ages since we last spoke.

I had forgotten that the gala my parents threw every year was coming up. It was supposed to be some charity event but instead it was a party where the wealthiest socialites of Toronto got together to talk business and flaunt their money. For me, it was an affair where I had to wear a suffocating gown and make stupid small talk with people who looked down their noses at everyone.

My mother worded it like I had a choice in going. I didn't. I was expected to go every year. Robert and Jennifer Davis couldn't have their only daughter not show up to the biggest socialite party of the year. With them having the biggest law firm in Toronto, there were expectations that I had to uphold. This gala being one of them.

"I'll have to see about work."

"You're still working at that place?" I didn't miss the disdain in her voice as she spoke about my job. A job she nor my father fully approved of. They wanted me to come work for them at their law firm. When I told them no, I disappointed them to no end, something they loved to remind me of whenever they had the chance.

"Yes, Mom, I am." I heard her scoff through the phone. It made me grind my teeth together. And this is why I was glad we only talked a few times a year and rarely saw each other in person. I could picture my mom clear as day sticking her nose up and glaring down at me.

"Well, make sure your schedule is clear for the 25th." Her tone left no room for argument. I was going whether I liked it or not. *"If you bring someone, try for a suitable date."* This time, I really had to clench my jaw together to stop from saying something.

A few years ago, I took Josie with me, needing someone by my side. One look at her and my parents immediately deemed her unfit. She didn't come from a wealthy family or a family of status, so in their eyes she wasn't good enough to be my friend. Or be in attendance at one of their functions. It had taken everything in me that day not to say anything.

"I have to go. See you in a few weeks." Not even waiting for a reply back, my mother ended the call. I pulled my phone away from my ear and stared at my screen until it turned black.

Always a joy talking to her. It was basically a call telling me I better be at the gala in a few weeks and nothing else. Not once did she care to know how I was doing or about anything in my life.

Tears pricked the back of my eyes. I wasn't sure why I still wanted their love and acceptance. I learned long ago that it would never happen, yet there was still a small part of me that hoped one day they would. I should know better than to get my hopes up about anything having to do with them.

Blinking back tears, I took a few breaths before focusing on the paperwork in front of me. There was no point in letting her get to me.

Just brush it off, Tasha.

God, I really did need this vacation.

2

TASHA

I hated packing. There was just something about it that was the absolute worst. I loved going on the trip, but having to somehow fit outfits, shoes, and makeup in a suitcase was the bane of my existence. And don't get me started on having to repack to come home or how you somehow had even less space and nothing seemed to fit right in your suitcase.

I was currently sitting on the floor of my bedroom with my suitcase on my bed, overflowing with clothes. I was taking a break, drinking a glass of wine, before I tackled folding it all and trying to make it fit. I was more than tempted to push it off and deal with it tomorrow, but I knew I was just putting off the inevitable.

Tomorrow was going to be a busy day making sure everything at work was settled while I was gone. I had a few patients that I still had to call and inform I'd be gone for a week. So packing tonight would be the smarter option for sure, especially since I didn't do it last night after work like I said I would.

I was in the middle of telling myself one more minute when a knock sounded on my door. Confused about who would be there, I padded over and peeked through the peephole. A grin stretched across my face at the sight on the other side of the door.

"Guys!" I yanked the door open to find three of my best friends. Josie Scott, Lydia Ellis, and Mila Jones standing there grinning with Josie holding a bottle of wine. "Did I forget girl's night?"

I stepped aside, letting the three in, and shut the door behind me.

"The guys wanted to do a last minute poker night, so I thought why not come and hang out?" Josie moved toward my kitchen in search of glasses.

"And to see if you've packed yet," Lydia whispered as she passed by. I snorted, not at all surprised. Josie knew I'd put off packing until the last minute. I followed the girls into my kitchen, glad that they dropped by—and if I was being honest, that they were giving me a distraction.

"Are you girls ready to go on vacation?" Mila asked as I helped pour four glasses of wine and handed them out.

"Yes. I need to be sitting on the beach drinking a margarita." Lydia let out a groan-like moan. "Haven't taken a vacation in so long."

"That's cause you are a workaholic." Josie shot Lydia a motherly look. Lydia may have been the oldest at twenty-nine and Josie's boss, but Josie was definitely the mom of our group.

"I won't deny that." Lydia just shrugged. Hard for her not to be a workaholic when she owned one of the fastest-growing magazines in Toronto. *Fusion Weekly* started off as a small magazine with few employees, but was now a magazine where people got to see everything that went on in the city. I wouldn't be surprised if Lydia's next move was getting it into all stores across the province.

"This will be the perfect trip for all of us to unwind." Josie said over her shoulder, headed for my living room. Mila flashed me a wide grin before schooling her expression. This trip had a lot more in store than Josie knew.

"Can't wait to show off some of the bikinis I bought. I've been hiding them from Bryton so he would be surprised."

"I did the same thing." Josie flung her legs onto mine as I settled on the couch. From the look on both Josie and Mila's faces, their boyfriends had no clue what was about to hit them. Mila's boyfriend, Bryton Young, star left winger to the Toronto Knights, was in for a big surprise.

When I met Mila a year ago, I instantly knew we'd be close friends. She had the same spontaneity about her that I had. The two of us were definitely the troublemakers of our girl group. Where Josie typically settled my crazy ideas, Mila encouraged them. Like the time we went to karaoke night downtown and got kicked out for dancing on the tables. Of course Josie nor Lydia participated, but Mila and I had a blast.

"Maybe I can find a hot Australian man while we're there," Lydia mused, sipping her drink on the other side of Josie.

"What about Landon?" Mila asked.

"What about him? He could fall into the ocean for all I care." Lydia shrugged. The relationship between her and Wyatt's older brother, Landon, was an interesting one. The two claimed to hate each other, but there was clearly something there. The sexual tension between the two was almost stifling.

"Uh-huh." I smirked over the lip of my wine glass. "Did you pack any skimpy bikinis?" I asked. When she went silent, all three of us howled in laughter. She could deny it all she wanted, but there was definitely something between the two of them.

As the conversation shifted and the girls kept talking, I found myself sitting there silently sipping my wine, replaying the conversation I had with my mother the day before. Her words still echoed in my head, as well as the feelings that stirred up every time I talked to my parents. In only a few words, she managed to make me feel like a child. A child who would do anything for their love, even though I knew I wouldn't get it. I was a grown woman, and yet here I was, still striving for my parent's approval and affection.

"Hey, you okay?" Josie sat up, nudging me with her knee. "You've been a bit quiet."

"Yeah, I'm good." I sent her a fake smile, one she clearly saw through. The look she sent me had me nodding. We'd known each other for so long. Just one glance and we knew what was going on in the other's head. The look in my eye was probably enough for her to know it was my parents.

Every time they called or forced me to attend some event for them, Josie had been by my side. There to cheer me up and make me feel better. Without her, I was pretty sure I would have gone crazy. After all these years, she was more of a sister than a best friend.

With a small sigh, she untangled her legs from her lap and moved to sit next to me, leaning into my side. Josie really was my ride-or-die. The moment I met her freshman year, the two of us bonded like no other. She was the yin to my yang. Where Josie was more relaxed and a rule follower, I was the opposite.

Part of why I liked to push the boundaries sometimes was to get a reaction out of my parents. To see if they paid enough attention to notice the things I did. One of the only times they noticed was when I dyed my hair bright pink before a big event they wanted me to go to. All I got was a look before they walked out the door, leaving me home without another word.

Josie and I evened each other out. I pulled her out of her shell a bit, and she kept me in line. She did a good job curbing my irrational ideas...usually.

Not wanting to focus on my parents anymore, I forced them to the back of my mind. They didn't deserve to take up space in my head. Not when I was surrounded by people who actually did care about me.

"There is one thing I, for sure, want to do while we're on vacation," Mila said a few minutes later. "I looked up a dance club a few blocks away from our hotel that we have to go to."

"Oh, a dance club." Lydia perked up.

"We can make it a girl's night or drag the boys, but it looks really fun."

"I'm in." Josie grinned next to me before gently nudging my shoulder.

"Me too." I nodded. "Let me propose a toast." I sat up and lifted my wine glass. "To an amazing vacation we won't forget."

"I second that." Josie clinked glasses with mine.

"To an awesome vacation." Mila and Lydia tapped their glasses against ours with the biggest grins in the world.

"And possibly getting dick!" Lydia cheered. Laughing loudly, we all clinked our wine glasses together and cheered.

A COUPLE OF HOURS LATER, we were still sitting on my couch, drinking wine and laughing about some story Mila was telling us. We were all a tiny bit tipsy, thanks to the two bottles of alcohol.

"We were in the middle of doing it when Bryton slipped and ended up smashing his forehead into the table. Cut his face and everything." Mila giggled as she continued her story. "But it didn't stop him, he just went right back to it."

"No, he didn't!" Josie gasped.

"Was still amazing."

All of us girls cackled at the image.

"I'll never see Bryton in the same light." I shook my head.

We were all busy laughing when a knock sounded at the front door. Stumbling past the girl's legs, I headed for it and flung it open. It took me a second to register who was just beyond the threshold.

"Hey," the deep voice said as I blinked up at the hulking body blocking the hallway.

"What are you doing here?" The words slipped out as I stared at Trevor Hall, star right winger to the Toronto Knights. Beside him was Wyatt, his best friend, who my eyes flicked to for a beat.

"Lovely to see you too." With a hand on my shoulder, Trevor gently moved me to the side so he could slip inside.

"Hey, Tasha." Wyatt, who was also Josie's boyfriend, smiled at me in greeting as he stepped into my apartment. Bryton followed behind him with a nod.

While my apartment wasn't that small, having three huge hockey players made it feel tiny. Stepping back into the living room, I scrunched my nose at the sight of both Josie and Mila kissing their boyfriends. On the far side of the couch, Lydia threw back the rest of her drink.

"What are you guys doing here?" Josie asked once she stopped sucking face with Wyatt.

"Knew you would be drinking so figured why not come and pick you up," Wyatt said with a shrug.

"Then what is he doing here?" I pointed to Trevor, who stood off to the side, hands in his pockets, as he looked around my apartment.

"Aw, did you miss me, Tasha?" The way he said it had me rolling my eyes, but it didn't stop the small flutter in my chest. Damn him for being so attractive. The scruff, the semi-crooked nose from playing hockey. There was even a small scar near his eyebrow that somehow made him look ten times hotter.

It had been a little bit since I last saw him. I was busy with work, and he was focused on practices with the team. With the season just around the corner, Coach Barnum had been working the team nonstop. The Toronto Knights may have won the Cup Championship last year, but that didn't mean they could go easy this next season.

I glanced away, trying my best not to flush under Trevor's gaze. I wasn't typically someone who got flustered, but for some reason, Trevor Hall made me blush like a teenage girl.

"Ready to go home?" Wyatt asked, holding Josie close. Again, I looked away at the way they both looked at each other. Sometimes, it was too much seeing how in love the two were.

"Yeah, but first," Josie stepped back so she could see all of us, "in two days everyone needs to be at the airport at seven a.m. sharp. That way, if any of you are late, we still have plenty of time."

"Jo, our flight doesn't even leave until nine thirty," Trevor said with a pout. I already knew he was giving Josie a look for having to be up so early. Not that I blamed him. To be at the airport at seven meant waking up at five to shower and ensure everything was ready to go.

"Trev, we all know you're going to sleep through your alarm. This way, you can still make it to the airport and not be late," Josie said, almost scolding him like a mother would.

Out of everyone, Trevor was definitely going to be the one late to the airport.

I was glad we had someone taking the lead with the vacation itinerary and making sure everyone was set to go. Knowing how our group was, we'd have someone oversleep and miss our flight or do something stupid. Josie was the perfect person to keep us all in line. Plus, no one was going to ruin this trip for her. They weren't allowed to.

"And don't forget your passports," Josie added, looking at each of us. I ducked my head at the way Trevor put his hand up to salute her. Mila giggled before smothering it in Bryton's shoulder.

"Kay, I'm out of here," Lydia said, standing up.

"We'll give you a ride," Wyatt offered.

In a matter of minutes, the girls had their belongings and filed out the door with the promise to talk in the morning. Josie gave me a quick hug before pulling Wyatt out the door, leaving Trevor and me.

I could feel his gaze on me as I moved around the living room, grabbing wine glasses to discard in the kitchen. This was the first time the two of us had been completely alone in the last five months. I'd done all I could to avoid it, especially since the awkward night we shared months ago during one of Josie's parties.

After what happened, I kept my distance. Partly because of my pride but also due to embarrassment. Keeping my gaze down, I finally spoke.

"Anything else you need?" My skin tingled under his gaze. Trevor was quiet for a moment before I saw him step toward the door out the corner of my eye.

"All good. Have a good night, Tasha." The way he said my name made my breath hitch in my chest. I glanced up and met his eyes right as he paused in the doorway. His green eyes were all I could see and focus on. The corner of his lip quirked into a smirk that made my stomach clench before he disappeared out the door.

I stared at the empty spot for a good minute before shaking my head. Going on vacation with Trevor was going to be interesting, especially since I was still trying to figure out how to fight the spark that lingered between us.

3

TASHA

"There you are! Where have you been?" was the first thing Josie said the moment she saw me at the airport.

"Uh, security?"

"It's seven thirty!"

I sent a look over her shoulder at Wyatt. He just shrugged and took a sip from his coffee. *Asshole,* I mouthed at him, which only made him grin.

"There was a long line at security," I said, which actually wasn't a lie. For being so early, you'd think there wouldn't be so many people but apparently not. The line to check my bag was just as bad.

"Where's Mila and Bryton?" Josie looked around me as if they would just suddenly appear.

"I saw them in line a few minutes ago. Mila said something about getting a coffee first." I held up my own cup of caffeine that I stopped to get once I was through security. I was going to need a lot of it to get through the day's flights. "Where are the others?"

"Landon went to the bathroom and Lydia went to the gift shop I think," Wyatt said.

"Oh." I looked at Josie.

"Lydia is avoiding Landon." Josie whispered. Ah. It was going to be an interesting vacation for the two of them since we were literally about to be on an island together for five days.

"Trevor texted me that he was on his way twenty minutes ago," Wyatt added.

"See, this is why I said to get here early," Josie muttered under her breath. Poor Josie was going to have an aneurysm before we even boarded our flight.

"Everything will be okay, babe." Wyatt wrapped his arm around her waist and tugged her back into him. I watched her relax in his hold. When he leaned down to whisper something in her ear, I looked down at my phone.

"They are disgusting," Lydia suddenly piped up next to me. I laughed at the way Lydia said it. With a mix of contempt and jealousy. I silently agreed with her, though.

Wyatt and Josie were probably the cutest couple I'd ever seen. The two of them melded so well together, and Wyatt literally worshipped the ground she walked on. I'd never seen my best friend so happy. From the moment the two met in their apartment building elevator, it was game over. Who knew getting stuck in an elevator with a stranger would lead to something so amazing?

Josie deserved that. She deserved a man like Wyatt. Someone who would put her first and love her until the end of time. He saw her broken pieces and helped her put them back together. The first time I ever saw them interact, I knew they were endgame.

While I was happy for them, there was this flare of jealousy inside of me. Not because I wanted Wyatt for myself. It was clear he only had eyes for Josie. But I wanted someone to look at me like he did her. Like she was the air he breathed. No one had ever looked at me like that. And sometimes, I wondered if I'd ever get lucky enough to have that same thing.

"At least I have you to get drunk with." Lydia nudged me with her hip, jerking my attention away from the happy couple.

"We can get drunk together," I promised. Being on a trip with two happy couples was definitely going to drive us to the bar.

"As soon as we land, I'm getting a margarita," Lydia said before moving around me to go put her bag down by Josie and Wyatt's.

With plenty of time before our flight, I let Josie know I was going to walk around for a few minutes. I didn't want to sit longer than I had to since our flight was going to be brutal. Twenty-four hours with two layovers. The itinerary literally said it took a full day to get there. Only Josie would pick the farthest place to vacation.

There were a few benefits that came with knowing Wyatt, Bryton, and Trevor, though. Being who they were, we were able to get first-class seats instead of being stuck in the back of the plane. At first, I was pissed at them for using their name to bump us up to first class, but after realizing the flight was as long as it was, I relented. Only because I didn't want to sit in a small cramped chair for twelve plus hours.

Walking around the airport for about thirty minutes, I finally made my way back to our gate. My body vibrated with excitement, with the intense need to get the show on the road. Arriving at the airport and having to wait was always the worst, especially when you got there hours before you were even set to leave.

The area around our gate was a bit busier when I got back, making me weave in between people and their luggage.

I could barely see my group of friends huddled slightly off to the side near a wide span of windows. I didn't miss the way some people kept looking in their direction as I got closer. Being the three biggest hockey players in Toronto, they all gained attention no matter where they went. I made a mental bet with myself that at least five people would come up to them before our flight was called.

I felt bad for them, seeing firsthand how intense the paparazzi and fans could be. There had been a few occasions when all of us got dinner and we came out of the restaurant to people snapping photos of us. Of course, I got it less than Josie or Mila since they were dating Wyatt and Bryton.

Unfortunately, I had experience with my picture being taken quite a few times, thanks to my parent's socialite parties, but having a camera shoved in your face is never fun or easy.

I am proud of Josie for handling it as well as she does, though. The first time the press learned about her and Wyatt's relationship she freaked, as would anyone, but now she wasn't bothered by it. Josie knew it came with the territory of dating the golden player of the Knights.

"I fully plan on sleeping the entire time." I caught the end of Bryton's sentence.

"Ask me again why we agreed to go somewhere so far away and fourteen hours ahead of us?" Lydia questioned.

"It better be worth it," Landon muttered. My eyes looked at the pair. For two people that claimed to hate one another, they stood awfully close. I noticed the way Landon kept peeking over at Lydia without her knowing. Just quick glances but enough to show he felt some sort of way about the firecracker that was one of my best friends.

"I brought playing cards," Trevor's voice spoke up a second later. My eyes drifted to him reluctantly. Looking at him, I had to stop myself from biting my lip. Clad in a pair of black joggers and a gray sweatshirt with his brown hair mused, he looked like he just rolled out of bed. But despite that, he still was the most attractive man I had ever met.

I hated that. Hated that he was attractive and a good guy. It wasn't often you found both in a guy, let alone a hockey player. Trevor may have been famous, but it didn't seem like it had gone to his head. It was clear he was a ladies' man but from what I saw over the last few months, he wasn't the cocky fuckboy that I initially thought he was.

All of that just made it harder to suppress certain feelings. Especially the ones that came up after he left my apartment two nights ago.

"Don't let Tasha play you. She's great at cards." Josie laughed as Trevor's eyes met mine. Ignoring the zap of electricity that ran through me, I let the corner of my lips tilt up in a smirk. Something close to surprise flitted across Trevor's face before he returned a similar expression.

"We'll see about that." I didn't miss the competitive look on his face. Of course, as a professional athlete, he was very competitive. Our game nights turned into more than a simple night of having fun. More often than not, they were comprised of yelling and claiming someone cheated or wasn't being fair.

"I'd hate to kick your ass," I said.

"Oh, kinky. I can bend over if you'd like." I narrowed my eyes at his words, my inner competitive side coming out. Kicking Trevor's ass at cards was the perfect way to start this vacation.

"YOU ARE CHEATING!" Trevor practically yelled.

"I am not!" I narrowed my eyes at his accusation.

"Yes, you are! There is no way you've won this many hands. Stand up." Trevor shot back. Trevor's hands came over to lift my leg, as if he'd find cards underneath me, causing me to slap it away.

"I am not standing up." I said.

"You're hiding cards under you, I know it." He reached for me again. I slapped his hand once more and shook my head.

"You just can't stand losing." I reached for the stack of cards on the little table dividing us.

"I can handle losing perfectly fine," Trevor retorted, making me snort. *Yeah, right.*

We'd been on the airplane for six hours already, even though it already felt like ten. Being in first class was definitely better than being in coach, though. Instead of being stuck in a small chair surrounded by people, I was seated in a pretty roomie area that offered more space to recline than I could imagine.

The first five hours weren't bad. We all had seats by each other so we could easily talk. I spent most of that time talking to Josie and Mila while Lydia slept. Almost the entire time Trevor kept prodding me to play cards with him. Every few minutes, he would poke my arm or interrupt my conversation with the others until I finally agreed.

So now, an hour later, we were playing our seventh round of blackjack. I'd won six of those seven, much to Trevor's dismay. With each hand I won, he grew more and more suspicious that I was cheating. Wasn't my fault he just sucked…and had a horrible poker face. Every time he had a bad hand, the corner of his mouth would twitch. When he had a good hand, his fingers would tap the cards. It made him all too easy to read.

"We can play something else," I offered, although I had no problem kicking his ass some more. I bet he was happy I declined putting money on the table. If I had, I would have quite the stash now.

"One more round," he all but demanded.

"Fine by me." I smirked, shuffling the cards in my hands.

"How did you get so good at cards?" Trevor asked, his eyes watching me shuffle. It was odd but the act of manipulating the cards soothed me. The sound, the feel of them in my hands.

"I had a lot of time when I was younger," I answered. Trevor sat there waiting for me to continue. "My parents weren't around much when I was little, and there was only so much TV or reading I could take. So, I learned how to play cards," I said with a shrug.

"You played by yourself?"

"Yeah." I avoided his gaze, knowing how pathetic it sounded.

I really didn't have the right to complain or do the whole *"woe is me"* thing because my parents weren't around. I still had everything I needed. Instead of giving me their time, though, my parents gave me everything else. Everything from the newest toys to a brand new car.

"Shitty parents are the worst." Trevor's response had my snapping my head up. He was looking at me with a knowing expression, like he knew what I was talking about. I opened my mouth to say something, but he stopped me. "What are we playing this time?"

He was changing the subject, and I found myself all too grateful for it. I didn't like talking about my family, and by the sound of it, neither did Trevor. With the corner of my mouth tilted up, I shuffled the cards one last time and dealt them out.

Looked like Trevor and I had something in common after all.

"Can I get you anything?" the same voice that was just there five minutes ago asked. I resisted an eye roll. The same flight attendant had come by our seats at least three times in the last twenty minutes. Each time asking only Trevor if he needed anything while ignoring me completely.

"I'm alright, thank you," Trevor politely declined.

"Just give me a wave if you do."

From the corner of my eye, I saw her place her hand on his arm and give it a squeeze. The flight attendant slowly let go and walked away, but I knew she was still staring at Trevor. Once she was out of hearing range, I snorted into my book.

"What?"

"Nothing." I kept my gaze on the book in my hands.

"Nuh-uh, you snorted. Why?"

I put my book down and glanced over the divider at him. "Are you blind?" The look he sent me had me holding back a laugh. "The flight attendant is flirting with you."

"She's doing her job." He shook his head.

"Yeah, cause asking someone if they need anything *four* times is her job."

"In case you didn't know, I am quite a big deal around here." He puffed his chest out and wiggled his eyebrows at me.

"Known as the biggest dork? Yeah."

"You're just jealous of my dorkiness." He said.

"That's not a word." I pointed out.

"It is now."

My lips threatened breaking out into a smile. I turned back to my book so he couldn't see the amusement written on my face. I hated how my guard dropped around him so easily. Just one of his earth-shattering smiles and the walls I'd built crumbled around my feet.

"I thought you might need one of these." That all too familiar voice spoke yet again. I looked over just as the same flight attendant walked up to Trevor. In her hands, she had a blanket even though she already passed some out a few hours before. I met Trevor's eyes and sent him a look that said, *"told you."*

"I…" For a guy who was such a ladies' man, he seemed unsure of what to say. The woman stared down at him with a look that said she was more than willing to meet him in the bathroom. Something flared in my chest at the message behind it.

"Actually, I'll take that," I said, standing up and extending my hand for the blanket. For the first time since she started coming over, she seemed to notice me. Her eyes looked me up and down, taking in my worn black leggings that were more gray from how many times I'd worn and washed them and the baggy sweatshirt I donned. I didn't exactly look my best, and the tilt of her lips let me know it.

It didn't faze me. I had plenty of people, mostly girls, look at me like that. You didn't grow up with parents like mine, going to socialite parties where every single person there judged you and still cared about what people thought of you. I had plenty of fake friends over the years to know a fake smile when I saw one. "The blanket?" I prompted, sending her the same terse smile back. *Don't play a fake game with someone who's played it longer.*

A flash of anger crossed her face before she schooled her expression and handed the blanket over, clearly not thrilled at me for interrupting her flirting with Trevor. Like she truly thought Trevor would instantly jump up and follow her back to the bathroom.

"Thanks." I sat back down and made a show of putting it over my legs. When she still hadn't moved, I raised an eyebrow. "I think we're good now." I didn't care that my voice came out rude or that my expression was less than friendly. Maybe now she'd get the hint. I was getting tired of seeing her come around every few minutes.

I understood that Trevor was attractive. Okay, he was more than attractive, but she didn't need to prance around and flirt with him every few seconds. Especially not when I was sitting right there the entire time.

The look she cut me only made my eyes narrow even more. Turning to Trevor, she plastered on her stupid smile and squeezed his arm again. Looking at Trevor, I noticed how uncomfortable he seemed as he leaned away from her. Clenching my jaw, irritation suddenly filled me. My eyes were glued to her hand on his arm as I sat up.

"I suggest you move your hand before I come over there and do it myself." My voice was like ice. Both her and Trevor's heads turned in my direction. "Your. Hand."

She looked at me and then her hand, still not moving it. From the corner of my eye, I could see Trevor trying to move his arm away, which just further pissed me off.

"I have no issue telling your supervisor you're harassing passengers." And I was dead serious. Just because she found someone attractive didn't mean she could go around touching them without their consent.

The color leached from her face at my words. I was normally the nicest person, but I could also be the biggest bitch you'd ever met. I had no problem being one either. She finally seemed to understand and snatched her hand back. I didn't look away from her as she slowly backed up a step.

"If we need anything, we will let you know." I didn't bother giving her a fake smile this time. She nodded once, my words finally seeming to sink in. "Until then, don't come back." I didn't miss the slight flinch on her face at my words. Not one part of me felt bad.

Without another word, the flight attendant left, this time not sparing Trevor another glance. Good.

Still feeling bothered at the way she touched him, I sat back in my seat, my hands shaking slightly as I grabbed my book once again. I could feel Trevor's gaze on me, but I forced myself to keep my eyes on the page I last read.

It took everything I had not to let certain memories flood my mind. Memories I tried so hard the past year to get rid of. Memories that ruined me inside and out.

"Thank you." Trevor's voice broke through the fog, threatening to drag me under. I gave him a small nod in return. "You didn't have to do that."

"Yeah, well, I don't like people touching others without their consent."

My words were still clipped as I stared at my book, all the words on the page blending together. Trevor opened his mouth as if to say more, but he seemed to understand I wasn't in the mood for anything else. Gripping my book with both hands, I ignored him and everyone around me as I tried not to drown in my past.

4

TASHA

Two layovers and many, *many* hours later, we were finally on our way to Whitsunday Island. Everyone was extremely exhausted, but I could feel the excitement building the closer we got to the hotel. Because of where it was, the only way in was on a boat, which only ran at certain times, so once we were on the island, there really wasn't a way off.

The tour guide on the boat listed off facts about the island, but I tuned him out as I gazed out at the water. I was squeezed between Mila and the side of the boat, the others scattered around with a few other tourists.

"The island has…" The guy was saying, but it went in one ear and out the other. I closed my eyes and leaned my head back, relishing in the way the wind whipped at my face as the salty breeze of the ocean filled my nose. The air nipped at my skin, causing goosebumps to pebble along my arms, but the sun brushed them away.

Turning my head to the side, I looked down at the water. The pictures I saw online did not do it an ounce of justice.

The closer we got to the hotel, the clearer and bluer it got. So clear that I wanted to dip my hand in.

We weren't even there yet, but that didn't stop me from noticing how much clearer my mind was already. After my moment with the flight attendant, things got awkward between Trevor and me. Once I calmed down enough to think rationally, a wave of embarrassment hit me in full force.

My past clouded my judgment and made me overreact. But that lady didn't need to be so touchy—not with anyone—so I didn't really feel all that bad about how I reacted. It was more embarrassing for me that Trevor witnessed it all go down. Looking back on it from a different angle, even his, I had totally acted like a jealous girlfriend when I was far from one.

Thankfully, I was spared more humiliation when I was seated next to Lydia for the next flight while Trevor sat with Landon. I knew I had to apologize and tried to make an attempt when we got off the plane, but it got so hectic collecting our baggage and making it to the boat in time for its departure that I wasn't able to.

Feeling someone's eyes on me, I looked away from the water and met a pair of stunning green eyes. The only eyes that seemed to make the ocean's color pale in comparison.

Trevor was sitting across the boat from me. His big body squished between Lydia and a random stranger. I had to pinch my lips together to stop myself from laughing at the way his body didn't fit on the little bench, his long legs cramped and almost pushing up to his chest. His six foot three frame barely fit on the already small boat.

An expression passed over his face, but before I could even process what it was, the feel of the boat slowing underneath me jerked my attention elsewhere.

"Once we dock, we will help you get off. Your luggage

will be taken to your rooms separately," the guide said as he moved around the ferry, giving instructions.

I was itching to get onto land and stretch my legs. According to Australian time, it was only two in the afternoon, even though to us, it felt like eleven at night. We all agreed to try and stay up to beat the jet lag so we could start our actual vacation tomorrow.

I already knew what I was going to do after we checked in. The beach was calling my name, my toes aching to feel the sand and water and the ocean breeze against my skin.

When we docked, I tried to wait patiently to get off, but when this older lady moved like a snail in front of me, I was seconds away from shoving her off myself. I would have done everyone the favor but forced myself to stay back a few steps and let her hobble off.

The moment my feet touched the ground, I let out a sigh. Finally, we made it. Seeing as I was one of the last ones off the boat, I made my way toward my friends, glad we didn't have to carry our bags to our rooms.

"We're here!" Josie squealed as we all stood around each other. Bryton let out an unenthusiastic, "Yay," that had me laughing under my breath. We were happy to be here, but having spent the last day and half traveling we were desperate for some shut-eye.

"How about we all go check in and clean up before meeting to get something to eat? Sound good?" Josie suggested.

There was a chorus of agreements before we all made our way toward what looked like golf carts waiting to take guests up to the hotel. I was tired but the fact that we were now here pushed the exhaustion away.

The ride to the hotel was thankfully short as the carts drove down the paved walkway that led to the hotel. We passed palm trees that extended higher than I could see.

Plush green bushes lined the pathway and I swore I saw a chipmunk run in front of us.

In no time, we were all walking through the front doors of the hotel toward the check-in desk. Josie really outdid herself picking a destination for this vacation. The hotel was incredible. Tall ceilings with glass chandeliers. The marble-looking floor was so squeaky clean I swear I could see my reflection in it. A glance out of the huge windows to the side showed the beach. It was literally only a few steps away.

I was so busy staring longingly at the beach that I missed the others walking ahead of me. By the time I made my way over, the front desk lady was handing Lydia our room key. Since Lydia and I were the only two not in a relationship, we were sharing a room. The same went for Trevor and Landon while Josie and Wyatt took their own room and Mila and Bryton got their own as well.

There was no point in spending extra money to get individual rooms when none of us really cared if we shared. Plus, we were all planning on spending the days doing stuff, not hanging out in our rooms.

Somehow, Wyatt managed to get all of our rooms on the same floor, no doubt using his name. From where I stood, I could hear Josie telling him he had to stop doing that. Her not caring if someone was rich or not was one of the reasons I loved her.

Growing up, most of the friends I had were only friends with me because my parents were wealthy or because their parents were friends with mine. They were always in it for something. So when I met Josie freshman year of university, I expected she would be the same.

Which was why I had no problem admitting that I was the biggest bitch to Josie. For the first few weeks, I flat out ignored her, figuring she'd be the same as every other person I met. But Josie, being Josie, proved she was far from one of those people who took advantage of someone's wealth and status. She never once cared about money with me.

I remember one time the two of us went out to dinner with a few other girls I knew. They all sat around waiting for me to pay. It was the first time I ever saw Josie angry. She snapped at the other girls, demanding that they pay for their own meals and not use me as a piggy bank. It was at that moment I knew she was my ride or die.

"Remind me to kiss Wyatt later for this room," Lydia said as soon as we stepped into our room moments later. I silently agreed. The room was huge. As soon as you walked, there was a living room that could easily fit all eight of us and then some. A kitchenette sat off to the side. To the left of us was a hallway that must have led to the bedrooms. And here I was thinking we'd be sleeping in a room with two queen beds and maybe a mini fridge.

Without another word, Lydia took off to claim her room as I walked over to the two sprawling windows where the view was breathtaking. The ocean was spread out as far as the eye could see, and I could almost hear the waves from here.

Again, the urge to go down and feel the water and sand washed over me. With plenty of time to meet up with the rest of the group, I quickly made my decision.

"I'll be back!" I yelled down the hallway to Lydia before swiping up the hotel key. My luggage wasn't even here yet so it wasn't like I could change anyway.

Heading out to the lobby, I followed the signs that pointed to the beach. The wooden pathway wrapped around the hotel before veering a little until the beach was in sight. I only passed a few people as I went.

The closer I got to the sandy shore, the more the tension in my shoulders eased. Right before reaching the sand, I slipped my flip-flops off and rolled my leggings up to my knees. The soft sand slid between my toes as I slowly waded through it toward the water.

The smell of salt hitting my nose made me smile. The lightest of breezes lifted strands of my hair off my face as I got closer to the surf.

There was something about the beach that I loved. The salty air, the grainy sand that sometimes was hard to walk in, the way it made you feel like you were insignificant to the rest of the world. My parents had a house that sat near the beach and any time I wanted to get away, I would head there and sit on the beach for hours.

Warm water lapped at my ankles as it rolled up onto the shoreline. Closing my eyes, I took a deep breath, the sound of the waves crashing filling my ears. Exhaling, I pushed away all the stress of the last few days. The conversation with my mother and the stupid gala I was going to be forced to go to when I got back. I pushed aside the fact that I was on vacation with a man I embarrassed myself in front of—not once but twice. The same man who did things to my stomach that confused the hell out of me.

I was going to enjoy my time away. Nothing was going to ruin it for me. Not my messed up family, my past, or the stupid feelings that appeared whenever I was around Trevor. This vacation was meant to be fun and relaxing, and that was just what I was going to do.

With that in mind, I opened my eyes and stepped further into the water, ready to make this the best vacation ever.

"WE ARE NOT SWIMMING WITH SHARKS." Josie looked at Wyatt like he lost his mind.

"Babe, it would be so fun." Wyatt tried again.

Biting into a french fry, I watched Wyatt try to convince Josie to go swimming with one of the most agile predators in the ocean. I could pipe up and tell him it was useless trying to get her to do it, seeing as she was deathly afraid of sharks but watching him practically beg was entertaining.

"It's completely safe. You're in a cage, and they can't get you," Wyatt continued. Everyone else sat around the table, eating and watching the two go back and forth. Earlier a worker at the hotel recommended a local restaurant a block away. It was a cute, hole in the wall restaurant that claimed to make *the* best fish and chips. Which they weren't wrong about.

"Have you never seen the videos on the internet?" Josie asked, almost breathless over Wyatt's idea. "The sharks can still get their faces in the cage! You could die."

"Think he knows Josie will ultimately win this one?" Bryton leaned over to whisper in my ear.

"Give it another minute and he will," I whispered back, shoving another fry in my mouth.

"A shark couldn't eat me. I'm way too fast." The entire group laughed at how ridiculous Wyatt sounded. "What, you guys don't think I could win against a shark?" He glanced at his teammates for backup.

"Well…" Bryton trailed off like he didn't know how to answer.

"Well, that's fucked up." Wyatt looked betrayed that no one, not even Landon, his brother, supported him.

"It's okay, babe, we'll still do something fun," Josie said, patting his hand as Wyatt leaned back with a huff. His dreams of getting up close and personal with sharks went up in flames.

Trevor piped in next, his words causing all our eyes to snap to him. "I would have gone with you."

"Nice going," I muttered under my breath as I kicked him under the table. If Josie could kill someone with a glare, Trevor would be six feet under.

"What? It could be fun," Trevor started to say, only for Mila to quickly interrupt.

"How about we go snorkeling?" When no one answered, Mila elbowed Bryton in the side. A strained groan fell from his mouth before he nodded his head in sudden agreement.

"That sounds like fun."

"I'd do it," Lydia added. Thankfully, that helped put an end to Wyatt's idea. While everyone started talking about snorkeling, a sharp pain blossomed over my shin and caused me to jerk in my seat. I looked up and glared at the only person who would kick me. I met Trevor's gaze as his eyes sparkled in amusement.

"What was that for?"

"Payback." He shrugged, taking a huge bite of his hamburger.

"I didn't even kick you that hard," I shot back.

He sent me a look that said, *"And?."*

"I can kick you somewhere higher if you prefer." I plastered a fake smile on my face, making my voice honey sweet even though I felt nothing of the sort.

"If you want to touch my dick, all you have to do is ask." Trevor's words made me choke on my drink. The idiot, having waited until I took a sip to say something in return.

"Tash, you okay?" Mila asked, softly patting me on the back as I tried to give my lungs air. Everyone looked at me while Trevor had a smug smile on his face.

"Wrong tube," I choked out, my coughing dying down. When everyone went back to their conversations and food, I sent Trevor a heated glare.

"Better watch your back Hall," I seethed in a low tone.

At my comment, he just grinned.

"Looking forward to it." His smirk had me rolling my eyes. I swear he got more annoying every time I saw him.

"Aside from snorkeling, what else do we want to do while we are here?" Josie asked.

"I think there are some good hiking trails we could walk," Landon commented.

"Hiking?" Lydia scrunched her nose up at his idea.

"Some of us like doing things outdoors." He sent the small dig back at her. If I thought Wyatt and Josie had a lot of sexual tension, it was nothing compared to these two. Lydia and Landon were clearly into each other but too stubborn to admit it.

They argued like an old married couple. Anyone could see the looks they sent each other when the other wasn't looking. It was only a matter of time before they both cracked and gave into whatever was going on between them. But Lydia was one of the most stubborn people I knew, so I wasn't holding my breath anytime soon.

By the time we finished dinner, we had a few ideas on what we could do: snorkeling, hiking, a boat cruise, a relaxing day on the beach, and a club that Mila had found.

I hung back from the group as we all slowly trudged back to the hotel, exhaustion palpable from the long day we had. The sun was beginning to dip, making the air a bit chillier. Wrapping my hands in the sleeves of my sweatshirt, I watched the two couples in front of me holding hands as they walked. The way their bodies seemed to gravitate toward each other was almost effortless.

Jealousy stabbed at my chest. I was happy for all of them, but it didn't stop the feeling of wanting what they had from consuming me.

"Why are you sulking back here?" a voice cut through my depressing thoughts. I let out an audible sigh as Trevor walked beside me.

"Is it your mission to always annoy me?" I asked.

"It's just so easy to." I glanced over to find him smirking at me. Shaking my head, I looked forward. He stayed quiet for another minute before speaking again. "I want to properly thank you for what you did on the plane."

"I actually want to apologize for that." I wrapped my arms around my waist. "I didn't mean to shove my nose in the situation." It had struck a nerve but just because I had an issue with it didn't mean Trevor did.

"You don't need to apologize for anything, Tasha," Trevor said. "The flight attendant was being too handsy and you were right for calling her out on it."

"Yeah, but—" A hand on my elbow pulled me to a stop.

"Tasha." Trevor's voice begged me to look up at him. Tilting my head back, I met his gaze. "You saw I was uncomfortable and did something about it. Don't ever be sorry for something like that," he said seriously. "Thank you."

The look on his face melted the growing guilt inside of me. Guilt for overstepping in a situation that wasn't any of my business. But hearing him say that eased my worries.

"She should have kept her hands to herself," I mumbled, the thought of her making me angry again. A chuckle drew my attention back to Trevor.

"There's the feisty side."

"I do not have a feisty side." Even I knew that was a lie.

"Uh-huh." The unconvinced look he shot me had me rolling my eyes and shoving him to the side with my shoulder.

"I'd stop while you're ahead." I started walking again, the others pretty far ahead of us now.

"You know, I think you like me, Tasha Davis," Trevor spoke after a moment.

"And where did you get that idea?"

"I have my ways," he answered vaguely, making me scrunch my eyebrows together.

"I think you've taken too many hits to the head. Are you mentally sound?" I asked in a serious voice, looking over at him.

"I can assure you I am perfectly sane."

"Hmm," I hummed.

"But even if you don't like me," Trevor's voice was suddenly right next to my head, his breath against the shell of my ear making me shiver. His voice turned husky, washing over my skin. "I plan on changing that before this vacation is over." I was still trying to comprehend his words when he pulled away from me, gave me a smirk, and jogged toward the others up ahead. I stared after him, his words sinking in.

I plan on changing that before this vacation is over. What the hell did that mean?

Despite my confusion, I couldn't deny the fluttery swoop in my stomach as I stared after him.

5

TREVOR

I really needed to look away from the blonde across from me, but my eyes wouldn't listen. When I did look away, it would only last a second before I was back to staring like a weirdo. I was screwed, and I knew it. I knew it the moment Tasha Davis stepped into my life. Well, more like bulldozed her way into my life.

When Josie talked about her best friend when we first met, I assumed she was someone similar to her—shy, soft-spoken. But none of those things described Tasha. The fiery blonde could crush a man in her high heels without a second glance. She was confident and wasn't hesitant to put a person in their place.

The moment I laid eyes on her, I knew she was going to come into my life and completely wreck it. And not a single part of me cared.

It was no secret that I had been with my fair share of women. But none of them sparked my curiosity as much as Tasha. There was something about her that made my eyes seek her out every time she walked into a room. I was drawn to her in a magnetic sort of way.

Tasha liked to act like she couldn't feel what was between us. That she couldn't sense the electrical current that glowed bright whenever we were around each other. I know she could, even if she wanted to deny it.

Like right now, sitting across from each other at the little diner the hotel had, there was something palpable in the air. I was glad I agreed to come on this vacation. It would give me a chance to have moments alone with her, which were hard to come by these last several months.

Any time we were alone in a room, she would make some excuse to leave or say that one of the girls needed her help. It was beyond frustrating because all I wanted was to have a conversation about what happened. But the last thing I wanted was to push her to talk when she didn't want to. So, for the time being, I let it go, but the two of us were stuck on this island for the next five days. She couldn't get away from me that easily. Just like on the plane.

When we got on, the first thing I noticed was that Landon was next to Tasha, while I sat next to Lydia. I didn't even hesitate in ripping his ticket out of his hand and shoving him mine. Like hell I would pass up the chance to sit next to her for hours. Even if that meant getting an earful from Landon.

I didn't even care that I got my ass kicked at playing cards either. I had no idea she was secretly some poker, card-playing master, but I would take getting my ass beat just to see the way she smiled when she won.

And what she did for me on the plane was... I couldn't really put it into words. I was uncomfortable with the flight attendant coming by every few minutes, purposely touching my arm and flirting. Being who I was, that kind of attention came with certain situations. It was nothing new. I'd gotten used to women blatantly flirting with me and grazing my arm or hand in an attempt to lure me to the bedroom. I just never had someone come to my rescue like Tasha did.

41

She didn't even hesitate to call out the flight attendant. She noticed my discomfort and put a stop to it. It was nice having someone have my back, and I won't lie, it was kind of hot seeing Tasha all worked up and jealous. At that moment, I wanted nothing more than to drag her across the divide on the plane and kiss her.

It was because of that I fully planned on using this vacation to my advantage. We were stuck on this island for the next few days, and somehow, I was going to show Tasha that I had no plans of giving her up anytime soon. Even if the thought of that slightly scared me.

"Everyone good with just laying around the beach today?" Josie's voice jerked my attention away from Tasha.

Today was our first official day on the Island and everyone was still jet-lagged, even though we went to bed early last night. Relaxing today sounded perfect. I said yes with everyone else at the table as my attention went back to Tasha who was quiet, seemingly lost in thought as she stared down at her food. "I heard there's a bonfire showdown on the beach tonight if anyone wants to go." Josie continued.

I really needed to get a hold of myself and stop staring. When she looked up, confused, having missed the conversation, I found myself smiling.

"You should start paying attention, Sunshine." The words left my mouth before I could stop them. Her gorgeous gray eyes met mine. Her face was free of makeup, and God, did she look beautiful, her blonde hair pulled into a messy bun on her head.

"Did you just call me Sunshine?" She raised an eyebrow at me.

"Yeah, and?"

"Out of all the names... Sunshine?" Her nose did this cute little scrunched up thing that made my heart race in my chest.

"It matches your hair," I tried to say casually but wasn't sure if it came out that way. I made myself look down at my food, needing to get myself under control.

"What did I miss?" Tasha asked, ignoring my comment.

"Honestly, nothing. Everyone's going to either spend the day on the beach or relax back at the hotel and then maybe go to a bonfire tonight." I told her.

"Sounds like you weren't paying attention either." The look she gave me had me holding back a smile. I loved when she teased me. Nothing could stop those same words from leaving my mouth.

"I can do multiple things at once, babe." I took a bite of my omelet as I relished in the way her eyes widened and her mouth opened a little. Getting any reaction out of her was one of my favorite pastimes.

My eyes darted down to her mouth. The dirty image of those lips wrapped around my cock had me shifting in my chair. Now was not the time to get hard. Shoving another forkful of eggs in my mouth, I tried to think of random things.

Locker room filled with sweaty hockey players. Max's hairy ass. Coach Barnum.

Eventually, it felt like cold water was being dumped on my head. Perfect.

Once the hard-on in my shorts calmed down a little, I turned back into the conversation at the table. Josie and Wyatt were whispering something to each other, looking every bit in love that they were. Wyatt and Josie were that couple that you couldn't help but look at and think, that's love. Josie truly was the best thing to ever happen to Wyatt.

When he got hurt during a game two seasons ago, it was like this part of him slowly seeped away. Getting hurt is never what a professional hockey player wants, especially one as hardworking and fierce as Wyatt. It was like he was lost for a little bit. Unable to play like he used to. Then he met Josie.

I don't know what it was, but she helped bring him back to life in a sense, and he helped her with the passing of her father. The two met at a time when they both needed someone. I wasn't sure if I ever saw a pair more suitable for each other.

Leaving them to their moment, I glanced at Lydia, who was glaring daggers at Landon. I didn't have to be a part of that conversation to know Landon probably said something to her. Wyatt's older brother could come off as an asshole. I mean, he was one but he was also a great guy.

He's had to be the father figure to both Wyatt and their younger brother, Mateo, since their father ran out. He's also become a brother figure to me throughout the years. Once you got past his hard exterior, you saw someone who would do anything for those he loves.

Although from the way he was looking at Lydia, I couldn't decide if he wanted to get as far away from her as he could, or if he wanted to pull her across the table and kiss her. Leaving those two to whatever that was, I turned back to Tasha, who was talking to Mila.

"I bet if one of the guys used their names, they'd gladly bring us some," I caught Tasha saying. The way Mila grinned, I knew the two were up to no good. I sat back and watched as Mila turned to Bryton.

"Babe." Mila crooned. The way Bryton looked at his girl-friend almost rivaled Wyatt and Josie.

"Yeah?"

"You know I love you, right?" Tasha covered her mouth as Bryton narrowed his eyes at Mila.

"What do you want?" Bryton asked.

"I can't tell my boyfriend I love him?" Mila battered her eyelashes.

"Again... What do you want?" Bryton repeated.

Mila let out a dramatic sigh, my own lips twitching. She knew how to lay it on thick. All four girls were trouble and they knew it.

"Us girls want to go to the beach. We had such a long flight yesterday, but we want margaritas while we relax." Mila pressed her chest against his arm as she traced his hand with her finger. "Think you could help us get a few delivered to the lounge chairs?"

"So, you want me to ask the poor workers at the hotel to keep bringing you girls drinks?"

"Uh...yes." She looked a little uncertain.

Mila could ask for the moon and Bryton would say he'd get it for her.

"I'll see what I can do," Bryton relented, earning a kiss from Mila in return. I shook my head. The boy was so in love. But as I looked over at Tasha, who was smiling widely, I briefly wondered if I'd ever get the chance to be that way with her.

6

TASHA

"I could get used to this," Josie commented as all of us girls laid out on the beach. I hummed in agreement, my eyes closed as I soaked in the warm sun. A girl could definitely get used to drinking margaritas while lounging by the water.

"What do you think the guys are doing?" Mila asked.

"Probably found some sport to watch," Lydia answered. I didn't have to look at her to know she was rolling her eyes. Not that she was wrong, either. They probably went to the bar in the hotel and found some game to watch.

"It's important for them to have time off before the season starts. I can already tell Wyatt is biting at the bit to get back on the ice," Josie said.

"Bryton is the same way. He's been driving me crazy being home. I'm not sure how much more hockey talk I can take. Every few minutes, he's telling me about some team and the stats or certain plays he can't wait to try out with the guys." Mila said with a sigh.

"Oh, you've gotten the play talk too?" Josie asked. "I love hockey, don't get me wrong, but I don't need to hear any more trick plays, please."

"Thank God we love them," Mila said with an amen following from Josie.

"Margaritas?" a voice spoke above me not even a second later. Opening my eyes, I found a worker from the hotel holding a tray filled with delicious-looking drinks. The margaritas screamed *tropical* with salt on the rim, pineapple on spears sticking out of the blended goodness.

"Oh yes!" Mila stood up and reached for one.

"Thank you." I smiled at the guy, grabbing one of my own. My last one was long gone, so perfect timing.

"Okay, maybe the guys are useful for something." Lydia smirked. Bryton definitely came through with getting us drinks on the beach.

"Well, here—cheers to amazing friends." Josie held up her glass with a wide grin.

"Cheers to that." I mirrored her smile, leaning forward to tap my glass with hers and the girls.

"We should leave the guys and move here," I commented, lying back down on my chair.

"You know, I can get behind that." Mila hummed, sipping her drink. "They won't survive without us, though."

"Especially Wyatt, he's like a little baby around Josie," I teased.

"I would deny that, but it's the truth." We all laughed with Josie. Both Wyatt and Bryton acted tough, hell they played hockey, but around their girlfriends they were softies. You could literally see the way their eyes lit up when they saw Josie and Mila. It was cute and nauseating at the same time.

"How is it going with Wyatt?" I asked Josie. We were so busy with work that we didn't get much time to properly catch up.

"Things have been great. He's just so…" Josie trailed off, her face practically glowing as she thought of her boyfriend. "I've never met someone like him before."

"Well, he has my approval." I said.

"Oh, now he has the approval? We've been together for almost a year."

"He had to prove himself." I shrugged, grabbing my suntan lotion to rub on my legs. After her last ex, I expected the best for my best friend. Never again would I see her so insecure about herself or made to feel like she was worthless. I wouldn't allow that if I could help it.

"I thought you immediately liked him." Josie said.

I did but that didn't mean I wasn't going to thoroughly question the man. What Josie didn't know was I met up with Wyatt after we first met and asked a few questions. Was I a bit excessive in my questioning? Hell yes, but it just proved Wyatt was a good guy. He took my grilling with ease and answered all the questions I threw at him, letting me know he was nothing like Josie's previous boyfriend.

Wyatt had my approval ages ago.

"You're my best friend, what do you expect?" I raised my eyebrow at her. Josie just shook her head at me, used to my antics by now.

"Want to talk about the other night?" she asked a moment later. I knew she was referring to me being off when she and the girls came over. Over her shoulder, Mila and Lydia talked, leaving the two of us alone in our conversation.

"My mom called the other day while I was at work." The word mom was like acid on my tongue.

"Figured as much. What did she want this time?" Josie turned on her chair so she was laying on her side, looking at me.

"To remind me to come to the gala in a few weeks." At my words, she rolled her eyes. "It was more of a...demand than a reminder. You know how she is." I sighed and relaxed back into my lounge chair, wanting to erase any and all thoughts of my mother.

"What did she say?"

"That I should bring a *suitable* date this time." I clenched my jaw as a familiar wave of resentment washed over me whenever I talked about my parents. "Oh, and a jab at my job. You know, the usual."

"Are you going to go?" Josie asked, but we both knew I couldn't say no. Not when it came to Robert and Jennifer Davis. Even now they still had a hold over me.

"I'm not going to let myself think about it. We're on this gorgeous island, and I'm not going to let them take that from me."

"That's the spirit. We're gonna have so much fun you won't even have time to think about your parents." She reached out and squeezed my arm with a smile.

I fully planned on doing just that.

I WAS FEELING PRETTY DAMN good, I wasn't gonna lie. The seven alcoholic beverages we had were finally kicking in, making me feel like I was on cloud nine.

"God, this sand feels so good," I moaned, wiggling my toes deeper into it. Grabbing handfuls, I started piling some on my legs. When I was little, I would try to cover every inch of my skin, until it cracked and fell apart. Didn't matter that the sand would take ages to wash off. No doubt I'd be regretting this later.

"It's like an exfoliant." Josie said beside me, sprinkling the rough grains on her own legs.

"We should bottle this up and take it home with us."

"We could start a business!" Josie exclaimed.

"We need a badass name!" I shouted, although I had no clue why. It was just us four on this part of the beach.

While Josie and I played in the sand, Lydia snored away on her chair, arms and legs spread out like a starfish, and Mila was busy texting on her phone. Judging from the look on her face, it was very inappropriate.

"Sand Band," I said, testing the name.

"Coochie Sand," Josie suddenly said, looking right at me with a serious expression.

"Coochie Sand," I repeated. Seconds later, the two of us burst into loud fits of laughter. Cackling so hard, I fell over to the side into Josie.

We held onto each other as we cracked up over what she just said. Every time we made eye contact, it only made us giggle that much harder.

"Coochie Sand," I wheezed.

A shadow appeared over me, which was weird since the sun was tacked in the sky and there weren't any clouds. And then that shadow spoke. "There you guys are."

Leaning my head all the way back, I found a pair of upside down legs right in front of me.

"Why are you in the sky?" I blurted. "Did you know your boyfriend can walk on clouds?" I elbowed Josie.

"That's so damn cool," she breathed. We were a lot more drunk than either of us realized.

"What are you two talking about?" The world started to whirl as I leaned my head farther back to see who was talking now, sand squishing further into my hair. It was a different voice than Wyatt's.

"TREVOR!" I yelled once I caught sight of his face. He stood above me, staring down with raised eyebrows. "What are you doing here!"

Beside me, Josie reached out and grabbed Wyatt's ankle.

"Don't worry, I'll keep you down on Earth."

"Oh shit, don't float away." My own arm shot out to grab Trevor's leg. "I got you!" An image of Trevor gliding up into space suddenly appeared in my head, making me giggle.

"You guys are drunk, aren't you?" Trevor asked. I barely heard him over my own fits of laughter.

"No," I responded at the same time Josie said, "Coochie Sand." Once again, setting us off into hysterics

"Yeah, they're drunk," I heard Wyatt say. Josie and I rolled around in the sand, laughing as Trevor and Wyatt watched us.

"How much did you guys drink?" Wyatt asked once our laughter died down a bit.

"We only had seven margaritas," Josie replied.

"Yeah, wasn't a lot," I chimed in.

"Uh-huh." Trevor said.

Wyatt and Trevor shared a look before coming around to our feet.

"Let's get you girls up and cleaned off." Wyatt suggested, as both him and Trevor reached for us.

Trevor grabbed my hands and gently pulled me upward with little to no effort. Wyatt did the same to Josie.

"But I was having fun," I whined as Trevor lifted me to my feet. He dropped his hands to my waist when I stumbled to the side. Woah, maybe I have had a lot to drink.

Glancing around, I saw Josie climbing on Wyatt's back, Mila kissing Bryton like her life depended on it, and Lydia cradled in the arms of Landon.

"I think you girls have had enough fun. Come on." With his hands on my bare waist—thanks to my skimpy bikini— Trevor maneuvered me toward my stuff. The calluses on his hands made me shiver. His hands were so big they nearly spanned around my entire waist. Immediately, inappropriate thoughts came to mind.

"You have very large hands," my mouth suddenly blurted, the alcohol controlling the words coming out of my mouth.

"Do I?" Trevor kept walking us forward, but I could see the smirk that graced his lips.

"Yeah, they're very manly too." I was definitely going to regret what I was saying when I sobered up. "Bet you know how to use them." If it wasn't for the alcohol swimming through my veins, my face would be the same shade of a tomato. But drunk me had no filter. She also didn't blush.

"Wow, you are way drunker than I thought," Trevor noted before stopping beside the lounge chair that held my stuff. "Think you can stand on your own for a second?"

I nodded despite the world spinning in circles.

I watched, fascinated, as Trevor picked up my beach bag and made sure everything was inside of it. My eyes were glued to his hands. Hands that were making me think things I shouldn't.

"Here you go." He held out the cover up I wore over my bikini on the way down to the beach.

I shook my head. "I don't want to."

"You're not walking around the hotel in just that." Trevor glanced at the pale blue bikini I had on. His eyes lingered on my chest and the tiny bit of fabric that covered my nipples.

"Here." He stepped forward for me to put my arms through it. I wouldn't say the see-through cover up covered anything, but the intense look on his face had me doing as he asked.

Once Trevor was satisfied that my body wasn't available for all to see, he grabbed my beach bag and held out his hand for me to hold. "Let's get you cleaned up."

I didn't even hesitate placing my hand in his. It was weird to think a person could feel something from just a palm slid against their own, but even in my drunk fog, I felt the zing that shot up my arm. The way my hand seemed to fit perfectly in his as he wrapped his fingers through mine wasn't lost on me either.

I was vaguely aware of our friends around us as we slowly made our way back to the hotel. At least it wasn't a long walk, but my foot coordination was slightly off, making Trevor tighten his hold on me.

"Drunk on our first day on vacation. Why am I not surprised?" Trevor teased.

"Hey, Mila was the one ordering all the drinks," I said, defending myself. "Who am I to say no?" Who passed on free alcohol?

"Hm."

"Don't be jealous." I patted his arm. A very nice arm, that was. "I can get you some. I know a guy." I even went as far as sending him a wink. The sober side of me wanted to smack my hand to my face to hide my embarrassment.

"I'll keep that in mind." I could tell Trevor was trying not to laugh as we made it up the walkway to the hotel.

"Party baby!" Josie suddenly yelled behind me. I glanced over my shoulder to see her waving her arm in the air as she was being carried on Wyatt's back. The look on Wyatt's face made me giggle. She yelled right in his ear, making him wince. When Josie got drunk, she tended to be louder than normal.

"Woo!" I echoed just as flamboyantly. A few heads turned to stare at us as we walked by. Wyatt and Trevor shared a look before shaking their heads. I had no clue where Mila or Lydia ended up, too busy trying to ignore the feel of Trevor pressed against me and failing. Between him and the alcohol, I wasn't sure which was making my head swirl more.

As we neared the front doors, we passed by one of the hotel workers carrying a tray of drinks. Trevor quickly flagged him down.

"Can we get a couple of water bottles by chance?" I

couldn't tell if he recognized Trevor or if he saw the desperation on Trevor's face more than anything, but he quickly handed over two waters from his tray. "Thanks, man."

I stood there watching, not fully registering anything, as Trevor graciously helped Wyatt open the water and hand it to Josie before turning to me."Drink this."

I stared at the water bottle in his hand like it was a snake.

"Why?" I frowned and narrowed my eyes at the drink. A margarita sounded better.

"Tasha, drink."

My eyes widened at the demand. The way his voice got low and husky made my entire body shiver, not with fear, no it was all excitement. Looking up at his face, I found him staring down at me with those gorgeous green eyes, his jaw clenched, clearly not budging.

"Tasha," he warned again. Reluctantly, I reached out and grabbed the bottle, downing half of it in one go. "Good girl. There you go." The praise did something weird to my chest and stomach.

I just stood there silently, staring up at him, the water bottle now clenched in my hands. Because of the damn alcohol, I couldn't quite grasp the emotions that brewed inside of me, nor the expression clearly written on Trevor's face.

"Let's get you back to your room, yeah?"

All I could do was nod as he put his arm back around my waist and started for the front doors of the hotel.

With each sip of the water, I started to feel a bit better, my head clearing slightly, which was probably a good thing. I already knew I embarrassed myself to no end in front of Trevor. Although, it really wasn't my fault that the margaritas were so strong. They sure didn't skimp on the alcohol at this place.

The ride up the elevator was slightly awkward. Josie and Wyatt stood off to the side, Josie now wrapped around his front like a koala bear. The two of them whispered to each other, and I looked away, minding my own business. I glanced down at my feet only just realizing I was barefoot.

Trevor stayed pressed against my side, arm around my waist as if he was afraid I would topple over at any minute. I wasn't going to complain. Drunk me was more than happy to have his arms around my body. Something sober me would never admit out loud.

I didn't say a word as the elevator slowly made its way up to our floor. I didn't trust what would come out of my mouth. Not when my stomach was tangled in delicious knots that only came from one thing.

Thankfully, the doors opened a moment later, cutting through the weird silence that enveloped Trevor and me. This was the closest we had been since that night five months ago. The closest I let us be without making some excuse to get away.

"Think you'll be okay to go to the bonfire in a few hours?" Trevor finally spoke when we reached my room, which was right across from his. I didn't know what time it was or how long we had been out on the beach. Didn't help that my body was still off from the time difference.

"Yeah, I'll be good." I just needed a nice long shower and maybe some food. Standing there, I brushed a bit of sand off my arm. More than likely, it was stuck to me in other spots too. If I didn't get cleaned up soon, it'd cause an uncomfortable and irritating itch that I wanted no parts of.

Trevor looked a bit doubtful but dipped his chin to his chest after a minute. Handing me my bag, he finally took a step back, the warmth from his body suddenly gone. I shifted under his gaze, not sure what to say or do.

As I fumbled in my bag for my room key, Trevor watched my every move. When my keycard unlocked my door, and I pushed it open, I glanced back over at him. Standing there in the hallway, hands now in his pockets, his broad shoulders were more relaxed.

"I'll see you in a bit?" He said it more like a question, and I found myself doing the most embarrassing thing ever—I gave him a thumbs up.

Yet, the longer we stood there staring at each other, the stronger the urge came to do something stupid. Like kissing him again. Needing to get away, I quickly turned and entered my room before shutting the door behind me.

I sagged against it, head whirling. *What was going on with me?* When I was around Trevor, I tended to lose the tight grip I had on myself. The one that kept me from doing anything out of line. It was like one look from him disarmed my entire security system. Didn't help that my slightly drunk self was more than happy to give up the password.

I still wasn't sure if that was a good thing or not

7

TASHA

I ended up spending a solid thirty minutes in the shower. Thanks to my drunk self lying in the sand, it took ages to get it out of my hair and all other places it shouldn't have been. By the time I stepped out of the stall, my skin was pink from the scrubbing myself.

Drinking so many margaritas in a span of a few hours probably wasn't the smartest idea. But it was nice to sit back with my best friends and not have a care in the world. We all needed it, and it was a good way to kick-start our time away.

With a headache starting to form, I wanted nothing more than to lay down and take a nap. But I knew if I did, I'd be even more off with the time change, and tomorrow, we planned on exploring the island. So as much as I wanted to sleep, I forced myself to get up and change out of my towel.

Not bothering to put in much effort, seeing as it was going to get dark out, I grabbed one of the twenty-something dresses I packed for the trip. I probably overpacked but you never knew what could happen. What if I needed twenty pairs of underwear, or I met some royal prince that invited me to dinner? I had to look nice cause you never knew.

Slipping on a light blue summer dress, I left my hair to air dry, the wet strands sticking to my back. Putting on a little bit of lip gloss, I called it good. After sliding on my flip-flops and grabbing my phone, I left my room. I glanced at Lydia's door across from mine, but it was shut. Right after I left Trevor in the hallway and started for my room, our door opened behind me to Landon carrying a mumbling Lydia.

When Landon saw me staring, he grunted and moved past me to put Lydia on her bed. Bet that will go well when she learns who brought her up here. She was probably still passed out. Letting her be, I grabbed my room key and headed for the lobby, texting Josie as I waited for the elevator.

I fiddled with my phone as I rode the elevator down. When I got to the lobby I didn't see any of my friends, so I awkwardly stood off to the side, waiting for replies to my texts. The main area of the hotel was surprisingly busy with guests coming and going. Some lingered with family as they chatted with each other.

"Feeling better?" My head shot up at Trevor's voice, relief washed over me at the sight of him.

"Where have you been?" I found myself asking, ignoring his question.

"Did someone miss me?" His eyebrow raised as his lip lifted in a smirk.

"You wish." I rolled my eyes, even though a small voice in my head told me yes. "Where is everyone?"

"Not entirely sure. Landon was in his room getting ready last I saw. Haven't heard from the others." Trevor shrugged. Subconsciously, I found myself looking him over, noting that he was wearing board shorts and a light jacket. His brown hair was a little bit curled, the sight of it making me want to run my fingers through it. It had gotten longer than normal but it fit him.

"I texted Josie, but she hasn't replied." I worried my bottom lip between my teeth.

"Probably still getting ready. Wanna head to the shore and wait?" As soon as the words left his mouth, someone shoved past me, hitting my arm and making me stumble right into Trevor. His hand grabbed my arm as my hand landed on his chest. I peered up at him from under my lashes. The smell of citrus with a hint of spice hit my nose. God, he smelled delicious.

"You okay?" Swallowing thickly, I nodded, stepping back. "Let's get out of here." Trevor gently steered me out of the hotel and toward the beach, his hand lingering at the small of my back before he dropped it.

We walked in silence for a bit, following the string of people also looking to spend the rest of their night by the water. Silence grew between us and I knew I had to say something.

"Thanks for helping me to my room earlier."

"Of course. Glad you guys didn't do anything stupid or get in the water."

"Excuse me. Stupid? We are smart drunks for your information."

"Josie told us about the swimming pool incident in uni. Not sure I'd say that was smart." Trevor said.

"First off, I didn't know you knew that story. And second, we got away with it, so." I shrugged.

"Let me take a wild guess that it was your idea?" He looked over at me with a raised eyebrow.

"Of course. Who else would have come up with such an iconic idea?" I grinned like a Cheshire cat. Trevor just shook his head at me. "You can't tell me you didn't do something stupid in school."

Out of the guys, I knew Trevor was the troublemaker. He

was probably the guy who went to tons of parties and slept around.

"I mean, everyone did," Trevor answered but didn't elaborate. I wasn't letting him off the hook, though, not when he already knew one of my stories.

"And? Not gonna share?" I nudged him with my shoulder. I could make out the bonfire up ahead as we reached the sand. Waiting for his answer, I slipped off my flip-flops and started in the direction of where we needed to go.

"Okay, fine," Trevor finally relented. Together, the two of us walked side by side. "It was my freshman year, we just won our tenth game, and decided to go out and celebrate."

I listened intently as he spoke. This was the longest we'd been around each other, and I didn't really want it to end. His presence next to me gave me this odd sense of security

"Long story short, I got super drunk. Drunk enough I barely remembered anything that happened. The next morning, Wyatt showed me his phone. Apparently, I thought it would be a genius idea to strip butt naked and run down the street singing at the top of my lungs."

He barely finished before I was laughing. The thought of Trevor streaking and belting out lyrics made me cackle.

"Oh, there's more." The grin on my face somehow got wider as he continued. "On the video, you can see me running down the street," Trevor paused for a moment as if preparing himself for the rest of the story. "At the same time, a family of four walked by with their kids."

I lost it.

Bending over, my whole body shook with laughter. He ran naked in front of an entire family? I lifted a hand as if to tell him to stop because I couldn't take anymore. I really couldn't, not when I could hardly catch my breath.

"Tasha," Trevor said but I couldn't stop. "It's not that funny."

"Y-yes, it is," I barely got out. I looked up with tears in my eyes to find him giving me a flat look, which just made me roar that much harder.

"Uh-huh, keep laughing."

"Oh God," I wheezed, hands on my waist as I tried to calm down. "Sorry, that was just—"

"I shouldn't have told you that story."

"Oh no, you definitely should have. Does Wyatt still have the video?" I wiped at my cheeks.

"Like I'm going to tell you that." Trevor quickly shut that down.

"Why not?"

"Knowing you, you'll send it to yourself and everyone else." He said.

"I..." He sent me a look. "Okay, fine, I would."

"Thought so."

"I'm sorry, that's too funny. You scarred those poor kids for life." I could just imagine those children seeing Trevor running around obnoxiously. "They probably never recovered."

"Gee, thanks." I sent him a silly smile in return. "Remind me to never tell you an embarrassing story again."

"Those are the best stories, though."

With the bonfire behind us, the two of us continued down the beach in the opposite direction. The setting sun warm against our backs. Despite the silence blooming between us, it was...nice.

After a few minutes, Trevor broke it.

"So, you're a therapist?" It hit me then that while we had known each other for a year, we didn't truly know one another. We never sat down and asked each other questions about our lives. We just knew the basics from when we hung out as a group. Shame instantly hit me. I should have made more of an effort to get to know him before now. I'd just been so focused on keeping my walls up to try.

"Guess in a way I am. I'm considered more of a counselor," I explained. "I can't prescribe medication, but I give advice and help people cope with their struggles. Like this young girl I'm seeing," I rambled. "When she first came to me she was so shy, couldn't even look up at me and had no friends at school. But now she's going to the mall with some girls from school and putting herself out there. It's just... It's amazing to see."

It was the best part of my job, seeing my patients overcome the challenges that brought them to me. Watching them grow—it was one of the reasons why I kept doing what I did.

"She sounds lucky to have you."

"It's all her. I just helped guide her in the right direction."

"No, take the credit. It's because of you she's doing so well." For some reason, his words made my heart squeeze tightly in my chest. "It sounds like you picked the right career."

"Yeah, tell that to my parents." I scoffed.

"They don't approve?" I could feel his eyes on me, but I kept mine down at my feet as they made imprints in the wet surf.

"That's an understatement. To them I should have followed in their footsteps and became a lawyer or some big wig to fit in with their friends."

All through high school, my parents pushed me to get straight A's, to be at the top of my class so I could go to Harvard like they did. I learned quickly that they only wanted to brag to their friends about having a "golden child."

I'll never forget the look on their faces when I told them I wasn't going to apply to an Ivy League college, and that I didn't want to follow in their footsteps. The look of disappointment on their faces was enough to almost make me take back what I said. Almost.

"You didn't want to?"

"God, no." The thought of having to spend my time around people who would use you for their own gain, or had to kiss their ass just to stay in their good graces made me want to throw up. I'd spent enough time around them, thanks to my parents, to know what it was like.

"That atmosphere, the people... It's not something I enjoy. I've been around it enough to hate it."

"So, your parents flipped, I take it?"

"To say the least. Now every time we talk there's always some jab regarding my job. That I 'gave away a good future and wasted my potential.'" Those were my parents' actual words. That they didn't raise a daughter to be like me. "But," I sighed, kicking at the sand, "I love what I do."

No matter how hard I tried not to let my parent's opinions affect me, they still did. Knowing they didn't approve of me and my job hurt more than cared to admit.

"Hey." A hand on my elbow pulled me to a stop. I glanced up to find Trevor looking at me intently. "If it makes you happy, do it. You don't need anyone's approval, not even your parents. If they can't see that, then fuck them."

My eyes widened a fraction at his words and the intensity of them.

"You make a difference doing what you do. Don't discredit that, Tasha." My heart squeezed tightly in my chest. Josie was the only person who ever told me my job mattered. Hearing it from Trevor, and the conviction in his words, made tears prick the corner of my eyes.

My eyes bounced between his, finding nothing but sincerity in them. Vulnerability consumed me as his unwavering gaze remained on me. I cleared my throat and looked away.

"Thanks." My words came out soft.

Wanting the attention off me, I started walking again, Trevor following.

"Sounds like you know a thing or two about shitty parents." I said a moment later. The only sound around us were the waves crashing against the shore. It was like we were in our own little world, and I found myself liking it. Something in the air made me slowly let my walls fall as we walked.

"Yeah," Trevor answered, his voice turning distant. I had a feeling he wasn't going to say much more on the subject. Not that I expected him to. This was our first deep conversation, so I didn't foresee him laying his entire past at my feet.

"My parents were alcoholics," Trevor said after a moment. "They weren't around much, and when they were, they were too hammered to do much."

I stayed quiet, letting him talk. I knew that sometimes people simply needed someone to listen without receiving any pity back. I also knew firsthand how annoying that could be—people feeling sorry for you.

"My mom would get sober once in a while, long enough to remember she had a son and get some groceries, before she fell off the wagon again."

"How old were you?" I asked softly, peeking up at him. His jaw was tense, and he was staring straight ahead, hands stuffed in his pockets.

"Eight."

My chest squeezed painfully. He was so young and had to deal with absent parents who relied heavily on alcohol to get them through. I didn't miss the underlying meaning of his words. That he had to fend for himself when his parents were under the influence. Just the thought of that made me want to embrace him in a hug and never let go. No child, let alone one that young, should have to take care of himself and his parents.

"So yeah, I know a thing or two."

I suddenly saw Trevor in a different light. Yes, he was still the cocky playboy hockey player but knowing a little bit of his childhood, I could tell there was a lot more than met the eye with him.

When Trevor's gaze met mine, something seemed to pass between us. I wasn't sure what it was but instinct told me that wouldn't be the last time I felt it.

TASHA

"**H**ow can you even think that?" I scoffed.

"Because it's true." Trevor shot back.

"It's the furthest from the truth." I countered.

"Doritos are the best chips." Trevor said. I looked at him like snakes were coming out of his ears.

"Doritos? Out of all the chips out there you choose them?" I retorted, the idea of Doritos being the best chip made my face crinkle.

"And you think Fritos are the best?" Trevor sent me a look of his own. One that told me he didn't agree.

"The chili cheese *twist* Fritos, first of all. And second, they are better than Doritos."

"What's so wrong with them?"

"They're just so..." I tried to come up with a better word. "Plain."

"I can't even look at you right now," he said dramatically, turning his body in the other direction.

"I didn't say they were disgusting, just plain."

"So, that means you think *I'm* plain." Trevor flung back.

"I mean..."

"I am not plain!" He turned around to gape at me, eyes wide in fake horror. I barely had time to look at his feet before he kicked a huge chunk of sand at me, hitting my dress in the process.

"Trevor!" I had already cleaned the stuff out of places that I didn't even understand how it got there. I didn't want to do it again.

"What?" He looked at me innocently, but the teasing smirk on his face was anything but.

"If you get sand in my freshly washed hair, you will feel a world of pain," I threatened, narrowing my eyes at him.

"Oh, really?" I watched him closely as he shifted in his spot on the log near the bonfire. I didn't trust him for one single second.

"Trevor," I warned. I watched as he bent to the side, grabbing a handful of the coarse but tiny grains. It was the kind that stuck to everything it touched.

Scrambling up off my seat, I took a step back, hands out in front of me. Eyes glued to his hand as some of it slipped through his fingers.

"Don't you even dare." I pointed a finger at him, but Trevor just slowly stood up. The fire behind him made him look like a menacing shadow. From the evil look on his face, he wasn't far from it.

"Don't do what?" he asked innocently as he stepped forward, mimicking my steps. There was no way in hell I was letting him near me with that. It took me ages to get the sand out earlier, and knowing Trevor, he'd make sure every inch of my hair was covered.

"I'm telling you right now not to do whatever it is you are thinking." I stumbled slightly as I kept my eyes on his figure. I didn't dare look away.

I knew the odds weren't really in my favor. Trevor was over six feet tall with long muscular legs that could easily reach me within a few steps. His body was basically a lethal machine, thanks to all his hockey training. Running in a medium that easily slipped away with each step was probably a walk in the park for him. Whereas for me, it would take extra effort on my part and probably make my legs replicate jelly for the next week.

"But you see, calling me names isn't very polite." He slowly advanced on me, easing me. I knew if I said anything it would only make it worse, but I never could control my mouth.

"I wasn't calling you names or referring to you as plain. I was just stating a fact." I could barely make out the expression on his face at my words.

"You're not really helping your case here." With each word, he kept walking in my direction. With the moon hanging high over the ocean, there weren't many people left on the beach and none spared us any attention.

"How about we come to an agreement?" I offered. Maybe I could talk myself out of this one.

"I don't think so."

"But—" Before I could finish, Trevor lunged for me.

Squealing, I dodged his attempt, pivoting on my heel and took off running. The sand was loose, which did not help as I struggled. I heard Trevor behind me and a quick peek over my shoulder told me he was right on my ass.

With wide eyes, I veered toward the wetter sand for better traction, pushing myself to run faster as my calves burned. There was no way in hell I was letting him catch me. Not with that sand still in his hand.

"Tasha!" Trevor yelled after me. "Get back here!"

"No!" I yelled back. Hearing him curse, I glanced over my shoulder again only to giggle at the sight of Trevor tripping. He fell to his knees. "Ha! Sucker!"

Laughing loudly, I kept running to put distance between

us. My legs were already getting tired, stupid self for not spending more time at the gym, but I pushed forward. The sound of the waves lapping at the sand muted the sound of Trevor getting back to his feet, making me run that much faster.

I wanted to believe I was running at super speeds, but the sand kept slipping away, making me stumble every other step and giving Trevor plenty of time to catch up. Damn him and his long legs.

"Just accept it, Tasha!" he yelled from behind.

"Never!"

I knew we looked like complete maniacs running down the coast yelling at each other, but I didn't care. For the first time in a long time, I was carefree.

My breathing got heavier and my calves started to cramp, making me slow down a little. I definitely was not a track star. But as I slowed, I didn't hear a sound from behind me. It didn't even seem like Trevor was behind me at all. Did he hurt himself when he tripped?

Coming to a stop, I went to turn around to make sure he was okay only for a pair of arms to wrap around my middle. I screamed as he lifted me off the ground and twirled me in a circle. I barely registered that he no longer had a handful of sand.

I couldn't help but squeal and laugh as I was twisted in the air. Trevor's arms were snug around my waist as he held me effortlessly against his chest. The feel of his breath on my neck made my skin break out in goosebumps.

"Should have said sorry," he whispered in my ear, bringing us to a stop. Before I could comprehend what he meant, we were moving again. My toes grazed the slightly chilly ocean water, making me squirm in his hold.

"Trevor." He kept a firm hold on me as he brought us closer to the water. This was worse than the sand. "Don't!"

"Are you going to say sorry?" My hands scrambled to grab his forearms, but my feet were already fully submerged. *Say yes, Tasha!*

"No." The word left my lips before I could stop myself. *Way to go.*

"Okay then." He swung me to the side as if getting ready to launch me in the ocean. Yelling, I gripped his forearms tighter, struggling to hold on.

"No, no, wait!"

Trevor stopped, leaving me hovering above the water, the waves hitting my shins. I brought my legs up in an attempt to keep myself dry.

"Yes?"

"I take it back."

"Take what back?" His lips grazed the shell of my ear as he spoke. Obviously wanting me to say the words out loud.

"There are two things." He whispered. When I hesitated, he started to swing me again.

"Fine, okay! You aren't plain!"

"Nope, that doesn't count." More of my feet dipped into the water as he waded farther out.

"Okay, okay. Trevor, you are not plain and neither are Doritos!" He paused. "Is that better?"

"Hmm," he hummed, his chest vibrating against my back. "It will do...for now."

"Then please let me down."

"If you insist." Trevor loosened his hold, lowering me a bit so waves hit my knees. Yelling, I gripped him once more.

"Put me down on dry land, you idiot!" I shrieked, kicking at the water.

Laughing, Trevor turned us both around and walked out of the ocean. Each step toward dry land made me relax more and more in his hold. *Stupid man threatening to drop me in the ocean.* As soon as he got us away from the water, I wiggled in his hold so he would release me.

As soon as my feet hit the sand, I let out a sigh. I loved the ocean, I did, but someone threatening to throw me in while it was dark? No, thank you. My mouth threatened to protest when Trevor's arms dropped from my body.

I liked his arms around me, maybe a little too much, but being in them was fogging my head. I needed my thoughts clear whenever I was around Trevor because it was really easy to give in, and the thought of that scared me. Getting attached too quickly never turned out well.

"You are so dead." I twisted around and glared at the man in front of me. I had to tilt my head back just to see at his face. Damn him and his height. Trevor had the balls to smile down at me like something was funny. "What?"

"You are as threatening as a squirrel," he replied, his smile somehow getting wider.

"Am not!" Putting my hands on my hips, I narrowed my eyes.

"Uh-huh."

Letting out a huff, I looked away. The way he was looking at me made my stomach flip and my cheeks to heat. His stupid smile was not helping.

Tasha no. Don't even think about it.

A cool breeze picked up, blowing salty air right from the ocean. I shivered as goosebumps rose on my skin, my thin summer dress doing nothing to hold off the chill. Didn't help that my legs were still wet from before.

"Here." I looked back at Trevor to see him shedding the windbreaker he had on. In a gesture that somehow made my heart race even more, Trevor held it open for me.

"But—"

"You're shivering," Trevor cut me off. He gave me a look that told me not to argue with him. I didn't have it in me to do so. Biting the inside of my cheek, I moved closer, sliding my arms into the sleeves and letting him pull it around my shoulders.

I was instantly enveloped in warmth and that familiar citrus yet spicy smell again. The same smell that was all Trevor. It took everything I had not to bring the sleeves up to my nose. Instead, I took small, deep breaths, basically inhaling his scent as if it was oxygen. Maybe I was crazy, or I was somehow still intoxicated.

"Thanks," I murmured. "What about you?"

"I'll be fine." He waved me off. "Want to head back?" He tucked his hands in his pockets, the T-shirt he was now in stretching across his biceps and chest. Averting my eyes, I nodded.

Our little moment ended. Disappointment washed over me because I wanted to stay in our little bubble where reality didn't seem to exist. Tonight, the walls came down just a little. It was like Trevor was softly, but firmly, hitting those walls and tearing them down brick by brick. I wasn't entirely sure if I was okay with that or not.

We walked side by side back to the hotel, stopping to grab our shoes and phones we left by the bonfire on the way. A few people lingered on the beach, which wasn't surprising since it was only eleven thirty. I hadn't realized how long Trevor and I had been out. Time seemed to pause yet fly by when we were together.

As we walked, our fingers brushed against each other, each time making my breath still in my lungs.

"Thank you for tonight," I finally spoke as we walked through the lobby of the hotel.

"Would you want to do this again tomorrow night?" Trevor scratched the side of his neck as he asked, almost like he was nervous to bring it up. I found it cute. Trevor never struck me as a guy who got nervous about anything, let alone a girl. I found myself liking the fact that I made him react like that.

"I'd like that."

"Okay. Good." The corner of his lip tilted up as he nodded. Turning my head to the side, I hide my own smile.

We stayed quiet as we rode the elevator up to our floor. My steps slowed as we headed for our rooms, trying to savor this last moment. I had a good night. No, a great night. It wasn't what I expected, but it turned out even better than I thought.

Coming to a stop in front of my room, I held back a sigh. With my head back, I met Trevor's eyes. I went to open my mouth to say something but all the words got stuck in my throat.

Trevor seemed to sense my trouble. The corner of his mouth lifted in a soft smile. When he brought his hand up, my breathing stopped completely. His fingertips softly grazed the top of my cheek before tucking a piece of hair behind my ear.

I couldn't stop the tremor that ran down my spine at his touch. My eyes fluttered as my breathing picked back up. My heart raced. Trevor's green eyes darkened as he stared down at me. The muscle in his jaw ticked.

I watched as he battled with himself before he dropped his hand back to his side and took a step back.

"Goodnight, Tasha." I couldn't form words as I stood there watching as he opened his door. I wanted to say something, but my mouth wouldn't work. He glanced at me over his shoulder one last time before stepping through the threshold, leaving me there in the hallway.

"Goodnight, Trevor," I whispered after he was already in his room.

9

TASHA

"Sorry about last night," Josie said the next morning as we all sat down for breakfast at the same diner from yesterday. I took a big gulp of my coffee before answering. I was in desperate need of caffeine. I couldn't fall asleep last night despite being tired, so I spent the majority of the night thinking about things. More specifically, Trevor. Being up early to go snorkeling also didn't help.

"It's okay." I waved her off. To be honest, I forgot the others were supposed to join us last night.

"What did you end up doing?" When she asked, my eyes drifted on their own toward the person sitting at the end of the table. Trevor was talking to Bryton, but it was almost like he could feel my gaze on him because a second later his head turned toward me. My breath stilled for a second as we stared at one another. The intensity of his green eyes had me glancing away.

"Just walked on the beach for a little bit," I answered, only telling part of the truth. Josie may have been my best friend, but for some reason, I wanted to keep what happened between Trevor and me a secret. At least for now. Wanting to change the subject I looked at her with a raised eyebrow. "And what did you do?"

The sheepish expression that crossed her face had me shaking my head and laughing under my breath.

"Of course you did." Should have known her not showing up to the beach last night meant her and Wyatt were busy doing something else.

"Sorry." She looked anything but.

"Are you guys ready for snorkeling?" Wyatt said a moment later.

Out of everyone at the table I was pretty sure I was the most excited. I'd never been and the thought of seeing sea life up close almost had me jumping in my seat. I was ready to eat and go.

"How long is it?" I asked.

"I'm pretty sure it's about three hours? The front desk said they'll take us to a couple of locations via boat so it could take a bit longer," Wyatt said.

Three hours of exploring the ocean and the sea bed was going to be amazing. I was seconds away from jumping up and saying screw breakfast, but I knew with a full day ahead, it'd be smart to eat. So instead, I reluctantly stayed seated and waited impatiently for my food.

Breakfast seemed to lag. My impatience didn't help but neither did the slight tension between Trevor and me. I kept finding myself looking over at him. Pretty sure I felt his eyes on me a few times as well.

I was pretty certain the tension was all in my head, though, cause no one else seemed to be acting weird. Not even Trevor. But I wasn't going to let myself dwell on it any longer. We were on vacation, and we were going to spend our day in the ocean so nothing was going to ruin my good mood. Not even overthinking.

Once breakfast was done, I all but sprinted for the elevators so we could go get changed. Behind me, I heard a chuckle so I flipped whoever it was the middle finger as I tapped my foot waiting for the elevator.

Trevor's voice wrapped around me from behind. "The tour isn't going anywhere."

"But the animals are," I retorted.

"The animals."

"Yes. Right now, there could be dolphins in the spot we're going, but by the time we get there, they could be long gone."

"Oh, don't want to miss the dolphins." He mocked.

"Don't tease me." I elbowed him in his ribs.

"I would never." But I could hear the amusement in his voice. Trevor lived to tease me.

"I'm being serious here."

"Don't worry, I'll make sure we get to the tour on time so we don't miss any of the ocean life." I looked over at him with my head tilted up slightly.

"Promise?"

"Promise." The look in his eyes as he stared down at me made my stomach clench. Swallowing, I forced my eyes away. My stupid heart fluttered a little in my chest.

"Is everyone ready to go?" the tour guide asked as we all sat around the stern of the boat. A moment ago, he introduced himself as Johnno.

I grinned as both Mila and Josie cheered. A nudge on my knee had me glancing over at Trevor. The moment we got on the boat, he claimed the spot next to me and refused to move.

"Told you I'd make sure we got here in time." And he did.

I had barely gotten my bathing suit on when Trevor started banging on our door, saying we needed to get going. He then proceeded to knock on everyone else's repeatedly until Wyatt yelled at him to quit it.

And once everyone was ready, he all but ushered us out of the hotel to the golf carts waiting curbside to take us to the dock. Knowing he was doing it all for my benefit made my stomach summersault with anticipation.

Instead of replying, I stuck my tongue out at him and looked away. We—my friends and I—were the only ones on the boat for the tour, which I was grateful for. Sometimes, it was the worst having random people with you. Not to mention how awkward it got when you were squished together. At least this way, we had the whole boat to ourselves and could have our fun without anyone interrupting.

I shared an excited smile with Josie as the boat's engine hummed to life. As soon as the boat jerked forward, my whole body pressed into Trevor's side.

I didn't say a word as I slid back over to my spot but felt Trevor's eyes on me again. It was like everything was intentionally pushing us together.

Trevor didn't say anything, but he kept his legs spread wide so his thigh pressed against mine. Glancing down, I found myself marveling at how big and muscular his thigh was. Hockey players were always in great shape but damn those thighs were thick. I guessed they had to be in order to skate around the ice for so long.

The longer I stared at our bare thighs touching, the dirtier my thoughts became. What the hell was wrong with me? Getting all hot and bothered by a man's *thigh?!* It had been too damn long, apparently, if I was fantasizing about a leg.

Thankfully the tour guide started talking again, making me shove all those kinds of thoughts to the back of my mind. Now was so not the time. I forced myself to pay attention as Johnno told us about where we were going and how snorkeling worked. But no matter how hard I tried, my thoughts kept veering back to the person sitting next to me.

"OH, I LOVE THAT ONE!" Mila gushed as all of us girls leaned over, looking at Josie's phone. Since the boat ride was going to take a little bit, Josie decided she wanted to take some photos of all of us, her inner photographer coming out. "Definitely send that one to me." It was a picture of Mila and Bryton together, looking gorgeous as always.

"Can I get a picture with my beautiful girlfriend?" Wyatt came up and wrapped his arms around Josie.

Taking Josie's phone, I carefully moved around the boat to get a good angle. Looking at the two, a smile appeared on my face. The way they looked at each other, it was clear as day they were in love. Wyatt looked at Josie like she was the air he breathed. Like nothing else mattered but her.

As I took picture after picture, my chest ached with happiness for my best friend. She had absolutely no clue what was going to happen in a few days. No clue that I had been going behind her back for the past couple of weeks. Knowing how happy she was going to be soon eased the guilt that came over keeping it a secret.

Leaving the two of them in their own little bubble I gazed around the boat, turning, I found Lydia and Landon standing beside each other, leaning their arms against the railing, looking out at the ocean. Landon was standing close enough that his arm brushed against hers.

Shaking my head, I brought Josie's phone up, taking a picture of the two. I was about to put the phone down when the two of them glanced over at each other at the same time. My thumb moved before I could think, snapping the picture seconds before they turned away. My lips tugged upward as I looked at the picture I just took.

Damn, maybe *I* should be a photographer, not Josie, cause it was perfect. The green island and water in the background as Lydia and Landon stared at one another was literal perfection. They were definitely going to thank me later for that one.

"I'm ready for my photoshoot." I didn't even look up as I felt Trevor come up behind me.

"Sorry, closed for business."

"But my face is primed and ready." I pressed my lips together to stop myself from smiling at his antics. "I'm a great model."

That I already knew. I had seen countless pictures of him in magazines and commercials. A photoshoot of Trevor in his boxers flashed in my head. A photo I may have spent quite a long time staring at.

"Tashaaaa." He dragged my name out in a whine. "I'll pose like one of your French girls."

The idea of making Trevor do what I wanted sounded very appealing. Turning, I gave him a shrug.

"Okay, French girl, let's go."

"I'm yours to do as you please." I didn't miss the way his eyes darkened or the underlying meaning of his words. Shaking my head, I waved my hand at him.

"Pick a spot." My eyes almost popped out of my head when Trevor reached behind his head with one hand and pulled his shirt off. The action alone was hot, but it was put on the back burner at the sight of his upper body. His *ripped* upper body, I might add.

My eyes didn't know where to look first as they moved from his wide shoulders to his biceps before finally landing on the six-pack decorating his abdomen. I eyed every bump and ridge down to the V-line that disappeared into his swim shorts. Tattoos littered his skin; chest, arms, ribs, even his upper thighs had a few. I wanted to get closer and see what each one was.

"You okay over there?" My eyes lifted to his as he smirked knowingly at me. Flushing, I ignored the teasing tone. *Focus, Tasha.*

Trevor brought his arms up, flexing his bicep and pointing with the other and posed. Putting the phone down, I raised my eyebrow at him.

"Seriously?"

"What? All the ladies love it."

Scoffing, I rolled my eyes. "Uh-huh. Just stand there and look pretty."

"You think I'm pretty, huh?" Trevor's arms dropped, and he sent me a wide grin. I took that moment to snap a picture.

"In your dreams."

"Oh, I dream about a lot of things, Tasha." I refused to look up at him and let him see how flustered he got me. Looking at the picture I just took, I found my new favorite photo. Trevor may have just been standing there but the smile on his face made my breath hitch. It was enough to make anyone's heart stutter a few beats. A part of me was giddy, knowing that it was aimed right at me.

Unable to help myself, I quickly sent myself the picture before turning back to Trevor.

"Want a few more?"

With ease, Trevor posed a couple more times. Each

picture was Instagram-worthy and would no doubt get thousands of comments and likes from women.

"Your turn," he said a few minutes later.

"I'm okay." I wasn't sure I could take a decent photo with Trevor behind the camera. "We're almost to the spot anyway."

Keeping Josie's phone tight in my hand, Trevor reached into his pocket and pulled out his own phone.

"Selfies it is, then."

"Wha—" Trevor snapped a picture of me just as I spoke. "Hey!" I glared up at him. He moved until he was behind me and squatting a bit down, his chest brushing against my back as he brought his phone closer to our faces.

"Smile." Fighting the urge to roll my eyes, I looked forward and did as he said.

Trevor leaned down and smashed his cheek next to mine, beaming widely at the camera. A hand suddenly tickling my waist had me throwing my head back laughing, eyes closed. I briefly heard the camera's shutter sound around Trevor's tickle attack.

Squirming away from Trevor's hand, I wrapped my arms around my waist to block his hands from trying that again. My cheeks hurt slightly from smiling as I looked at him. Quicker than I could process, he brought the phone up and snapped a picture of me.

And then ever so slowly, he lowered it, his eyes glued to my face.

"Perfect." His voice was soft, but I still heard him. I opened my mouth to talk—I wasn't sure what I was going to say—but the tour guide took that moment to announce our arrival. Disappointment flooded through me at our stolen moment.

"Is everyone ready to dive in and get some snorkeling done?" Johnno, our tour guide asked. "We're going to get you guys all geared up and go over some things." He clapped.

As we all got ready, my excitement grew. I had always wanted to go snorkeling. Growing up, I went on quite a few vacations with my parents, but I wouldn't classify them in the same category as this one. More than anything, they were business trips.

My parents would come home and say we were going on a trip, get my hopes up that the three of us would be a family and go see all the sites, only to crush my dreams when they would end up in meetings all day. I always ended up stuck in the hotel with my nanny. I wasn't even allowed to go outside.

I used to plead with my parents to take me to places. Beg for them to take a day off and spend time with me. To come see me do cool tricks in the pool when I went swimming. But every single time, I was told that if I wanted the things I had in my life then they had to work.

Once I turned eleven, my parents stopped taking me on trips altogether. They left me home with nannies and maids. Left for weeks at a time while I stayed home alone. For so long, I was angry at them. Hurt that they left me behind, but I grew to accept it. To accept that we weren't a real family, no matter how much I wished we were.

After I turned sixteen, my parents had me join them on trips once in a while but only for them to show off that we were a happy little family to their friends or business partners. I'd be stuck sitting at awkward dinners with people I could care less about with my parents glaring at me every few minutes if I so much as chewed too loudly or said something they didn't like.

So, to be on an actual vacation with friends meant everything to me. To be out doing actual things and not holed up in the hotel.

"We are a little bit away from the shoreline because we

have found that this spot has the most active sea life. With snorkeling, we usually skim the surface of the water but if you are confident enough, you can swim a bit deeper in the water," Johnno explained.

For the next few minutes, all of us were handed flippers, goggles, and breathing tubes. I had to keep myself in check so I didn't interrupt the directions being given to us. I just wanted to be in the water.

Clad in a multi-color bikini and my gear, I was set to go. I knew I looked like a dork, but glancing over at the others, I wasn't the only one. It took a lot of effort not to laugh at Trevor as he struggled to put his goggles on, his face getting squished.

"We are going to fall backward into the water. Trust me, you don't want to go feet first, it doesn't feel good." Johnno chuckled. "Who wants to go first?"

"Tasha does." A hand on my lower back gently pushed me forward, Trevor smirking down at me. I elbowed him for volunteering me first.

"Gee, thanks," I mumbled, stumbling toward the guy. It wasn't easy walking in flippers.

"You got this, T." Josie grinned at me as I walked past. I may have wanted to get in the water, but I didn't want to be the first one to embarrass myself.

Standing next to the tour guy, I noticed he was actually cute. He appeared a little bit younger than me, but that was easily overlooked with his attractive Australian accent and the fact that he looked pretty damn good without a shirt on.

"Come to the edge of the boat." I felt eyes burning my back as the guy put his hands on my waist and helped me to the edge. "The best advice I can give is not to hesitate and just fall back. Best to just get it over with." He flashed me a kind smile.

The girls gave me a thumbs up as I sat there. Suddenly

feeling nervous, my eyes darted around until I met Trevor's. His head tilted to the side as if he could sense I was nervous. He gave me a small nod of encouragement, and for whatever reason, it seemed to ease the tension in my shoulders.

"Here you go." Johnno reached up and helped me fix my goggles until they were snug. "Don't want any water to slip in." Sending him a grateful smile, I took a few deep breaths. "Ready?"

With one last nod, I shimmied back farther.

"Want me to give you a push, or do you want to just fall back?"

"Push, please," I said after a moment. Just like jumping out of a plane, best to have someone shove you and not over-think it.

I barely got the words out before I was forced backward. I fell into the water so ungracefully, closing my eyes tightly even though I had my goggles on. Kicking my legs rather awkwardly, I pushed to the surface, breathing in a mouthful of air. I hadn't expected the water to be so cold. It was supposed to be pretty warm but the chill sent a shock through me, my skin breaking out in goosebumps.

"Woo, Tasha!" My eyes snapped open as I looked up at my friends still on the boat. A giant smile formed on my face.

I moved around the water to warm up and get used to the flippers on my feet while the others got ready to get in. It felt weird swimming with things hooked to my feet. I moved around like a little kid trying to swim for the first time. I could tell I was using my arms more than my legs.

"Fuck, it's cold!" Lydia yelled, causing me to laugh, my head dunking under the water. "Why didn't anyone say the water was cold?!"

"It's not that cold, don't be a baby," I heard Landon say, shortly followed by an, "Oh shit," as he, too, got in the water.

"Fucking idiot," Lydia muttered as she swam by me. Grinning, I moved onto my back to float, enjoying the sun on my skin as it warmed me up. I hadn't been floating long when I felt the water around me ripple just a little. Before I could open my eyes, I was suddenly up in the air before crashing back into the water with a loud splat.

Paddling to the surface, I took a deep breath, turning my head to glare at none other than Trevor. Trevor, who was grinning ear to ear. Of course the idiot still looked cute with the goggles covering half of his face.

"Why did you do that?!" My voice came out muffled, thanks to the goggles.

"No reason." He shrugged like he did nothing wrong. The little smirk on his face had me moving before I could think. Surprised at my advancement, Trevor didn't have time to move as I placed my hands on his head and shoved down hard, forcing his head under the water.

Keeping his head under for another second, I quickly let go and swam backward. That's what he got. He came back to the surface sputtering while it was my turn to grin. This time when Johnno interrupted, I didn't mind.

Sticking my tongue out at Trevor, I turned to our guide.

"We will swim a little in that direction." He pointed ahead of us. "On the way, keep your eyes open for stuff below us. You never know what we will see."

"We aren't going to see sharks, right?" Mila asked.

Johnno hesitated for a split second.

"Fuck no." Lydia said with a shake of her head.

"Don't worry, we don't typically see any around here. But with the ocean, we never know so keep your eyes open and shout if you do see anything." Johnno was quick to explain.

"Don't let the sharks come up and bite you." Trevor's voice sounded right beside me as my side was pinched. Jerking, I sent a wave of water toward him.

"Don't. You're gonna jinx us!"

"I'll protect you from the sharks." The others around us started swimming, cuing Trevor and me to follow.

"Great, I'm going to die."

"You have such little faith in me. I'm hurt."

"You think you can fight off a shark?" I asked, swimming after the others.

"I mean, there's a good chance I could die."

"No, you would die." I hurled back.

"Don't tear me down, Sunshine." The grin on Trevor's face grew.

"I'll say a heartfelt eulogy at your funeral."

"Gee, thanks." He deadpanned.

"You're welcome." I flashed him a grin. "Now try and keep up, shark boy."

We only swam for a moment before Johnno told us to put our breathing tubes on.

With all my stuff in place, I put my head in the water, making sure to keep my eyes peeled. I hadn't realized we were so close to the bottom. Right below us was the sea bed. If I could have squealed, I would have.

One second, the ocean seemed barren, and the next, it was filled with sea life. Fish of all different colors and sizes swam around below us. Some darting around really fast and others slowly swimming along.

Trevor was closest to me as I reached out to tap his arm, pointing at a fish that looked like Dory from *Finding Nemo*. It was even cuter in person.

Swimming around, I marveled at everything I saw, including the different types of rocks and algae. With the water being so blue, everything seemed crystal clear, perfect for snorkeling. The sun shone through the water, lighting it up in a way that was breathtaking.

The next little bit was a blur. I completely lost track of time as we all swam around the reef, pointing at all kinds of things: starfish, crabs, and even an octopus that swam by us. But my favorite was the giant sea turtle that slowly swam directly below me. It was the most incredible thing I'd ever seen.

Once we all got more comfortable, the guys started swimming deeper in the water. We swam close enough to the shore that diving deeper made it possible to see even more things on the floor bed.

As time went on, my arms and legs tired but I kept swimming around, wanting to soak up every last minute.

"Would you guys like a group photo before we head back?" Johnno asked as all of us came back up to the surface, taking our goggles off. He barely got the words out before Josie was yelled out a yes. I watched, surprised, as he lifted up what looked like a big camera from the water.

Had he been taking pictures the whole time? I made a mental note to ask when we got back to see if he took anything good for us to keep.

Gathering around each other in the water, I bumped into Trevor's side. With my arms getting more tired by the second, I immediately attached myself to him. Throwing my arms over his shoulders, I practically climbed on his back, feeling the hard muscle beneath my hands.

"And what do you think you're doing?" His head tipped back a bit to look at me.

"I'm tired," I simply said, facing Johnno for our picture. With a shake of his head, Trevor looked forward. Trying my hardest to ignore the feel of Trevor's wet skin on mine, I grinned at the camera.

After our picture, we all tiredly swam toward the boat which was thankfully not too far away. And by "we all swam," I meant I held onto Trevor the entire time and made him swim me back. I occasionally kicked my feet but Trevor did all the work while I laid my head on his shoulder. A thousand thoughts ran through my head as we returned to the boat.

As I kept my head on Trevor's shoulder, I had the sudden urge to tell him everything. To explain what happened that night between us. He deserved to know why I was distant. I kept going back and forth in my head, but I couldn't deny I felt the happiest I had been in a long time and maybe, just maybe, that was because of him.

10

TREVOR

"I could eat an entire buffet right now," Bryton said next to me as the boat headed back to the island. I ignored him and the others, my eyes landing on the blonde siren across from me.

Tasha leaned against Josie's side, looking adorably tired as she talked about who knew what. Something tugged in my chest as I stared at her. Her blonde hair hung down her back in waves, slightly dry but still wet enough to cling to her skin. Her shoulders and face had a light red hue to them from being out in the sun. She looked downright beautiful. And no one needed to get me started on her slender bare legs draped over Josie's. Legs that I wanted straddling mine.

Sitting there, I could still sense her on my back. The feel of her slick skin against mine as she held onto me, chest pressed to my body. It had taken everything in me to act normal. Like Tasha Davis hanging onto me was something that happened every day.

I thought back to last night on the beach. It was the first time Tasha and I had been alone like that without any of our friends nearby. Oddly enough, it didn't feel weird or awkward between us. We were just two people on a beach.

It was nice learning more about her. Seeing what made her the way she was. Tasha was so closed off at times, never really showing how she felt and rarely talked about herself. At least not when I was around. From what I saw Josie was the only one she was really close with. Knowing she hid so much of herself just made me want to know even more.

"Dude." My shoulder was shoved, my eyes moving to Bryton next to me. "Could you be more obvious?"

"What?"

"You're staring at Tasha like some creep." Bryton remarked.

"I'm not."

"The fact we've said your name five times and you didn't respond says you are." Bryton gave me a look.

Shit.

"When are you going to admit you feel something for her?" Wyatt asked.

"I don't feel anything for her," I lied right out of my ass.

"Yeah, and I don't love Josie." Wyatt shot me a look. "We're your best friends, Trev. You can't lie to us."

"I don't know what I feel," I grumbled. That part was true. I liked her. Liked her more than I should, considering that she could barely stand to be around me. But last night and today sparked confusion because she was acting differently. Almost like she enjoyed my company.

I never met a girl that knew how to get under my skin so much. She somehow crawled her way inside of me and didn't seem to be going anywhere anytime soon. I didn't think she even knew just what she did to me.

"Don't know what you feel as in you like her but don't want to, or you just want to sleep with her?" Bryton asked.

"Josie will have my balls if you sleep with her best friend

and make things awkward," Wyatt said, narrowing his eyes at me.

"I'm not going to sleep with her. I mean, I would like to obviously but..." I trailed off, unsure of what I was saying. Wyatt, Bryton and Landon stared at me, waiting for me to continue. With a sigh, I finally told them about what happened months ago.

"We kissed and everything was going great and she just froze. One second she was into it and the next she was running to her car." I couldn't lie and say I wasn't hurt. If I had done something to hurt her or make her uncomfortable, I would have liked to know before she ran off.

"Well, that explains the awkward tension between you," Landon commented.

"She has pretty much ignored me ever since." It may have sounded cocky, but no woman had ever done that. Typically, I couldn't get them off of me. Take the flight attendant on the way here, for example, who Tasha told to leave me alone.

"She seemed all over you today," Landon pointed out. She was definitely being more touchy the last few days but that just made everything even more confusing.

My eyes cut back to Tasha, laughing at something Lydia said. I wondered what was going on inside that head. What was the reason behind her ghosting me? Did I do something? The thought of hurting her in any way didn't sit well with me.

"Maybe you should just ask her," Landon said with a shrug, as if doing so was easy.

"I'll ask her as soon as you admit you like Lydia," I shot back, raising my eyebrow at him. The look he sent me had me smirking. "Thought so."

"God, between the two of you, I'm lucky I have Mila," Bryton remarked, looking over at his girlfriend with what could only be described as adoration.

"How are things with you guys?" I asked, glad to have the conversation directed away from me.

"Great. Actually," he looked over at the three of us, lowering his voice, "I'm going to ask her to move in with me."

"That's great, Bry." Wyatt patted him on the shoulder with a grin. I sent him one of my own. Mila and Bryton were perfect for each other.

Bryton kept his relationship with her hidden from us for a while. We knew something was up when he would bail on going out after a game or showed up to practice with a grin on his face. One day, Mila came to a game and the next she was a part of our little group. The two just melded together perfectly.

I'd never seen Bryton so happy. He was always more of the quiet type. When we did go out to celebrate, women flocked to him but he rarely gave them the time of day. He would just smile politely and make a little small talk but that was it. He's taken a few girls home but anyone could tell he didn't want that type of life. Then he met Mila.

"We basically live together anyway, but I want us to get our own place together."

"Proud of you, man." Landon tapped Bryton's leg. It sounds weird but Landon has always been that older brother figure to Bryton and me. Neither of us had someone like that in our lives and Landon filled that role.

"When are you going to ask her?" I asked.

"I think tonight. I don't want to overshadow Wyatt's day tomorrow." I caught his nervous undertone as he spoke.

"Don't worry, she'll say yes. You two are practically married anyway." Wyatt added. Which was true. They had been together for well over a year now.

"I couldn't live without her." Something about his words settled in my chest, making me once again glance at Tasha. Not that I was thinking about marrying Tasha any time soon, but it made me wonder if there was a chance I could have what Bryton and Mila had.

"WHERE ARE YOU GOING?" Landon glanced over from his spot on the little couch our room had.

"I'm just going for a walk. I'll be back in a bit," I lied. I wasn't in the mood to explain where I really was going. Plus, I wasn't sure Tasha would show. After dinner, I tried to catch her eye but she was too busy talking with Josie. Who knew if our plan to meet up again tonight was still on.

Landon looked at me skeptically but didn't say anything as I grabbed a jacket and headed out of the room. I was more than tempted to knock on Tasha's hotel door, but if she was anything like me, she probably didn't want Lydia to know where she was going. So, ignoring the urge, I made my way down to the lobby.

I stood off to the side, waiting for Tasha, when I heard my name.

"Trevor Hall!" Glancing over to my right, I noticed a group of three guys staring at me in shock.

"Dude, you are the best right winger in the league!" I chuckled under my breath at their expressions. Each one seemed starstruck as they walked over to me.

"Congrats on the Cup win, man. That last shot right when the buzzer went off was epic!"

Even after all these years of fans coming up to me, I wasn't entirely used to it. Hearing someone go on about how talented and amazing you were was awkward. I never really knew what to say back. I typically just smiled and said thank you.

"Thanks. It was a group effort," I replied politely.

"Can we get a picture with you?" one of the guys asked.

"Of course." I never said no when people asked for a picture or for me to sign something. We had great fans. The least I could do was take a quick second to say hi and pose for a picture. While the three tried to decide who would take the picture, a new voice interrupted them.

"I'll take it." Tasha stood off to the side, looking between the guys and me. My eyes ran over her body, taking in the jacket she was wearing. The same jacket I put on her last night. It hung off her slim frame and if it wasn't for the sweats she had on, it would have looked like she didn't have pants on.

The sight of her in my jacket sent a wave of possessiveness through me. I really liked the way she looked in it. The fact she was wearing it tonight made my lips twitch. While I was busy staring at Tasha, the three guys handed her a phone and came to stand beside me.

"Say, *Go Knights,*" Tasha said, holding the phone up. I caught her teasing smirk, knowing she did that on purpose. Resisting the urge to roll my eyes, I went along and said the phrase with the three guys.

Tasha liked to torture me as she took quite a few photos before finally putting the phone down.

"Thanks for the pictures, man." All three shook my hand. "Bring us back another Cup win."

"We'll try." I said, shaking their hands. Almost like kids in a candy store, the three grabbed the phone from Tasha, talking animatedly as they walked off.

"Wow, who knew you were so famous," she teased, coming up to my side.

"You're looking at the second most followed hockey player in the league." I flashed her a smile and put my arms out.

"And humble."

"The most humblest."

"That's not even a word dumb ass." Tasha shook her head, but I saw the ghost of a smile on her face.

"Ready?" I put my hands in my pockets, trying my hardest to resist the urge to grab her and pull her toward me. With a small nod, she headed for the door leading outside.

The sun had long since set as we walked the path toward the beach once again. I peeked at Tasha from the corner of my eye. Her blonde hair was pulled into a messy bun, and under the lights, I could see her cheeks were a soft pink color from being out in the sun.

A part of me was worried she wouldn't show, but walking side by side with our brushing, I was glad she did.

"Penny for your thoughts?" I asked. We'd been walking for a little bit in silence.

"Just a penny? Worth at least a hundred bucks or so."

"Smart ass." I bumped her shoulder with mine. "Seriously, what has you so quiet?"

We walked a little bit farther, shoes in hand, sand squishing between our toes, the waves crashing the only sound around us. I waited patiently, not wanting to push her to talk if she didn't want to.

"I never apologized for what happened that night we...."

"Kissed," I supplied.

"Yeah, that."

"You don't have to." I shook my head, but she cut me off.

"I do. I left without an explanation, and I'm sorry."

"Did..." I hesitated for a moment. "Did I do something?"

"No, it wasn't you," Tasha rushed out. "I..." I could tell she was struggling with what she wanted to say.

"If it's uncomfortable to talk about, that's fine, we don't need to. I just wanted to know if it was something I did, so I can make sure I never do it again." I gently pulled her to a stop with her elbow.

"The thing is I *want* to tell you. You deserve to know because you didn't do anything. I just… I don't know how." When she glanced up at me, her eyes were watery. The sight felt like someone reached into my chest and gripped my heart in their fist.

"I've only ever told Josie, and I don't want you to look at me or think of me differently because you probably will, and I can't stand that," Tasha rambled, looking anywhere but at me.

"Hey." Reaching out, I gently grabbed her chin and tilted her head back. "I will never judge you. For anything. Ever. You may not know me that well, but you will learn I don't judge someone based on their past. Got that?" My thumb smoothed over her skin. She gazed up at me with wide eyes but nodded.

Letting her chin go, I started walking again, thinking maybe it would help her talk if I wasn't staring at her. A few more minutes passed in silence before Tasha cleared her throat as if readying herself for what she was about to say.

"A month or so before I met you, I was out at a club with some friends. I tried to get Josie to go, but she was so cut off from everything. I could barely get her out of her apartment unless it was for work. So, I went with some other friends, and we were dancing, having a great time."

From the corner of my eye, I watched as she kicked at the sand, hands clenched at her sides. A sense of dread washed over me at her story.

"Somehow, we got separated. One moment I was dancing with my friends, and the next I was in a darker corner of the dance floor. A random guy came up and started grinding on me, even though I told him no." The way her voice dropped as she spoke made the hair on the back of my neck stand up. Please tell me this wasn't going where I thought it was.

"He, uh… He didn't like me saying that. Because of where I was dancing, no one saw him grab me and drag me toward the bathrooms in the back."

"Tasha." My voice came out in a strangled whisper, the dread in my stomach growing with each passing second. Tasha all but stopped walking as she stared straight ahead, almost lost in the memory.

"He pushed me against the wall…" She trailed off, unable to say more.

I was clenching my jaw so hard it felt like my teeth were on the brink of shattering. My chest heaved as images of Tasha flashed through my head.

Tasha. Fuck.

Trying to gain a bit of control, I turned to face her. Even though it was dark, the moon highlighted the tears running down her face. Tears that had no right being there. The words left my mouth before I could stop them.

"Did he…?" I couldn't even bring myself to finish saying it. She shook her head.

"H-he touched me, but I kneed him in the balls and ran." Red hot anger flared in my chest. Furious at the person who dared to lay a finger on her.

"Tasha."

"When you kissed me, I got a flashback and freaked out and ran. It wasn't you I swear I…" Tasha rambled. I noticed more tears welling in her eyes as her breathing picked up. I didn't hesitate in grabbing her by the arms and pulling her into my chest. She was stiff as a board in my hold.

"It's okay."

"No, it's not." Her body shuddered as if she was finally letting it all out. I wasn't fazed when her hands came up and hit my chest. "It's not okay!"

Tears ran down her face as she hit my chest harder. I stood there, arms holding her close. There was no real impact to the hits. If I had to stand there all night and let her get her anger out, I gladly would.

After a few minutes, I felt her body sag against me as the anger faded and the tears came harder. I wrapped my arms tighter around her frame and held her as she cried into my shirt. It took everything I had not to let my rage show. The last thing Tasha needed was to think my feelings were directed at her.

Bending my head forward, I placed it in the crook of her neck. It felt like a knife being stabbed into my chest repeatedly at the thought of what happened to her. That some *boy* thought it would be okay to lay a finger on her.

I wasn't sure how long we stood there, but Tasha slowly calmed down. I wanted nothing more than to keep her in my arms and make sure nothing and no one touched her. Eventually, she slowly pulled back. She met my eyes and once again my heart squeezed. Those gorgeous gray eyes were red and swollen from crying. Even so, she was beautiful.

Bringing my hands up, I gently cupped her face in my palms. My thumbs brushed away the wetness on her cheeks. "You are so strong," I spoke softly.

"But I'm not," she croaked.

"Yes, you are. And when you think you aren't, I will be right here to remind you." And I meant every single word.

"You think too highly of me." Tasha sniffled.

"You think too little of yourself." My thumb caught another tear. Her eyes fluttered closed, and she leaned into my hands. "I'm so sorry," I whispered.

No wonder she ran away that night. Kissing her probably took her back to that moment, and here I was being selfish thinking about only myself. It never hit me that maybe she was going through something traumatic.

Having her in front of me, touching her, eased the pressure in my chest. She was here, and she was safe.

My arms moved to cradle her against me, feeling her relax as the minutes passed. The crashing waves made it feel like we were in a little bubble of our own. We stayed just like that for a while longer. When Tasha started to shift in my arms, I knew it was time to head back. After our long day and this, I bet she was exhausted.

"Let's get you back," I spoke softly as I reluctantly dropped my arms. With a small nod, she stepped back. My eyebrows raised when she laced her arm with mine and started back toward the hotel.

We were both quiet as we walked back, but I found myself glancing down at her every few seconds. My heart broke knowing what she went through, but I also knew she wouldn't like me feeling sorry for her.

Every time I glanced down at her, my heart thudded in my chest, but I pushed it aside. The last thing Tasha needed was me trying to be more than her friend. Because she needed a friend more than anything right then. So, while I wanted more, I would push that aside and be what she needed instead.

11

TASHA

"Then he asked me to move in with him!" Mila gushed, the widest grin on her face. She was giddy as the four of us walked down the cobblestone street that weaved its way through the little town on the island. "He said he wanted to buy a house for the two of us."

I smiled at the way she was almost bouncing on her toes as she walked. She was like the energizer bunny this morning. Not that I blamed her. Moving in with your boyfriend was a huge step. She and Bryton were the cutest couple; he basically worshipped the ground she walked on.

"We're so happy for you." I grinned at her.

"Told you this vacation was going to be good for us." Josie beamed, looping her arm through mine.

At her words, my head moved on its own, glancing over my shoulder at the person walking behind me. The sight of Trevor made my stomach flip. Last night didn't go as planned. After going back and forth during dinner, I made the decision to tell him, despite being scared out of my mind. I didn't want him to look at me differently, but he did deserve an explanation.

It felt oddly nice to tell someone besides Josie. It had been weighing down on me for months, and while I wasn't healed from it, I did feel a bit lighter telling Trevor.

What happened that night in the club was... There really weren't any words to say what it was. It should have never happened to anyone, and yet it did. At first, I felt ashamed. Ashamed that I put myself in that situation because I should have known better. The shame and the guilt was what kept me from telling Josie immediately. I also figured that as a counselor, I should be able to deal with my own trauma.

It wasn't until one night when the two of us were sitting in her living room having our weekly wine night that I broke down and told her everything. It was her words that night that helped me. It wasn't my fault. It would never be *my* fault. But even I knew it would take some time before I fully believed that.

So, I took Josie's advice and went to Florida where my parents had a condo. They rarely ever went there, so I was safe to go and be alone. I hated not having anyone with me, but in the end, it really helped.

When I finally came home, I felt better. A lot better. I wasn't going to let one moment define me or my future. So, in a whole new headspace, I was happy to get back to my daily rhythm. Happy to get back to my life.

But then, when that night with Trevor happened, I wasn't expecting to freak out on him. I hadn't been with anyone after being assaulted, so feeling someone's hands on me sent my mind reeling. I did the only thing I could in that moment and ran

Later that night, all I could picture was Trevor's face and how he would react if he knew the truth. If he knew the reason I freaked out, he'd probably think I was damaged goods. I highly doubted Trevor would want to be with someone like that. And as much as I liked him, I couldn't subject him to that.

With all that in mind, I kept my distance. I forced aside my attraction and kept our interactions to a minimum. But being on this island… Things were starting to shift. The hold on my feelings was slipping with each day that passed. I didn't know if Trevor sensed it last night, but I did.

"I'm excited to finally see the island." Lydia's voice broke me out of my trance. Looking away from Trevor, I nodded along with the others. Having spent the last few days at the hotel, it was nice to finally see more of what Whitsunday Island had to offer.

In my hand, I held a pamphlet that we got from the hotel this morning. It labeled some of the popular places to see, recommended restaurants, and a small map of the town.

"Where to first, ladies?" Wyatt came up, putting his arms over mine and Josie's shoulders.

"Should we look at some of the stores first then maybe go see some sights?" I suggested, catching Wyatt's eye.

"Works for me." He grinned, dropping his arm from my shoulder and steering Josie toward a store in front of us. I stared after the two with a grin.

"Think she knows?" Trevor's voice spoke next to me a second later.

"I don't think so. I think Bryton asking Mila to move in has helped to distract her from the possibility of anything else happening."

"Look at my boys growing up."

"When's your turn," I joked, elbowing his side.

"Ha ha." He looked down at me. "I'm fully grown." Trevor gestured to his body.

Scrunching my nose, I shook my head. "Physically, yes. Mentally…no."

"That hurts, Sunshine."

"Good." I flashed him a grin before starting after the others who were already ahead of us.

"You know, I think you're jealous."

"Oh, am I?"

"Yep, you want to be me. I get it." He said it so seriously.

"Again, I am?" I asked.

"You just see how awesome and amazing and think to yourself, 'Damn, I want to be him so bad.' I don't blame you."

My lips twitched as he smiled broadly at me. I knew what he was doing. Without saying the words, he was letting me know that last night would stay between us, and we didn't need to talk about it unless I wanted to. And right now... I didn't want to talk about it. I wanted to push that conversation to the back of my mind and just enjoy today.

"Uh-huh. I think it's the other way around. I think you want to be me." I remarked.

"Why would I want to be you?" he asked.

"Cause I'm prettier." Trevor looked me up and down before shrugging.

My mouth fell open at his words. "You did not just say that!"

"I only speak the truth." Trevor answered.

"Okay, I see how it's going to be. Watch your back, Trevor Hall." I narrowed my eyes at him. I would get him back for that comment. Giving him a fake stink eye, I brushed past him into a store.

The cute little shop we were in was your typical touristy place. Filled with shirts that had the island's name on them. Little souvenirs and trinkets. They even had an adorable stuffed turtle that I secretly wanted to get. I walked around on my own until I heard Trevor's voice.

"What do you think of this?" I turned and paused at the sight before me.

Standing there, he wore a hat that had feathers sticking

out the top. It was clearly a few sizes too small and barely rested on top of his head. With my attention on him, he did a little pose with his hands on his hips.

"So cute." I said.

"I think it matches my outfit." The bright purple hat didn't match his green shirt. At all."It's missing something." I tapped my chin as I walked toward him, a rack filled with sunglasses catching my eye. With an idea popping into my mind, I searched for the ugliest pair. Upon finding pink ones that had little stars on the sides, I grinned.

Turning to Trevor, I stood up on my toes, reaching to put the sunglasses on his face. I purposely picked a pair that would fit a toddler, not a six foot three grown man. They barely perched on his nose and didn't even cover his eyes.

"Perfect." I beamed up at him.

When Trevor popped his hip out and pretended to fling hair over his shoulder, I lost it. He looked beyond ridiculous but in a cute way. The only thing missing was a feather boa to tie it all together.

"Think I'm ready for the runway?"

"Oh, definitely. Give Gigi Hadid a run for her money." I grinned ear to ear.

"You know it, honey." He made his voice higher pitch as he brushed past me, walking down the aisle with a sway in his hips. A *huge* exaggerated sway. My laughter echoed around the shop, and I tried to stifle it but with each sashay and flick of Trevor's hands, I couldn't help it.

"Work, work, work," Trevor said under his breath as he strutted. A few people in the store started staring at us, but Trevor paid them no mind.

When he came to a stop in front of me, I clapped and gave him a nod of approval.

"Beautiful."

"I know." He winked, taking the hat from his head,

and placed it on mine. My breath caught in my throat when Trevor crouched down, getting level with my eyes before gently taking the sunglasses and sliding them on my face. His fingertips softly grazed my cheeks as he pulled back.

"Think they fit you better." The grin on my face faltered at the intensity in his eyes. His gaze held me, his eyes lingering with an intensity that sent a chill through me. He looked at me as though he wanted to consume me entirely.

Swallowing thickly, I watched as Trevor's eyes followed the movement. His jaw muscle twitched before he blinked and took a step back.

"Let's see your model pose." He said. Ignoring the fluttering in my chest, I flashed Trevor a wide smile.

When he pulled out his phone to take pictures of me, I rolled my eyes but started masquerading around. Each pose was crazier than the last. Trevor pretended to be my photographer as he gave me instructions and snapped an endless amount of pictures. After a few minutes, I was laughing too hard to continue.

"Should have been a model, Sunshine," Trevor said, plucking the hat from my head and returning it to the rack.

"I know I missed my true calling." I laughed, shaking my head. Glancing around, I looked for the others but found no one. "Where is everyone?"

With Trevor taller than me, he looked above my head and down the aisles.

"I think we've been abandoned," he remarked.

"They just left us?" Making a face, I reached into my pocket for my phone. Finding a text from Josie, I quickly clicked it and read what she wrote.

Looked like you and Trev were having a great time, so we all went ahead to look at more shops. Text me in a bit. Have fun!

She followed the text with a winky emoji. I couldn't

decide if I was pissed at the group for leaving us or happy to hang out with Trevor alone. Probably a mix of both.

"Yep, we've been left," I said, shaking my head as I pocketed my phone.

"Let them miss out on the fun we're having." Trevor waved it off. "Let's go do whatever we want."

The thought of doing something spontaneous with Trevor made butterflies erupt in my stomach. Before I could overthink, I said, "Let's go explore."

"Look how stunning," I breathed. The sight before me was absolutely beautiful. One of Whitsunday Island's secret waterfalls was directly in front of us, looking everything like the locals told us about.

The waterfall cascaded down into a crystal-clear lake, rocks and moss growing all the rocks surrounding the pool beneath. The sound of the waterfall hitting the rocks a gentle roar. The sun filtered through the tall trees, highlighting the water. The scene felt like a hidden paradise.

When Trevor and I set out on our solo adventure, we explored the little town, visiting a few more shops and some historic buildings. It was surprisingly fun walking around with Trevor. He really was the type that went with the flow and made anything enjoyable. We were the typical tourists as we took picture after picture of the beautiful town. There was so much to see.

We had stopped to grab something to drink when we overheard locals talking about a waterfall. Being the nosey person that Trevor was, he interrupted them and asked them about it. Of course he charmed the pair, especially the wife, and they gladly told us about a secret path that most tourists didn't know about.

"The hike was worth it, wasn't it?" I didn't miss the mocking tone Trevor had.

One thing the couple didn't tell us was how rigorous the way up would be. It was all uphill with some rocky terrain. Thankfully, I wore tennis shoes, but I wasn't prepared for the walk to be that hard. Or for how out of shape I was.

The whole time, Trevor just casually strolled ahead as if the incline didn't bother him at all. He barely broke a sweat while I followed behind panting so hard my ribs hurt.

"Think the complaining was necessary?" he continued. Without looking away from the waterfall, I gave him the middle finger. Trevor laughed, the sound echoing around us.

I may have complained a little bit—okay, more like a lot. About halfway, I started getting tired, sweaty, and hungry. It was Trevor's bright idea to come, so it was only fair I gave him my wrath. But seeing the waterfall did make it worth it.

"Want to sit down for a minute?"

I barely let Trevor finish his sentence before brushing past him toward a big rock near the water. My legs were tired and definitely needed a break before heading back.

"When we get back you are so buying me some food," I grunted as I heaved myself up and sat down. The rock was a little slick from the water raining from the waterfall. Thank God I decided to wear a tank top and shorts, or else I would have died. There was no way I'd be hiking in a dress, either.

"I'll get you the biggest pizza we can find," Trevor promised, taking a seat beside me. At the mention of such food, I almost moaned. That would be so good right now.

The two of us sat on the rock, looking at the waterfall in comfortable silence. Trevor's big frame took up most of it, so our legs were touching. We were the only ones nearby, and we didn't pass a soul on the way up. It was so peaceful here.

The sound of the waterfall and birds overhead was like our own little nirvana.

"I can admit the hike was worth it," I said after a moment. From the corner of my eye, I saw Trevor open his mouth to say something. "Don't even say it," I interrupted him before he could.

"Say what?"

"I just know you're dying to say it but don't you dare." He knew exactly what I was talking about.

"I wasn't going to," Trevor said with a shit-eating grin.

"Uh-huh."

We lapsed into silence, but Trevor let out a giant sigh next to me. I ignored it at first but then he did it again, this time bumping his knee with mine. On the third sigh, I threw my head back and groaned.

"Fine, just say it." He waited for me to look over at him.

"Told you so." *There it was.*

"You just had to, didn't you?"

"Only cause I was right." I swore Trevor's grin grew wider.

"It was your bright idea to go on a five-mile hike. ONE WAY! We weren't even prepared." I exclaimed, throwing my hands up.

"Five miles isn't even that long," he had the nerve to say.

"Says the guy who works out every day. Us normal people don't do that."

"I don't workout every day. I take Sundays off."

"Oh, cause that's so much better." I rolled my eyes. I knew being a hockey player, they had insane workout schedules and meal plans. You couldn't play at the top of your game if you weren't healthy.

"You can come workout with me sometimes if you want."

"I wouldn't want to embarrass you with how much I can

108

lift," I teased. Yeah, cause that was the real reason I didn't want to go workout with Trevor.

"Oh yeah?"

"Yep. These muscles don't build themselves." I brought my arm up and flexed.

"I can see that. Although, I think mine are better." Trevor mirrored my action, making his T-shirt strain against his muscles. The sight of his forearms and biceps made my mouth dry but like hell if I was going to let him see how he affected me. Why did he have to be so attractive with those damn tattoos?

"I don't see anything? You sure there's muscle there?" I made a show of squinting my eyes as if I didn't see anything. The guy was insanely huge and had biceps the size of my head.

"You're a little shit." Using his shoulder, he shoved me to the side. I was already close to the edge, and since the dude was stronger than he realized, I tipped to the side, ready to fall off the rock. Before any noise could even leave my mouth, a pair of hands grabbed me by the waist and yanked me back.

I smashed into Trevor's side with a yelp. If I had fallen off the rock, I would have ended up in the water. Turning in his hold, I slapped his arm. "You almost made me fall in the water!"

"Yeah, but I saved you, didn't I?"

"You are so mean!" With each word, I smacked his arm harder, which only made him laugh.

"It's not like you would have died."

"We don't know what's in the water! I could have hit my head on rocks or something." When he just kept laughing, I shoved him. Catching him by surprise, he tilted to the side. I did nothing but sit there and watch as he slipped and fell right into the water.

Trevor landed with a loud splash. Scooting forward, I peered over the rock as Trevor's head reemerged. Wiping water from his face, he glared up at me.

"Sorry," I squeaked. I didn't mean to shove him hard enough to fall in.

"Tasha."

"I truly am sorry." But the damn smile on my face appeared again.

"That was on purpose." He pushed through the water toward me.

"It really wasn't." My eyes roamed his face, stopping on the hair stuck to his forehead before finding his shirt glued to his upper body. I swallowed thickly at the sight of the fabric clinging to his abs and chest.

"I don't believe you." He came to a stop right below the rock and stared up at me. There was something about seeing him fully clothed and wet. Who knew a T-shirt could form so well to a body? No wonder guys liked wet T-shirt contests.

"How's the water?"

The look on Trevor's face had me snorting. He looked less than amused. "Help me up, will you?"

"No. I'm not that much of an idiot." I shook my head. I knew if I tried to help him, he'd pull me right into the water with him.

"I won't." Trevor promised, extending an arm up.

"Yeah, I still don't believe you." Gesturing to a few smaller rocks to the right of us, I said, "Try getting up over there."

"Wow, you push me into the water and won't even help me out? You really are mean."

"I didn't push you in!"

"Come on, Sunshine, please? The water is getting colder." I stared down at him with a raised eyebrow. "I promise on all things holy that I won't pull you in," he added.

Seeing nothing but sincerity on his face, I let out a sigh.

"Fine, but if you pull me in, you will regret it." Moving to the edge of the rock, I got on my knees and held out a hand. I wasn't sure how much help I'd really be. I watched him wearily as he put one hand on the rock and the other grabbed mine.

I pulled his arm up hard, trying my best to help lift him out of the water, but the guy weighed a shit ton. Trevor did most of the work in lifting himself. Helping was pretty much worthless.

Water ran off his clothes and soaked the spot we were just sitting on. Seeing just how soaked he was, I was glad I put both of our phones in my little bag the last time we stopped to catch my breath.

"Have a nice swim?"

"Want me to throw you in?" he threatened.

"You wouldn't." I narrowed my eyes at his threat.

"Oh, I would."

I took a small step back, shaking my head. "Nope, you promised."

"But I—" Trevor started to speak, but the sound of one of our phones ringing cut him off. Surprised we had service, I reached into my bag and pulled out my phone. Lydia's number flashed across it.

"Hello?" I quickly answered.

"Where the hell are you? We've been trying to call for the last half hour."

"Sorry, we haven't had service." Movement out of the corner of my eye caught my attention. While Lydia talked away in my ear, all I could focus on was Trevor grabbing the neck of his shirt before pulling it up and over his head.

My mouth instantly went dry. *Holy fuck.* Nothing could top the way he looked shirtless covered in all those tattoos. My eyes followed the path of a line of water droplets as they ran down his chest and in between his abs. *The things I would do....*

"*Tasha!*" Lydia's voice snapped me out of the dirty thoughts racing through my mind.

"Yes?" I answered but my mind was elsewhere.

"*You guys need to get back.*" My mind worked overtime trying to remember what our plans were for the rest of the day. "*The lighthouse,*" Lydia emphasized.

Shit, the lighthouse.

"We're leaving right now. I'll text you as soon as we get close."

"*Try and hurry cause we can only hold off for so long.*" Her voice went soft. I knew what she meant as I quickly said bye and hung up the phone.

"We got to go." I moved to step around Trevor.

"Why?"

"Lighthouse," was all I said.

"Oh shit."

"Here, hold this so I can get down." Not even thinking, I handed over both my phone and my bag to Trevor. I was so busy looking down that I didn't see the smirk on his face, which was a huge mistake.

I had absolutely no warning as Trevor's hand touched my shoulder and gave me a shove. It wasn't a soft shove either. I barely shrieked before my body crashed into the water. Breaking the surface of the water, I sputtered before turning my gaze to Trevor. He stood above on the rock, staring down at me with a wide grin.

That fucking asshole.

"How's the water?" He had the balls to throw my words back at me. A wave of calmness settled over me as I swam toward him.

"You are so dead." My voice came out even, which only amused Trevor even more. He extended his hand out to help me up but I ignored it, grabbing onto the rocks and pulling myself up instead. My wet clothes weighed me down.

I stood in front of him, completely drenched. My hair fell out of its ponytail as I leveled him with a glare.

"If we didn't have to get back I'd be shoving your head under the water right now." We didn't have time to mess around, but boy, was I tempted to tackle him right back into it.

"You looked a little warm. Thought I'd help out." Trevor shrugged. The movement brought my attention back to his bare chest.

Shaking my head, I pulled my hair over my shoulder and squeezed out the excess water. I felt it trail down my spine and the back of my legs, making me grimace. My socks squished in my wet shoes. Great, now I'd have to walk in them.

"You better watch your back." I was going to get him back one way or another. Grabbing my phone and bag from his hand, I turned on my heel and started for the trail.

"You're welcome!" Trevor called out as I walked off. The only response I could muster was lifting both hands and giving him double middle fingers, Trevor's laughter following me back down the path.

TASHA

"**W**hat the hell happened to you two?" was the first thing out of Lydia's mouth. Four pairs of eyes turned to look at Trevor and me as we came to a stop in front of our group of friends. I couldn't even begin to imagine what we looked like.

"This idiot," I jabbed my thumb in Trevor's direction, "decided it would be a fun idea to go on a hike. And then proceeded to shove me into a pond."

"You shoved me first!" Trevor was quick to say.

"No, I didn't! You lost your balance and toppled over." I said as I turned to face Trevor in disbelief.

"Well, then you *lost your balance* too." He shot back.

My mouth fell open at his words. "You are such a liar!"

"Is that why you're covered in dirt?" Mila butted in. I glanced down at my soil-covered legs.

The trail back to town was pretty much loose gravel, which just clung to our wet shoes and legs. Didn't help that the wind decided to pick up and pelt us. And add in the fact that we got lost for a good twenty minutes as well. My shoes, legs, and even my clothes were encrusted with what now looked like dried mud.

My clothes had spots that were still soaked and my hair was practically a bird's nest. Trevor fared a bit better but even he was covered. Between the two of us, we looked rough.

"It looks like you guys rolled around a mud pit," Landon commented.

"Gee, thanks," I deadpanned, self-consciously touching my hair. Wasn't exactly how I wanted to look for this, but there wasn't time to go back to the hotel and clean up. A hand on my lower back had me turning to find Trevor close by.

"You still look beautiful, Sunshine," he whispered in my ear. I blushed at his words.

Trying to turn the attention away from me, I peered around Mila. "It hasn't happened yet, right?"

"Not yet. Wyatt took her into a shop just a moment ago so we can get into position." Thank God we didn't miss it.

"Okay, everyone fan out around the lighthouse," Mila whispered, even though she didn't need to. Josie's camera hung around her neck.

Excited for my best friend, I echoed the grin on everyone's face. Josie had no clue what was going to happen, but lucky for her, all of us were going to be there to witness it.

Up ahead along the pathway was a gorgeous lighthouse that overlooked the ocean. It was situated up on a hill so it stood above the town. Its beautiful white stone and red roof stood out amongst the greenery of the island.

Leaving our spot from the pathway to the lighthouse we all branched out. As I speed walked toward a spot to hide, I briefly admired the tall piece of architecture. It truly was the perfect place for this. We were all kind of flying by the seat of our pants since we had no way to practice what was coming.

Claiming a spot near the base of the lighthouse, I had the perfect view of the ocean straight ahead, along with the cobblestone path and rock wall that was just in front of the lighthouse for tourists to sit and admire the view.

Glancing around, I saw Mila to the left of me a little bit, tucked against the building with Josie's camera poised. Lydia was standing lower down the hill by the pathway trying to act normal. I had no clue where the guys were, but I briefly caught a glimpse of Bryton's head over a bush further down the hill. We were all spread out along the lighthouse to get all the angles.

Poised and ready to go, I waited. I couldn't believe this was finally happening. For years, Josie and I talked about finding someone to spend the rest of our lives with. A guy who was everything we wanted and more. And Josie found that. She found her person.

I'd never met someone who put my best friend above everything. Wyatt was the kind of man you searched your whole life for, and I couldn't be happier that Josie found him without having to waste years of her life giving other guys, who weren't right for her, endless opportunities. Back in uni, Josie was with such an asshole. He made her feel less than, and I vowed to never let another man make her feel like that again. When it came to Wyatt, I didn't have to worry about that.

Blinking rapidly, I tried to get rid of the tears that threatened to spill. I was just glad I was here to witness their special moment.

Another minute passed before I heard Josie's voice coming up the pathway to the lighthouse. Thankfully only a few other tourists were scattered around but none were near enough to ruin this perfect moment.

Josie and Wyatt appeared down the path, headed for the rock wall overlooking the ocean. The lump in my throat grew as I looked at my best friend. As briefly planned I lifted my phone up, pressed record, aiming the camera at the two of them. All of our friend group were supposed to record this moment from every angle so Josie could watch it back later.

"This place is stunning!" I heard Josie gush as she walked over to the rock wall, her gaze on the ocean.

As Josie talked, Wyatt peeked over his shoulder, catching sight of me. I sent him a thumbs up and smiled. He sent me a small, nervous one in return and patted his pocket.

"I almost don't want to go home."

"We can always come back soon," Wyatt said, coming up to her side.

"Maybe we can make this a yearly trip." From here I could hear the giddy-ness in Josie's voice.

I watched silently as Wyatt gave himself a little pep talk, his lips moving like he was muttering something under his breath. When he inhaled deeply, I knew it was time.

"Josie." Wyatt gently grabbed her waist and turned her to face him. The smile she had on her face made my heart squeeze. "You know I love you, right?"

"I would hope so. Especially after last night." I almost choked out a laugh. Josie definitely didn't know everyone was within hearing distance. Chuckling, Wyatt nodded.

"I made a promise to your dad that I would make sure you felt loved every second that you're by my side. And the thing is Josie," his hand came up to brush against her cheek, "I don't want you to ever leave my side."

My throat closed as tears once again pricked my eyes. I willed my hand not to shake my phone.

"I want to wake up to your horrible singing every day. I want to see the way your tongue sticks out of your lips when you're thinking about something. I want everything that is you for the rest of my life."

When Wyatt kneeled down onto one knee, my grin

almost split it in half. Josie covered her mouth as she stared at Wyatt in shock. I kept my camera on them as Wyatt reached into his pocket.

"So, Josie, will you—"

"Hell yes!" Josie interrupted Wyatt before he could finish. She threw herself at fiancé, who barely managed to stay upright. I could tell Josie was crying as her body shook. My own tears ran down my face.

Wyatt must have whispered something in her ear because she pulled away and nodded, extending her left hand. From here, I could hear her gasp as she stared down at the ring Wyatt slid onto her finger. The ring I helped Wyatt pick out a month ago.

It was a gorgeous pale pink diamond, resting on top of a rose gold band. It was beyond gorgeous and huge and absolutely perfect for Josie. I told him the day we looked at rings that Josie was more of a simple ring person, but he claimed he wanted the best of the best for her. We ended up compromising on one big diamond instead of multiple. This one was 100 percent made for her.

When Josie pulled Wyatt up into a kiss, I heard a loud cheer. Not even a second later, the guys came into view, pretty much tackling our newly engaged friends. I kept recording as they yelled, Trevor picking Josie up and twirling her around.

I waited until Lydia and Mila came out to congratulate the two, wanting to get it all on video, before finally putting my phone away. Walking down to where everyone was I caught Josie's eye. All it took was one smile before the two of us ran toward one another.

Her body slammed into mine as I wrapped my arms around her tightly. I hugged the girl who was more my sister than anything else, practically squishing her. Pulling back a few minutes later, I sent her a watery smile.

"You're getting married."

"I am." I reached up and wiped a tear off her cheek. "You did all of this, didn't you?"

Smiling, I shrugged. "Wyatt did most of it, but I wasn't about to let my best friend get engaged in some gross, sweaty hockey arena." Josie laughed, tears still leaking out of her eyes. "And your boyfriend may be great but he doesn't know how to pick out a ring to save his life."

"It's beautiful."

"You're welcome," I joked.

"You'll be my maid of honor, right?"

"Oh, I already got my maid of honor badge." The two of us shared another smile. "I'm so happy for you, Jo."

"Me too." Seeing the look in Josie's eyes almost made me cry. She looked happier than I'd ever seen her. After every-thing she'd been through, she deserved to be happy. It was then she seemed to take in my appearance.

"And what happened to you?" She raised an eyebrow at me. Feeling Wyatt's eyes on me, I shook my head.

"It's a long story. I'll tell you later. You better get back to your boyfriend—wait, I mean— *fiancé.* He looks seconds away from pulling you out of my arms." I whispered the last part.

"Love you, Tash."

"Love you too." Josie pecked my cheek before turning and heading back to her now fiancé. Almost immediately, Wyatt pulled her into his arms. With a soft ache in my chest, I stepped forward and lifted my phone to take more pictures.

"Okay, picture time!"

"I WAS surprised you never found out," Lydia said a couple hours later as all us girls sat at the hotel bar.

"I had no idea. I mean, Wyatt was acting a little different earlier but that was it."

"Wyatt called me at least three times, worried that you knew or had found the ring." I said. Every other day, I swore Wyatt was texting me to make sure Josie hadn't found out. I eventually just took the ring and put it in my drawer by my bed. The day before we left, I went by their apartment and gave Wyatt the ring before Josie got home from work.

"He's so cute," she mumbled, looking down at her ring for the hundredth time in the last twenty minutes. Not that I blamed her. It was absolutely gorgeous.

"I'm just happy we pulled it off. The videos and pictures we got were pretty good," Mila said as she sipped the last of her cocktail.

"I was surprised the guys were able to get such good pictures," Lydia commented. The pictures the guys took almost looked better than Mila's. Who knew they could take good photos?

"Speaking of," Lydia looked over at me, "what exactly happened with you and Trevor?"

"Yeah, why did it look like you rolled around in the dirt together?" Josie leaned forward in her chair as she asked. All eyes landed on me as they waited for an answer. I was tempted not to say anything but with the way they were all staring, I knew I couldn't get out of it.

"After you guys left us at the gift shop, thanks for that, by the way." I narrowed my eyes at Josie, who just grinned in response. "Trevor and I walked around for a bit before he overheard a couple talking about a waterfall trail." I found it comical how each of them listened so intently as I spoke.

"Anyway, we somehow ended up on a ten-mile hike

round trip together. Trevor nudged me and almost sent me into the water so I shoved him back…and he fell in."

Josie and Mila snorted as Lydia shook her head.

"Not my fault the guy has no balance. But Trevor being Trevor, he shoved me in as payback. Long story short, we had to hurry back into town, and with the way the wind blew, we ended up covered in dirt. That's all that happened."

"Nothing else?" Mila asked.

"No."

"You're so blind." Lydia shook her head at me.

"What?"

"You have no idea how smitten Trevor is with you." Josie sent me a small smile.

"No, he isn't. He lives to torment me."

"Definitely blind." Lydia restated.

The boys took that moment to come over, cutting our conversation off. My eyes instantly found Trevor. He was mid-conversation with Landon as I sat there staring at him. I could still picture him shirtless, water running down his abs. I had to shake the image from my head and look away before he could see the slight blush on my cheeks.

I didn't know what was going on or what was in the water on this island, but the last few days, I found my walls crumbling. The feelings I kept buried were resurfacing, and I was helpless to stop them. I wasn't even sure if I wanted to stop them.

"Ready to go get dinner?" Josie shook me out of my thoughts. Nodding along with the others, I quickly drank the last of my cocktail and stood.

With the long day and Josie and Wyatt's engagement, we all decided to go to dinner at a place the hotel front desk recommended. It was apparently a pretty high-end establishment and the perfect place to celebrate an engagement.

I felt more than saw Trevor coming up to my side. The others walked ahead of us as they talked.

"Got all cleaned up," he commented. I smoothed my hand down the front of my pale yellow dress. The silk clung to my skin, showing off my developing tan. I didn't typically wear the color since it clashed with my blonde hair, but with the way Trevor was looking at me, I was glad I decided on it for tonight.

After taking pictures of Josie and Wyatt, I immediately came back to the hotel to shower off all the mud and dirt. Ironically, the mud was just as hard to get off as the sand.

"You did too." I glanced over at him. Of course he looked downright hot in his white linen pants and dark blue button-up. The sleeves were rolled up to show off his forearms, along with the tattoos that were there. Something was wrong with me as I felt my underwear dampen, all from the sight of Trevor. *Get it together, Tasha.*

We didn't say anything else for a moment as we left the hotel. I could feel him glancing at me every few seconds, making me wonder what he was going to say.

"Ever going to admit you purposely pushed me in the water?" he said a moment later. *Yep, there it was.*

"Nope, cause it wasn't on purpose." I was being truthful. I really didn't think he would fall into the water with the shove I gave him. Typically, the guy was an immovable wall. I mean, his nickname on the ice was *The Beast.*

"Uh-huh."

"You're the one who pushed me in on purpose." I nudged him with my shoulder as we walked.

"Cause you did it first."

"No I didn't! You're just clumsy." My voice rose a pitch.

"Well you're—"

"Are you two done bickering like an old married couple?" Wyatt called out. Both of our heads turned to find everyone

staring with raised eyebrows. Having been caught, I incon-
spicuously kicked the side of Trevor's shoe with my heel.

"Ready to eat? I'm starving." I suddenly said. Leaving
Trevor's side, I saddled up to Lydia's and hooked my arm
through hers. With the restaurant a few blocks ahead I all but
dragged her forward. I felt multiple pairs of eyes on me as I
walked but only one burned more than the others.

13

TASHA

"Everyone ready to go?" Josie asked as I bent over to lace up my heels.

"Ready," Lydia, Mila, and I echoed. Everyone added finishing touches to their makeup and outfits.

Today was our final day and night on Whitsunday Island. At dinner last night, we all agreed on going whale watching and doing more exploring before going to a local club tonight. It was the perfect way to end our trip. One last day to celebrate Josie's engagement before going back to the real world.

We all had a blast whale watching. We ended up seeing four humpback whales break through the water that were apparently passing through during migration. Probably one of the coolest things we'd done on this trip, snorkeling aside.

After a full day of exploring more of the town, we were now all getting ready to go to the club. We were set to meet the guys downstairs in five minutes for the short walk from the hotel.

Straightening up from putting my heels on, I smoothed

my hands down the sides of my skirt. Since it was our final night, it was a perfect time to finally dress up.

"What do you guys think?" Mila asked as she came out of the bathroom with flawless winged eyeliner and mauve pink lips. She had an obsession with lipstick and always carried no less than three colors in her purse at all times.

She wore a short silver dress with a plunging neckline, something only she could pull off. Her dark skin practically glowed as her gorgeous curls went down her back, a few tendrils framed her face. Her six inch heels made her even taller. Mila looked drop dead gorgeous.

"Damn Mila." I whistled, causing her to grin widely.

"That dress suits you perfectly." Josie echoed.

"I need those heels." Lydia added.

Mila preened under our compliments. While she went over to her purse on the couch Lydia got up and headed for the bathroom, her dress catching my eye.

Her red dress was so different yet perfect for her. While it had long sleeves, the front dipped down between her breasts and the skirt had a revealing slit, showing off plenty of leg. It cinched at the waist, showing off her body in ways she typically didn't. Her short blonde hair was piled into a cute updo. Interested to see how Landon dealt with how hot she looked tonight.

"Excited for tonight?" I turned to ask Josie next to me. She was in the middle of slipping on her heels when she answered.

"It's going to be fun, but I'm sad it's our last night here though."

"The last five days have flown by." I said in agreement. Feels like we just got here. So much has changed since we stepped foot on the island. Mila and Bryton were moving in together. Josie and Wyatt were engaged. Trevor and I...well that was still up in the air. As for Lydia and Landon, the two still couldn't decide if they wanted to hit or fuck one another.

"Think Wyatt will like the dress?" Josie asked, standing and doing a little twirl.

The soft white dress she wore hugged her frame perfectly. The material was silky, bunched on one side to show off more leg with little sparkly tassels hanging down. The dress contrasted beautifully against her tanned skin. It was unlike anything she typically wore but it fit her so well. Like me, she kept her long brown hair down. She looked like a bride to be.

"He's going to love it." I promised. Josie grinned in return.

While everyone dressed a bit fancier, I chose something more casual. The black top I wore was only held by a single string around my neck and my back, leaving almost my entire back bare. It plunged just enough to show off my cleavage. I paired it with a simple black skirt that showed off my legs. With a pair of red bottom heels I was good to go.

Within ten minutes we were all ready to go. Glancing at my friends I saw how hot we looked. We were all so different from one another, but damn, we would be turning heads tonight. Or more like *our* men's heads.

I couldn't be bothered to carry a bag, so I stuffed some money in my top and held my phone. If anything, I'd make Wyatt pocket my phone since he'd most likely have Josie's. No one wanted to be out dancing with a purse hanging from their shoulder.

Arm in arm with Josie, we all made our way down to the lobby where the guys were waiting for us. The club was only a block away, thankfully, since we were all wearing high heels. The walk back was going to be a bitch after.

Our heels clicked against the marble floor, drawing the attention of all four guys standing there, and even a few guests in the lobby. My eyes sought out one person in particular. Trevor's eyes met mine, and it felt like it was just us as the others faded away.

Trevor's eyes raked up and down my body, his jaw muscles twitching. I could have sworn I heard him mutter a 'fuck' under his breath. I felt my cheeks heat up at the way he kept staring. Almost like he wanted to devour me right then and there.

While he was busy checking me out, I did the same back. Trevor's brown hair was styled back but a few pieces hung on his forehead, my fingers itching to push it back. He had a slight bit of stubble on his face which only enhanced the dirty thoughts running through my mind.

A black dress shirt fitted his upper body, the sleeves rolled up, showing his forearms and the sexy as hell tattoo sleeve he had. It was almost like he paired his outfit with mine. A small part of me purred at the thought. He finished his outfit off with a pair of black linen pants that almost looked like dress pants. He literally looked like he walked off the set of a photoshoot.

"Hey." His words brought me out of my blatant staring.

"Hi."

"Looks like we're matching." Trevor swept his eyes up and down me. The way they lingered on my legs made my pulse jump.

"Means we're secretly the coolest."

"Oh, 100 percent."

Trevor's face was serious for a moment before breaking out in a smile.

With the others heading for the doors, I was forced to look away from Trevor's smile. A smile that made my heart flutter in an embarrassing way. When he turned around, my gaze immediately dropped to his ass.

"Nice ass," I muttered, not even realizing it came out of my mouth.

"You want to do what with my ass?" Trevor looked at me over his shoulder, eyebrows raised. Of course he was close enough to hear that. "Didn't know you were into that kind of stuff, Sunshine."

"What? No!"

"It's okay, I'm not kink-shaming. You do you."

"I'm not…" I shook my head, but he stopped me.

"Don't worry, Sunshine. I won't think of you differently, I promise." Trevor smirked. "But kinky."

"You… I…" I couldn't get the words out. Not when he winked at me and then turned away.

"Come on, Sunshine. You can tell me all about your kink on the way."

Narrowing my eyes, I stomped past him. "I hate you," I muttered under my breath. I was more embarrassed that he heard me admiring his ass than anything else.

"No, you don't." Trevor followed after me. I didn't have to look at him to know he was grinning like an idiot.

"I truly believe you've been hit in the head too many times. Brain damage has occurred."

Trevor easily kept up with my long strides. "I told you I wouldn't judge. I'm just curious." From the corner of my eye, I watched him smirk over at me. "So do you like to be the one doing the fucking or is it the other way—" Before he could even finish, I sent my elbow right into his ribs.

"I am so done with you," I said, my expression neutral. He just responded with an even wider grin.

Ahead of me, Mila and Bryton walked hand in hand. Bryton bent down to whisper something in her ear. Lydia and Landon were walking side by side, despite the two of them saying they hated each other. I didn't miss the sneaky glances they gave each other. Maybe something was secretly going on between them now that we were on vacation.

Josie and Wyatt hung back near us. The two of them were

128

a picture of pure happiness. Josie's face was going to fall off from how much smiling she was doing. Wyatt was no better. Staring down at his fiancée like if he looked away, she would disappear.

The walk to the club didn't take too long. In less than five minutes, we were nearing the doors. With each step closer, I felt the all too familiar pressure in my chest. I'd only been to a club once since that night and could sense the same anxiety filling me. It was only because Josie was by my side that I didn't turn and high tail it out of there. I also had my mantra to fall back on—*I am safe, I am safe, I am safe.*

I knew it took time to get over traumatic experiences. Hell, I preached that to my own patients, yet sometimes, I couldn't seem to take my own advice.

"Hey." Josie's voice snapped me out of my head. "Can I talk to Tasha for a second?" she asked Trevor, who nodded and went to walk by Wyatt.

Looping her arm through mine, she spoke softly. "You okay?"

"I'm fine. You don't need to worry about me." I squeezed her arm and sent her a smile. It was her night, and I wasn't going to take the moment from her.

"I'll always worry. But if at any point you want to go, just let me know and we can leave." And she meant it. I knew if I looked uncomfortable, she would haul me out of there with no hesitation.

"I will," I promised, even though if it came down to it, I wouldn't. Not tonight. "Let's celebrate your engagement!" I grinned, changing the subject.

Josie looked at me with worry and hesitation on her face, but I gave her a little nudge. I was going to be just fine. She didn't seem convinced, but she eventually left my side and walked back over to Wyatt.

As the others reached the door to the club, I lingered back a second.

Don't think about it, Tasha. You are okay. Nothing will happen.

I knew I would be fine, I just needed to convince my mind of that. I was going to let loose and have fun tonight.

"Hey," a voice said softly next to me. Swallowing, I looked up at Trevor. "I got you."

Those three words seemed to settle into my bones, easing the tension in my shoulders. I don't know if it was the way Trevor said them or the look on his face, but I knew he meant them. He wasn't going to let anything happen to me when he was around.

"Okay?" His eyes never left mine.

"Okay."

With an encouraging smile, Trevor put a hand on my lower back and steered me into the club.

14

TASHA

"God, that burns."

I coughed as I took another shot of tequila. I was already three shots in and each one seemed to sting worse than the last. Yet when Mila slid another shot in front of me, I knocked it back.

I looked around the club, still pleasantly surprised at how nice it was. It was bigger than it looked on the outside and despite it being the only club here on the island. Cleaner than any I'd ever been to, and while it was packed with people, it didn't feel like we were sardines on top of each other.

The dark red walls gave the place a more moody vibes, paired with the low lights hanging above us. It wasn't too dark that you couldn't see in front of you, but dark enough it set the mood to something sexier.

"I'll be right back!" I yelled over the loud music as the others got ready to go on the dance floor in the middle of the room.

"Want me to—" Josie started to say, but Trevor interrupted her.

"I got her." I shivered as Trevor came up behind me, his

chest grazing my shoulder blades. With a firm hand on my back, he helped guide me across the room toward the bathroom.

From the moment we entered the club, Trevor has stayed by my side. He went up to the bar with the others to get us drinks, making sure I stayed in the booth but kept his eyes on me the whole time. Just like he promised.

Trevor was a wall of pure muscle and towered over almost everyone. He easily paved a way for us through the crowd.

"Are you doing okay?" Trevor leaned down and whispered in my ear. Surprisingly, I was. We'd only been here a little bit, but I felt good. No panic attacks yet. I knew I had Trevor to thank. His words and the fact he stayed by my side so far had eased the tension inside of me. I knew nothing was going to happen as long as he was there. I was already too tipsy to think too hard about that.

"I am." I tilted my head back and smiled up at him. Even in the dark club, his eyes seemed to shine at my words.

"I'll be right here when you're done."

I had to physically force myself to walk through the bathroom doors because if I stayed there for another moment I would have done something incredibly stupid. The alcohol running through my system slowly made my logic fade to the background.

While I washed my hands, a group of girls stumbled over to the sinks, talking loudly. I tried to ignore them, but I couldn't help but overhear what they were saying.

"Did you see how hot he was?"

"I would let him throw me against a wall."

"Those tattoos."

I immediately knew who they were referring to. Who was standing outside the women's bathroom with tattoos and was extremely attractive? That would be Trevor. Looking through the grungy mirror, I listened to the girls rave about him.

In a weird way, I felt a bit smug at them talking about Trevor. He was attractive and always grabbed women's attention when he was out, but they weren't the ones going home with him. He wasn't going to walk *them* back to their room and make sure they were okay. Nope, that was *me*.

So, they could say what they wanted, but they had no chance.

Smirking to myself, I let them walk out in front of me, catching sight of Trevor leaning against the wall waiting for me. Unable to help myself, I firmly pushed my way through the girls standing there. I felt their eyes snap toward me as I went up to him, sending him a wide smile as I hooked my arm through his.

With a quick glance over my shoulder, I caught the glares from the girls, but my smug grin only got wider. I refrained from winking at them, and instead tugged Trevor away from the bathrooms, back to where our friends were waiting for us.

I knew I practically staked my claim on someone who wasn't even mine, but I couldn't bring myself to care. Not right now anyway.

"What was that about?" Trevor asked, to which I just shrugged.

"Nothing."

When we reached the booth that we managed to snag, I noticed only the guys were seated. None of them even glanced at Trevor and me, their eyes glued to the dance floor in front of us. Without looking, I knew my girls were dancing.

With each passing second, I felt the tension between Trevor and me grow. I know he knew what I did a second ago was anything but innocent, which meant I needed to get away from him before I did something even more stupid. Without looking at him, I left him at the booth with the others and made my way toward my girls on the dance floor.

Upon seeing me, all three girls cheered. I looped my arm through Josie's and let the music sink into my body as I let go.

SWEAT RAN DOWN MY BACK, making my hair stick to my neck and shoulders. My feet were starting to hurt, but I barely noticed it as I stumbled in the direction of our booth. Josie giggled against my side.

"Oh, shots." She reached for one as Wyatt spoke.

"Want some water, babe?" Josie shook her head at his words, not even looking at him as she grabbed the clear glass and knocked it back. I followed her lead and took two, barely feeling the burn this time.

I caught my breath before Lydia was beside me, tugging on my arm, bringing me back to the dance floor before I could say a word.

"I love this song!" she yelled.

The two of us found a spot not too far from our booth, Lydia's arms going around my neck as we danced together. The music was so loud that she had to bend her head to yell into my ear.

"Trevor hasn't taken his eyes off of you."

At her words my head instantly turned toward our booth, eyes landing on Trevor. True to her words, he sat there, watching me dance with Lydia. The heat of his stare burned my skin, even from afar.

Still moving my body, I watched as he brought his beer

bottle to his lips, taking a long pull. I didn't know what it was, but the action was erotic. My mind instantly went someplace dirty.

I was definitely feeling the effects of the alcohol as I found myself moving my hips more. My eyes were hooded as I kept my gaze on Trevor, my body grinding and rolling. A jolt of satisfaction ran through me at the way he leaned forward, forearms braced on his knees, eyes glued to me.

I couldn't look away even if I tried. Under his gaze, I felt sexy. Sexier than I ever felt in my life. I knew I was pretty. I wasn't blind. I knew guys loved my long legs and blonde hair. Saw my face, the same features as my mother, and thought I was a model. I was used to *those* stares. But not the way Trevor was looking at me.

Looking at me like he would go to Hell and back just so he could watch me.

The alcohol in my system fueled my confidence. Lifting my hands up, I swayed my hips, loving the way Trevor's eyes tracked the movement. With my heart racing, I closed my eyes and turned.

My head whirled at the movement, making me stumble, but a pair of arms caught me. Opening my eyes, I jerked out of the person's hold and looked at the person standing there.

Johnno. Our snorkeling guide from the other day.

He recognized me at the same time I did as a wide smile took over his face.

"Nice to see you again!" he yelled.

"You too!" With a mind of their own, my eyes raked over him. He was wearing a button-up shirt and shorts. His tan face and hair slick with sweat. While he was still very attractive, I couldn't help but compare him to Trevor. Couldn't help but see Trevor's green eyes where Johnno's brown ones were.

Speaking of Trevor.

I glanced over my shoulder and looked for him, only to pause at what I saw. He was still sitting at the booth but a girl was leaning forward, grinning down at him while her hand was on his arm. I watched with a sinking stomach as he smiled up at her. Smiled.

I didn't know why but seeing that felt like a blow to the stomach. His smile appeared genuine, and he didn't seem to be moving away from her. Hurt and irritation washed over me.

Anger and alcohol wasn't the best combination to have filling my veins as I whirled to face Johnno.

"Dance with me," I all but demanded. I barely gave him time to nod before I was moving my body against his. If Trevor wanted to flirt with someone, then so could I.

I had no right to be jealous but telling myself that did nothing to help the envy that bloomed in my chest. Trying to shove it aside, I turned around until my back was pressed against Johnno's chest. His hands landed on my hips, guiding them back against him.

Closing my eyes, I tried to get lost in the moment. I had an attractive guy behind me who was more than happy to be dancing with me. But as soon as I closed my eyes, the person dancing behind me wasn't Johnno. No, it was Trevor. It was *his* muscular arms holding me against his chest. *His* breath on my neck.

I lost myself in the image. My alcohol-induced brain ran with the fake scenario as I moved my hips back into Johnno.

I was so lost in my head, the music pounding through my body, that I didn't feel the hands on my hips disappear. It wasn't until warmer breath fanned over my neck that I blinked out of my fantasy. I stiffened as hands wrapped around my waist. My mind took a moment to realize I wasn't imagining a different set of hands on me.

"Sunshine." Even though the voice was deeper and

136

huskier, I would have recognized it anywhere. I relaxed into Trevor's hold, but my heart raced at the weight of his hands on me.

Trevor moved one of his palms across my stomach, stopping right below my breasts. His hands were so big that just one spanned almost all the way across my torso.

"If you wanted to be touched, all you had to do was ask."

A moan almost escaped from my mouth. At his words and the tone he used. My eyes fluttered as well as my stomach. *Damn.*

"What do you think you're doing, hmm?" With one hand under my breasts and the other on my hip, he gently coaxed my hips to move. I felt ready to faint as my ass pressed into his groin. My skirt had ridden up to where I could feel the fabric of his pants against the back of my thighs. My nipples threatening to poke through the little fabric of my top.

"You should know better than to tease me, Sunshine." My eyes closed on their own as he whispered in my ear. His breath tickled my neck, making me hyper aware of how close he was

The bratty part of my brain was working just fine as I opened my mouth to respond.

"I wasn't the one flirting with a random stranger." My voice came out breathier than I intended.

"So you were jealous." Trevor's grip on my hip tightened just slightly. Somehow, his voice got even deeper.

"No." But we both knew it was a lie.

"If you would have looked you would have seen me turn her away the moment she touched my arm." My skin heated when his nose grazed the top of my shoulder and skimmed the distance up to my neck. "Jealousy looks good on you, Sunshine."

God, I loved when he called me that. I may have said I hated it the other day but I lied.

"But know that no one is allowed to touch you when I'm around." The conviction in his voice was clear as day.

If I wasn't already a puddle in his arms, I was now. I was near detonation with the way he was gently, but firmly, grinding against me. I'd done more with guys on a dance floor but this with Trevor was by far the sexiest thing I'd ever done. Ever felt.

"Understood?"

"I... Uh..." I couldn't get the words out. My brain was complete mush.

"I'll take that as a yes." He chuckled against my skin.

Yep, I was done for. I was going to explode into a ball of need. I wanted Trevor right then. Wanted him more than I ever wanted anyone else. It took everything in me not to turn around and kiss him. To press myself against him.

The thoughts that swirled in my head were dangerous. If I let myself give in, I'd be done for. I'd lose whatever sort of friendship the two of us had developed over the last few days. And as much as I wanted to believe that Trevor liked me, I wasn't sure he did.

Yes, he was here with me, but we were in a different place, a different country. Would our feelings be the same once we got back home, back to the real world?

And as much as I wanted to not think about the future, I had to. Because Trevor had the ability to take my heart and break it into a million pieces.

Using all of my willpower, I forced myself out of his hold. My head whirling as I quickly stepped away, heading to our booth. On the way, a waitress walked by carrying a tray with shots. I didn't hesitate in reaching out to grab one, only for another hand to snatch it first. It was Trevor's. He wasted no time in knocking back the shot, my eyes glued to the way his throat rippled as he swallowed.

With heat crawling up my spine, I turned on my heel and continued my way back to the others.

"Where's Josie?" I questioned Landon, the only one sitting at our table.

"They left a few minutes ago," he said, his eyes not leaving the dance floor.

"Oh." I swayed to the side as the effects of all the alcohol took hold. I was a lightweight, so drinking so much was probably not the smartest idea. Big hands grabbed my hips to steady me. Trevor's citrus-y scent filled my head. "I think it's time to go."

"What? No." I shook my head but had to close my eyes as my head dizzied.

"Time to go, Sunshine." I opened my mouth to argue but when the world started to tilt on its axis, I knew he was right.

Trevor talked with Landon for a moment before gently steering me for the door with an arm around my waist. "Let's get you back to the hotel." His voice was soft. A big difference then what it was a few minutes ago on the dance floor.

Using his big frame once more, Trevor led us through the crowd of people until we reached the doors. Immediately, the brisk air cooled the sweat clinging to me, bringing my temperature down a few degrees.

Still keeping his arm on my waist, Trevor guided me down the sidewalk leading back to the hotel.

"Did you know I danced back in the day?" I suddenly said after a moment when the silence stretched between us. The sober part of my brain wanted to reach out and slap drunk Tasha. I needed to learn to control my mouth when I drank.

"Oh yeah?"

"Yep." I nodded my head rapidly. "My mom put me in ballet classes for years."

When my mom first signed me up for them, I was thirteen. I loved it and even made a few friends in the class.

Every few months, we would have recitals and all the parents would come and watch their kids. My mom and dad came to the first one but that was it.

The next recital—four months later—my mom dropped me off at the doors and drove off. I thought she was just going to find a parking spot but as I went on stage, I looked everywhere for her just to come up empty. Then, I thought maybe they were somewhere in the back, but when it was over and everyone ran to their parents, who congratulated them on their performance, I stood there. Alone. My parents were nowhere in sight.

It wasn't until twenty minutes after the recital that my mom showed back up and ushered me into the car. Not a single word was said about my dance. Not even a, "How did you do?"

After that, ballet turned into a way for my parents to get rid of me for a few hours. It also gave them bragging rights —that they had a daughter in dance. Like they knew if I could dance or not. I stayed in the class until I was sixteen, when I learned that the *real* reason my parents signed me up was to get close to another girl's father, who, apparently, was a millionaire that they thought would be useful as a friend.

"Bet you were great."

"Best in the class." I stuck my chin out proudly. "Watch this."

Stopping in the middle of the road, I moved my feet into first position, the back of my heels almost touching. It was hard to do in heels, but I lifted myself up onto my toes. I went to lift my leg up but my skirt was too tight and my balance was completely off. Stumbling to the side, I couldn't help but laugh.

"Oh yeah, so impressive."

"I know, right." I smiled. Totally missing the sarcasm in

140

Trevor's voice. "I quit just to spite my mom." The words left my mouth on their own.

"Wow, such a badass."

"The biggest badass. I used to dye my hair a lot to piss off my parents," I said as we started walking again. "I once went pink and my parents practically banned me from being seen with them. Worked in my favor cause I didn't have to go to any stupid events," I rambled.

"Wait, I have a picture!" I patted my hips and then cupped my chest, looking for my cell. "Where's my phone?" I turned in a complete circle, hands still on my breasts.

"I have it, Sunshine." Trevor gently grabbed my elbow. I forgot I left my phone on the table near the others so I wouldn't lose it. Didn't even notice Trevor had grabbed it.

"Oh, good. Can't lose that. It's got all my dirty pics." I sent him a wink. God, I had no filter when I drank. Beside me, Trevor cleared his throat, his eyes widening as he looked at me.

"Yeah, you need to get some sleep."

"But I'm wide awake!" I made a show of making my eyes big.

"For now." He steered us onto the sidewalk yet again— because I kept veering off into the street—the hotel up ahead. We walked in silence for another minute as I stumbled along the cobblestone pathway.

"Why aren't you all over me like you were at the club?" Again, the word vomit. Trevor just laughed under his breath at me.

"You don't need that right now. And despite what you think, you are definitely not sober." Walking through the hotel doors, I stumbled slightly, making Trevor wrap his arm around my waist again and tug me to his side. "I made a promise to watch over you tonight and I intend on keeping it."

Why does he have to be such a gentleman?!

I was quiet as we rode the elevator up to our floor. My head was in an almost drunk haze, but it only magnified the dirty things that ran through my mind. Especially when those big hands of his grabbed my hand and tugged me out of the elevator. His hand engulfed mine and made me wonder what he could do with them. He had big hockey player hands. Maybe I just unlocked a new kink.

"Keycard?" Trevor's voice pierced through my dirty thoughts. Shaking my head, I reached into my top, pulling it out. It was warm and a tiny bit sweaty thanks to being next to my boob all night.

Without batting an eye, Trevor took it from me and opened my door, letting me stumble past him inside. Needing to get my heels off, I barely made it three steps before I was bending over and unlacing the torture devices. How I managed to get both shoes undone without falling over, I had no clue.

I briefly heard a low grunt behind me, but as soon as I flung my heels off, all I could think about was how much better my feet felt. I wiggled my toes and moaned.

"You go get changed while I get you some water," Trevor said.

I didn't need to be told twice to get out of these clothes. While it wasn't the most uncomfortable outfit I'd worn, it wasn't comfortable either. Plus, who wanted to stay in sweaty, gross clothes? Not me.

When I got to my room I quickly changed into an over-sized T-shirt to sleep in. I was pretty impressed with myself. I only managed to trip twice and fell onto the bed once. Not bad.

"Are you dressed?" Trevor's voice came through the doorway.

"Yep!" I sat on the edge of the bed, legs dangling off the side.

"Here, brought you these." Trevor walked in, holding a glass of water and something else. My stomach churned slightly at the thought of water, and I shook my head.

"You'll thank me later, Sunshine. Drink." The command in his voice had me instantly reaching out, taking the water and the Advil he had.

"Good girl." The praise had my toes curling. I took another few sips. "Think you'll be okay tonight?"

"Unless you want to stay the night." The voice that came out of my mouth was anything but innocent. The flirty tone seemed to shock him as his eyebrows raised. Biting my bottom lip, I tilted my head back to look up at him. My inner voice screamed at me to stop talking. "We could stay up awhile longer."

I watched as Trevor's eyes darkened and his jaw clenched. He was staring down at me with a look that screamed yes, but he stayed where he was. He looked like he was at war with himself before he shook his head.

"As tempting as that is—no."

"Why not?" One hand left the cup I was holding and trailed up my bare legs to the hem of my shirt. This was drunk Tasha talking now.

"Because..." Trevor stepped forward, bending down slightly as he reached out. I thought he was going to touch me, but he just grabbed the glass of water from my hands. Our fingers brushed, sending a zing up my arm. I watched him move and place the glass on the bedside table before coming back to stand in front of me.

"Because why?" I prompted.

"Because," squatting down in front of me, Trevor gently lifted my chin with his hand, "when I take you, I want you completely sober."

15

TASHA

My ringing phone jerked me awake. With a pounding head, I blindly flopped my arm out to grab my phone. It took a moment to find it and bring it up to my ear, my eyes still closed.

"Yes," I croaked after barely swiping the screen to answer it.

"Morning!" Josie's voice chirped through the speaker.

"No." She was too happy in the mornings. Even in university, she was up and ready for her eight a.m. classes at the crack of dawn. I was fine getting up early, but it was best if no one talked to me for a good fifteen to twenty minutes.

"Ready for some breakfast?" At the mention of food, my stomach gurgled and my head throbbed. I definitely drank way too much last night. I answered her with a groan, which just made her laugh.

"I know, but you need something to eat, and it's almost eleven. Come down and meet us at the little diner in the hotel."

"Do I have to?"

"Yes. Everyone will be here in a minute, so get your ass up."

The thought of getting up was not appealing. *"The sooner you get here, the sooner we can sit on the beach until we leave."*

Josie knew my weak spot. Relaxing by the water before we had to go sounded pretty damn good right then. Especially with a long ass flight ahead of us.

"Fine. I'll be down in a bit."

Dropping my phone on the bed, I stretched, still wishing I could lay in bed longer. Forcing myself to get up, I was glad my head didn't spin. Nothing was worse than getting dizzy while hungover.

Padding over to the bathroom, I briefly remember putting PJ's on last night but the rest was a bit of a blur. A quick glance in the mirror showed the huge T-shirt I had on was inside out. Yep, definitely put this on drunk. I cringed seeing my smudged eyeliner and what looked like lipstick around my lips. Great.

Feeling beyond disgusting, I took a quick shower since I didn't take one the night before. Knowing the others were waiting for me, I washed quicker than I would have liked, forgoing cleaning my hair. I could have spent another thirty minutes under the warm water. Not in the mood to get dressed up, I threw my hair into a high ponytail and slipped on a sundress. If we were going to go sit by the beach, I'd come back and change anyway. Not bothering with makeup, I grabbed my shoes and purse before leaving my room.

I must have looked pretty bad because the couple with two little kids in the elevator sent me some questionable looks. Almost like they've never seen a hungover person before. It took everything I had not to say something, but thankfully the elevator stopped at the lobby and I was able to high tail it out of there.

It wasn't hard to find the table with my friends at the hotel restaurant. I was the last one to show up, and judging by the looks of Mila and Lydia, I wasn't the only one who was hungover. I couldn't even remember when I got back to the hotel or how.

"Hey, sleeping beauty." Josie grinned up at me as I slid into a chair across from her and Wyatt. I briefly registered that Trevor was on one side of me and Landon on the other. The sight of coffee in front of me instantly taking over everything else.

I gave a little nod to the others as I poured some sugar and cream into my coffee before taking a big sip. I heard a chuckle from beside me as I sat there, a coffee cup cradled in my hand, looking like death warmed over.

"You okay?" Trevor whispered next to me. Taking another huge gulp, I nodded. Once I downed about half the cup, I started to feel better. The caffeine worked its way through my bloodstream.

"Ready to order?" The waitress appeared at the end of the table. I had a feeling they put off ordering for me.

While everyone told her what they wanted, I quickly scanned the menu. Everything made my stomach stir with nausea but I knew I had to eat something. "I'll just have a bowl of fruit and some toast." I told the waitress before she left.

"Seems like everyone had fun last night," Bryton remarked, a wide grin on his face. Next to him, Mila looked worse than I did. She was leaning against his shoulder and looked half asleep.

"It was amazing," Josie answered, then continued talking about how much fun the vacation had been.

As I refilled my coffee, I felt Trevor lean in close to my side.

"How did you sleep?"

"Good. Everything's a bit of a blur though." He chuckled at my words. "Do you know how I got to my room?"

"I brought you back." At his words, I suddenly remem-

146

bered walking back to the hotel with him. A nagging voice kept telling me I did something stupid and embarrassing, but I couldn't remember for the life of me what that could have been.

"I didn't... I didn't do anything bad, did I?" For the first time since sitting down, I looked at Trevor. At the sight of him, a memory flashed across my mind of the two of us at the club. We were dancing, and he whispered something to me.

Tasha, remember!

"Depends what your definition of bad is." The look on Trevor's face did nothing to ease my worry.

The longer I stared at Trevor, the more I was able to put the pieces of last night back together. I recalled dancing with Johnno, getting jealous of the girl touching Trevor, and then him appearing behind me, his words once again flashing through my mind.

I cringed at the memory of trying to dance in the middle of the street. And then I remembered what happened in my room last night. What Trevor said to me.

Because when I take you, I want you completely sober.

I could tell Trevor knew exactly what I was thinking as the corner of his lip tilted up. Oh God. *Oh God.* I threw myself at him last night. My drunk self invited him to spend the night, and he had to gently let me down.

Humiliation washed over me. *What the fuck were you thinking, Tasha?!* I looked down into my coffee mug, unable to hold Trevor's gaze. I winced as I remembered pushing my shirt up my legs in an attempt to be sexy.

I was so embarrassed. Of all people, I had to throw myself at Trevor. Trevor—the same person I had finally gotten to a good place with.

"Tasha—" Trevor started to say but the waitress came with our food, interrupting him.

147

I silently thanked her for her timing. I could feel Trevor staring as I kept my eyes on my food. For some reason, it wasn't just humiliation that made it hard to look at him. It was the way I felt about him and how those feelings came rushing back to the surface.

Feelings that had been steadily growing the last few days. I wanted to ignore the way my stomach fluttered whenever I was around him. But it was hard to push away when he made sure to keep an eye on me just like he promised. And the way our bodies molded together in an almost perfect way on that dance floor….

While I may have been a bit drunk, I knew I didn't imagine the way my body heated up at his touch. Hell, just a simple look from him was enough for me to feel tingly all over.

In the light of the day, it was hard to ignore the rush of feelings I was now experiencing. I knew Trevor was being a gentleman by not accepting my advances last night while intoxicated, but it didn't lessen the sting of the rejection. Especially now that I was 100 percent coherent.

My overthinking self started to spiral. Last night, these feelings, being hungover— it was all too much. So, I did what I did best. I shoved it all down and ignored it. Ignored Trevor.

For the rest of breakfast, I kept my attention on eating or talking to the others. Whenever I noticed Trevor try to start a conversation with me, I would insert myself in another.

I knew it was rude, and I was probably overreacting, but right then, I couldn't deal with it all. Everything I felt for Trevor was now being drudged back up in full force. All the walls I put up, all the little lies I told myself, were quickly vanishing. I wanted him. Wanted him when I shouldn't have.

Liking Trevor should have been off-limits. With Josie and Wyatt being engaged, if we were to get together and it ended badly, it would make the whole friend dynamic weird. Cause who's to say this would end up as more than just sleeping together? Trevor didn't seem like the type to want more than that.

On top of that, I had my own issues that he shouldn't have to deal with. My parents. Trust issues—thanks to past boyfriends that cheated and used me to get close to said parents. Sometimes, I could be too much. Too hard to love.

With the self-deprecating thoughts swirling in my head, I couldn't help but think it was best I kept my distance from Trevor altogether.

BY THE TIME we boarded the first plane to get home, I was beyond exhausted. Lying around on the beach helped my hangover but didn't stop my mind from going a million miles a minute. Now that I was fully aware of my feelings for Trevor, it was ten times harder to ignore him.

Probably should have been an adult and just talked to him. Anything other than ignore him. But I tended to dissociate when I became overwhelmed. The rest of the flights back home I either slept or read my book.

When we landed hours later, I was more than ready to get home. I was grateful Josie planned the trip to where we had two days to recover from the time change before heading back to work. I needed sleep and time alone to figure things out. Time to figure out if what I felt was only because we were on vacation or not. If I even wanted to be more than a friend to Trevor.

It was well after two in the morning by the time we got to baggage claim. Thankfully, no one was there since it was so late, and we didn't have to worry about fans recognizing the guys.

Spotting my bag, I reached to grab it only for a different hand to beat me to it. I knew that tattooed arm.

"Here you go." Trevor's voice was thick with fatigue as he placed my heavy bag in front of me. Tilting my head back, I met his gaze. Day old stubble covered his face, my hand itching to reach out and touch it.

"Thanks," I said softly, our fingers brushing as I grabbed the handle. The way his eyes roamed my face made me want to grab him and kiss him. I almost did until I heard Josie behind me.

"We're going to head out." Sending me a tired smile, Josie pulled me into a tight hug. "I'll text you in the morning."

"Be careful getting home." Giving Wyatt a smile of my own, I stepped back, watching the newly engaged couple walk hand in hand toward the doors leading outside.

"Do you want me to take a cab with you?" Trevor asked behind me. As much as I wanted to say yes, I knew I shouldn't.

"That's okay."

"Really, I don't mind." Trevor tried again.

I shook my head. I wasn't sure what I would have done if the two of us were stuck in an Uber together.

"Trevor, you're exhausted and you live fifteen minutes from my place. Go home and get some sleep." I could tell he wasn't happy about what I said, but he took a step back. "I'll see you later."

"Tasha, wait." I hesitated for a second before turning around. Trevor stood there, an unreadable expression on his face as he held out something in a white plastic bag. "Here."

My curiosity won out as I took the bag from him. Reaching in, I felt something fuzzy, the sight of what it was making my eyes widen. I pulled out a stuffed animal in the form of a green turtle. The same stuffed turtle I was eyeing at the gift store a few days ago.

My throat closed and my eyes pricked with tears. He bought me a stuffed turtle.

"I... I..." I didn't know what to say. Pressure clogged my throat as I struggled to come up with words. I really needed to get out of there before I did something stupid. "Good-night," I said like a complete idiot, turning on my heel and strutting away.

I felt Trevor's eyes on me as I walked. I held the stuffed turtle to my chest as I headed for the exit to the airport, every step making me feel like I just made a huge mistake.

By the time the Uber parked in front of my building, I wanted nothing more than to crawl into bed. Maybe it wasn't the smartest idea to vacation somewhere in a different time zone. After paying the driver, I dragged my suitcase through the doors, waving to the doorman, and into the elevator.

Looking at my phone, I found myself clicking through my photos. I flipped through ones of us at the club, at the beach, and selfies with the girls until I landed on one I forgot I took.

A picture of Trevor when we went hiking to the secluded waterfall. We had stopped for a second to catch our breath—okay, my breath—and I brought my phone up to see if we had a signal. I remember Trevor standing there, joking about something when I ended up snapping a quick picture before he noticed.

Afterward, we got too busy with the hike and the proposal that I forgot to look at it. Thankful that I was alone in the elevator, I zoomed in, staring at Trevor's face. God, he really was hot. With his brown hair curled at the back of his neck, those bright green eyes focused on me. It truly should have been a crime that he was so good looking.

I was so busy staring at the photo that I almost missed the elevator doors opening to my floor. Pocketing my cell, I headed for my apartment. It was still dark outside when I entered my bedroom, rolling my suitcase off to the side. I'd deal with that tomorrow after I got some much needed sleep.

With a quick wash of my face and a change of clothes, I was ready to fall into bed and snooze until the late afternoon. Plugging my phone in, my eyes lingered on the stuffed turtle I placed on my nightstand. The thought of Trevor going out of his way to get it for me was enough to bring tears to my eyes.

I lied there staring at the turtle until I fell asleep with only one thing on my mind.

Trevor.

16

TASHA

For the second day in a row, I was woken up by my phone. Letting it ring, I rolled over, burrowing deeper in my bed. There was no way I was getting up, not when it felt like I had just fallen asleep. When the ringtone stopped, I hummed, feeling myself slowly going back to sleep, only for it to start again.

Nope. Not answering.

Wasn't until it started for the third time that I groaned, rolled over, and grabbed my phone from my nightstand. Whoever it was better have a good reason.

"What." My words came out harsh.

"Is that how you speak to your mother?" The voice on the other end of the line made my heart stop. I was not expecting my mother to be the one calling me.

"Sorry." I cleared my throat and started again. "Good morning, Mother."

She made a sound between a hmm and a tsk. *"I've been trying to reach you the last few days."*

My eyes were still closed as I responded. "I told you I was going on vacation with some friends." Of course, she didn't remember that part. Too busy only talking about her and my father's gala to pay attention to what I said.

"Anyway." Immediately glossing over what I just said, she continued. *"Your father and I have been talking, and we think the gala is the perfect time to make the announcement."*

There was something about her tone that had my eyes opening. Nothing ever good happened when my mother used that tone. Like the time I was forced to do an apprenticeship at their law firm right out of high school when I didn't want to.

"What announcement?"

"Your engagement."

My entire body froze at her words. Engagement?

"What the hell are you talking about?" I demanded.

"Language," my mother scolded. *"We've talked about this."*

"No, we haven't. What engagement?"

"I told you. With the merger happening with Caplin Brown, we all want a united front, so the decision was made that you and his son will marry." My mother said it so casually, like she didn't just drop a bomb on me. Like she didn't just make a life-altering decision for me.

"Did you just say that in order for your firm to merge, *I* have to marry someone's son?"

"Yes. Now, they are going to be at the gala in three weeks so the two of you can meet before we announce the engagement. I..." My mother kept talking but I was long gone.

My parents wanted me to marry a stranger so they could merge their company with another? There was no way they actually agreed to that.

"Did you already agree?" I interrupted my mother mid-sentence.

"Of course." Red hot anger grew in my throat.

"You agreed without even asking me."

"It's not a big deal."

"Not a big deal?" The voice that came out was one I never used on my mother before, but I was fuming. "This is my life, Mother, not yours to throw around."

"Tasha Nichole Davis, you will not speak to your mother like that."

"I am *not* doing it."

"Yes, you are."

"I am an adult, Mother, and capable of making my own decisions. That also includes who I am going to marry. And I am not going to marry some stranger to benefit *your* company." I made sure to put emphasis on 'your' because it certainly wasn't mine. I wanted nothing to do with it. Never had.

"Tasha—"

"I am your daughter! Not some pawn for you and Dad to use whenever you please." My whole body shook with rage.

I was hurt. Beyond hurt at how easily my parents agreed to some deal without even telling me. They wanted to use me for their own gain. Again. And they truly thought I would be okay with that. That I would roll over and be like, "Sure. Sounds good."

"I—"

"The answer is no." With that, I hung up before she could say anything else. My phone fell to my bed as I sat there, my chest heaving with each breath.

My parents wanted to marry me off. They were practically selling me as if I was a piece of property and not their blood relative. They were willing to sacrifice my life, my future, and my chance of falling in love so they could prosper. I knew my parents were ruthless but not this much.

Trevor's face flashed through my mind. Doing what my parents wanted would mean I'd have to give him up. He wasn't even mine but the thought felt like someone reached into my chest and tore my heart out. I would lose him before I even had him.

Gasping for air, I shook my hands out. No. I wasn't going to allow that.

I was not letting my parents dictate my life. And definitely not who I would be with. Not when the person I wanted was right in front of me and all I had to do was reach out. To hell with my parents. To hell with *everyone*.

I was up and out of my bed in a matter of seconds. Throwing on a pair of shorts, I grabbed my phone and shoes, not even bothering to brush my hair or change out of my sleep shirt. Snatching my keys, I all but ran out of my apartment. Forgoing the elevator, I booked it down the stairs and outside to my car. I barely noticed the splatter of rain against my head as I ran across the parking lot.

I was numb as I got in my car, started it, and pulled out, heading in the direction of the only person I wanted to see. The only person who mattered.

The ride passed by in a blur, it was only 8 o'clock in the morning so the roads weren't too busy yet. I was stuck in a state of disbelief, anger, and hurt. Before I knew it, I was shutting my car off and walking up the front steps of Trevor's home.

It was a cute white brick house that had large windows and a beautiful patio out front. What stood out the most was the dark blue door. The same blue color as the *Toronto Knights* colors. I wasn't sure if it was intentional or not.

I was drenched from head to toe from the pouring rain, but I didn't care as I rang the doorbell. Didn't care that I literally rolled out of bed and probably looked like a drowned rat.

When he didn't immediately answer, I rang the doorbell again, blinking away the water running down my face. A very drowsy, very ruffled Trevor answered the door. It took him a second to understand that I was in front of him.

"Tasha?"

"I..." My breaths were ragged, almost as if I ran all the way there.

"Are you okay?" Trevor looked more awake as he opened the door farther, his bare chest coming into view. I shook my head at his question.

I wasn't okay. Nothing was okay right now.

"My parents want to marry me off to some random guy." The words flew from my mouth. My voice was hoarse, like I'd been screaming, when really, it was from the burning hot fury inside of me. Saying it out loud sounded even crazier than my mother saying it on the phone.

"What?" Trevor took a step toward me, confusing marring his features.

"I said no." I shook my head, water flying from my hair. My body shook but I wasn't sure if it was from the rain, the adrenaline, or what I was about to say. "I told her no because I'm tired of them trying to dictate my life. Tired of letting stupid things stand in the way of what I want."

Trevor stood there in his doorway, staring at me as I continued while drenched to the bone.

"But I realized when I hung up with her that I'm letting my fear of getting hurt stand in the way of what I truly want."

"What do you truly want, Tasha?" Trevor's voice was soft, but I heard it as if he was whispering it in my ear. I didn't even hesitate in answering.

"I want you."

"Me?" He took a step forward. I nodded, feeling like my heart was in my throat. I couldn't read his face to know if I said the right thing, or if I was about to have my heart stomped on.

"Are you sure?" Trevor asked, taking one more step

outside, the rain now hitting his bare chest and instantly soaking him.

"Yes." My heart pounded so hard in my chest.

The longer Trevor looked at me, the less confident I became. I was probably making a huge mistake. Maybe I ruined my chance with him by having my walls too high. I started to take a step back when Trevor spoke again. What looked like determination flashed across his face.

"Good, because I've wanted to do this again since that night five months ago." Without another word, he covered the distance between us, hands cupping my cheeks before planting his lips on mine.

The moment our lips met, everything around me went silent. The anger sizzling at the back of my throat extinguished, and all I could focus on was Trevor's lips against mine.

My hands slid up his slick chest as he tilted my head back to get a better angle. When his tongue gently traced the seam of my lips, asking for permission, I couldn't stop the moan from spilling out of my mouth and into his.

Fuck, he could kiss. Last time, I freaked out and left before I could truly appreciate it. But not this time. No, there would be no leaving.

Pulling back to get some air, I kept my eyes closed, my entire body sizzling. I gripped Trevor's biceps to keep myself grounded. The swipe of his thumb on my cheeks prompted me to open my eyes.

Trevor gazed down at me with a soft look on his face. His hair stuck to his forehead, rain clinging to his eyelashes. My eyes tracked a trail of water dripping down his jaw, my lips practically begging to follow after it.

"Let's get you dried off," he murmured.

I nodded, not trusting my voice

Stepping into his apartment, I awkwardly stood on the

mat right by the door. Aside from the fact I was dripping water everywhere, this was the first time I'd ever been inside his place.

"Coming?"

"Uh..." I glanced down at my soaking wet clothes dripping onto his rug.

"It's just water, Sunshine. I can clean it up later." The soft smile he sent me almost made me melt into a puddle of goo. Slipping off my shoes, I gently placed my hand in his.

I wanted to look around at the place, but all I could focus on was his back as he tugged me after him. The muscles moved with each step he took. My eyes trailed down to the waistband of the sweats he wore. I admired how they hung low on his hips. I mentally scolded myself for not paying more attention when he was facing me a moment ago.

Walking into his room, my eyes immediately darted to the bed in the center of the room. Swallowing thickly, I stood in the middle of Trevor's room, my mind trying to play catch up.

"You can wear these," Trevor said.

I drew my eyes away from the bed to the clothes in his hands. It was suddenly sinking in that we were really doing this.

"Hey." Trevor's voice was soft as he stepped toward me, stopping when his chest was inches from mine. His hand came up and gently grabbed my chin, tilting my head back to look up at him. "Nothing is going to happen if you don't want it to." His eyes bounced back and forth between mine. "And as much as I want to throw you on the bed and continue what we started outside," those eyes darkened slightly, "we both are exhausted. So go get dried off and changed. I'll be here when you get back."

How is it that he knew exactly what to say? Despite wanting to also continue what we started a moment ago, he was right. Now that the anger dissipated, it left exhaustion in its wake. One look at Trevor's face, and I knew he was just as tired as I was.

"Okay," I replied softly. Sleep and then we could talk about...us.

"Take as long as you need."

Before I could reply, he bent down and pecked my lips. His mouth curved upwards when he stepped back. The whole thing was so boyish and cute, I couldn't stop the grin that spread across my face.

Taking the clothes from Trevor, I slipped past him to the bathroom hooked to his bedroom. I dared a peek over my shoulder and found him watching me. Picking up my pace, I quickly entered the bathroom, shutting the door behind me. I glanced at my reflection in the mirror, and while I was soaking wet and my hair stuck to my face, the look in my eyes caught my attention.

Despite everything that happened that morning, my eyes appeared brighter. My hand came up to touch my lips, still tingling from the kiss in the rain. A kiss that I would not be forgetting about any time soon.

Not wanting to keep Trevor waiting, I quickly peeled off my wet clothes, taking a moment to debate on keeping my underwear on or not. Even though it would be a little weird, I slid them down my legs and pulled on the T-shirt.. While the boxers were a bit big, they were surprisingly comfortable.

In the confined bathroom where no one could see me, I tugged the collar of the shirt up and sniffed it. It smelled just like Trevor, citrus-y and spicy, it was almost intoxicating. The front of it had the Toronto Knights logo, making me grin. Yeah, I was not giving this back any time soon.

Using his brush—a huge no, usually, but there was no other option—I quickly pulled it through my hair and put it back into a bun. I sighed at my reflection. The shirt hung down to my knees, covering the boxers completely. I looked like a little kid putting on her parent's clothes.

Gathering my wet clothes in my arms, underwear hidden in the middle, I slowly opened the bathroom door and peeked out. Just as I slipped out, Trevor walked through the doorway holding two glasses of water.

"Make yourself at home while I go put those in the dryer." With empty hands, Trevor reached to grab my wet clothes but I turned him down.

"It's okay. You don't have to."

"I don't mind, really." With a genuine smile, he took them from me and left me alone in his room.

My inner snooper appeared, and I wasted no time walking around his room slowly, taking it all in. I didn't know why but I was surprised at how...bland it was. He had a nightstand on each side of his bed along with one lamp. He had a giant TV hooked to the wall opposite of the bed. Below it was what looked like a chest filled with movies and a gaming system.

The only thing noteworthy were the few pictures he had scattered around. Leaning down, my lips twitched at the photos. All of them were of the guys and Trevor. There was one with Wyatt and him where they looked barely out of high school. I noted that even younger Trevor was cute. He was definitely the type you'd have a secret crush on, along with every other girl in the entire school.

While he was cute back then, now there was something more...rugged about him. Obviously, he was more muscular and had tattoos. It was clear he was someone who only got better with age.

The next picture was him with Wyatt and Bryton. They stood with their arms around each other, still clad in their hockey uniforms, grins so wide. Trevor and Wyatt looked a bit older in this one, so it had to be more recent.

"We took that picture right after we won our first Cup Championship." Trevor appeared behind me. I didn't even try to hide that I was snooping. "You can take the bed. I'll be out on the couch if you need anything." While it was thoughtful, that wasn't what I wanted.

"No." Walking over to the bed, I sat down, swinging my legs over.

"No?" He watched me get comfortable in his bed, eyebrows raised.

"No. Get in here." I patted the spot next to me. While we may not have been doing what either of us were probably wanting, this was the next best thing. I wanted—no, needed —to be close to him. Just so I knew that I wasn't dreaming or making it up.

"Tasha, I—"

"I want you to." He still had a skeptical look on his face. "Please."

He finally relented as he rounded the side of the bed and slid in. Even though the sun was up, his room was pleasantly dark thanks to the black-out curtains over his windows, so falling asleep wasn't something I was too worried about.

"Sorry for just dropping by," I whispered a few minutes later as the two of us laid on our backs.

"You never have to be sorry."

Three more minutes passed before I opened my mouth again.

"Thank you for the clothes and drying mine."

"Tasha." Trevor chuckled.

"Yeah?"

"Go to sleep."

"But I—" I didn't get the words out before I was pulled toward him, my body practically landing on top of his.

"Shhh. Sleep." A heavy arm settled around my waist, keeping me in place against his side.

I laid there stiff against him as I inwardly freaked out. I tried my hardest not to think about the hard muscle under my right hand that was placed on his bare chest.

"Relax," Trevor whispered, his hand softly squeezing my hip.

Taking a few deep breaths, I forced myself to loosen up in his hold. Mixed with the warmth radiating off of his body and the protective way he was holding me, I soon found myself dozing off, my exhaustion finally catching up with me.

TASHA

This time when I woke up, there were no interruptions from my phone. Instead, it was quiet, which was slightly odd considering my apartment was right next to a road that constantly had high amounts of traffic. It took a moment to remember what happened earlier. The phone call from my mom, driving all the way to Trevor's apartment, our kiss in the rain.

Sitting up, I looked around only to find the bedroom empty. The spot next to me was still a little warm so Trevor must not have left too long ago.

Unsure of the time, I quietly slipped out of bed, although I wanted nothing more than to stay in it all day. The dude had the comfiest bed I'd ever slept on. After a quick use of the bathroom, I left Trevor's room. I could hear the patter of rain against the roof and windows, the dark clouds making it hard to tell the time of day.

Coming out of the bedroom, my curiosity came back in full force. With Trevor nowhere to be found, I finally let myself peek around his place since I didn't get the chance when I came in earlier. Trevor living in an actual house was surprising. Most people our age lived in apartments since it was cheaper and easier to take care of. He was away for games a lot during the season, so it made me wonder who took care of the place when he was gone.

All on one level with at least two bedrooms, it was almost like the little bungalow was made for a couple. I was too busy ogling Trevor early this morning to take the time to notice how well-decorated his living space was. I wasn't sure if he did it himself but I was impressed with the gray colored couch that took up most of the living room. It could easily fit ten people and looked just as comfortable. There were pictures of wintery mountains and scenery hanging on his walls.

The sound of clinking pans drew my attention toward an archway off to the side of the living room. Following it, I walked through a wide threshold and came to a stop on the edge of a gorgeous kitchen. A huge island sat right in the middle with barstools on one side. Deep blue cabinets contrasted beautifully against the white granite.

Immediately, my eyes landed on the figure leaning over the stove. Still dressed in a pair of gray sweatpants and no shirt, Trevor stirred whatever he had on the stove, totally oblivious that I was behind him.

The corner of my lip tilted up as I leaned against the wall, watching him. Damn, the sight of a shirtless man in the kitchen was enough to make any girl swoon but seeing a muscular back with tattoos was a whole other thing. All I wanted to do was run my nails down that back and see what was under those sweatpants. Who knew I'd be so attracted to hockey players?

I could get used to seeing that view.

The thought came out of nowhere, surprising me. But what was more shocking was how it didn't scare me as much as before.

"What are you making?" I asked a moment later. At the sound of my voice, Trevor flinched, whirling around with a spatula in his hand. He had it raised as if to defend himself. "If I was an intruder, you'd already be dead." I raised an eyebrow at him, crossing my arms.

"I'll have you know, I am quite skilled with a spatula." I knew he was trying to sound intimidating but it only made me grin.

"Yeah, okay." Pushing off the wall, I walked farther into the kitchen, going around the island. "Is that…eggs?"

"Thought you'd be hungry." Reaching up, Trevor rubbed the side of his neck, looking almost embarrassed. It was beyond sweet he thought to make me something.

"I am."

"Take a seat, m'lady." With a fake British accent, Trevor gestured to the barstools.

"Thank you, good sir." Who was I to say no to a hot guy making me food?

I was more than happy to sit there and watch Trevor move around the kitchen. The sight had me clenching my thighs together under the counter.

"If you keep looking at me like that, I'll burn the eggs," Trevor told me, his back facing me.

My cheeks heated at being caught staring. "I wasn't looking," I lied, making him chuckle.

"Suuure. So that wasn't your eyes I felt undressing me?" He glanced over his shoulder at me, smirking.

"Must have a ghost in here." I shrugged, making a show of looking around.

"Uh-huh." Still smirking, Trevor leaned over the counter and placed a yummy-looking omelet in front of me.

"Thank you." My heart stuttered in my chest at the act of him cooking for me. Avoiding his eyes, I took a bite. I couldn't look at him without wanting to kiss him. The two of us probably needed to talk about a few things before we... continued on that path.

"This is really good." I hadn't realized just how hungry I was. I only ate a few bites at the diner in the hotel yesterday, too busy freaking out about Trevor and me. "Didn't know you could cook."

"There's a lot you don't know about me." I glanced up to see him bent over, arms on the counter, as he watched me.

He wasn't wrong. There was a lot I didn't know about Trevor, but I wanted to learn everything. How he took his coffee. What his favorite pre-game snack was. That was, if he wanted to share those things with me.

"Did you mean what you said earlier?" Trevor suddenly asked. Lifting my head, I met his gaze. Those gorgeous green eyes stared at me with an emotion I couldn't place. Fear? Disappointment?

It would be easy to say no. To sweep it all under the rug like I did for so long and ignore the way I felt about him. How I felt from the moment we met. But I meant what I said earlier.

I was tired of being scared. Of letting my parents and fears dictate what I did with my life. I was done letting that moment in the club ruin my chances of having someone. I wasn't even sure if Trevor wanted to be with someone like me—someone broken—but now was my opportunity to find out.

"I did."

My words lingered between us. I refused to look away from him, hoping he knew that I was serious.

I waited impatiently for him to say or do something. Each passing second made my anxiety skyrocket. Just when I thought he wasn't going to reply, he stood to his full height. I watched his every movement as he rounded the side of the island. I swiveled the barstool to face him as he came to a stop directly in front of me.

Swallowing, I held still as he stepped between my legs, bending down just a little to see my face as his arms came around me, hands on the counter behind my back. I was fully surrounded by all that was Trevor Hall. He was so close all I had to do was lean forward an inch and our lips would have touched.

The muscles on his arms flexed as he caged me between them, making my breath hitch in my throat at how close that powerful body was to mine.

"Are you completely sure that's what you want?" he asked. The vulnerability in his eyes almost took the breath out of me.

"I've never been more sure of anything in my life."

My words seemed to split whatever control Trevor had on himself. Bringing one hand up, he cupped the side of my jaw, tilting my head back. I wasn't sure who leaned in first, but the moment our lips met, everything else faded.

The kiss was soft at first, but then it turned into something hurried and rough. It almost felt like I was being punished with how he kissed and nibbled my bottom lip before sucking it into his mouth. This was my consequence for not letting him do it sooner. Somehow, my legs ended up wrapped around his waist, his erection pressing against me through the boxers I wore.

When I opened my mouth so his tongue could sweep against mine, a groan reverberated deep in his throat. My hands finally got their wish as they moved up his bare abdomen, the hard muscles flexing under my fingers.

As my fingers traced the indentations leading to the waistband of his sweats, Trevor's hand slid down to my neck. He grabbed a handful of hair at the back of my head. Our lips lost contact as he tugged softly but firmly. An involuntary moan left my lips.

My eyes fluttered open as Trevor leaned over me, eyes dark, lips quirked up into a smirk.

"Tell me to stop." His voice was so deep as he spoke. As if he was trying his hardest to hold himself back. "Tell me to stop, or I'm going to take you right here, right now."

I struggled to get words out.

"I don't want to hurt you," he added. I knew he was talking about what I'd gone through in the past year. The thought of being intimate freaked me out a little still but nothing about Trevor scared me. I knew he would never hurt me and that he would stop if I so much as uttered the word no.

Bringing a hand up, I softly touched his face. My heart threatened to explode at how sweet the man in front of me was. How could I have missed how incredible he was?

"You would never hurt me." Making sure he knew what I was saying, I tilted my hips up, grinding softly against the bulge pressed against me. His grip in my hair tightened slightly. Loving the reaction, I bit my lip and moved my hips again.

His shoulders were strained with tension as he held himself still, his eyes locked with mine. The muscle tight under my palms. I needed this. I needed him. Right. Now.

Dropping my hand, I trailed it slowly down his chest as I leaned forward, lips grazing his. "Please."

Trevor groaned, that one word his undoing. Pulling my head back farther, he trailed his lips down the column of my throat, hips pressing into mine so I couldn't move.

I breathed heavily as he planted open-mouthed kisses along my neck. The slight stubble on his face tickled my skin. When he reached a spot on the side of my neck, my back arched. My hard nipples rubbed against the shirt I was wearing.

When he sucked on the side of my neck, I moaned loudly. My eyes closed as he sucked the sensitive skin. He pulled away from my skin with a chuckle.

"That's the sound I've been dying to hear."

"Maybe you should have tried harder," I quipped.

In response, he let go of my hair only to reach down and grab my hips, pulling me straight off the stool and into the air. In one second, I was sitting on a barstool and in the next the back of my thighs touched the cold granite island.

Before I could fully register the chill that soaked into my legs, Trevor's mouth was back on mine. God, I could kiss his lips all day if he let me. They left mine a second later, making me groan. When I didn't immediately feel his lips again, I opened my eyes, watching as Trevor moved to kneel between my legs.

"W-what are you doing?" My voice was breathless. My cheeks heated up at the thought of him there, pressing his mouth to a part of me that no man had been in a long time.

"Tried harder," he repeated, following it with a tsk and a wink.

I swore I stopped breathing as he grabbed the waistband of the boxers he lent me and started tugging them off. I was completely bare underneath and the thought of him seeing that had me squirming. Oh God, he was about to see my pussy. Up close and personal. There truly was no going back now.

As if sensing my thoughts, Trevor's eyes met my own. He never looked away as he pulled them off and dropped them to the ground. His thumb softly rubbed my inner thigh, the action soothing the tension in the air. And in my throat.

The sight of him kneeling before me was by far the hottest thing I'd ever seen. I was embarrassed to admit how much I needed him. The way his pupils were blown and the hungry look on his face he needed me just as much.

I did nothing but watch as he gently pushed my knees apart, baring me to him. Trevor let out a low groan, eyes fluttered shut for half a second. "So fucking pretty."

Leaning back on my elbows, I tried my hardest not to close my knees as he reached out, his fingers brushing the wet spot between my thighs. Just that one simple touch had me whimpering.

Looking up at me from under his lashes Trevor leaned down, trailing kisses up my thigh before finally reaching my pussy. With the flat of his tongue he licked my pussy in one long lick. My eyes immediately rolled back, and I let out a moan that filled the kitchen.

Holy fuck.

I felt Trevor's chuckle against my skin before his mouth met me again. As if punishing me again, he teased my clit with one little flick before moving a few inches down, spearing my pussy with his tongue. I slowly swirled my hips, rubbing myself against his face as I continued to whimper and moan and let myself have this moment.

Trevor's hands came up and hooked around my hips, keeping me firmly in place. There was no getting away. No running in the opposite direction while pretending my feelings for him weren't real.

I reached down and threaded my fingers through his hair, tugging at the soft strands. All my insecurities flew out the window as Trevor feasted on me right there on his kitchen island like I was his breakfast.

Trevor's low groans and my whimpers echoed around us. Each flick of his tongue made me louder and louder. The moment I felt two fingers slide inside of me, I was done. My hands gripped his hair tighter as my legs clamped around his head, my whole body shaking.

My vision narrowed and my body tensed as a wave of pleasure unlike anything I have felt before came over me. Meanwhile, Trevor never let up. He continued licking and finger fucking me. The way Trevor kept his fingers curled inside me I was left on the edge. I only had a moment before another orgasm hit me. Trevor drew it out as long as he could before he finally slowed. He had to pull his head out from between my legs and remove my hands from the hold I had on his hair.

I laid there, spread out on the counter, breathing heavily while my legs shook. My entire body was jello, and I was more than content not moving an inch. A soft smack between my legs made me jerk up, eyes flying open.

Trevor stood, putting his hands on the counter by my head, caging my body in.

"Did I try hard enough that time?" My mind was still trying to process the orgasms to remember what he was talking about. A handsome smirk blossomed on his face. "I'll take that as a yes."

"That was…"

"Did you think we were done?"

I met those gorgeous green eyes as he gave me that smug look. His expression was a promise that told me this was just the beginning. My breath hitched in my throat as Trevor leaned down until his lips barely grazed mine.

"We aren't done until you're begging me to stop." At his words, my body lit up all over again. Right when I thought he couldn't get any hotter. "Does someone like that?" His lips barely touched mine as he spoke softly. I nodded, eyes fluttering closed. He wasn't even touching me, and I felt like I was going to combust.

"Use your words, Sunshine."

"Please." It came out as a plea but I didn't care. I needed

him inside me. And I needed more than his fingers. "Please, Trevor." At his name leaving my mouth, he closed his eyes.

"You are going to be the death of me, Tasha Davis."

This time when our lips met, it felt different. For once, I wasn't scared of it.

I pulled back just enough to whisper. "Take me to bed." His body shuddered as if he'd been waiting a long time to hear me say those words.

Without another word, he scooped me up off the counter. Wrapping my legs around his waist, I planted soft kisses along his neck as he walked us to the bedroom. It was almost torture having the fabric of his sweatpants rub against me.

I fully expected Trevor to throw me on the bed, but when he gently laid me on my back, I felt like my heart was going to burst.

"I need to see all of you." His voice was hoarse as he hovered above me. Trevor's hands grabbed the hem of the shirt I was wearing but he hesitated, looking up at me. The fact that he tried to be gentle and considerate was...something I never experienced with a man before. It quite literally left me speechless, which was something he was good at doing—leaving me without words.

Placing my hands over his, I sent him a soft smile.

"I'm okay." And I was. Before, the thought of being intimate would make my heart race and my palms sweat. All I could think about was that guy in the club and his hands in places they shouldn't be. I think when I kissed Trevor all those months ago, it wasn't just the assault that made me run away. It was also how easy it was to be with him, how easy it was to forget things.

I felt safe. Whole. Protected. Wanted. There was no fear there. Not with Trevor.

Seeing the truth on my face, he slowly pulled the shirt up. He placed a kiss on every inch of my skin. By the time I had the shirt up and over my head, I was panting all over again. I thought I'd be embarrassed lying completely bare in front of him but I didn't.

How could I when he looked down at me like I was a goddess? Like every part of me was made for him to cherish.

"Mine." He said it so softly, I almost didn't catch it. Before I could fully register the word, Trevor's mouth captured one of my breasts in his mouth. All thoughts flew out the window as his lips covered my nipple.

Before today, I never knew it was possible to feel so good just by having my breasts touched and played with. I did nothing but lie there, hands brushing over his shoulders, down his tattooed arms, as he licked and nipped at my chest. And that was exactly what he did. When one wasn't in his mouth, he softly rolled the other between his fingers.

It didn't take long for me to arch my back and beg for more.

"Trevor. Please." I barely recognized my own voice, thick with need. When he pulled away, his pupils were so big I could barely see the green in them. He looked seconds from devouring me.

Clearly feeling the same as me, he moved off the bed, hands grabbing the waistband of his sweatpants before pulling them completely down. With no underwear to contain himself, his cock sprang free. I wasn't prepared for the sight of him. He was long, hard, and perfectly thick.

Instantly, my mouth watered and my thighs clenched together. How I was supposed to take him inside of me I had no idea, but boy, was I ready to find out. I quickly moved to my knees and reached out to touch him. He gently grabbed my wrist and stopped me.

"Later. If I don't get inside you right now, I'm going to lose it." Desperation clear as day clung to his words.

"Later," I promised, and I fully intended on following through.

"I want you on top. I want you to be the one to set the pace, so if you want to stop, we can. Just say the word."

I didn't know what to say to that, so I did the only thing I could. I grabbed his face and kissed him. Hopefully showing him what his words meant to me. The kiss didn't last long.

Once Trevor was lying on his back, I checked him out the exact same way he did to me moments before. Every part of him was honed to perfection. Wide shoulders, abs that glistened and begged to be licked. All thanks to hockey. And all of it was mine.

With plenty of time later to explore every inch of him, I crawled on top of him and straddled his legs. Trevor breathed just as hard as I did. That didn't change as I slowly reached down and grabbed his cock. His body jerked, his abs contracting with the movement, as the sexiest moan fell out of his mouth.

I slid my palm up and down his shaft, his thickness heavy in my hand as I teased him. Feeling every ridge and vein. Then, I lifted up and aligned myself with his tip.

His big hands rested on my hips, stilling me for just a second. "Condom?"

"IUD," was all I said as I lowered myself over him, his silky soft skin gliding against mine. Meeting his eyes, I didn't look away as I sank down onto him, every inch filling me. I remained still as I tried to find my breaths. I let myself adjust before the need to move took over.

Placing my hands on Trevor's chest, I slowly started to thrust my hips.

The groan that left his mouth brought a smirk to my face. Trevor kept his hands on my hips but stayed true to his word. He let me set the pace and rhythm, even though I could tell he was trying his hardest not fuck me harder.

After a few minutes of riding him so slow it was almost torturous, I put him out of his misery. Leaning forward, nipples brushing against his chest, I lowered my mouth next to his ear. "Fuck me," I whispered.

It only took a second for the words to sink in before he drove up into me. Letting out a loud cry, I held on as he did exactly what I asked of him.

His dirty whispers had my body humming with need.

"Fuck yes."

"Look at how well you take me."

"So fucking tight."

They all drove me closer to the edge.

"Cum for me."

I didn't need to be told twice. I exploded a second after that. Everything went dark as I rode out my orgasm. Trevor's grunts and moans echoed in my ears as I clenched tight around him. A few hard thrusts upward and I felt him finish deep inside of me, his whole body tensing under me as he rode out his own orgasm.

It was highly likely that when I thought back on our first time together, I'd say I blacked out. But really, it was just the sensation of euphoria skipping through my veins that had me seeing black.

Not even a few moments later, Trevor's tongue licked up the side of my neck. Using his chest to help me reposition myself, I slipped off of him and to the side, using his arm as a pillow as we both looked at each other. When our eyes locked, I felt that long-lost piece in my heart fall back into place.

TASHA

"**Y**our parents are serious about an arranged marriage?" Trevor asked.

"Apparently. I shouldn't even be surprised." I traced my finger along the lion tattoo Trevor had on his shoulder that wrapped down to his chest. I was currently lying on top of him, one leg hooked over his, a sheet barely covering us.

It was close to three in the morning, but neither of us seemed keen on going to bed. My body still hummed after the last round we had. I lost count of how many times Trevor made me come with the way his fingers traced up and down my spine. I knew there would be at least one more before we went to sleep.

"They've done this before?" he asked.

"They've tried to set me up with their friend's sons before, but that was more subtle than this. We'd usually go to dinner and he'd be there so I'd have no choice but to talk. Or I'd be required to attend one of their events, and they'd nudge me to go start a conversation."

"Wow, that's..." Trevor seemed unsure what to say to that, his words trailing off.

"Yeah," I mumbled.

"Your parents sound great," Trevor joked.

"Don't they?" I snorted. My fingers kept tracing his skin almost like if I stopped, he'd disappear. "Do you talk to your parents?" The words left my mouth before I could stop them.

I knew the subject of family was sensitive for him since he told me a little bit about them in Australia. I didn't want to bring up something unwanted, but I also wanted to learn more about him. Learn what made him into the man he was today, even if that meant getting to know all the bad parts.

Trevor's fingers stalled on my back, and he laid still below me. When a minute or so passed with no word, I knew I overstepped. It was too soon for me to ask that kind of question. I should have known better.

"Sorry, I—" I made the motion to get off his chest, but I didn't make it far before Trevor's hand on my back kept me rooted there on my stomach. I peered up under my lashes at him, hoping I hadn't upset him.

"The last time I spoke to my parents was right after I got drafted." Trevor stared up at the ceiling, his fingers once again tracing a path on my skin. I listened as he spoke, lying my chin on my hands on his chest.

"I hadn't heard from them in months. They didn't even call to congratulate me on the day of the draft, so I don't know why I thought they would because they never called... for anything. When I got drafted, I was with Wyatt's family on their couch, cameras pointed at us, and I waited. It's not every day you get your name called for the third pick, let alone with the same team as your best friend."

The way he talked about Wyatt and his family gave me the inkling that he cared deeply for them. They may not have been blood related, but they showed up more than his own parents did.

"Anyway, it was a few weeks after when I finally heard

from them. Not to congratulate me, though." My chest tight-ened at the hurt in his voice. "They wanted to know how much money I was promised and if I could give them some."

I made a noise—one that had to have shown how appalling I thought that was—but stayed quiet.

"Apparently, they needed money for rent. Their landlord was about to kick them out, but I also knew the real reason they asked for it. They needed it for drugs." Trevor shook his head, his jaw tight. "Nothing about me making it to the league or being proud of me. Just how much I could transfer over into their bank account."

My heart broke. All he wanted was his parents to tell him they were proud of him, to see that their son did something with his life. Yet all they wanted was money for drugs, and they knew Trevor had the means to provide that.

"So, I paid their rent for a year and gave them five thou-sand dollars. Didn't hear a single thank you. After that, I cut them off. Blocked their numbers and left them alone."

When I first met Trevor, I only thought he was a fuckboy. He was always that funny, lighthearted, takes nothing serious type of guy. But I clearly had it all wrong. He may be all those things, but he's also selfless and caring. Even when some people didn't deserve it.

I knew there was nothing I could say right then, and I had a feeling he wouldn't want any of my sympathy either. So I did the only thing I could. I placed kisses on his chest, moving up his neck until I reached his lips, kissing him softly.

"You're amazing, you know that?" I whispered when I pulled away.

"I think I need another reminder." Trevor grinned at me. The haunted look in his eyes slowly disappeared. Smiling, I kissed him again. "One more."

Laughing, I gave him a little peck.

"That one doesn't count." He said.

"It does! Our lips touched."

"Nope."

I barely grazed my lips on his before pulling away."Better?"

Trevor shook his head before suddenly flipping me over and onto my back. His muscular body hovered over me.

"Not even close." When his lips met mine, it was slow and teasing. His tongue softly grazed the seam of my lips. I opened my mouth, expecting our tongues to meet but instead Trevor sucked my bottom lip between his.

"Now it's my turn to remind you how amazing *you* are."

My face split into a grin as Trevor kissed his way down my body, showing me *exactly* how amazing he thought I was.

"I SHOULD PROBABLY HEAD HOME."

We were currently lying in his bed, legs tangled together as we watched TV. We hadn't left the bedroom unless it was to shower or grab the food we ordered.

"Why?" The way he said it was like I was purposely leaving him. I didn't want to go as much as he didn't like hearing me say that.

"Because," I shifted so I could see his face better, "I have work tomorrow and you have practice."

It was hard to believe it was already Sunday and we had to get back to real life. The two of us had been so wrapped up in each other to remember life outside of his apartment.

The last day was nothing short of amazing. It was so easy being around Trevor. It literally felt like we'd been together for years, not days. It's crazy to think that just a week ago, we

180

hadn't spoken much and now here I was, wrapped in his arms, not wanting to leave. Despite how fast things escalated between us, it felt...right.

Being with Trevor felt right.

"How about we both skip work and practice and stay in bed." He wiggled his eyebrows making me laugh.

"As much as I want to do that, and trust me, I do." I really, really did. "We can't. I've been gone from work for over a week and you know Coach will have your ass if you miss practice, especially with your first game a week away."

"Why must you be right?" Trevor groaned, throwing his head back into the pillow.

"You'll find I'm always right." I smirked. He pinched my side, making me squirm away from him while giggling.

"You could always stay and go home to change in the morning." The offer was tempting but I knew we both needed sleep and a little time away from each other. We'd only gotten a total of five hours of sleep—roughly—in the last two days. Plus, this was all so new that we needed to spend a little time away from each other without the other clouding our thoughts.

"You know I would if I could." I also didn't want to be the reason he was dead tired tomorrow at practice. So much for spending the weekend getting extra sleep.

Since it was getting late, I reluctantly made myself get out of bed. I sidestepped Trevor's hands that tried to pull me back down. If I didn't leave now, I would fall back in bed with him and never leave. I needed to be strong for the both of us.

Trevor sat up in bed, watching me slide on my shorts. Shorts I hadn't worn since I got there. When I started to pull his shirt off, his voice stopped me.

"Keep it." Biting my lip to stop myself from grinning like a

181

fool, I kept his borrowed shirt on. Now I truly wasn't giving it back.

Eyes lingered on me as I moved around trying to find my shoes and the shirt I came wearing. Grabbing my phone from his bedside table, I noticed quite a few texts and missed calls. My phone was the last thing on my mind since admitting my feelings to Trevor.

I looked over the texts from Josie and the girls, not at all surprised there was nothing from my mother.

"You don't have to go." Trevor reached and grabbed the back of my thighs, tugging me between his legs. He tilted his head back to look up at me, the look on his face slowly breaking my resolve.

"I know," I whispered. My hands came up to softly graze his cheeks, the stubble rough against my palms.

"You're not..." Trevor stopped himself from finishing, looking almost hesitant.

"Hm?" I waited patiently as he tried to figure out the right words. After a moment, he seemed to steel himself for whatever he needed to get off his chest.

"You aren't going to go home and regret this, are you?" I'd never seen him look so vulnerable. The question took me by surprise, yet not really. I knew with everything that happened between us, it would make sense for him to be wary. Worried that I'd run again.

The thing was, I wanted Trevor from the moment I met him. I just got scared and let my past get in the way. Now that I knew what it was like to have him, I had no plans of letting him go. Something he was about to learn.

"No." My fingers ran through his hair. "I think you're stuck with me for a while." I felt the tension slowly seep from his body at my words.

With a small smile, I bent down, placing a kiss on his lips. Each kiss set my whole body on fire in a way I'd never felt before. I half expected my foot to pop up, just like in the movies.

A moan formed in my throat as Trevor deepened the kiss, his fingertips digging into the back of my thighs. He was seconds away from pulling me onto his lap, I knew it. And if he did, I knew I wouldn't be leaving his bed anytime soon. I was very easily going to become addicted to having sex with Trevor. It was that good.

When I pulled away, Trevor groaned, dropping his head against my stomach. I was glad to see I wasn't the only one affected.

"Sunshine."

Sunshine.

It was my new favorite word.

"I have to go." Trevor let out one more groan before loosening his grip on me. "Come on, you big baby." Grabbing his arms, I tried to pull him off the bed, but he didn't move an inch as I tugged. He sat there watching me with an amused grin.

"God, what do you eat?" I groaned, planting my feet and pulling harder.

"Are you saying I eat too much?" he said, acting offended.

"Yes."

"That's a mean thing to say, Sunshine."

"Yeah, but it's true." I flashed him a grin.

"This is all muscle, I assure you."

I scoffed at his words.

"You would know. You're the one who licked my abs just a few hours ago," Trevor said with a smirk, making my cheeks flush. "Cat got your tongue?"

"Fine, you can get up on your own." I stuck my tongue out at him, acting like a little kid, as I turned on my heel and headed for the door.

Just as I predicted, I only made it to the hallway before

Trevor grabbed me by the waist, turning me around until my back was pressed against the wall. He towered over me, one hand on my waist and the other on the wall above my head.

"Just going to leave without a goodbye?" His face hovered over mine, his bare chest taunting me.

"Bye," I said cheekily.

"I'd be very careful, Sunshine." His warning tone had me biting my lip.

"Or what?" Trevor's jaw clenched as he nudged my legs apart before wedging his knee between them. I was trapped between the wall and his body, his knee pressed against my center.

"You'll learn the hard way what happens when you talk back to me." Never before had just a few words made me so wet. The rebel side of my brain told me to push him. Push him enough to see what would happen.

Almost like he heard what I was thinking, the corner of his mouth quirked up. He applied more pressure against my pussy. His hand grabbed my hair, pulling it tight into a fist as he gently but firmly tilted my head back.

"Someone likes the thought of that, don't they?" I went to nod, but he shook his head. "Words. I want to hear you say it."

I was pretty sure I would have melted into a puddle if he wasn't for him holding me up.

"Yes." It came out in a breathy whisper.

When Trevor ran his lips down the side of my jaw to my neck, my eyes closed on their own. In just a short amount of time, Trevor already knew my weak spots. He wasn't even kissing my neck, just barely gazing his lips against my skin.

My hips had a mind of their own as I ground against his knee, the fabric of my shorts rubbing me just perfectly. I didn't care that I was probably soaking through them onto his sweatpants. Especially not when Trevor started sucking on the spot between my neck and shoulder.

"I can feel you soaking through my pants," Trevor whispered in my ear. "I've barely even touched you," he taunted, hand tightening in my hair.

"So needy," he murmured, his voice vibrating against my ear, sending a shiver down my spine.

"So needy," he hummed, the sound vibrating against my ear, sending a tremor through me. Panting, I brought a hand up to grip his bicep, needing something to hold on to as the pleasure in my lower belly grew.

I probably should have been embarrassed at how fast I melted under his touch but I wasn't, not when the need to come grew by the second.

My body tightened as my orgasm grew. I was seconds away when the pressure between my legs suddenly disappeared. My head was in the clouds, too distracted to fully comprehend what happened as that pressure in my lower abdomen suddenly vanished. I blinked up at Trevor, who smirked down at me.

"Maybe now you'll learn not to talk back."

Realizing what he did, I gaped up at him. *He did not.* He did not just get me to the edge and then stop. At the look on my face, he chuckled, letting my hair go and stepping back.

Letting out a huff, I crossed my arms, body still on fire and tingling."That was mean."

"So mean," he agreed as he pecked my lips before nodding his head toward the front door. "Let me walk you out."

I wanted to be mad at him for teasing me and then acting like it didn't happen. But that was next to impossible when he flashed me that wide grin and held his hand out for me to take.

"You better watch your back. I'll get my revenge soon." I

lifted my chin with a confident flair as I placed my hand in his. I already had an idea in mind.

"I look forward to it."

Rolling my eyes, my lips tugging up into a smile, I followed him out of his house, grabbing my things as we went and headed to my car still parked out front.

It was dark outside, nearing eight thirty p.m., so none of his neighbors could see how disheveled I looked. Once I placed my stuff in the passenger seat, I turned around, head tilted back to see Trevor's face. His hands found their place on my hips.

"Text me when you get home."

My heart fluttered at his words as I placed my own hands on his bare chest. I really didn't want to leave. "I will. Have a good practice tomorrow."

"Have a good day at work tomorrow." His eyes looked right into mine as he squeezed my hips gently.

Knowing that if I didn't leave I would drag him back inside and ride his cock until dawn. Who knew I would become so addicted to Trevor in just a matter of days?

Lifting up onto my toes, I pressed a soft kiss to his lips. We pulled away a moment later, both knowing I had to go. Sending him one last smile, I slid into my car, Trevor holding the top of the door for me before shutting it. Rolling my window down, I gazed up at him.

"Goodnight."

"Goodnight," he echoed.

Before I could convince myself to stay, I pulled away from the curb, watching Trevor's figure in my rearview mirror until I turned at the corner.

As I drove home, I had a permanent smile on my face. For the first time in a long, long time I felt truly happy. All thanks to one person.

TASHA

"**I**'m so glad you're back. I can't lose my favorite doctor."

I grinned over at Mr. Waltham as he lowered himself into the chair. Mr. Waltham had been coming to me for almost six months and was probably one the sweetest old men you'd ever meet.

"You could never lose me, Henry."

He pointed at me, wagging his finger. "Best doc in town."

No matter how many times I told him I wasn't really a doctor he still called me one. I'd long since given up trying to tell him otherwise.

"How are we doing today?" With my notepad in my lap, I leaned back in my chair.

"Good, good. I got a new neighbor."

"Oh really?"

Mr. Waltham was one of my...more eccentric patients in the way that he didn't really need therapy. At the age of seventy-five, he mainly came to have someone to talk to. Someone to interact with on a weekly basis. He had some of the best stories and lived in a retirement community that wasn't far from my office. He claimed half the people there were too snooty for him.

He was a soldier in the Vietnam War and had been married to his wife for over forty years until she passed away a few years ago. When he lost her, he lost the one person he could talk to everyday.

I told him he didn't need to come in weekly, but he just shook his head and came anyway. I felt bad that he was paying for weekly sessions just because he was lonely, but I wasn't going to turn him away when he needed someone. He could come as long as he wanted.

That was one thing I told myself when I got this job. No matter the person or the problem, they could come to me as long as they felt they needed to. I would never turn someone away if they needed help.

"Her name is Rosette. She moved in a few weeks ago." My eyebrows raised at the mention that his new neighbor was a lady. It was the first time he spoke about another woman that wasn't his late wife. I was a little surprised this was the first time he'd brought her up if she moved in a few weeks ago.

"Have you gone over and introduced yourself?"

"Why would I do that?" Mr. Waltham looked at me like I should have been the one in the seat he sat on. Like our roles should have been reversed.

"So you can meet your new neighbor." I held back a grin. He was typically a social butterfly. Always telling me about some new person he met, even if that person was some kid he met at Applebee's.

"You may find that you have something in common with her," I continued. Mr. Waltham just shook his head. I had a feeling he liked this Rosette and that is why he hadn't brought her up before now. My eyes dropped to his lap, observing as he fingered the wedding ring on his left hand. My heart squeezed.

"Is it because of Carol?" I asked softly. In the last six months, he'd talked non-stop about his wife. Telling me story after story about how they met, how they used to go dancing, and how she was the greatest love of his life.

"It's still hard to believe she's gone." His voice turned soft. "Some days, I wake up and roll over thinking she'll be there, smiling over at me like she always did. We did everything together."

"Are you afraid that Carol would be upset if you talked to your new neighbor?"

"No." Mr. Waltham shook his head again. "She probably would have hit me on the head for not going right over and introducing myself." When he chuckled, I gave him a genuine smile. One that would encourage him to keep talking.

"So, why not go over?" I could tell my question hit close to home as he leaned back against the chair with a sigh.

I knew why he didn't talk to his neighbor. He just didn't want to say it out loud. The moment he actually spoke to another woman, it would solidify the truth—that Carol really was gone. In his mind, it was likely he thought he'd be cheating.

"You know," I sat forward, hands on my lap. "People always say time heals. It heals pain, sadness, anger. In a way, they're right, time does heal but it's different when it comes to grief. Grief doesn't go away overnight and while time can dilute it and make it a little easier to manage, it doesn't disappear one day never to return again."

I sent him a soft smile as I spoke.

"There is always going to be a part of you that misses Carol and grieves her loss. Ten years from now, you will still feel that grief but instead of that gut-wrenching pain, it's going to turn into a small ache. An ache that will remind you that she's no longer here, yes, but it won't consume you."

I swallowed thickly as I watched him tear up across from me.

"You going over to talk to Rosette doesn't mean you still aren't grieving. It also doesn't mean that you've suddenly moved on from Carol." I knew that was his biggest fear. Giving someone else his love.

"I'm not saying you need to ask Rosette out on a date but having a conversation won't hurt. Maybe you'll find yourself a new friend. Or," I reached across to softly touch his hand, "if the day comes that you feel something more for a woman, that's okay, too." His hand closed around mine as he nodded.

"There is no timeline for grief. And the same goes for moving on."

We sat there in silence for a few minutes, Mr. Waltham's hand clutched in mine. I could tell he wasn't the type that liked to cry as he got himself together.

"Thank you, Doc."

"Anytime. And if you need anyone to talk to, I am always here," I promised.

Helping him stand up, I walked him to the door. He seemed...lighter than when he first walked in. Like my words helped ease something inside of him.

"Same time next week?"

"Of course, Doc."

Giving me one last smile and pat on the hand, Mr. Waltham headed for the front doors of the building. Shutting my own office door, I leaned my forehead against it with a sigh. That was an unusual visit for him. I just hoped what I said helped a little.

Hearing my phone ring, I quickly went over to my desk and answered it.

"Hello?"

"Hey."

The voice on the other side made my heart sputter.

Trevor.

"Hey." This was probably the first time we'd talked on the phone, just the two of us.

"How's work going?" For some reason, those words made my throat close up. No one other than Josie ever asked me how work was. My own parents despised my job so of course they wouldn't ask.

"Um, good. My patient just left, so I've got about an hour before the next one. How was practice?" I tried to keep my voice casual but was pretty sure I was failing.

"You okay?" Trevor completely passed over my own question.

"Yeah, I'm fine."

"Fine doesn't always mean okay." I heard shuffling in the background as he spoke.

"When did you get so analytical?" I leaned my hip against my desk, holding my phone closer to my ear. Weirdly, just hearing his voice made me feel better. It was days like today, having to help bear the weight of a loss, that made my job hard and draining.

"I have many layers." I could practically hear the smirk in his voice, even though I couldn't see him. *"Seriously though, you sound upset. Did something happen?"*

"Just a hard day with a patient."

"Well, I think I know how to cheer you up."

A knock sounded at my door. I already knew it was going to be my assistant telling me she was going on her lunch break. With my phone still pressed to my ear, I headed for the door.

"And what is that?"

Waiting for his response, I opened the door only to stop in my tracks. Trevor stood in front of me, holding up a bag of food with his phone to his ear.

"Lunch."

I slowly brought my phone down, staring at him in surprise. He was the last person I expected to see.

"Hope it's okay that I just dropped by." He had a hesitant look on his face, like he was expecting me to turn him away. Why the hell would I do that? He had been stuck in my mind from the moment I got home last night. Plus, he brought food.

"It's more than okay." I beamed. Him showing up was exactly what I needed. "Come in."

I stepped to the side for him to pass by, my assistant standing right behind him with an approving look on her face. She sent me a wink before I shut the door. Facing Trevor, I noticed how his presence filled my entire office.

"I stopped by Rick's and thought you could use something to eat." Trevor rubbed the side of his neck, the motion making him irresistibly cute. At the mention of Rick's food truck, my stomach growled.

One of the best things to come out of Josie and Wyatt's relationship was finding out Rick's Food Truck existed. Rick owned one of the best food trucks and had some of *the* best hamburgers in Toronto. I became a regular after the first time Josie took me there.

"Sounds perfect." I woke up late this morning and hadn't had time to grab a proper breakfast before my first appointment, so I was starving.

"I got onion rings too."

My mouth instantly watered at his words. I was a sucker for Rick's onion rings.

"I could kiss you right now."

"Which reminds me." Trevor grabbed my hand, twirling me to face him. He wasted no time leaning down to kiss me.

The feel of his lips against mine made me forget everything that was going on in my mind. It was like he silenced it all, and all I could do was focus on him. Trevor filled my senses as I kissed him back. I grabbed the front of his shirt as I pressed into him.

Finally pulling away, my eyes fluttered open to meet his. The smile on his face did something to my stomach.

"Now you can eat." I stood there, gaping at him, my mind trying to catch up. Whenever Trevor kissed me, it was like my brain turned to goo.

"I had no idea my kisses were good enough to make a person forget about one of Rick's hamburgers.

"Oh, hush." Ignoring his gaze, I took a seat, reaching for the to-go boxes. As soon as I opened the container with onion rings, I dug in. I could have eaten them every single day for the rest of my life.

"Gonna share?"

I shook my head, stuffing another ring in my mouth. "Get your own."

"Wow, that's the thanks I get for bringing you food?" His expression morphed to something of mock hurt. We both knew it was just a ruse.

"Fine." With a sigh, I grabbed an onion ring, purposely picking the smallest one, extending it out. "Here." He took it with a raised eyebrow. "Be happy you got one."

Shaking his head, the two of us dug into our food. I kept glancing over at him, still shocked he was actually here but glad he was.

"Thank you for the food," I said after a little bit.

"Of course. Although, my intentions were a bit selfish." Trevor looked down at his food, his cheeks a little pink. "I wanted to see you." As if my heart could flutter anymore.

"Well, feel free to be selfish more often."

"Will do." We shared a smile. I felt like a teenager sitting in front of her crush, blushing while a kaleidoscope of butterflies flapped in her stomach.

"How was practice?"

"Good. Coach was a hard ass, as always." Coach Barnum was known for being an ass but winning multiple Cup Championships, I think you kind of had to be.

"Ready for your first game next week?" I may not have been as big of a hockey fan as Josie—the girl could make someone deaf with her screaming while watching the games —but I knew enough. Kind of hard not to when you lived in the hockey capital. Plus, Josie practically forced me to watch games with her, so I managed to pick up what actually went on in a game.

"Yeah, we have a new defensive player and he's not bad, but he keeps letting goals through. He needs to lean more into the goalie and keep his stick straight." While I learned a lot about the game, there were still things I didn't know- like the importance of a player keeping his stick at a certain angle. "He'll get there, though."

I caught the last part of his sentence, but I was too focused on how endearing he looked when he talked about hockey.

"You love it, don't you?" At the look on his face, I clarified. "Hockey."

"I do." The smile that appeared on his face made me want to smile. "I didn't even play hockey until high school."

"Oh?" Toeing my heels off, I curled my legs underneath me.

"I grew up in Elora, and there was only one ice rink in the entire town. It was always packed, but in order to skate, you had to pay." Trevor grabbed a french fry as he spoke. "Since I didn't have a lot of money growing up, I couldn't ever go and skate. Even when my friends wanted to go, I couldn't. I did sneak in a few times, though."

"Such a rule breaker," I teased.

"When I got to high school, my only priority was to grad-uate and move. My sophomore year, my school started their

194

first hockey team, so I went to tryouts. Found out I was pretty damn good."

"Played ever since?"

"Pretty much. Somehow got a scholarship to Toronto to play, and the rest is history."

"Bet you're glad you went to tryouts that day." I said.

"It was more about being away from my house. It was easier to be at the rink sometimes."

It meant a lot that Trevor was here opening up about his parents. It wasn't easy to talk about certain situations. While I knew there was more to the story about his parents I would let him tell me on his own time.

"So..." When Trevor changed the subject, I let him. "Why were you upset earlier?" Of course, he didn't forget.

"It was nothing." I waved him off.

"If it made you upset, it's not 'nothing.'"

"My patient from earlier lost his wife a few years ago." I couldn't say too much because of doctor-patient privilege. I may have only been a counselor, but it was still an invasion of privacy and against the law. "It was a rough day for him. I tried to be of help, but I'm not sure I was."

My biggest fear slipped past my lips without realizing it. I had never fully admitted that out loud before, not even to Josie. That I questioned my ability to guide a person through their struggles in a way that had them coming out on top on the other side of it. That I was just sitting there spouting bullshit. That I wasn't making a difference.

"Hey." Trevor's voice was soft as he stood up, moving to squat in front of me. He placed his hands on my knees, drawing my attention to him. "Tasha, you are great at what you do."

"I—"

"No. Don't even think about putting yourself down. You care about your patients, which makes you great at your job."

His hands squeezed my thighs. "Sometimes, just having their words listened to is all people need. They need someone who will care enough to stop and listen and understand."

Trevor had absolutely no clue how much his words meant. How they helped ease the pressure in my chest.

"How do you always say the right thing?" I whispered, my own hands coming down on his. When I first met Trevor, I never once thought he'd be someone I could confide in or who would say the right thing to make me feel better. There was so much more to him than I ever knew or let myself know, for that matter.

"It's one of my many talents."

I chuckled at his response. "Thank you." I met his eyes as I squeezed his hands.

He was the first person that wasn't Josie that made me confident in my job. That I was making a difference when I second-guessed myself.

I'd always been someone who pushed for perfection. If I couldn't do it perfectly the first time, I beat myself up about it for weeks at a time. My parents strived for that same thing, which I guessed was where I got it from. Always having to get straight A's, be in advanced classes, learn languages.

I may not have had the job they wanted, but I still had that urge inside of me to be perfect at it. Even more so to show them that I was doing just fine in the career that *I* chose. I was always trying to prove myself with everything I did.

"Always."

The urge to kiss him grew more and more the longer he stayed in that position. Him squatting between my legs made him perfectly in line with my lips. My hands moved on their own, leaving his hands to softly touch the scruff on his face. "I like this," I murmured.

"Yeah?"

"It suits you." It made him look more rugged.

"I'll make sure to keep it then." At that point, the two of us spoke softly. My palms smoothed over his face while his hands ran over my thighs ever so slowly. Even wearing my work slacks, his body heat seeped through the fabric.

"I want to kiss you." The words left my lips in a whisper making him chuckle.

"You don't need to ask permission, Sunshine."

I didn't let myself be embarrassed as I brought my lips to his. Not when kissing Trevor made everything inside of me settle down. It wasn't a sexual kiss as his lips moved gently against mine. It was crazy how fast I went from pushing Trevor away to needing him. But not a single part of me second-guessed it.

Pulling away from each other, Trevor gave me that smile that made my heart race. I could definitely get used to him coming to my office for lunch.

TASHA

"Please tell me this jet lag is kicking your ass too." Josie groaned over the phone later that night.

"I'm exhausted." Partly because of what she said but Trevor was to blame for the other part. Josie didn't need to know that, though. Not yet.

I wanted to tell her everything, but I held back. This thing between Trevor and I was too new to tell anyone. A part of me wanted to keep us a secret for as long as we could before anyone else interfered.

It wasn't like I didn't trust Josie. I trusted her with my life. But I also knew she would march right up to Trevor and demand what his intentions were. She'd make sure he treated me right. And I fully planned on letting Josie loose on Trevor but now wasn't the time.

For now, I wanted it to be just us two. So, if that meant keeping it from Josie, I would. Even though she'd be pissed at me when she found out. I just needed to know if the feelings between Trevor and me could really become something.

"Maybe next time we stay in the same time zone."

I chuckled at her words. It was her idea to go to Whit-sunday Island in the first place.

While Josie chatted away over the phone, I got started on my laundry as I waited for my takeout to come. I was too tired to even think about cooking.

As soon as a knock sounded on my door, a weird noise came through the phone. It only took a second for me to realize what was going on. I could hear Wyatt saying some-thing in Josie's ear, followed by a soft whimper. I made a disgusted face.

Opening my door, I was greeted by Trevor, holding two to-go bags.

"Thank God," I said by way of greeting, motioning for him to come in. Trevor looked at me with raised eyebrows as he closed my door behind him.

Josie's whimper turned into something louder, making me want to gag.

"Okay, well I'll talk to you later, Jo. Have fun." Not even waiting for her response, I hung up. "Disgusting," I muttered with a shake of my head.

"What was that about?"

"I think Josie and Wyatt were getting it on while I was on the phone with her." Trevor just laughed before I said, "Next time you can be on the phone when they do that.". Wanting to get the conversation off whatever Josie and Wyatt were doing, I looked at the bags in Trevor's hands.

"Twice in one day. Are you secretly an Uber Eats driver?"

"It's my side gig." He grinned. "I actually ran into the delivery guy when I came up the stairs."

When Trevor left my office this afternoon, neither of us had said anything about seeing one another tonight, but I was glad he showed up.

"And you brought food, too." I noted two different names

on the bags. One from the Chinese place down the street and one from Chick-Fil-A.

"Didn't know you already ordered something." Trevor shifted his weight on his feet, seemingly embarrassed.

"Well, I, for one, am starving. There better be some fries in there."

"Obviously."

Grabbing a bag from him, I led him to my living room. My place wasn't as big or nice as Trevor's. It was just a two bedroom apartment with a more open floor plan. My kitchen opened up to a little dining area and the living space. The two bedrooms were off to the left of the kitchen down a short hall.

I wouldn't say my place was a mess, but I did have stuff scattered around. I did like to keep things clean and organized but as soon as I had my own place, I made it *mine*. I put the decorations I wanted, even if they didn't match. It wasn't as glamorous as my parents place but I didn't need it to be.

Growing up in my parent's house—well, more like a mansion—things were kept immaculate. The place was always meticulously decorated and everything had a place. A maid would come and clean the house every week until it was immaculate.

It wasn't a homey house. No part of it screamed that a loving family lived here. We only ate at the dining room table a handful of times and only if clients came over. More often than not, I ate alone in my room.

I told myself that when I got my own place, I would make it the way I wanted. I would make it feel like a home. And I did.

"You know, if you keep bringing me food, I just might fall in love with you," I spoke over my shoulder.

"Maybe that's my plan."

It was working.

"Sorry for dropping by unannounced…again." I didn't think I could ever be mad at Trevor for just dropping by.

"Don't be, I'm glad you did."

I'd never had a guy bring me food or show up without having to be asked. Part of it was me. I always kept guys at arm's length, not fully letting myself be open. The other half of it was the men I dated. They were never the type of guys you'd fall in love with and marry. I knew that, which was why I picked them.

But I was tired of the meaningless guys. I wanted someone who showed up, or wanted me for me. Just like the man standing in my kitchen right now.

I was a little self-conscious about having Trevor in my apartment. I couldn't remember the last time a guy was over, but Trevor wasn't just some guy. It wasn't lost on me that one of the star players for the Toronto Knights was showing up at my door and bringing me food.

I may not have been the biggest hockey fan, but even I knew that Trevor Hall was a big deal. Since Wyatt and Bryton were off the market, Trevor was now considered the most eligible bachelor on the team. Countless times, I'd walked past billboards with his face and abs, hearing girls go on about how attractive he was. I knew for a fact tons of women would have killed to be me.

"So, tell me," I said once we had eaten a little. The TV played mutedly in the background. "What do you do when you aren't at practice or playing hockey?"

I was always curious what they did in the off season or in between games. There was only so much practice and working out you could do. Although, they did get paid enough to never have to work another day in their lives.

"You wanna know if I have a side job?"

"Yep. Are you secretly a stripper?"

"With a body like mine, I could be." He gestured to his abs.

"It's not that spectacular." I rolled my eyes at him, eating another mouthful of noodles.

"I recall you saying differently just the other night." He raised an eyebrow at me. Damn him and his nice eyebrows.

"Nope. Wasn't me." I shook my head, putting my food on the table.

"Oh, it wasn't you that pushed me onto my back and proceeded to *lick* my abs?" At his words, my face heated. I knew my cheeks were bright red from the smirk on Trevor's face.

"Pig," I muttered, kicking his leg. His hand grabbed my foot faster than I could retract it. "Don't you even dare!" I tried to wiggle my foot free when he brought his hand up to it as if he was going to tickle me.

"Admit that my abs are delicious," he threatened with his hand inches from the sole of my foot. I narrowed my eyes at him as he smirked at me.

"You can't threaten me."

"Are you sure about that?" He brought his hand closer, causing me to squirm. Okay, maybe he could but he didn't need to know that.

"Yep." I stuck my chin out but kept my eyes on his hand.

"I don't believe you." While his hand didn't move, his other hand cupped my ankle, his fingers softly stroking the skin. He was purposely distracting me. "Let's hear it."

"Never." I tried to act tough.

"Fine. Have it your way." Before I could say anything else, he started tickling my foot.

My whole body jerked and a very unladylike squeal came out of my mouth. "Trevor!"

He kept a tight grip on me as he continued. I fought

against his hold until I managed to kick him in the chest hard enough that I sent him to the floor with a loud thud.

Breathing heavily, I sat up, looking down at him as he laid on his back, eyes closed.

"Trevor?" When he didn't respond, I moved closer. "Trevor?"

Noticing that the table was moved a little to the side, I jumped off the couch.

"Trevor!" Oh God, what if he hit his head on the corner of the table? Starting to freak out, I stood over him, hands moving around, not really sure what to do. "Trev—" I was cut off when a pair of hands grabbed the back of my calves, yanking me down.

I landed on top of him, straddling his waist, hands on his chest. A mischievous smirk appeared on his face as he looked up at me, his hands moving to rest on the tops of my thighs.

Seeing that he was perfectly fine, I slapped his chest.

"You asshole! You made me think you were hurt!" I continued slapping him while he just laughed underneath me. "You're so mean."

"Well, I got you where I wanted you, didn't I?"

"You could have just asked!" I glared down at him, trying my hardest to ignore the hard muscle under my hands and the thing that pressed itself against me through my shorts.

"If I asked you to do something, you'd do it?" His tone changed as he stared up at me. His grip on my thighs tightened just slightly. I knew what he meant as my chin dipped in a slow nod.

"So, if I asked you to straddle my face you would do so without hesitation?" My eyes widened. "You'd sit on my face as I eat your pussy?" His words were crude, but I couldn't deny the zing that went straight to my core.

The thought of doing that had me soaking wet. The image that popped into my head made my hips move unconsciously. I hadn't even noticed they swirled over him until a sharp smack on my ass jerked me out of my thoughts.

"Yes or no, Sunshine." The command in his voice made me bite my bottom lip.

"Yes." The word left my lips without a second thought. The hand on my ass squeezed, followed by a low hum in Trevor's throat.

"Take off those little shorts that have been teasing me all night and come sit on my face."

"Right here?" I gestured to my living room.

"Yes." God, that demanding tone of his was going to be the death of me.

"I…"

He must have seen the slight hesitation on my face. "You're in control here, Tasha. I might ask you to do things, but if you aren't comfortable you say no and it all stops. Understand?"

I had noticed that he didn't do anything unless I gave permission. That alone meant more to me than anything else.

"Understand."

"Now, don't make me ask again."

That did it. I quickly got off his lap, moving to the side so I could take my shorts off. Those intense eyes watched as I hooked my thumbs in my shorts. I made a show of bending over until my shorts pooled around my ankles, gracefully lifting my legs out. The small tank top I had on did nothing to hide my lacy underwear.

The way Trevor's eyes moved up my legs, darkening at the sight of my red panties, made me feel like the sexiest woman in the world. He looked seconds away from pouncing on me. It made me feel….powerful. Wanted.

I knew Trevor told me what to do, but I was the one in control. After everything that happened, I needed it. To know that I could stop at any moment, and he wouldn't be upset.

Trevor never once looked away as I peeled my underwear down my legs. I could tell he was holding himself back as I took my time, his eyes lingering on my legs in a way that I loved.

"Get over here." Trevor's voice was hoarse.

I had never actually done this before. I'd always been in a missionary position when I was with a guy. So as I went to straddle his head, I wasn't entirely sure what to do or where to put my hands. I tried my hardest not to let my thoughts distract me from the moment.

I hovered above him, my bottom lip between my teeth, thighs flexed to keep me up. Trevor's hands grabbed my thighs.

"Never hover," was all he said before he yanked me fully down. My hands grabbed the side of the couch in surprise, a squeak leaving my lips.

Everything ceased to exist the second I felt his tongue touch me. My eyes rolled back as I gripped the couch like my life depended on it. There were no words to even begin to describe what coursed through my body.

My hips moved on their own, my pussy grinding on his face. The thought that I was practically suffocating him was shoved out the window as he grabbed my ass, urging me to grind harder.

My moans filled the room as Trevor hummed below me, clearly in no rush for me to get off. One of my hands left the couch, reaching down to grab his head to pull him even closer. Every groan from his throat vibrated against me. His tongue went from my clit and back down every few seconds. My wetness moved across his face as I shamelessly rode him.

It didn't take him long to get me to the edge. Not after the way he teased me at his place yesterday and this afternoon in my office. Pretty much all I could think about all day was Trevor. Of this moment.

My release hit me faster than ever before. No sound left my mouth as I came all over his face—head thrown back, eyes squeezed shut, thighs shaking.

Feeling the swipe of a tongue on my clit, my whole body twitched, and my eyes snapped open. Slowly, I untangled my hands that had a death grip on Trevor's hair. One second, I was sitting on him, and the next, I was lying on my back on the rug. My head whirled from the orgasm. So much that I wondered how he flipped us so easily.

Trevor hovered above me, the look on his face prideful. His hair was sticking up where I gripped it, his face had a glossy sheen, even his beard, but it was the look on his face paired with the way he touched me that had me arching underneath him.

I almost felt like I should have said something, but I had no words. All I wanted right then was to feel him inside of me. Trevor brought his thumb up, rubbing it across my bottom lip. Before he could pull it away, I wrapped my lips around his thumb and sucked. The groan that left his mouth had me smiling around his thumb as I grazed my teeth against the pad.

"On your hands and knees."

It took a second for my mind to catch up.

"I said," he pulled his thumb from my mouth, "on your hands and knees."

I didn't even hesitate in sitting up, grabbing the hem of my tank top and pulling it off, those dark green eyes of his staring through me.

I barely got to my hands and knees before he was grabbing my hips and yanking me back roughly. Glancing over my shoulder, I noticed he didn't even take his pants fully off.

A tight grip on my hair yanked my head back, arching my

back even more, my ass perfectly raised in front of him. He quickly spanked me, emitting a moan from deep in my throat.

"You have no idea how bad I wanted to bend you over your desk earlier and fuck you," Trevor whispered in my ear as he bent over me, wedging himself between my legs. I could feel his hard cock pressed against me. Could feel just how hard he was. "To make you moan so loud that everyone in the building knew what I was doing to you."

I wasn't sure I'd ever get enough of his dirty talk. The way his voice got all husky and low.

"And then to see you answer the door in those tight shorts. You would have given the delivery guy a little show." I wiggled my hips back against him as he spoke, making his grip tighten on my hair and hip.

"You are mine, Sunshine. You'd do well to remember that." Those words had me groaning, bucking my hips again.

Trevor wasted no time in slamming his cock right into me. The force knocked the breath from my lungs, making me grip the rug as I stretched to accommodate his size.

He felt so good. Like he was meant for me.

Once again, I circled my hips, earning a hiss from behind me. Another smack landed on my ass before Trevor started thrusting. This wasn't sweet and slow. No, it was fast and rough. Exactly what I wanted.

"Good girl," he said above me. "You're taking me so good."

His provocative words were more electrifying than anything I'd ever known. Everything with Trevor felt more intense, like my past experiences were nothing compared to this.

"Look at you, taking every inch of me."

It didn't take long for me to peak again. I swear, just one little word from Trevor was enough to get me there. I felt like I was floating as I moaned so loudly I was pretty sure my neighbors could hear.

Trevor didn't slow as my pussy gripped his length. With a handful of my hair, I had no choice but to let him fuck me as I came. Through it all, Trevor filled me, fucked me, praised me. His moans filled my ears. His hands on my hips were almost bruising as he came, collapsing against my back as he came down.

Both of our bodies were slick with sweat, our panting filling the room. Trevor rolled off to the side on his back as I stayed on my stomach trying to get my breathing back under control. There was no way I was getting up any time soon.

"That was..." When Trevor couldn't finish his sentence, it made me laugh.

"I know." Crossing my arms under my head, I turned to look at him. His dark hair was stuck to his forehead, and his eyes were shining. I had seen Trevor happy but this was... This was different. The look on his face was one I couldn't describe, but I had a feeling I had the same expression on mine.

"Would you like to stay?" I whispered.

Reaching out, Trevor rubbed my cheek with his thumb. "I would love that."

TREVOR

B eing on the ice was my happy place. My mind emptied, and the only thing I had to focus on was the puck in front of me.

The rink was cold, but it helped cool off the sweat running down my back. My hair was sticking to my forehead under the helmet as I skated, pushing hard against the ice to reach the puck. I was breathing hard, but I welcomed the burn that settled into my chest and thighs.

Stealing the puck from my teammate, I skirted around him, my eyes searching for one person. Catching sight of Wyatt, I brought my stick back and snapped it forward, sending the puck straight for him.

With a quick flick of Wyatt's wrist, the puck shot right into the goal. Grinning under my helmet, I skated over to my best friend, slapping him on the back. Bryton landed a hard smack to my helmet as he skated by.

The sound of the whistle called the end of practice.

"Good job, boys!" Coach yelled from the side of the rink. Three hours later and practice was finally done. Despite being exhausted, I felt great. Our first game was Monday, and I was stoked to finally be back on the rink with hundreds of screaming fans.

The image of Tasha sitting in the stands shouting my name came to mind, making my heart stutter for a beat. I've never had someone in the stands to cheer me on. Sure I had Wyatt's mom and brothers but they were here *for* Wyatt, not me. My parents never came, too strung out to care. Having Tasha there for *me* would be everything. I just had to ask her and hope she wanted to.

Taking my helmet off, I shook out my hair, sweat sticking to my forehead as I skated slowly around the rink.

"What has you in a good mood?" Bryton asked, coming up to my side.

"Yeah, you've been smiling nonstop the last week," Wyatt interjected.

"No reason," I lied. I knew the reason. It was because of Tasha.

The last week had felt surreal. Every day, Tasha and I hung out. Whether that was because I dropped by her office for lunch or because we went to each other's place for dinner. And, of course, food always turned into much more but neither of us were complaining. Not in the slightest.

"You've been MIA all week." I could feel their eyes on me as we took another lap around the rink to cool off.

"I was recovering from jet lag. Aren't you guys?" It wasn't that much of a falsehood. I'd just been recovering from jet lag with Tasha.

A few nights prior, the two of us decided to keep whatever was going on between us a secret. Just for now. We both knew we couldn't hide it forever—the paparazzi and our friends were bound to sniff it out. We just wanted to keep it on the low for the time being.

It did suck not telling my boys. Every day at practice that week, I had to bite my tongue from saying something. But until Tasha and I agreed to tell our friends, I wouldn't say a word. Even if I did want to shout from the rooftops that Tasha Davis was mine.

We had yet to actually classify what we were, but I was pretty sure we both knew it was beyond just a hookup. Tasha was mine in every sense of the word.

"Getting Mila out of bed this week has been a chore." Bryton laughed, shaking his head at his girlfriend.

"How is finding a house going, by the way?" I asked.

The three of us skated to the side of the rink where our water bottles sat, leaning our sticks against the wall along with our helmets. We were the last on the ice as everyone else headed for the locker room.

"Good, actually. I think we found a house we both like." Bryton grinned. It was still crazy to think that Bryton was buying a house with his girlfriend. Wyatt was engaged. Felt like yesterday all three of us were single, hitting up the bars on weekends.

"I'm happy for you, man." Wyatt clapped Bryton on the shoulder.

"Are you and Josie going to move before you get married?" Bryton asked.

"We aren't sure yet." Wyatt shrugged, chugging his water. "Her apartment is the last thing her dad gave her. I don't think she wants to leave it."

"She can always keep it so when she gets tired of your ass, she has another place to stay," I joked.

"Ha ha." He shoved my shoulder as I laughed. "My fiancée loves me, thank you very much."

"Oh, I know." I thought back to Monday night and the phone call I interrupted between Tasha and Josie.

"What?"

Realizing I said that out loud, I pushed off the side wall.

"I need a fucking shower," I told the guys as I skated toward the locker room, leaving the two to follow me off the ice.

"Want to go get drinks tonight?" Bryton asked from behind me.

"Sorry, I can't tonight," I told him. I had other plans that were more important.

"Oh, Friday night plans." I could practically hear the smirk in Wyatt's voice. No doubt thinking I was going out to hook up with someone. If only they knew that person was Tasha.

"Yep."

Tasha only had one patient this morning, so as soon as I got home, showered, and changed, I was taking her out. It was going to be our first date, and I had big plans for it.

Yesterday, when I told her I was taking her out today, she got so giddy. She asked me at least a dozen times what we were doing until she finally gave up when I wouldn't reveal anything. But I knew she was going to love it.

"Apparently, Tasha is going out tonight too," Wyatt said, looking at me as if to gauge my reaction. To see if I would be jealous or not. If it wasn't me that she was going out with, I probably would have been. "I overheard Josie on the phone with her this morning."

"Oh?" I tried to make myself sound curious as I headed over to my cubby to take my hockey gear off.

"Josie said Tasha hasn't dated in a long time and wouldn't tell her who it was. Have you guys heard anything?"

"Not a clue but Mila may know," Bryton said as I shook my head, trying my hardest not to grin like an idiot.

Grabbing the back of my soaked white T-shirt, I yanked it over my head and threw it near my bag. Behind me, I Wyatt and Bryton changed, so I made quick work of putting on my other shirt. If either of them looked at my back, they would have seen scratches all over it, courtesy of my little blonde spitfire.

I made quick work of changing and putting my gear away. The sooner I got home and ready, the sooner I got to see my girl.

"I'll catch you guys later," I said, grabbing my bag as I headed for the exit. "Tell the girls hi for me." Before they could respond, I walked through the doors.

I had to get ready for a date.

"YOU STILL AREN'T GOING to tell me what we're doing?" Tasha asked again. I shook my head, keeping my eyes on the road.

I could understand her curiosity, though. We'd been on the road for almost an hour, each mile getting farther away from Toronto.

Tasha let out a sigh and laid her head back, looking out the window. With my hand on the steering wheel and the other on her thigh, I glanced over with a soft grin. While it was only noon, the sun was mostly blocked by gray clouds. A few rays of sunshine broke through, hitting Tasha just right. From where I was sitting, she looked stunning. Like an angel, sunlight ricocheted off her face and body where it was able to slip through the windows.

I took my hand off her thigh but she didn't even notice, too busy staring at the passing trees. Even though I knew it was against the law, I reached for my phone next to me in the console. There were only a few other cars on the road with us and no one close.

Clicking the camera icon, I brought my phone up and quickly snapped multiple photos of Tasha. She was too beautiful not to photograph.

My thumb clicked away as I took shot after shot, not even sure how many I took as I kept glancing at the road in front of us. Tasha turned to look at me but I didn't stop.

"Are you taking pictures of me?" She smiled. I snapped a photo at that exact moment, getting that gorgeous smile of hers.

After one more picture I finally put my phone down. I would gladly fill my phone with photos of her.

"My turn." Before I could protest, Tasha snatched my phone and aimed it at me.

"Really?" I raised an eyebrow at her, tilting my head to the side.

"Yep." She beamed at me on the other side of the camera. I could only grin back. She really had no idea what she did to me.

I was no stranger to a camera. I'd done multiple photo-shoots for magazines, billboards, as well as ones for the team, but having Tasha take pictures of me was different. It felt more personal.

I let Tasha take picture after picture. If she wanted me to pose a certain way, I did so without saying a word—well, as much as I could with being behind the wheel. When she seemed satisfied with the pictures she got, she finally put the phone away. Leaning back against the headrest, I glanced over to find her eyes still on me.

"What?"

"Nothing. Just watching."

"You know that's kinda creepy, right? Just staring at someone as they drive." I retorted.

"You won't tell me where we're going, so I gotta entertain myself somehow," Tasha said with a shrug.

214

"There's a radio right there."

"Fine, then. I'll just annoy you with some music instead."
Beside me, Tasha paired her phone to the stereo. "Let's see
how you like this one."

The moment Taylor Swift's "Cardigan" came on, I wanted
to laugh. Oh, Tasha.

"Sucks for you." I sent her a grin. "I love me some Tay
Tay."

Before she could say anything else, I started belting out
the words. I was so off-key as I sang. I was a horrible singer,
but that wasn't going to stop me. I sang the lyrics, knowing
the song word for word. I mean, who didn't love Taylor
Swift? Tasha laughed as I kept going. I could have listened to
her laugh every second of the day.

I didn't miss a single word or beat as the song came to an
end. With a proud smile on my face, I looked over at her and
found her grinning ear to ear. *She had the most perfect smile.*

"You are horrible." She laughed.

"I think you mean fantastic."

"Fantastically horrible," she amended, to which I agreed.

"You're damn right."

"How do you even know that song?"

"Because Tay is the queen." I snapped my fingers, making
her laugh even more. "Plus, she has some decent songs to
workout to." And she did. My workout playlists consisted of
everything from R&B to Disney songs. If you were lifting
weights or running you couldn't listen to boring slow songs.

"You are such a dork." Tasha shook her head at me.

"You love it," was my response back. With my phone still
in her hand she flipped through the pictures she just took as I
placed my hand back on her thigh. I had no problem with
her going through my phone if she wanted. I had nothing to
hide.

We lapsed into silence, a random song playing in the

background. It wasn't awkward silence either. Being around Tasha made content, like neither of us had to fill the quietness with awkward conversation. We could just be around each other.

We drove for another twenty minutes before I saw the sign that told me I needed to turn. We were a long way from Toronto where it was more dense with trees, and the homes were mainly cabins or farmhouses.

"So you ready to know where we're going?"

"I've been ready since yesterday!"

"I thought since it's an unseasonably warm October day, we should be outside. And the other day, you told me how you've always wanted to go to a pumpkin patch and get a pumpkin. So, I thought why not?."

The smile that formed on her face at my words let me know I made the right choice in choosing a date at a local pumpkin patch. Earlier this week, we were lying in bed talking about random things when Tasha brought up that she'd never carved a pumpkin.

Said her parents thought it was pointless so she never got the chance. I could hear the longing in her voice as she spoke about it, and I knew right then that we had to go.

And there was also the fact that I only carved a pumpkin once or twice in my life. When I met Wyatt in university, he brought me over to his mom's house. At the time, Matteo was only twelve, and they had a tradition where they all went and picked out a pumpkin, brought it home, and had a contest to see who carved theirs the best.

They gladly took me in with open arms and let me tag along with them. Even at nineteen, it was a blast. Plus my pumpkins typically won the contest.

Tasha was practically jumping in her seat as I turned down the road that led to the patch. There were only a few cars, seeing that it was nearing one o'clock on a Thursday, which worked perfectly. The two of us could hang around for as long as we wanted without anyone seeing us.

Parking the car, Tasha looked out the front window in excitement. Turning to face me, she sent me the widest grin.

"Let's find the biggest pumpkin here."

22

TASHA

"Look at this one!" The pumpkin in front of us was literally the size of a boulder.

"Maybe we should pick ones that'll fit in the car," Trevor suggested. This may or may not be the fifth big pumpkin I'd asked for us to get. Each time Trevor said no. Apparently, one the size of a car wasn't allowed.

The two of us walked around the pumpkin patch for a good thirty minutes. Trevor tugged a wagon behind him that already had his pumpkin since he picked it out fifteen minutes ago. There were plenty to choose from, but I wanted the *perfect one.*

Trevor leaned down to pick up a decent-sized pumpkin. "How about this one?"

"It doesn't have a good stem, though." I thought, at that point, Trevor would have been over it and ready to go, but he just smiled and put the pumpkin down.

I weaved in between rows as the gray clouds about us got darker. I was glad I decided to wear jeans and a sweater, not the cute dress I initially picked out.

When Trevor asked me out on a date, I never expected we'd end up on a farm. I wasn't sure what he had in mind, but this was beyond what I could've imagined.

We were doing things a bit backwards. Sleeping together and then going on a date, but I didn't mind. We were doing things our way, and I liked it.

I looked around for another few minutes before spotting the pumpkin I wanted. It was perfect—light orange, tall and wide, and a stem that curled at the end. Bending down, I grabbed it.

"This one." I declared to an amused Trevor as I held it up. He reached out and took it from me, putting it on the wagon next to his.

"Ready to go?" With rain threatening overhead, it was time to go, even though I wanted to stay forever. I always enjoyed getting out of the city and enjoying somewhere more peaceful.

"Let's go." Placing my hand in his, the two of us made our way back to the front of the farm to pay for our pumpkins.

As we walked hand in hand, a sudden image popped into my head, making me pause. I could see it. See us a few years from now doing this exact thing every October. Us walking around and laughing, taking pictures on top of giant pumpkins with gourds surrounding them. It was bizarre, but I could see it so clearly.

Glancing up at Trevor, I realized the thought of being with him years from now didn't freak me out. Instead, I was almost giddy from the idea.

"GETTING HUNGRY?" Trevor asked as we got back in the car. Pumpkins secured in the backseat.

"Starving."

"I have the perfect place in mind."

As Trevor started driving back in the direction we came in, I frowned down at his hand that was resting on the gear shift. With a huff, I reached down, grabbed it, and moved it onto my leg.

Beside me, Trevor chuckled, squeezing my thigh softly.

"The hand goes here. Always."

"Noted."

Aside from the fact that physical touch was one of my love languages, I just liked having Trevor touch me. It made me feel safe.

We drove for another ten minutes before we hit a little town. It was one of those towns you read about in books where only a few hundred people lived and everyone knew everyone. We must have been driving down the main road because shops lined both sides of the street.

Trevor turned the car into what looked like a cute diner, the sign out front reading Lucille's. When Trevor told me to stay put, my lips twitched into a smile. I waited as he came around the front and opened my car door for me like a true gentleman.

"M'Lady." Trevor bowed, holding his arm out.

"Thank you, good sir," I replied back in a fake British accent.

With a shared smile, the two of us walked hand in hand inside the diner. The moment we stepped through the doors, I was hit with that homey vibe that only family-owned diners had.

The place was small and almost every seat was filled. We managed to find a booth near the back and took a seat. Glancing around, I noticed all the stuff on the walls. From what I could see, there was a mix of pictures, posters, and jerseys.

"The Boone family used to bring me here with them when we went to the pumpkin patch," Trevor said out of the blue.

"Oh really?"

"His family pretty much took me in even though I was nineteen and in college. Evelyn would all but demand I come to their house during the weekends for dinner and on holidays. We would do the pumpkin patch then hit up this place afterward."

The way Trevor spoke about Wyatt's family brought a smile to my face. He clearly loved them like his own. It came as no surprise that Wyatt's mom, Evelyn, would take Trevor under her wing. She was literally a mom to everyone. Every time I saw her she treated me as if I were her own.

"Well, I'm honored you brought me here." I placed my hand on his across the table. It was clear this place meant something to him.

"Now, let me tell you a secret about this place." He leaned forward with a grin. Intrigued, I leaned close to him, waiting for him to share. "They have *the* best pie shakes."

"Pie Shakes?"

"They put actual pie slices in their shakes." My eyebrows raised at his words. Now that sounded good.

"Since you seem to know what's good here, I'll let you order for me."

"What if I choose something disgusting?"

"I trust you." I shrugged. My words seemed to make him pause. He looked at me with an expression I couldn't place. Before I could say anything, the waitress appeared next to us.

"What can I get you two sweethearts?" I smiled over at the cute older lady standing by the table. Her gray/white hair clipped back, eyes crinkled as she stared down at the two of us.

I watched as Trevor smiled up at her and rattled off a bunch of food. When the lady walked off with our order, I raised an eyebrow at him. "You do know there's only two of us, right? Not an entire hockey team."

"You haven't eaten today. Don't think I haven't noticed." He shot me a look. "Plus, I had a grueling practice, and I'm starving."

"Coach pushed you guys hard huh."

"Yeah, typical with our first game on Monday. But what's more interesting was Wyatt talking about you." I had a feeling I knew what they were talking about. Earlier, Josie called to see if I wanted to hang out with her and Wyatt, but I made the mistake of telling her I had plans.

Immediately, I was bombarded with questions. I knew invading questions would only make her more curious, but I just wanted to focus on today and the time I was going to get with Trevor. I also knew she would tell Wyatt, who would probably talk to Trevor and Bryton. The three of them were worse than girls when it came to gossiping.

"Josie is probably coming up with tons of ideas on what I'm doing right now." I knew my best friend like the back of my hand.

"Think they'll figure it out on their own?" Trevor questioned.

"Knowing our friends, probably." We shared a grin as our waitress came back, this time with a tray filled with shakes.

"Here you sweethearts go."

The light orange shake with what looked like pieces of crust made my mouth water when she put it in front of me. The best part was they even came with extra shake on the side in the metal container.

"Thank you so much." With a promise to bring the rest in a moment, she left us.

"So, that one is peach pie." Trevor gestured to the one in front of me. "And this one is pecan pie."

I wasted no time in swiping my finger across the whipped cream on top, sucking it off my finger. I did that a few times before I noticed how still Trevor was across from me, his knuckles white as he gripped the counter, eyes glued to my mouth.

Maybe now was the perfect time for my revenge. He teased me, so now it was my turn. Keeping my eyes on him, I scooped another dollop of whipped cream onto my finger. Slowly bringing it to my parted mouth, I made a show of sliding my finger against my tongue before closing my lips and sucking the whipped cream off.

Seeing his reaction made me want to grin. I told him I'd get him back for teasing me in the hallway of his place a week ago.

Letting my finger go, I went to do it again, but this time, I leaned over the table, dipping my finger in the creamy topping of the shake in front of him. Flashing him a grin, I sat back with my finger sliding back into my mouth. I moaned low in my throat and closed my eyes. Across from me, he groaned.

Opening my eyes, I let my finger go with a pop. Trevor looked seconds away from launching across the table at me.

"What?" I asked innocently.

"You're playing with fire, Sunshine."

"I'm not doing anything." I played innocent as I licked my finger once more. His eyes tracked my every movement. "I'm just eating the food that you ordered for me."

"I can put that smart mouth to better use if you prefer."

His words had me clenching my thighs under the table. *Goddamn.* But I wasn't about to let him get to me.

Pulling the milkshake in front of me closer, I dipped my head down. Eyes glued to his, I twirled my tongue around the straw before wrapping my lips around it. Trevor made a move to get out of the booth when the waitress appeared once more. Perfect timing.

"Looks delicious! Thank you so much." I grinned widely up at her as she placed multiple plates on the table. From the corner of my eye, I watched Trevor shift in his seat, most likely having to fix himself under the table.

"Hope you guys enjoy it!" With one last smile, she left.

"Ready to eat?" I turned to Trevor with a teasing grin.

"You'll pay for that later." His tone held a promise that he would get me back for what I just did.

"Whatever you say." I winked at him.

This time, I leaned forward and took an actual sip of my milkshake. My eyes widened at the taste, looking at Trevor. "Woah, that is so good."

"Told you."

Taking a few more sips, I reached for the basket of onion rings. Trevor ordered a bunch of things that he knew I liked —French fries, sweet potato fries, onion rings, fried pickles, even a plate with mini sliders on it.

With a growling stomach, I dug into the food, Trevor doing the same across from me. I liked that he didn't need to fill the silence, the two of us having become more comfortable around each other this past week. I almost felt as comfortable around him as I did Josie, which was a big deal.

"Man, I'm going to have to go to the gym tomorrow to work off all this food." I groaned a bit later, completely full. Between the two of us, we managed to eat everything, including the two shakes that we shared.

"You know, you could come workout with me tomorrow."

"Workout together?'

"Yeah, why not." Trevor shrugged.

"You'll make me do tons of push-ups, won't you? Some of us aren't professional athletes."

"Don't worry, I won't go hard on you."

Yeah, I didn't believe that for one moment. Although, working out together could be fun.

"As long as you don't get me up at the crack of dawn."

With that look on his face, I knew I would probably regret agreeing.

23

TASHA

"You still aren't going to tell me where we're going?" I asked a little bit later. Once we had paid at the diner, Trevor ushered me back to the car without telling me where he was taking me next. At first, I thought we were heading back home, but he pulled off the freeway before our exit. Since the sun was almost set, it got increasingly harder to pay attention to our surroundings and make a guess.

He flashed me a grin, squeezing my thigh. "You'll like it, I promise." I really shouldn't have been surprised Trevor planned a whole day but the fact that he did was super sweet. I never went out with someone who planned a date that took up the whole day. Most of my dates had been meetups at bars or coffee shops.

I was excited to see what else he had planned. When he pulled into a dark, empty parking lot, I looked out the window with a raised eyebrow.

"If you wanted to kill me, the pumpkin patch would have been a better option."

"Too many people." His voice was so serious, I couldn't tell if he was joking.

"You do know I wouldn't make a good kill, right? I wouldn't fight that hard so there really wouldn't be a thrill."

I glanced out the front window, barely making out a dark building up ahead. There were only a few lights on, but you could tell no one was around. If he did want to take me out, he could've totally gotten away with it. No one knew I was with him.

He must have felt my apprehension because he laughed and turned the car off.

"I'm not going to kill you." He opened the door and started to get out, looking at me over his shoulder. "Not yet, at least." He slipped out and shut the door behind him. I sat there gaping as he came around to open my door.

"Come on, Sunshine." Reaching in, he unclipped my seat-belt and tugged me out of the car.

"Walking around an empty building doesn't sound all that fun. How about we just go for a ride?" I suggested. "Yeah, a nice long car ride sounds amazing."

I dug my feet into the ground, but Trevor easily pulled me along like I weighed nothing. Coming to a stop in front of the doors, he pulled out a key, which made me even more confused. I looked to see if there were any signs on the door or building but there was nothing.

"Are we breaking in?" I asked. I wasn't actually scared Trevor would do anything but I was curious what we were doing in a place like this.

"If I remember correctly, you broke into your uni's pool."

"Yeah, but I knew that building! Not this one," I argued.

"Do you trust me?" Trevor stepped through the door, holding his hand out for me to take. I only briefly hesitated before raising my arm and linking my fingers with his.

"Of course."

"Then come on." A kid-like smile appeared on his face

when I placed my hand in his. That smile was slowly becoming my favorite thing.

Trusting that we weren't breaking and entering, I let him lead me inside. We passed a front desk and a hall of empty rooms. In the dim lighting I could see the white walls had pictures on them. The carpet beneath our feet was worn from use. I got the feeling we were in some sort of athletic club or community center.

Trevor led us farther inside, only a few lights guiding us. Stopping in front of two double doors Trevor turned to me. "Okay, close your eyes." I sent him a look that clearly said, "Are you kidding me?"

"Sunshine, trust me."

With a sigh, I closed my eyes.

"No peeking." Gripping my hand a bit tighter, he opened the doors in front of us and tugged me inside carefully.

I kept my eyes shut despite every part of me dying to open them. We walked for a bit before the air around us dropped in temperature. Scrunching my eyebrows, I shuffled my feet as Trevor made sure I didn't run into anything.

"Okay, here we are." He slowed us to a stop as I felt him move behind me, his hands coming to rest on my hips. "You can open your eyes," he whispered in my ear.

A little nervous about what was in front of me, I peeled open my eyes. My lips curled up into a smile. Of course, I should have known.

Across from me was an empty ice rink. Lights filled the arena, bouncing off the freshly smoothed ice. Turning in his arms, I peered up at him. "An ice rink, huh?"

"Wanted to bring you into my world a little." Trevor shrugged. His words caused butterflies to erupt in my stomach.

A part of his world.

Almost like he planned on keeping me around a while longer.

"Let's go skate." Lifting up to my toes, I pecked his lips before stepping back. With a matching grin, Trevor led me over to the benches that were off to the side. A bag was already sitting there waiting for us, along with some hockey sticks leaning against the wall.

"Made a few calls to get us some skates," Trevor explained as he saw me eyeing the bag. Taking a seat on the bench, I watched as he bent over and reached into it, pulling out a pair of white ice skates meant for me. He really did plan everything.

While he rummaged for another pair, I untied my combat shoes. I went to grab a skate to put on but a pair of hands beat me to it. Before I could say anything, Trevor kneeled before me, grabbing my ankle and pulling it toward him.

I sat there motionless as he carefully slid my foot into the skate, tucking my jeans into the sides with precision before doing the same with the other foot.

"The trick with skates is you have to make them tight enough that your foot won't slip out, but not too tight where your foot goes numb and the back digs into your heel," Trevor said as he tied up the laces. "These are pretty new skates so they might hurt a little."

I tried to focus on what Trevor said, I really did, but all I could think about was him on his knees in front of me. It did something to my stomach and the cavity inside of my chest where my heart lived. Those broad shoulders were even bigger up close, and I could see his biceps flexing under his long sleeve shirt.

"See how they feel." He tapped the sides of my thighs for me to stand up. Using his shoulders for balance, I stood up, tilting to the side a little because I wasn't used to balancing on such a thin blade. Trevor gripped the back of my thighs to keep me in place.

Trying to ignore his big hands gripping the back of my legs, I lifted one foot and the other to show him I was good to go.

"Perfect. Let me get mine on." Trevor moved to sit on the bench with his own skates. I realized he didn't know I knew how to skate. Meaning, I could definitely have some fun with this. I mean it wasn't every day a professional hockey player taught you how to skate.

In a matter of seconds, Trevor had his skates all laced up. I knew exactly what those fingers could do but the sight of him doing that was oddly erotic. Standing up, he extended his hand out for me to take.

With a smile, I put mine in his. I had to press my lips together not to laugh as Trevor slowly led me toward the ice, treating me like a newborn deer that didn't know how to use its legs. I stumbled a few times, which made Trevor grip my hands tighter.

My heart was ready to burst when he got on the ice and turned to help me. He was being so kind and sweet, having zero clue he was worming his way into my heart inch by inch.

It had been so long since I was last on the ice that I wobbled, hands white knuckling his. Okay, maybe I wasn't going to have to fake not knowing how to do this.

"I got you." Peering up at him, I knew those words were meant for more than this moment. He had me on the ice, but he also had me in life.

I ducked my head so he couldn't read the emotion on my face.

"Just hold onto me." Holding my hands, Trevor started to skate backward, towing me along with him. "The front of your skate should always be pointed forward," he instructed.

The ice was perfectly smooth, making me wonder what kind of strings he pulled that made it possible for us to be here after-hours. But then again, just one word from him and people threw themselves at his feet. The lights overhead were slightly dimmed, which gave off a more romantic vibe.

"There you go," Trevor said with approval as we moved at a crawl. I couldn't deny it, the praise made my heart—and other parts of me—warm. "Keep your knees slightly bent."

Looking up, I found him so focused on my own feet, a little frown on his face. Like he was worried I was going to fall and hurt myself. *Fuck.* I was falling for him. And not in a cute little crush way. No, this was way past that. The thought scared me because this man in front of me had the potential to break my heart into a million pieces. But as he flashed me an encouraging look, I found that I didn't quite care if he did.

Pushing those feelings to the back of my mind, I squeezed his hands and looked up at Trevor. While this was sweet, it was time for some fun.

I slowly pulled my hands from his as he looked at me, confused. "Hope you're ready.

"Ready for what?"

"To get your ass beat." With a mischievous grin, I quickly darted past him, pushing off the ice with my skates. The first few seconds were a bit wobbly before I got my feet under me. Just like riding a bike.

"What the hell!" Trevor yelled behind me, making me laugh loudly.

I skated around the outside of the rink, remembering what it was like to be on actual ice. Trevor easily caught up with me, coming up close and sending me a bewildered look. "Since when do you skate?"

"Since forever."

"I..." He seemed at a loss for words.

"Aw, did you want to be the hot hockey player that teaches the innocent girl how to skate?" I made a little pout.

"You think I'm hot?" He broke out into a grin, lifting an eyebrow.

"Of course that's the only thing you got out of that." I shoved him, hoping he'd stumble, but of course the prick stayed upright. The dude was pure solid muscle, and he made skating look like walking.

As my legs remembered how to skate, I picked up the pace. The sound of the blade cutting through the ice met my ears. I could see why Trevor loved being on the ice. There was something about it that was calming. Like everything faded away as soon as your skate smoothed over it.

"Who taught you to skate?" Trevor asked a moment later. The two of us stayed side by side as we went around the rink.

"I actually went out with a guy on the hockey team in uni. I was a sophomore, and he was a senior, so of course when he asked to teach me I said yes." I rolled my eyes at the memory. At the time, I was crushing hard on the guy. Thinking a guy on the hockey team would want to date me. Boy, was I wrong.

"He took me to the arena on campus a few times, and I picked it up pretty quick." I shrugged.

"And?" Trevor prompted.

"And nothing. The moment he got in my pants, he was out. The whole thing only lasted, like, two months." After him, I learned that if a guy was going to use me I might as well use them first. So I gained the reputation of getting a man and spitting him back out the next day. It was easier than being hurt.

"Sounds like he was a prick."

"Oh, he was. Thought he was going to make it to The League but he wasn't even picked." I snorted. "I think he works at a car dealership now."

"And here you are with a *real* professional hockey player," Trevor boasted, flexing his arm.

"Ah, there's that ego."

"It's not ego if it's true." He wiggled his eyebrows.

"I truly think you've been hit too many times."

"All good." Trevor tapped his head with his fist. "All about confidence, baby."

Slowing down, I tilted my feet to the side so I could come to a stop. Trevor did the same beside me.

"You know," I peered up at him, skating toward him so our chests were inches from touching. "I think you're all bark and no bite."

"Is that so?" I watched as his jaw clenched, a flare of hunger in his eyes.

"You've gone a bit..." I made a show of looking him up and down, the corner of my lip tilting up. "Soft."

"Soft?" When his voice grew deeper.

"It's okay. I guess I can get used to this soft version of you."

"I'd be very careful if I was you, Sunshine."

"Oh, but where's the fun in that?" I smirked. Sending him a wink, I pushed off my toe pick and darted away. I heard his skates against the ice as he skated after me.

"Tasha," he taunted behind me.

"You're too slow," I teased over my shoulder.

My thighs were starting to burn, and while I was halfway decent at keeping up my speed, I wasn't a pro like Trevor. I knew he was taking it easy on me. Even though I knew it wasn't smart, I threw another jab over my shoulder. "Come on, Grandpa!"

Too busy cackling at my own joke, I didn't notice Trevor was behind me until a pair of hands grabbed me by the waist and lifted me in the air. I shrieked as Trevor twirled me around. How he managed to do that and stay upright on the ice was beyond me.

My squeal turned into fits of laughter as Trevor kept me suspended in the air and skated forward.

"Let me down!" I tried to sound threatening but my laughter ruined it.

My entire back was pressed against his front, which made it hard to concentrate, especially when his muscles flexed to keep me up off the ice.

Trevor slowed down and came to a stop at the edge of the rink. I'm not sure how he did it, but one moment I was in his arms, and the next, I was being turned and plopped down on the edge of the sideboard. My ass was hanging off since it was barely big enough for me to sit on.

I gaped up at Trevor, finding myself at the perfect height for him to stand between my legs. Placing his hands beside me, he caged me between the sideboard and his body, bending so his head was level with mine.

"Did you call me a grandpa?" He was close enough that his breath fanned across my face. Those eyes pierced mine. I wasn't about to show him how much he affected me.

"I did." I stuck my chin out. "And?"

"You have a grandpa fetish? Wow, that's dirty."

"Trevor!" I smacked his arm as he threw his head back laughing, the sound seeping into my bones. Man, I loved his laugh.

"You are so gross!" I crinkled my nose, but a smile still played on my lips.

"You love it." Dipping his head, he captured my lips with his, caging me underneath him. My hands moved up the front of his shirt slowly. I could feel the hard muscle of his pecks.

The way Trevor kissed me made my toes curl in my

skates. The swipe of his tongue against my lips pulled a moan from my throat.

As Trevor kissed me slowly and softly, I realized he was right. I did love it. I loved a lot of things he did and maybe, just maybe, I could let myself fall in love with him.

TASHA

"It's okay, you got this Tasha. Just keep going." I muttered under my breath. Well, more like wheezed out.

I was currently running on a treadmill, trying my hardest not to look like I was dying. I was pretty sure my life flashed before my eyes a few minutes ago, but with the Greek god beside me, I had no choice but to act like it was easy.

I went to the gym somewhat regularly. Okay, maybe like twice a week if I was feeling productive, so I wasn't in the worst shape. Or so I thought. Working beside Trevor was like being on a whole different planet.

The dude was a machine. No wonder he had a six-pack and biceps the size of my head. Damn my competitive side for thinking I could keep up with him. Who the hell did I think I was? Chris Hemsworth?

I was fully regretting agreeing to workout with him this morning. I regretted it the moment he woke me up at six o'clock in the morning. On a Saturday! We didn't go to bed until one in the morning having done...other things after we got home from our date. How he still had enough energy to come to the gym was beyond me.

It was like God was finally pitying me as Trevor slowed his treadmill down. Saying a silent thank you, I stopped mine and leaned over to catch my breath. *Holy shit.* That was the most cardio I'd done in forever.

"Doing good?" Trevor asked. I didn't even lift my head to answer, I just gave him a thumbs-up. "Great. Onto abs then."

"Abs?" I looked over at him with wide eyes. I thought we were done?

"Yeah, it's full body, remember?" The teasing look on his face proved I wasn't doing a good enough job of hiding how out of breath I was. Trevor was just standing there, his breathing labored but still under control. Like he hadn't just run five miles after doing legs and arms.

"Oh, right. Abs. Woohoo. My favorite." Stepping off the treadmill, my legs trembled. I was going to be so sore tomorrow between skating last night and this. It was almost like Trevor was trying to kill me. Instead of murdering me like a normal assassin, he did it using a workout.

By the time I felt secure enough on my feet, Trevor was already waiting over on the mats.

"I'm gonna kill him. Get the girls to help me hide his body," I muttered as I grabbed my water and made my way to him. "No one will know."

At least with abs, we got to lay down. Although, I wasn't sure that was a good thing either.

"Okay, let's do ten moves, four times, a minute each," Trevor rattled off. "Then we'll call it a day."

Okay, yeah, I could do that. Only a few more minutes to go.

Trevor showed me the moves before setting the timer on his phone. Thirty seconds into the first move, I was once again plotting Trevor's death. I was dying. That was how well it was going. I always thought the grim reaper would come for me when I was old and asleep. Not while I did a damn ab routine.

Beside me, Trevor mumbled encouraging words, but they had the opposite effect. I was inwardly cursing and threatening him. If I wasn't clenching my jaw so hard and trying to keep my breathing even, I probably would have said the things out loud.

As I struggled, Trevor repeated the moves like no big deal. The only plus side to all of it was a shirtless Trevor. He took it off a good hour ago when we were doing legs, so at least I had something glorious to look at as I slowly died.

More than once, I found myself looking over at him, enjoying the way his abs contracted and glistened with sweat. His entire upper body was slick, and in some weird, gross way, it was fucking attractive. I think I was delirious because there were quite a few times I caught myself thinking about wanting to lick his abs.

Just as I was about to call it quits, Trevor's timer went off, letting us know we were done. I flopped onto my back with ragged breaths. I was soaked head to toe, and I knew I didn't look half as good as Trevor did. I was pretty sure I could wring my sports bra out.

"You did so good," Trevor praised. The only response I had to that was sending him the middle finger.

My arm flopped back to my side as I laid there utterly spent. I was never working out with him again. Nope. Never.

"I told you, you didn't have to do what I did." Trevor laughed beside me.

"No, you didn't."

"Yes, I did, and you said, 'This will be the easiest workout I've ever done.'"

Shit, I did say that.

"Potato, Patato." I waved him off.

238

"Come on, let's get you up and showered." Trevor chuckled, getting to his feet.

"I'm good. I'm just gonna hang here for a bit."

"You're going to lay on a sweaty gross mat for a while?"

I scrunched my nose up at that. On second thought, yeah, I didn't want to lie there for longer than I had to.

"Fine. Help me up, you big goof." I raised a shaky arm.

With a sigh, Trevor hauled me up in one quick motion. Grabbing our stuff, we headed out of the gym and toward the elevators. Instead of going to the arena Trevor always used, where most of the hockey team trained, we decided to use the one in my apartment building. I was thankful for that decision so I didn't have to sit in my sweaty clothes for longer than necessary.

I clung to Trevor's arm as we got in the elevator. My legs shook, my arms shook, my whole body was exhausted. As it should be since we worked out for almost two hours straight. I leaned my weight against him, my fingers itching to touch the hard muscle I was pressed against. He had that post workout pump going on that made his muscles pop even more than usual.

The moment we stepped into my apartment, I wanted to lie down, but I knew I had to shower. Watching Trevor walk in front of me as he headed to the kitchen, his bare back on full display, I bit my lip, an idea forming.

"Trevorrrr."

"Yeah, baby?" He didn't turn around as he reached into the fridge for a cold water bottle.

"I need to shower."

"Okay, you can go first." Again, he didn't turn around. Making my voice honey sweet, I leaned against the counter.

"My arms and legs are too shaky. I could use some help." I tried not to snort at the way he whirled around, the water bottle halfway to his mouth.

When he didn't say anything, I grabbed the bottom of my sports bra and pulled it off. Trevor stared at my breasts, his jaw somewhere forgotten on the floor. I didn't feel an ounce of embarrassment standing topless in front of him. Any insecurities I had before Trevor were long gone. Especially when he made it well-known how he enjoyed every part of my body.

Keeping my eyes locked onto his, I hooked my fingers in the band of my workout shorts and tugged them off, kicking them to the side. This morning, I was half awake getting dressed, so I didn't bother putting on a pair of underwear.

Standing there completely naked, I watched as Trevor drank me in. His eyes lingered on my breasts before finding the spot between my legs. With a teasing smirk, I took a step backward.

"I'll be waiting." With that, I turned and started for my bathroom, adding a little extra sway to my step. I was almost certain his eyes were stuck on my ass.

I barely turned on the water and stepped under the stream before I felt Trevor behind me. Something silky smooth and hard pressed against the top of my ass, making me grin. That didn't take him long.

As his arms came around my waist, I arched my back, pressing my behind into his crotch and bringing my arms back and around his head. His mouth came down and pressed soft kisses along my shoulder.

The water warmed, spraying down on us as we stood there pressed against one another. His hand was light as a feather as he ran it up and down my stomach and under my breasts before moving back down.

"Hold still for me," he whispered against my neck.

I stayed where I was, halfway under the water, as Trevor reached around me to grab my loofah. He poured a generous amount of body wash on it before coming back to me.

He stepped back just a little as the loofah grazed my shoulder blades. My eyes closed as he gently washed my back.

I couldn't help but sigh when he took his sweet time washing my ass. Paying it extra attention. He even made sure to get the back of my calves before moving back up my body.

"Hands on the wall, baby." Using his knees, he nudged my legs apart. With my hands on the wall, my ass arched out.

I waited eagerly to see what he was going to do next but when the roughness of the loofah rubbed against my pussy, I let out a gasp. I was not expecting that.

Gently, but firmly, he rubbed the soapy loofah between my legs. Each pass over my clit made me moan. Putting one of his hands on my ass, Trevor leaned over my back.

"Maybe we should see if you can come without me touching you." As he spoke, he rubbed in between my legs just a tad bit harder, making my toes curl at the sensation. I never would have thought the roughness of a loofah could feel so damn good.

"You have two minutes to come or I'll stop." The threat behind his words told me he wasn't joking. I knew from experience he would leave me on edge until he was good and ready for me to finish.

My moans echoed through the shower as I used my hands to steady myself, moving my hips back to meet his hand. My eyes squeezed shut as I quite literally humped the loofah. The rough texture of the loofah was unlike anything I've felt before. Twisting my hips to hit it directly on my clit. The friction made me whimper low in my throat.

"Come on, baby. One minute left."

Gritting my teeth, my hips moved faster and faster. I had to come. No, I *needed* to come. Groans mixed with high pitched whimpers left my mouth as I climbed closer to my peak. I was right there.

"Thirty seconds." Trevor's voice was unrelenting. "You better come."

His words were my undoing. With a cry, my orgasm rippled through me. My legs trembled, and my hands struggled to hold me upright. My moan was so loud, I was fairly certain the neighbor next door heard.

A warm, hard body pressed against me, keeping me up as I started to float my way back down to reality. I was a panting mess but that felt fucking incredible.

"Good girl," Trevor hummed against my neck. The loofah passed over my core one last time making my body jerk. Setting it aside, Trevor gently turned me around to face him, pressing my back against the wall.

Placing his hands on the side of my face, he used his thumbs to tilt my head back to look at him.

"So fucking perfect." His words made me melt. Placing his lips against mine, I sighed against him, my arms wrapping around his torso. I could kiss his mouth forever.

When he pulled away, I pouted. My disappointment was short-lived, though, as Trevor grinned down at me with a look in his eyes.

"Now to wash the front."

***

"WE CAN CARVE the pumpkins tomorrow if you want." Trevor said.

"Oh yes! But let's do it at your place since you have front steps to put them on." I suggested.

It was now nearing noon and the two of us were in the kitchen making lunch. Well, Trevor was cooking. I was sitting at the bar watching him, trying not to drool over the way his muscles flinched and contracted as he cut vegetables and lifted the frying pan to sauté them. The same back that had red lines running down them, thanks to me.

I felt a swell of pride at that. Those were from me. No one else. It was kind of like I staked my claim on him.

"Sounds good."

After our shower, the two of us ended up in bed. Well, after Trevor bent me over the bathroom counter and fucked me. And then we ended up in his bedroom doing some other things that didn't include sleeping.

After such an eventful morning, I was starving. Trevor, ever so graciously, offered to make us something as I sat there enjoying the view.

"I wanted to ask. Why do you live in a house and not an apartment?" I was just curious because most people our age didn't have the means to afford a house. And seeing as it was only Trevor, wouldn't it have made more sense to rent an apartment?. Although, maybe that wasn't what he wanted. And besides, it wasn't like he wasn't rolling in cash.

Trevor was quiet for a moment before responding.

"Growing up wasn't easy. Aside from my parents forget-ting to buy food, they sometimes forgot to pay rent. There were a few occasions when we had to sleep in the car." I could tell he wanted to come off like it wasn't a big deal, but I heard the hurt in his voice. It may have happened years ago, but it was still hard to think and talk about.

"A couple of times I'd come home and find the door locked. My parents were too drugged out to open it for me. I'd sit outside for hours until they realized I was out there." I stared at the back of his head as he continued. "When I got enough money, I bought the house. I wanted something that was all mine that couldn't be taken away."

I swallowed back the tears that gathered in my eyes. He didn't need my pity, but I understood. Understood the need to have something that was yours. To make it the way *you* wanted it without fearing someone would take it away or criticize you.

"I get it," I spoke softly.

Letting the conversation drop Trevor finished up lunch while I grabbed plates. He dished the homemade style hash onto a plate before the two of us headed for the living room. With no desire to sit at the table, the two of us got cozy on the couch.

I couldn't stop the hum of satisfaction from leaving my mouth as I stuffed my mouth. The potatoes, the peppers and onions were incredible. I was going to make him cook for me from now on.

As we ate and watched TV, Trevor got quiet. I glanced over at him, finding his eyebrows drawn in as if he was deep in thought.

"Hey," I nudged his shoulder. "What are you thinking so hard about over there?" There was definitely something on his mind.

"It's nothing." He brought a hand up to his neck, shaking his head.

"But...?" I prodded, knowing there was more than what he was saying.

He let out a sigh, looking over at me. "I was wondering if you wanted to come to the game on Monday."

He looked at me in an unsure way, almost like he was expecting me to say I wouldn't want to. My heart squeezed at the fact that he wanted me to attend. I was already planning on going. He just didn't know that yet.

"Of course, I'd love to."

"Yeah?"

"Gotta root my man on for the first game of the season." The words slipped from my lips before I could stop them.

Trevor grinned widely at me. "Your man, huh?" My cheeks grew hot as I rolled my eyes.

"You know what I mean."

"Uh-huh," Trevor teased. "I have a jersey you can wear too."

"Oh, gonna make me an honorary Trevor Hall fangirl?"

"Can't have my girl wearing someone else's jersey." Trevor winked. My insides warmed at his words.

My girl. I think I could get used to hearing that.

TASHA

"I love my fiancé, but the guy is driving me nuts." Josie groaned.

"Ready for the game tomorrow, huh?" I joked.

My best friend shook her head across from me as she took a sip of her coffee. "Don't get me started."

This morning, when Josie called and asked to go to coffee together, I immediately said yes. The two of us haven't seen much of each other lately. She wanted to hang out the other day, but I had my date with Trevor, so I was in desperate need of some girl time.

"I need some girl talk that isn't hockey." Josie said.

"Perfect, because I was just about to ask if you've thought about the wedding yet." I commented, sipping my coffee.

"Oh yes!" Josie sat forward with a wide grin. "Wyatt and I both agreed we don't want something huge. Just family and friends."

I nodded in agreement. I couldn't see Josie with a huge wedding anyway.

"Are you guys thinking soon?" The thought of my best friend getting married made me almost giddy. The two of us talked about our weddings before and the fact that she was about to walk down the aisle with the love of her life was a little mind-blowing.

"Okay, it might sound a bit crazy but..." Josie hesitated making me nudge her under the table with my foot. "We're thinking five months from now."

My eyes widened. Five months. Five months to get a dress, a venue, send out invites, order flowers.

"Okay, that's..." I trailed off.

"I know. It's a lot." She sent me a sheepish grin. "But we don't want to wait."

Even though she was sitting, I narrowed my eyes at her, looking her up and down.

"You aren't pregnant, are you?" Josie sipped her drink, damn near sputtering it out when my question clicked in her head.

"Tasha!" She coughed into her napkin and looked at me with wide eyes.

"What?" I shrugged. "The way you two go at it like bunnies." Although, I wasn't any better at the moment. Josie shook her head at me, her cheeks pink.

"No, I'm not pregnant. We both want kids but not right now."

"Well, whenever you do have kids, I call godmother" I fully planned on being the cool, fun aunt.

"Noted." Josie laughed. "But that reminds me." She sobered up, reaching across the table to grab my hand. "I know I asked in Australia, but I want to make sure that you really want to be my maid of honor. You're my best friend, but I don't want you to feel like you have to be." Josie started rambling.

I squeezed her hands to get her attention. "Jo."

"You're literally a sister to me. I wouldn't have made it through the last few years without you." Tears appeared in her eyes as she spoke. My own started to tear up. "You pulled me out of a dark place, not once but twice. When my dad passed you were the only person I had left. I want you by my side when I get married."

"Of course, I will." I sniffled. "Can't get married without me." Josie laughed as she wiped her eyes. Pulling my hand from hers, I wiped my cheeks.

"Damn you, Josie Scott for making me cry." Who would have thought a simple question would get me to burst out in tears? I wasn't prepared. Neither was my mascara that was probably smudged under my eyes.

"At least you look like a cute panda," Josie joked, cleaning her own from under her eyes.

"Of course I do, but seriously, I'd be honored to be your maid of honor."

"Good, cause I'm going to need someone to help me veto Wyatt's ideas." We both shared a look. Men were pretty helpless when it came to planning a wedding.

"You're going to hire a wedding planner, right?" There was no way Josie and I, even with help from the other girls, could plan an entire wedding in five months.

"Yeah, we're meeting with someone on Tuesday."

"Okay, one thing down, hundreds to go." Even though there was a lot to do, I was beyond excited to help my best friend get married. I was going to do everything I could to make sure it was the best day of her life.

The two of us talked more about wedding stuff as our food came. Trying to come up with a game plan on where to start first, when to look for dresses, if they wanted an engagement party, and everything else. The entire time we talked, Josie had a permanent smile on her face.

I never saw her so happy. She was always stressed and worried about her father, going every weekend to see him to make sure he was taking his medicine and doing okay. She gave up so many weekends to be with him. Always pushing aside her happiness.

Then, when she dated her asshole of an ex, I thought she finally found that happiness. I thought she was finally with someone who could make her smile and give her the world. Who would treat her like she hung the moon. But I was so wrong. He gave her none of that.

I will never forgive myself for not noticing the signs. For being so wrapped up in my own life that I didn't notice my best friend, my sister, being hurt by that monster. I hadn't known the extent it went until I saw the bruises until later on. I had been sick to my stomach when I found out what had happened behind closed doors. Even now, I could barely stomach the thought.

When I apologized for not being there for her, she told me there was nothing to apologize for. But if I hadn't been so selfish and wrapped up in myself, I would have seen what was going on long before. I'll never forgive myself for that. Even if I did get revenge on Josie's behalf.

Josie will never know what I did to her ex for laying a hand on her. I plan to never tell her the strings I pulled using my parents' last name in order to make sure the guy's life was ruined. To this day, I'll never regret what I did. Especially sitting here across from her and seeing her smile like that.

"So tell me, what's been going on with you? Feels like we really haven't talked much," Josie said a moment later.

My stomach knotted in guilt. Since we've been back from our vacation, we've only talked once on the phone mixed with a few texts. I'd been busy with work and spending most of my time with Trevor. I hated that I was keeping stuff from her, but at least I could tell her one thing.

"I actually have something to tell you."

Josie leaned in, gazing at me with an arched eyebrow.

"I got a call from my mom a few days ago." Josie rolled her eyes. After everything, Josie was not a fan of my parents.

"What do they want now?"

"They want me to marry the son of some business partner." Josie's jaw dropped at my revelation, her expression one of disbelief.

I'd been doing my best to shove aside the whole thing since I last spoke with my mother. The fact that my own parents would arrange a marriage for me without even asking was like a stab in the back. I could take the jabs about my job or being forced to stupid events to show off but this... This I couldn't do.

"You're kidding me right?"

"Wish I was."

Trevor did a great job at keeping my mind off of it, but I couldn't help but still think about it.

"They want you to marry someone you're not even in love with? For what?!" Josie exclaimed.

"So their companies can merge." I grimaced. "Sounds like the plot to some bad romcom."

"They do realize it's the twenty-first century, right?"

The whole thing made me sick to my stomach. There was no way I was going to go through with it. I wasn't a puppet that my parents could control.

"What did you say to them?"

"I told her no." I watched as Josie broke into a grin, and I couldn't help but mirror it as the reality of telling my parents no fully sank in. I never blatantly told them that. I'd been so caught up in Trevor that I didn't realize what I had done.

"I can't believe you said that to them" Josie had the proudest look on her face. We both knew how much of a pushover I became when it came to my parents. The need to always please them took over whenever they called. But not this time.

"I'm so proud of you. I should go give your parents a piece of my mind." I couldn't help but snort at the idea of Josie marching up to them and telling them off. She was the least intimidating person I knew.

"I would pay to see that."

"Excuse me, I could do it." She narrowed her eyes.

"Of course you could." I patted her hand, which just made her huff at me. She muttered something under her breath.

"Bitch."

"Hoe."

We shot fake insults back at each other until we were laughing too hard to continue. I missed this. I missed being around my best friend who could instantly make me feel better. I really wasn't sure what I'd do without Josie in my life.

"Ready to head to the house?" Josie asked once we calmed down. With a nod, I finished the rest of my coffee and got to my feet. My legs protested, the muscles severely sore from the workout yesterday with Trevor. My entire body felt like it had been hit by a bus.

"You okay?" Josie frowned as she looked over at me.

"All good." I waved her off. "Decided to workout yesterday. Wasn't a smart idea."

"See, that's why I don't workout." Josie laughed. I was inclined to agree, especially after waking up this morning barely able to move.

"It's just going to be the group right?" I asked as we left the coffee shop, heading for my car parked down the street.

Apparently, Wyatt's family has a tradition of doing a family BBQ the day before the first game of the season. It was also supposed to be a small engagement party for Josie and Wyatt.

I hadn't known anything about it until Josie texted me last night asking me to come. I was a bit bummed Trevor and

I had to postpone our pumpkin carving date today, but he promised we'd do it later this week.

"Yeah, it's just Mila, Bryton, Trevor, Landon, Mateo and Evelyn."

I was glad it was going to be our regular group and not other people from the team. Not that I didn't like the guys on Trevor's team, but there was only so much staring and horrible pick up lines I could take.

"Oh, did you hear?" Josie said a second later when we got in the car.

"Hear what?" I briefly glanced over at her before focusing on pulling out into oncoming traffic.

"Trevor had a date Friday night." I smothered my smile at her words.

"Oh."

"Wonder who it is." Josie frowned. "Think it's serious?"

"Uh…"

"It has to be if he hasn't told Wyatt or Bryton," Josie went on, Oblivious that the person he was seeing was sitting next to her.

I itched to tell her, but Trevor and I said we wouldn't tell anyone yet. I'd hate to tell her when he isn't ready. I wanted to talk to him first before I said anything.

"You know, maybe we should set him up with someone." At her words, I gripped the steering wheel tighter. The thought of Trevor being with someone else did not sit well with me. Someone else kissing him, seeing the side of him that only I saw.

I quickly pushed those thoughts aside. I was not going to think about him being with another woman. Not as my feelings for him grew with each passing day.

Thankfully, I was saved from the conversation as we pulled onto the road leading to Wyatt's mom's house a few minutes later. When I pulled up to the curb, there were already cars parked all around.

"We're here," Josie called out as we stepped through the front door.

Walking into the house Wyatt grew up in made my chest ache. The cream walls were littered with photos of the Boone brothers. The deep brown hardwood floors were newer since Wyatt forced his mom to let him do updates on the place.

You could tell the place was loved. It was an actual *home*. Not some mansion that was filled with emptiness. There was a bit of clutter throughout the house but it was a type of clutter that came with a home that was well lived in. I couldn't help but wonder what it would have been like to grow up inside of it.

We walked down the hallway towards the kitchen in the back. I stepped through the archway just as Evelyn, Wyatt's mom, stepped away from the stove.

"There's my favorite." She pulled Josie into a tight hug, rocking her back and forth for a moment.

Wyatt appeared from the other side of the room. "I thought I was your favorite?"

"You mean least favorite," Landon pipped in, walking into the kitchen.

Evelyn rolled her eyes at her sons as she let Josie go and held her arms open to hug me. Giving me a bright smile, she pulled me into her arms. It was a hug only a mother could give. Not having gotten many from my own mom, I held onto Evelyn a tad bit longer.

"Are you taking care of yourself?" Evelyn asked, pulling back to look at my face. I nodded, but I wasn't sure she believed me. Those blue eyes of hers seemed to stare into my soul.

I changed the subject. "Thanks for letting me come."

"Of course." Rubbing my arm, Evelyn stepped back and moved over to the counter. The gorgeous white counters with grey throughout was filled with different kinds of snacks. Everything from chips and salsa, to devil eggs, to cheese balls. Evelyn always went full out when guests came over.

My eyes flitted over the rest of Evelyn's kitchen. The dark gray cabinets were gorgeous and not too dark for the space. Especially with the huge windows off to the side. While the kitchen has been updated it was still that older family home where a wall cut off the dining room and living room from the kitchen.

As I glanced over at the archway to the living and dining room area and found just the person I was looking for. Trevor leaned against the wall looking absolutely delicious. He shouldn't have been allowed to look like that.

And he was all mine.

I couldn't bring myself to argue with my inner voice. Not when he flashed me a smile that was reserved just for me.

"Where's Mila and Bryton?" Josie's voice pulled my focus away from Trevor. Her and Wyatt were standing off to the side of the island. Landon was leaning against the counter by his mom.

"He texted saying they'll be here in a bit," Trevor answered. Like a magnet, my eyes went back to him. I wanted nothing more than to go over there and kiss him. Since I couldn't I stepped towards the island, swiping a cracker.

"I have some snacks for you guys to munch on while we wait to start the burgers." Evelyn said as she placed yet another plate on the counter.

"Please tell me you made chocolate cake, Ma?" Landon asked, looking around the kitchen. These guys and their damn chocolate cake. Apparently, Wyatt and Landon's mom made *the* best chocolate cake you'd ever eat.

Someone always brought it up and raved about how amazing it was. Even Josie jumped on the chocolate cake train. I had yet to actually try it.

"Don't any of you even think of finding it and taking some before tonight." Evelyn pointed her finger at each of us. Landon, Wyatt and Trevor put their hands up as if they were innocent. I grinned at their expressions, knowing full well they would try and find that cake.

The sound of the front door opening and closing got all of our attention, especially when one voice in particular yelled out.

"The party has arrived bitches!" Mateo, Wyatt's younger brother, came waltzing into the kitchen. As soon as he saw his mom, his eyes widened. "Landon don't swear in front of Mom!" Mateo quickly turned to Landon and shoved his arm.

"You little shit." Landon wrapped his arm around Mateo's neck, tugging him into a choke hold.

Across the counter, Evelyn just sighed. "I'll be back in a minute. Try not to kill each other." With that, she left us all in the kitchen.

Somehow, Mateo managed to wiggle out of his brother's hold, stepping away with a wide grin. He turned toward Wyatt, holding his arms out as if to hug him, but when Wyatt stepped forward, Mateo shoved him to the side and grabbed Josie, yanking her into a tight hug and lifting her off the ground. "There's my girlfriend."

I'd been around enough times to know Mateo only said that to mess with Wyatt. It was hilarious to watch the eighteen-year-old flirt with Josie. I leaned back against the cabinets, watching the two of them.

"Geez, have you grown since I last saw you?" Josie took a step back, looking him up and down.

"So kind of you to notice. Yes, I have." Mateo lifted his arms up and flexed his biceps. "Grew these guns."

I snorted under my breath, but I had to agree. He definitely put on more muscle since he started uni a few months ago. His shoulders seemed wider and his face looked thinner like he was slowly growing into himself more.

"I'll let you touch them later if you want, gorgeous." He winked at Josie, making her laugh.

"Can you stop flirting with my fiancée?" Wyatt grumbled, stepping behind Josie to wrap his arms around her waist.

"Oh shit." Mateo looked between the two of them with wide eyes. "You finally did it, baby bro!"

A deep chuckle sounded by my ear, and I instantly knew who it was, the swirl of Trevor's cologne filling my nose. He leaned against the cabinets next to me, his arm grazing mine. I hadn't even noticed he had moved across the kitchen toward me.

"I'm older than you, dimwit," Wyatt shot back.

"Well, you see, I would have put a ring on Josie's finger way before now, so I think I am, in fact, more mature than you."

"You can't even grow a beard," Wyatt deadpanned.

Mateo let out a fake gasp. "Hey, I can! You see this?" He stuck out his chin and pointed. "Hair." Both Josie and Wyatt leaned forward to see.

"I see nothing." Wyatt shrugged.

Mateo pouted, looking directly at Josie. "Jo, he's being mean." The kid should have gone into acting as he fake-worried his bottom lip and pretended to swipe away a tear that definitely hadn't fallen onto his cheek.

"It's okay, I see hair, Matty." When Josie pulled him into a hug, I watched as Mateo sent his brother a smirk.

"It's like he wants his ass kicked," I muttered to Trevor. He chuckled beside me, the sound wrapping around my body like a blanket.

I quietly watched as Mateo showed Landon his nonexistent beard. I felt fingers nudge mine, making me glance to the side. Gesturing with his head, Trevor motioned toward the doorway leading out of the kitchen. Once he slipped through, I looked back to make sure everyone else was occupied.

Mateo was busy looking at Josie's ring with Wyatt, and Landon was looking at his phone. Slipping out unnoticed, I quickly followed after Trevor, reaching out to grab his hand. Feeling like a kid sneaking around, I clamped down on the laughter bubbling in my chest.

Trevor glanced around before grabbing the door handle of some random room and shoved the two of us through. I stumbled in as he hurried to shut the door behind us. Out of every room, he chose the bathroom.

"Hey." I greeted.

Trevor turned me to face him, his hands on my waist. I rose up onto my toes and wrapped my arms around his neck, bringing us closer. "Hey. How was coffee with Josie?"

I smiled at the way he always asked about my day, even if we were only apart for a few hours. "It was nice getting the chance to hangout, just two of us."

"Good." His hands slid under my sweater, softly caressing my bare skin before he lifted me up to sit on the edge of the bathroom counter. "You have no idea how hard it was not to kiss you when you walked in," Trevor whispered. His eyes darted from my lips to my eyes.

My fingers played with the hair at the nape of his neck as I looked at him. He had no idea how bad I wanted to kiss him too.

He dipped his head, bringing our lips that much closer but not touching. The need to kiss him grew by the second. I didn't even care that we were hiding in the spare bathroom with our friends just around the corner.

"Kiss—" I didn't get to finish my sentence before his lips were on mine. *Finally.*

I wrapped my arms tighter around his neck, pressing my front to his. His lips were meant for mine. Every time we kissed, my body came to life like a flame. Like he woke up some part of me that I didn't know existed.

I moaned softly in his mouth as he stepped between my parted legs. The rational part of my brain knew we couldn't do that here, but that didn't mean I couldn't tease him a little. Especially not when Trevor groaned against my mouth, tugging my hips even closer to his. God, I'd never tire of how vocal he was when we kissed and did other things.

We were too lost in what we were doing to hear the bathroom door open. Wasn't until the person said something that the two of us sprung apart. "What the fuck?!"

TASHA

O ur heads snapped to the side. Mateo stood in the doorway with wide eyes as he glanced at Trevor and me. The three of us just stared at one another without saying a word.

"You do realize there are germs in here, right?" Mateo said, breaking the silence. If I wasn't so caught off guard, I would have laughed.

I looked over at Trevor, unsure of what to say. Having a secret relationship with each other was now blown.

"Well, this is awkward." Mateo rolled back and forth on the balls of his feet. "I think I'm just gonna..." He pointed over his shoulder, giving us a tiny smirk before shutting the door.

"How much do you wanna bet he's off telling everyone right now," Trevor commented. I dropped my forehead on his chest with a sigh. It wouldn't be bad if everyone knew, it just wasn't the way I wanted everyone to find out.

"I mean, it's not the worst thing," Trevor whispered, his hands softly rubbing my sides. "Now I can touch you without worrying if someone will see."

That's true. We wouldn't have to keep our distance from one another, which seemed like an impossible task.

Josie's words from the car popped into my head. I didn't want Trevor seeing or talking to some other girl. The thought alone felt like someone was stabbing my chest. Before we went out there to all of our friends, I needed to know one thing.

Pulling back so I could see his face, I steeled myself for what I was about to ask. This could very well be the moment that changed everything between us. He could either say yes or no, and we'd be over.

"Trevor I..." I struggled to say the words. What the hell was wrong with me? I didn't struggle with what I wanted to say or going for what I wanted. When I wanted something, I went for it without second-guessing myself. Yet here in front of Trevor I was scared to talk. He turned me into a nervous school girl.

Trevor patiently waited for me to continue. His hands never once stopped their movement against my skin.

Tasha. Woman up and do it.

"Before we go out there, I need to know something." I stared up into the eyes I came to fall for. "What we're doing isn't just a...fling, right?"

"A fling?"

"Yeah, like are we exclusive?" My heart pounded in my chest as I spoke. "I just don't want to go out there and tell our friends if this is just a temporary arrangement." Yep, I was rambling.

"Tasha." Trevor's hands left my hips and came up to cup my face. "You really have no idea what you do to me, do you?"

My hands moved to grip the front of his shirt as he continued staring into my eyes.

"This is not a fling. Not to me." My heart soared at his

words. This wasn't a fling to me either. "I'm only going to say this once, and I'm sorry if I come off as a possessive douchebag."

Positioning his thumbs under my jaw, he tilted my head back, leaning down farther so he wasn't towering over me more than he was before.

"I want you to be mine and mine only."

"Why me?" The words left my lips before I could stop them.

"Because, for the first time in my life I don't wake up thinking about hockey. I wake up thinking about you. You are *mine,* Tasha. No other guy gets to look at you. Talk to you. Touch you. Is that understood?"

His admission did something to my insides. The words themselves were beyond possessive and demanding, but not necessarily in a 'I own you' type of way. Trevor was staking his claim, yes, but he also made me feel like I had all the power. It only made me want him that much more.

I liked the sound of being his and only his.

"Sunshine." His voice pulled me back from thoughts. "Understood?"

"Understood," I breathed. "Same goes for you. You're mine." I spoke with the same amount of intensity. If he was going to be possessive then so was I.

His lip lifted at my tone.

"I'm yours."

His mouth met mine, his tongue dancing over my own as if he was signing his name on a dotted line, as if we just sealed a deal. Before the kiss turned into something more, I pulled back with a smile.

"Okay, let's do this." I said.

"We'll just act normal and see if they say something. Maybe the idiot didn't say anything." Trevor suggested.

"You've met Mateo, right?" I laughed. I was pretty sure he had already told everyone.

Pecking my lips one last time, Trevor gently picked me up off the counter and sat me on my feet. Giving me a reassuring smile, he opened the door, glancing around in case anyone was right there. Taking a deep breath, the two of us left the confines of the bathroom and headed back toward the kitchen.

I could hear everyone talking as we got closer. *Okay, here we go.* Bracing myself for the questions to be thrown at us, Trevor and I slipped into the kitchen.

Everyone was standing around the counter talking with Mila and Bryton. Apparently, that had shown up while we were in the bathroom. No one seemed to notice the two of us, which I took as a good sign. Acting normal, I moved to stand beside Josie while Trevor approached Bryton.

I caught the end of what Josie was saying. "I would love it if you were one of my bridesmaids."

"Of course!" Mila squealed, pulling Josie isn't a tight hug. "We gotta start planning the bachelorette party!"

I laughed along with Josie, loving how that was the first thing Mila thought of. As the two of them kept chatting, I looked around to see if anyone was acting differently but they were all lost in conversation. None of them seemed to have noticed Trevor and I were gone.

I caught Trevor's eye and sent him a questioning look. *What the hell?* Maybe Mateo didn't tell a soul. Trevor just shrugged in response, clearly as surprised as I was. I wasn't going to question it, though. If he didn't tell anyone, then Trevor and I could do it on our own when we were ready.

Slowly, all of us started filtering out to the backyard, ready to get the BBQ started. Seeing a cooler filled with drinks by the table, I made my way over, desperately needing a drink. Reaching to grab a beer, a hand nudged mine. I looked over, finding Mateo grabbing his own beer.

"What?" Seeing me, he shot me an innocent grin.

"You're only eighteen," I reminded him. I had nothing against him drinking, but I was pretty sure Evelyn would skin him alive if she caught him with alcohol. That was if Wyatt or Landon didn't do it first. It didn't matter that he was of legal age in Canada.

"I'm a university student, babe." Mateo popped off the bottle with a twist of his wrist. Clearly wasn't his first time opening a beer. "Want to be with a real man?"

The smirk on his face made me grin. I couldn't deny that Mateo was good looking. He definitely had the Boone gene. Strong jaw, high cheekbones, sandy blond hair that he cut shorter, which made his face seem thinner than the last time I saw him. Those blue eyes drew a person in immediately. If I was his age, I would no doubt have a huge crush on him from looks alone.

"You think you can handle a woman like me?" I leaned my hip against the table, sending him a teasing smirk.

"Oh, I can treat you real nice. I've been told I make a great boyfriend."

"You know your mom's opinion doesn't count, right?" I said.

"I'm a momma's boy, what can I say? She taught me to treat women the right way."

"Did she?" As I leaned toward him, he nodded, his eyes widening a fraction. "That's a quality I look for in a man." I batted my eyelashes at him, knowing exactly how to hook him in.

Suppressing a grin, I traced a finger down his arm, causing him to swallow hard and look at me with wide, startled eyes.

I continued. "Someone who's strong, smart, caring, and can have a good time."

"We can leave and go have fun somewhere else." He offered.

I leaned in closer so I could whisper. "Not in this lifetime kid." Stepping back, I snatched the beer from his hand and walked off with a smirk. From behind me, Mateo sputtered out a reply that sounded a lot like a string of mumbled words.

"You're gonna fall for me one day, I know it!" he yelled.

Turning around and walking backward, I sent him a grin. "Thanks for the beer!"

Mateo stood there grinning widely as he stared after me. That kid was trouble. I probably shouldn't have teased him when he knew about Trevor and me—and had yet to tell everyone, but the opportunity was too good to pass up.

As I walked back toward the girls, Mateo's whining faded.

But then someone said, "No, not happening." Glancing over, I watched as Landon ripped another beer from Mateo's hand.

"That kid, I swear," Wyatt muttered, standing behind Josie.

"I love him," Josie said with a shrug. Wyatt tugged her back against him, leaning down to whisper in her ear. She giggled. I smiled at the sight before looking around for Trevor.

He was standing over by the grill with Bryton and Landon. I didn't spare the other two a glance as I took in Trevor. It was surprisingly nice out today, which was perfect for a BBQ. But it also meant that Trevor was wearing a T-shirt that showed off his arms and his tattoos. Tattoos that I spent multiple nights tracing with my fingers and tongue.

Even though he was only wearing a simple blue shirt and jeans, he looked delicious enough to eat. Every part of me wanted to go over there and wrap my arms around him but I couldn't. Not until we shared our news. Mateo obviously kept what he saw to himself. Although, I was tempted to say screw it and waltz up to him anyway just to see what everyone said. Or tug him back into the bathroom and have my way with him. Both were incredibly tempting.

As if sensing the weight of my gaze, his gaze shifted to me and those eyes of his slid up and down my body. I was pretty sure he was thinking the same thing I was. I had never craved anyone like I did Trevor. I just wanted to be around him and touch him every chance I could get.

For the next little bit, all of us stood around talking and drinking as the guys worked the grill, conversation jumping from subject to subject. Trevor and I slowly gravitated toward each other as everyone talked. He started off across the way from me until he was right there, his arm brushing against mine.

"Make sure you guys do well this year. I'm set to win my fantasy league," Mateo told Trevor, Wyatt, and Bryton.

"You do know it's practically cheating since you know us, right?" Bryton commented.

"It's not cheating. I'm just playing smart." Mateo pointed at Landon. "He does it too!"

Landon casually sipped his beer, looking like he couldn't give two shits. "And?"

"If I'm cheating, then so are you."

"I only have Trevor on my team." Landon said.

"Wait, hold on." Wyatt looked at his older brother. "I'm not on your fantasy team?"

"You're one of my backups," Landon said it so casually while Wyatt gaped at his brother.

"A backup?"

"Have to keep my options open." Landon shrugged.

Mateo smirked at the fact the attention was off of him. He was such a pot stirrer.

"Trevor? I'm your brother."

"Can't help that I'm better than you, B." Trevor smirked beside me.

"Oh, you think so, huh?" Wyatt turned to his best friend with a raised eyebrow.

"If the shoe fits." Trevor shrugged, totally taunting Wyatt. "I am bigger than you." I mean, Trevor was a tad bit taller, and his shoulders were wider than Wyatt's. Other than that, they were pretty similar.

Wyatt stepped toward Trevor with a playful smirk. "I could take your ass any day." Beside me, Josie took a step back. Mila and I followed her lead as the two stared at one another. I had a feeling they were about to wrestle each other.

"Then come at me." Trevor retorted. Yep, that did it.

Josie grabbed my arm as the guys reached for each other, trying to put the other in a headlock. I could tell the two of them were laughing as they grabbed at one another. Mila, Josie, and I stayed off to the side as the rest of the men cheered them both on.

"AHHH!" Mateo suddenly let out a battle cry as he ran and launched himself on Trevor's back.

"Oh no, you don't." Bryton jumped into the fray, reaching to grab Mateo. With a groan, Landon downed the rest of his beer, setting the bottle down before joining in with the rest of them.

The other girls and I stood there watching as our guys tackled each other, all four of them acting like teenagers. By the laughter that came from them, I could tell it was all in good fun, though.

"Remind me again why I love him," Mila remarked,

watching her boyfriend grab Mateo and tackle him to the ground.

"Because they're good in bed," Josie answered. I laughed as Mila agreed. I mean, they weren't wrong. Just the thought of what Trevor did to me this morning had me clenching my thighs together in anticipation of next time. I wanted to be woken up with him between my legs everyday.

"Hands off the booty!" Mateo yelled.

"I'm not touching your ass!" Bryton yelled back.

"Well, someone is!" Mateo retorted.

"That would be me," Trevor answered from the bottom of the pile.

"Okay, you can keep touching." Mateo remarked.

"Fuck no!" I watched as Trevor struggled to break away from the dog pile.

"What is going on out here?" Evelyn appeared out of nowhere. All of the guys froze, heads turning to look at her. She stared at all five of them, disappointment written in her features. "You guys should know better." Evelyn shook her head.

"Yeah, guys. Pfft." Mateo scrambled away, acting as if he didn't get the others involved and participated himself. He sent the others a smug look over his shoulder as he went over to his mom, dropping a kiss on her cheek.

"Are you guys done yet? We're hungry." Mila interrupted the glaring that went down between the guys.

"Yeah, come on, *children*. We wanna eat." I laughed under my breath at Mateo. He was looking to get his ass beat, and from the looks everyone was giving him I'd say it was a good possibility.

As the guys got up off the lawn to help finish the food I made my way over to Trevor, who stayed on the ground laying on his back.

"Didn't know you liked to touch other men's butts." I grinned, standing above him.

"My hand was stuck." Trevor glared up at me which only made me smile even more.

"Uh-huh. It's okay I won't judge you. It's totally natural."

"Tasha," he warned. I loved when he said my name like that.

"Keep doing you." I shrugged, ignoring his warning tone. In one smooth motion, Trevor got to his feet. This time he was towering over me. He stepped forward until his chest was inches from mine and I had to crane my head back to look at him.

"For that comment, you are going to feel my hand on *your* ass tonight." He lowered his voice to a whisper. He may have spoken softly but the promise was clear as day. Biting my bottom lip I leaned closer so he could hear me. His gaze flickering to my lips.

"I look forward to it."

His jaw clenched as I took a step back. With a wink, I turned on my heel and headed toward the table where the others were at. I probably made it worse for myself tonight but I always liked to do things that I shouldn't.

With the burgers now done, everyone made their plates and picked a place to sit. By the time I made my own plate the only place left was next to Trevor, which I obviously didn't mind one bit.

Under the table, he nudged me with his knee before placing some pickles on my plate. My lips twitched. He knew I liked pickles while he hated them. I nudged him back with my knee in thanks.

Everyone made idle conversation as we started eating. Every so often I'd look over and meet Trevor's eye, the two of us sharing a secret look before turning back to my plate.

Under the table he hooked his foot around my leg, subtly sliding my chair closer.

"So," Mateo suddenly poke up, the conversation around the table quieting. I took a big bite of my burger waiting for what he was going to say. "When is everyone going to find out Trevor and Tasha are screwing each other."

My hamburger stuck in my throat. Silence hung above the table for all of a second before every single head turned to look at Trevor and I. Trevor patted my back as I choked, coughing into my napkin as I struggled to breathe. That little shit. I should have known he would keep it to himself until the perfect opportunity to announce it to everyone. I narrowed my eyes at him as he sat at the other end of the table with a smirk on his face. Oh, I was definitely going to beat his ass.

"What?" Josie spoke first.

I looked over at Trevor with wide eyes. Well, shit. In the bathroom earlier, we planned for this but right now with everyone's eyes on me, I was frozen. This was a big thing to hide. It wasn't like we stole a piece of cake.

Trevor gave me a small smile, grabbing my hand with his on the table, squeezing it reassuringly.

"Tasha and I are together." He declared.

The two of us looked over at our friends, who all just sat there staring at us. My eyes were on Josie waiting to see her reaction. Another full minute passed of silence with no one saying anything. *Did we break them?*

"Thank god," Josie spoke first.

"Finally!" Mila echoed.

I stared at my two best friends with raised eyebrows. That was not the response I was thinking we'd get. I was expecting surprised looks, questions thrown at us, but everyone was just sitting here like it wasn't new news.

"Damn it," Wyatt cursed at the same time Bryton groaned.

I looked at Trevor, beyond confused.

"What is going on?" Trevor spoke the words before I could.

"You lost me a thousand dollars!" Bryton pointed at the two of us.

"You didn't need to bet that much." Mila pointed out to her boyfriend.

"Mateo cheated!" Bryton accused, looking at Mateo.

"I did not!" Mateo shook his head.

"Guys," I spoke above them as they all started talking and pointing fingers at one another. "Guys!" I yelled. Their mouths slammed shut and they looked over at me. "What in the world is going on?"

"Months ago we made a bet to see how long it would take for you two to get together. We've had to keep extending it," Josie explained.

"Took your sweet ass time," Bryton mumbled.

"You gambled on us?"

"Just a friendly wager. None of us could interfere." Wyatt shrugged as if it wasn't a big deal.

"So us," I gestured between Trevor and I. "Isn't a big shock?"

"We already knew you'd get together." Mila waved us off. "Plus, Trevor told the guys you two kissed months ago."

Our friends made bets on when we would get together behind our backs. For months! I wasn't sure if I should be offended or impressed.

"Ignore them." Evelyn reached over to squeeze my arm. "I'm happy you two are together." I shot her a small smile in thanks. "Even if I lost."

"You bet!" Trevor looked at her with wide eyes.

"I overheard them talking about it and thought, why not?" Evelyn didn't even look sorry.

"Is there anyone who didn't place a bet on Tasha and I?" Trevor asked.

Everyone looked at each other before shrugging, even Landon. Well, no wonder none of them looked at all surprised when Mateo blurted it out.

"Well...okay?" I guessed that went better than expected? I wasn't even sure about anything right now. I was fully expecting everyone to be shocked or something more dramatic than this.

"Guess we worried about nothing," Trevor said, looking just as confused as I was. And here we were worried about how to tell them. A lot of stress for nothing.

"Apparently so." A smile started to grow on Trevor's face.

"You know what this means, right?" He leaned toward me, hand coming up to softly grab my chin. "I can kiss you anytime I want."

"I like the sound of that." I grinned as his lips pressed against mine. Like every time we kissed my stomach erupted into butterflies. I didn't even care that our friends were sitting right there watching.

Trevor pulled back until his lips just barely brushed mine. I wanted to pull him back but now was not the place to do that. Pecking my lips one more time he sent me one more big smile before turning back in his seat. He laced his fingers through mine and kept it on the table.

I met Josie's eye as she grinned at the two of us. She sent me a wink before mouthing 'we'll talk later'. The fact that she wasn't angry that I kept this from her eased the guilt in my chest.

"Wait, how did you know about them?" Wyatt looked over at Mateo and asked.

"I walked in on them in the bathroom earlier." Mateo looked at Trevor and I. "Screwing in the bathroom, how unsanitary." He scrunched up his nose.

"Watch your mouth." Evelyn reached around Landon to smack his arm.

"Why am I being punished when it was them! You need to disinfect that sink now!"

"Oh, hush!" Mateo huffed at the look he was given. He muttered under his breath about things being unfair. I smiled at the karma. That's what he gets for telling everyone about us.

"So how did it happen?" Mila asked after a moment. She rested her chin on her hands as she gazed at the two of us with a wide smile.

"The day after we got back from Australia." Going to Trevor's place after that call with my mother was a spur of the moment but it turned into something great. I needed that push. Needed to get my head out of my ass and go after what I wanted. While the motivation behind me going over wasn't the best, it's become the best decision I'd ever made.

"Wait, if they've been together for over a week, that means you two didn't win," Wyatt started to say to Mila and Josie.

"We said when they *admit it* the person who is the closest wins." Mila shook her head. "They are just now admitting it, so we won."

"Still bullshit." I loved how upset Bryton was out of everyone.

As everyone started arguing and talking over each other again, I leaned against Trevor's side. Oddly enough, I was content. Yeah, everyone found out in a weird way but now that they knew, Trevor and I don't have to hide it anymore. Knowing our friends didn't care just made the whole thing a lot easier.

"Wait," Mateo suddenly asked, "Does this mean we have to get rid of the Bang Bet Club group chat?"

TASHA

G ame day.

This wasn't my first hockey game, but it was my first time going as Trevor's girlfriend. Girlfriend. Wow, that sounded weird, yet natural. Trevor Hall's girlfriend. It did have a nice ring to it.

We were lying in bed after the BBQ, talking about our friends making bets on us, Trevor's fingers tracing my spine, when he turned to me and said those three words.

"Be my girlfriend."

He said it so casually it took me a minute to realize he was being serious. When I glanced up, he was already looking at me with a smile on his face.

"Be mine," he added.

"As in?" It was like my brain couldn't comprehend him wanting to be with me.

"As in, make it official." His fingers never stopped moving along my back. The thought of exclusivity stirred something warm in my chest.

"Does that mean I get to call you my boyfriend?" I asked.

"Yes. I'll even get 'Tasha Davis's boyfriend' tattooed on my forehead."

I laughed. "Good."

"So, is that a yes?" Trevor waited for my response.

"Promise to make me food all the time?" Trevor grinned at my request. "Of course."

"Then it's a deal." I mirrored his smile before he pulled me in, sealing it with a kiss.

Thinking back to last night made me grin like an idiot. I seemed to be doing that a lot lately, thanks to a certain someone. I was glad he decided to ask me when we were alone, instead of in front of our friends like he previously planned. It was a moment meant for just the two of us.

"Why am I so nervous?" I played with the hem of the jersey I was wearing as Josie, Mila, and I waited to go through security outside. Up ahead, the arena was lit up, ready for hundreds of fans to go inside.

The place was packed. Everyone we passed was dressed in the Toronto Knights team colors—a sea of blue and white. A good chunk even had their faces painted. Waiting in line, we were surrounded by people who wore Boone, Hall, and Young jerseys. It was moments like these that reminded me just how popular the guys were. Wyatt, Trevor, and Bryton were the faces of the team. They weren't just some random players.

"Don't worry, it gets easier." Josie patted my arm, sending me a reassuring smile. I wasn't the one playing, but I felt like my heart was going to break free from my chest.

When I left Trevor's place earlier so he could get ready, he was cool and collected. He seriously didn't seem fazed at all. And then there was me, who was internally freaking out for him. It was the first game of the season. First time the Knights would be back since winning The Cup Championship.

I couldn't even imagine the pressure they had on their shoulders. Having won it all, they were expected to excel again and win another championship. I had faith they could do it, but that didn't mean I wasn't nervous for them anyway.

"Will it ever go away?" I asked the girls.

"Not really," Mila answered. "You just get better at ignoring it."

"That's not reassuring at all!" I called after her as she walked through after a security guard checked her purse. Josie laughed as she followed behind, then it was my turn.

Only holding my phone, we made it through the check quickly before making our way into the arena. Josie and Mila were here more than I was, so I let them lead us to where we were going.

Before I left this morning, Trevor reminded me he reserved a seat for me front and center. And not to forget to wear his jersey so everyone would know I was taken.

"Our men are going to kill it." Mila beamed as we walked down to the lower level.

The closer we got to the stands, the louder it got. The game wasn't set to start for another half hour, but the place was almost filled. Fans filled almost every seat, ready to cheer their team on. I'd never seen fans so passionate about something.

"Hey, Terry." Josie greeted a security guard who stood down by the lower level. I assumed he normally watched over the same section if she knew him by name.

"Hello, ladies." Terry grinned at us. "Ready for the game?"

"Oh, you know it," Mila replied back.

"Gonna be a good one."

As the three of us came out of the tunnel toward our seats, I was hit with exactly how loud the arena was. I forgot how bad it echoed, and it would only get worse when the team came out.

We walked to our seats that were right up front behind the plexiglass. I could feel eyes on us but that came as no big surprise. Josie and Mila were known among Knight's fans. It was expected since Mila dated Bryton longer than Josie and Wyatt had been together. When the two of them were first caught hanging out, people went insane over it.

Josie didn't care that much about the attention anymore. She was used to the staring, which came with the territory of dating a star hockey player. I had a feeling I was about to be put in the spotlight after tonight.

There had been a few articles written about me after attending a few games with Josie. Mostly wondering if I was sleeping with any of the players when I was just there to be with my best friend. But after tonight, that would change, especially when they caught sight of the person's jersey I was currently wearing.

I wasn't too worried about it, though. I'd grown up in the spotlight since I was young. I had cameras in my face at events and articles written about my family. It came with who my parents were. I didn't care what people wrote about me either. They could say what they wanted, believed what they wanted. As long as the people I cared for loved me as I was, I didn't care.

If some random hockey fans wanted to come at me for dating Trevor then let them. He was dating *me*, not *them*.

"How does it feel being Trevor Hall's girlfriend?" Josie asked. After eating, Josie pulled me aside at the BBQ, and we talked for a bit. I apologized for keeping it from her, but she wasn't upset. She was just glad I was happy and letting myself get close to someone again.

"Weird?" I shrugged, not really sure what the right word was for it. "I mean, it felt right but also odd." I had shut myself off from any possibility of being with Trevor and now here I was, falling for the one guy I said I wouldn't.

"You two are very cute together. I don't think I've ever seen Trevor so happy." Mila beamed, leaning around Josie to glance at me.

"We are pretty hot together." I grinned. "I think we're gonna rival hockey's cutest couple." I nudged Josie's shoulder.

"Yeah, right." Jo rolled her eyes. "Wyatt and I are the golden couple."

"Uh, excuse me? Bryton and I are the 'it' couple, thank you very much." Mila noted.

"Eh, you guys keep those titles. Trevor and I are going to be the power couple." Now that had a spectacular ring to it.

The two snorted.

"Uh-huh." Jo patted my arm in a condescending way.. "We'll see about that."

Moments later, I felt the shift in the air as the game was about to start. There was an electric hum in the atmosphere, like the calm before a storm. The crowd's murmur grew, voices rising in excitement, and the arena lights seemed to shine a little brighter, casting sharp shadows across the rink. I could feel the tension, a quiet buzz that makes the hairs on the back of my neck stand up. It's as if everything is holding its breath, just waiting for that first puck drop.

Sharing excited grins with the girls, I turned back to the ice as the lights dimmed and the announcer's voice through the speakers above us. I barely heard a word the guy said as he talked about both teams before introducing our oppo-nents. As they skated onto the ice, the crowd's boos were so loud it was all we could hear.

When it was our team's turn, the tension in the air became almost tangible.

"Welcome your Cup Champions!" The crowd roared so loud, the ground beneath us shook, the plexiglass in front of us rattling.

Player after player skated onto the ice, but I only had eyes for one. He was one of the last ones out.

"Your favorite left winger, who holds the title of most assists—*Bryton Young!*" Mila screamed, jumping up and down. I laughed as the people around us cringed away at the volume of her voice. Not that I blamed them, she could burst an eardrum with her yelling.

"Now, give it up for your right winger, a *beast* on the ice— *Trevor Hall!*" I shot to my feet, clapping my hands as I shouted for my boyfriend.

I gave shit to Mila for screaming so loud but mine rivaled hers. Pretty sure I was going to lose my voice by the end of the night. Everyone else around me cheered for Trevor.

My eyes were glued to number eighteen as he skated out onto the ice, tapping sticks with his teammates. Even under all the gear, Trevor was massive compared to some of the players. He truly was intimidating out there on the ice.

"And now, your captain, who led the team to another Cup win—*Wyatt Boone!*" I almost went deaf as the stadium ignited into a fit of cheers. . If I thought Trevor and Bryton's cheers were deafening, it was nothing compared to Wyatt's. Beside me, Josie went crazy for her fiancé.

I watched as Trevor skated toward me, everyone else around me fading as I focused on the grinning face beneath his helmet. He came up near the glass, knocking on it once before zipping away.

Bryton was next to come up and acknowledge his girl-friend. He winked, and she blew him a kiss. Then, it was Wyatt's turn. He slid to a full stop in front of Josie, tapping the glass three times before she did it back, their own little ritual before every game.

We stood there, watching as our men skated around the rink, warming up. I kept my eyes on number eighteen as he skated. He looked so natural being out on the ice, hockey stick in his hand as he slapped pucks around to his teammates.

From the many, *many* conversations I had with Trevor about hockey the last few days, I knew the team had a few new players they drafted this year, but they managed to keep all their original players. Apparently, it was something that didn't happen all that often.

Which was good because they all worked together like a well-oiled machine. They all knew each other so well, on and off the ice. The better the team got along outside of the game, the better they worked together when it counted.

Before our vacation to Australia, the guys held practice for two weeks straight, doing mini camps that were mandatory for everyone to attend. With new players, they had to work extra hard to come together. But from what Trevor said, the new guys meshed really well.

"So, number fifty is new and so is number seventy-seven." Josie pointed out the two as they skated past. "Seventy-seven was a trade from another team. He's apparently been in the league for a few years now, but number fifty is fresh out of the draft."

Josie listed off a bunch of facts about the players and the other team. I was almost sure all that information came from Wyatt.

"You should become an announcer," I teased. "I think you know more about the teams than they do."

"Wyatt's an excellent teacher." Josie blushed.

"Bryton teaches me *all* night long about how great hockey players are," Mila piped up.

"Trevor certainly has no issue letting me know how endless their endurance is." I added.

"Very good endurance." Josie nodded. All three of us stared at one another before laughing. Sitting with my friends and joking about the guys made me happy they knew the truth. I didn't have to sit and pretend like I didn't wake up this morning wrapped in Trevor's arms.

We spent the next few minutes talking back and forth and taking pictures. I managed to take a gorgeous selfie of all three of us, which I quickly posted and tagged them in. Who would have thought a hockey arena would have the best lighting?

Movement on the ice drew our attention as the teams moved to their sides, ready to play. My nerves skyrocketed as Trevor moved to stand next to Bryton and Wyatt. I watched as the three of them knocked each other's sticks before the referee blew the whistle.

Everyone took off at the sound, their skates tearing up the ice. The screams around me ricocheted off the plexiglass when the first body hit. We were seated so close I could hear the smash of the player's body against it.

Being this close to a hockey game was almost unreal. You could practically feel the intensity radiating off the players. You got a firsthand look at how fierce the game really was. I didn't fully understand how physical the sport could be until I started attending with Josie.

When Josie and I lived together, she would make me watch games with her, but if I thought some fans were insane, they had nothing on Josie. The girl would scream her lungs out at the TV, so into it you couldn't tear her away from the game. After getting our third complaint from our neighbors, I banned her from watching it with me and told her to yell into a pillow instead.

It was literally her dream to be here cheering with the rest of the fans. I couldn't deny that seeing it in person was better than watching it on a television screen. There was something about getting swept up in the whole thing with everyone else. I had to admit, it was almost addicting.

"Pass it," Josie muttered under her breath.

My eyes tracked Bryton, who currently had the puck. He barreled down the ice toward the goalie, an opposing player hot on his heels. The other guy went for Bryton only to be shoved into the plexiglass. The hard hit echoed around us. The person who hit him skated off seconds later, not bothering with a second glance. I caught sight of the jersey number and smirked to myself when I noticed Trevor's last name on the back.

That was my man.

Trevor's hit helped Bryton slap the puck to Wyatt who easily scored. The three of them worked so well together it was mesmerizing getting a front row seat to see it. It was like they knew where the others were without even looking.

Trevor would get the puck, skate forward a few steps, before hitting it toward Bryton without even turning his head. If Wyatt had the puck, the other two were right behind him, slamming players against the wall.

I yelled alongside Josie and Mila as our men played. By the time it was intermission, the Knights were up 4-0. While the team went to cool off, the three of us made our way up the stands to get drinks, my throat dry from all the yelling.

"How are you doing with your parents?" Josie asked as we waited in line for a beer.

"I don't know," I admitted. "The gala is coming up, and I'm going to have to go." There was no way I was getting out of that one. My parents would come get me whether I kicked and screamed or not. I had planned on not seeing or speaking to my parents after the whole arranged marriage thing but with the gala that wasn't going to be possible.

"Wait, your parents host the Davis Charity Gala?" Mila looked at me with wide eyes. I nodded. "I can't believe I never put two and two together. Of course." She smacked her hand against her forehead.

My parents' charity gala was pretty well known. When

the wealthiest of Toronto's elite all got together it was usually a big deal.

"That's one of the biggest events of the year!" The look on Mila's face was priceless. I guessed for those who had never been, the event was a big deal.

"It's not that great, trust me," Josie said. She only had to go once to know it wasn't all it was made out to be.

"You've been?" Mila looked at the two of us like we were suddenly celebrities.

"I went as Tasha's date a few years ago. I mean, the food was pretty good." I snorted at her nonchalance. Although, she was right. The food they catered was pretty damn good. "But the people, not so much. They are the snootiest, bitchiest people."

"Well, damn. Now I don't want to go."

"Trust me, you aren't missing out on much. If I didn't have to go, I wouldn't." I replied.

"Are you going to take Trevor?" Josie asked.

I thought about asking if he'd want to go, but I wasn't sure it was something he'd like to do. Getting dressed up and standing around having to make small talk with random people wasn't everyone's cup of tea. Plus, if he came, he'd meet my parents. I wasn't worried about how he'd act. No, I was worried about how *they* would.

I waited until we got our beers before answering.

"I'm not sure I want to throw him to the wolves." Cause that's what I would be doing. I knew he could hold his own, but it wouldn't be a pleasant night in general. "And that's not even including my parents."

"I would kill to see your parent's faces if you showed up with Trevor on your arm." Josie shot me a mischievous grin. I mean that would be a huge plus. Even if they found out about us before then.

I knew I'd have to make a decision soon, but as we headed

282

back to our seats, I pushed it aside for the time being. I'd ask Trevor another day. At that moment, I just wanted to focus on my man winning his game.

THE THIRD PERIOD of the game was brutal. As soon as the other team hit the ice, they came out with vengeance. Trevor and Bryton seemed to be getting double teamed, and slammed into the glass with more force than necessary. Each one rattled the plexiglass I almost thought it would break.

I flinched with every hit Trevor took, clenching the arm of my seat. God, no wonder Josie got so nervous during games.

The score was now 5-3 with only fifteen minutes left of the game. Next to me, Josie was yelling for Wyatt as he skated back onto the ice, zipping down the rink toward the net. Everyone else from our team was occupied with their own opposing player to cover him.

I watched as Trevor managed to break free from the two guys trying to block him. He booked it across the ice toward Wyatt, moving faster than I thought possible. All three barreled toward Wyatt.

"Come on, come on," I muttered under my breath, white knuckling my armrests.

Trevor came up to the guy right behind Wyatt, knocking him with his shoulder. The guy stumbled to the side, but he reached his arm out, grabbing Trevor by the top of his jersey and pads. They were right in front of us as I watched him yank Trevor, trying to throw him off his feet.

The guy apparently didn't realize just how big and strong Trevor was. One second he was gripping Trevor's jersey, and the next, he was getting slammed into the glass directly in front of me. It rattled so much I swore I felt it as whistles started blowing.

From where I was sitting, I could see the pissed off look on Trevor's face, under his helmet, as he said something to the guy. Definitely wasn't something nice by the looks of it.

Trevor was yanked backward and let the guy go as a referee came forward holding up a penalty card. I shot up out of my seat along with everyone else. The yells were deafening as Trevor shook his head and pointed at the opposite team.

"He didn't do anything!" I yelled.

He didn't. The other guy was the one who started it first, pulling on Trevor's jersey, which was not allowed.

"What the hell!" Josie shouted beside me. I stood there, stunned, as the referee called him out and pointed toward the penalty box. I didn't have to hear Trevor to know he was cursing. The other guy totally got away with it while Trevor was required to sit in the box for the next ten minutes.

The Knight's might have been leading but ten minutes without one of our best players wasn't ideal. It could give the other team plenty of time to score.

Wyatt and Bryton came up to Trevor's side, patting his shoulders as they steered him away from the referee before he could say something that would get him ejected. I wish I could hear what they were saying as Trevor shook his head and skated toward the box.

"Stupid ass ref," Josie grunted as she sat back down.

I kept my eyes on Trevor as he took his helmet off and sat down in the box. His hair was dark with sweat and stuck to his forehead. Even from here I could see his jaw was clenched.

There had to be nothing worse than sitting out and

watching your team play without you, especially with only fifteen minutes left in the game.

While the game continued, I kept one eye on Trevor. Watched as he kept shaking his head, putting his hands in his hair as he struggled to remain still.

The minutes ticked down until Trevor had only one minute left in the box. The Knights did a good job at holding off the other team, but they got close to scoring a few times. These last five minutes were going to be rough.

I couldn't help but grip Josie's arm as Trevor's time was up, and he shot out of the box like a bat out of hell. The other team had no idea what they just did by putting him there.

His teammates tapped sticks with him before lining up for the puck drop. I could almost feel the tension in the air as they prepared for the final face-off. The crowd around me grew even more frenzied.

The Knights gained back the puck easily as they all worked as a team, moving around the ice like one unit. Those ten minutes in the box really lit a fire under Trevor. I swore each hit was twice as hard as they were at the start of the game.

As the clock ticked down to thirty seconds, all of us were on our feet. Beside me, Josie and Mila were yelling just as loud as I was.

The other team stole the puck and darted down the ice toward our goalie. Even if they scored, they wouldn't win, but they made it personal by putting Trevor in the box so there was no way they were going to allow even one goal at this point.

I watched with bated breath as they neared the net. Trevor, Wyatt, and Bryton swarmed the guy. Snapping their sticks as they wrestled the puck away. Just as the buzzer went off Wyatt managed to get the puck and sent it all the way across the ice in the other direction.

5-3 was the final score.

I turned to Josie and Mila with a scream. The three of us threw our arms around each other, jumping up and down. I could barely hear anything over the roaring of the crowd. The girls and I babbled about the last play as the teams shook hands. I turned back to the rink after a moment to see the players starting to leave the ice.

Looking over to my right, I noticed the tunnel where the players came and went. A few players were already walking through the tunnel back to the locker room.

Without a second thought, I ran toward the spot, weaving in and out of people getting out of their seats. I didn't know what came over me, but I needed to see Trevor. Needed to touch him. I noticed a few fans were leaning over the edge, dangling their hands to get a high five from the players.

Before anyone could get the spot I wanted, I shot forward, colliding with the wall. It was the perfect place where I could lean over the railing and see who was getting off the ice.

I only had to wait a second before Bryton came into view. He noticed me right away and sent me a smile. I gave one back and patted his arm as he passed by. Next was Wyatt, who gave me a nod. Not even a second later, I caught sight of the one person I was waiting for.

With a smile that split my face in half, I waited for him to notice me. Almost like he could tell I was there, he lifted his head and met my eyes. The smile that broke out across his face made my heart pound.

There he was.

With two huge strides, he came toward me, thrusting his hockey stick into someone's chest. Going up onto my toes, I reached out to him. In one swift motion, he grabbed me and hauled me over the railing. My legs automatically wrapped around his waist and my arms came around his neck, my fingers gripping the back of his sweaty head but I didn't care. Not as he grinned down at me with the world's biggest smile. And it was all for *me*.

"Good game," I murmured.

"Did you enjoy it?"

I nodded. "Especially when you rammed that dickhead into the glass." Trevor threw his head back, laughing at my words. Then I said, "You're crazy."

"Crazy for you," he shot back, making me laugh in return.

"Cheesy." I leaned my face closer to his, my eyes flickering down to his lips for a split second. "But good, cause I'm crazy for you too."

As our lips met, I swore I heard the sound of cheers, followed by some whistles. But I didn't care. Didn't care that there was a possibility tomorrow morning everyone, including my parents, would know about Trevor and me.

What did it matter?

Everyone deserved to know that Trevor was all *mine*.

28

TASHA

Trevor Hall—star player for the Toronto Knights—made a big splash when he was seen kissing Tasha Davis. Daughter to Robert and Jennifer Davis, owner's of Toronto's elite law firm–Davis & Associates. We are unsure if the pair are a couple or if it's another fling for Hall, but the two definitely put on a show for fans.

A picture of Trevor and I kissing was posted right below the article.

"At least it's a good photo," I muttered as I stared at the article written about Trevor and me. I knew there would be something written about us after kissing at his game, so I wasn't all that surprised when Josie sent it to me. I was a bit surprised at how long it took them to print it.

It was currently Sunday night, and I was sitting on my couch, stuffing my face with ice cream as I went over work stuff. I was going to go hang out with Josie but with a new patient coming tomorrow I wanted to be prepared. And I was sulking.

Trevor was away for two hockey games, spanning five days, leaving me home alone. I understood why Josie and Mila hated away games so much. Not having Trevor around sucked. I'd gotten so used to being with him everyday. Either going to his place or coming here, making dinner together, and watching TV on the couch.

It was probably healthy having some space and not spending so much time together, but that didn't mean it didn't suck. He wouldn't be back until tomorrow afternoon, which felt like a lifetime. So, I was trying to distract myself with work, but every few minutes, I found myself looking over at my phone.

I told myself I wasn't going to bother Trevor, but the urge to text him was growing by the second. I looked over my patient's file one more time before I gave in. Reaching for my phone next to me, I sent him a text. It was a little after eight, so he should still be up.

Forcing myself not to stare at the screen until he replied, I gathered all my work files and put them off to the side. I wasn't getting anything else done tonight.

Curling up with a blanket, I switched the TV to a random movie as I waited for my phone to buzz. Thankfully, I didn't have to wait long.

Trevor: I was just about to text you.

A stupid smile graced my face at the text.

Tasha: Great minds think alike. What are you up to?

Trevor: Lying here listening to Bryton snore like a gorilla. If we didn't need him tomorrow for the game, I would put a pillow over his head.

I snorted, picturing him doing just that.

Tasha: If you put a blanket over his head, and he suffocates, it's technically not your fault.

Trevor: That is a very tempting idea. Here.

A second later, a video appeared in the text thread. The

sound of snoring came through my speaker, the screen black before the camera was flipped around and Trevor came into view. The back light of the phone lit up his face enough that I could see him roll his eyes. The video ended with his face staring back at me.

Even lying there, about to sleep, he was absolutely irresistible. He'd only been gone four days, but I drank in the sight of him. Did he get even hotter while he was gone?

Clicking on my own camera, I took a quick selfie of just my face. I didn't look the greatest with my greasy hair pulled up into a bun, face free of makeup, as I wore my pj's, but I hit send anyway.

Tasha: You need earplugs!

It took a minute for Trevor to reply and when he did, I felt myself flush.

Trevor: Wish your thighs were my earmuffs.

I read his text again and again, my thighs pressing together involuntarily. His innuendo was clear as day as I immediately pictured his head between my legs, thighs clamped around him to keep him in place.

Tasha: Don't start something you can't finish.

Trevor was such a tease, even if he wasn't sitting next to me. I wouldn't put it past him to get me all hot and bothered and then say goodnight.

Trevor: Who says I won't.

As I struggled to come up with a reply, Trevor sent me another.

Trevor: What are you wearing?

I couldn't help but snort at the comment. Such a guy question.

Tasha: Nothing but a lacy thong.

Couldn't be further from the truth. I was in a pair of baggy sweats and one of Trevor's T-shirts that was huge on me. Not to mention my fuzzy socks that were bright red. I was far from sexy at the moment, but I was cold and didn't have my boyfriend, who was a human furnace, to keep me warm.

Trevor: I'm thinking more along the lines of...sweats, a shirt, and a fuzzy blanket. Accurate?

Even though he couldn't see me, I raised an eyebrow, quite impressed. We'd spent so many nights together lately that he came to know what I slept in. That was, if I wasn't naked and sweaty beneath him.

Tasha: Caught me but you missed the fuzzy socks.

I took a quick picture of my feet and sent it.

Trevor: That just made me harder.

A giggle escaped my lips. I wanted to call and hear his voice but with Bryton in the same room that would be awkward as hell.

Tasha: Feel free to jerk off to that picture.

I made sure to add a winky face and eggplant emoji before I hit send. I could just picture Trevor lying on the bed, propped up, shirtless, looking sexy as hell.

Tasha: Aren't you going to give me something in return?

Five minutes passed without a response. I blindly watched the TV but my mind was going wild with ideas on what he'd send me. When my phone finally buzzed, I snatched it from my lap so fast. As soon as I clicked on the photo, my mouth went dry.

It was a picture of him lying back on some pillows, abs on display with tattoos littering his skin. I didn't even hesitate to save the photo. It would make a great screensaver.

Trevor: Wishing you were here.

If he wasn't four hours away, I would have been in my car driving to see him. Again, away games sucked ass.

Tasha: Hurry home to me tomorrow.

Trevor: I'll be back before you're done with your patients.

With a cheesy grin, I settled back into the couch with my

phone glued to my hand. If he couldn't be here, I'd settle for his cute texts.

"THE GUYS ARE ALMOST ready and will meet us at the club," Josie said as I leaned over to finish my makeup in the mirror.

The guys got back three hours ago. The first game they played three days ago, they lost but yesterday's game they annihilated the other team. Sadly, I only caught snippets of them between patients. But I was finally realizing why Josie got so into hockey when watching. I found myself yelling at my phone multiple times. I was starting to become one of *those* people. Although, I couldn't bring myself to care because I was cheering for my boyfriend.

"Are you ready for tonight?" Josie asked from behind me. Glancing over my shoulder, I sent her a confused look. "This will be your first real outing as a couple with Trevor. Wouldn't be surprised if the paparazzi showed up."

I had pushed aside the fact that Trevor and I were now Toronto's newest obsession. Every day, my phone had tons of new notifications from Instagram with new followers. Almost every single picture on my page had comments from people, a mix of good and bad. After reading some, I vowed not to do it again. There were only so many 'she's too ugly for Trevor' comments one person could take.

I wasn't surprised by the reaction, though. Trevor was a big deal around here. Add in the fact he hasn't had a serious girlfriend in years, and it made front-page news. It felt like the two of us had replaced Josie and Wyatt as the headline couple. That was, until they announced their engagement. Then Trevor and I would be long forgotten.

"It will be fine." I waved her off. "I knew what I was signing up for." It came with the territory when dating famous hockey players. I could handle a few cameras pointed at me.

"When are you going to announce your engagement?" I asked as I straightened up, smoothing my hands down my dress.

"We're taking pictures on Sunday for it, and then we'll do a big announcement."

"You can't just post a picture of the ring, huh?"

"Wy's manager said it's better for us to do it and get ahead of the papers and social media," Josie said with a huff. Oh, everyone was going to have a hay day when their announcement dropped. "But for now, we're enjoying our engagement just the two of us."

"It's never too late to dump Wyatt and marry me instead."

"We can elope." Josie shot me a grin.

"Just get me a big ring, and I'm all set."

"Pretty sure people thought we were together in uni." Josie snorted.

"Remember that party we went to senior year at the soccer frat house?" I asked, moving across her bedroom to grab my purse.

"The one after midterms right?"

"Yeah that one. We were having fun, minding our own business dancing when that frat guy came up to us and asked for my number. He wouldn't take no for an answer." I rolled my eyes at the memory.

"I'll never forget the look on his face when you told him we were together and then wrapped your arms around me and kissed me. Pretty sure he came in his pants then." Josie laughed.

"Then he asked for a threesome." I chortled.

Josie sighed a moment later. "Man that feels like a lifetime ago."

"I know. And now here you are about to be married."

"We've definitely come a long way." She wasn't wrong. Our lives have completely changed since then.

Leaving her vanity Josie came to my side, hooking her arm with mine. "Meeting you was the best thing to ever happen to me, Tash." Her words made my eyes prick.

"You're the best thing to ever happen to me too, Jo." We gave each other watery smiles before I cleared my throat. "We are not messing up our makeup." Pulling apart we wiped under our eyes.

"Ready to go?" I asked a moment later.

"Let's go get our men."

As soon as the Uber came to a stop in front of the club, I was up and out within seconds. With Josie at my side, we looked around for familiar faces, my gaze snagging on a small crowd forming up ahead. I instantly knew who was there.

Not wanting to lose each other, Josie and I clasped hands and headed for them. Behind us, I could hear people muttering about cutting in line, but I didn't pay them any attention. The closer we got, I heard the names Boone, Hall, *and* Young being tossed around. Yep, that was them.

Not caring about the people crowding around them, I pushed my way through, elbowing a few people as I went. I heard protests as I tugged Josie behind me before we finally got to the front of the crowd. I briefly registered people standing there with oversized cameras but someone else stole my attention.

My eyes landed on Trevor as he stood in front of me alongside Wyatt, Bryton, and Mila. He spotted me within seconds and took two large steps toward me, wrapping his arms around my waist, tugging me into his chest.

I didn't waste a second before pressing my lips to his, the tension in my body immediately disappearing as I wrapped my arms around his neck. The two of us sighed like he'd been gone months. After a moment, I pulled back enough to look up at his face.

"Hi." I grinned.

"Hi." He mirrored it. God, he was handsome.

"You played amazingly." I boasted.

"You watched?" The surprise in his eyes had me nodding.

"Of course. I watched in between patients."

"You're incredible," Trevor breathed, staring down at me.

"Of course I am."

As the others started for the club, I stepped back, grabbing his hand and following after them. The crowd easily parted to let us through, cameras clicking away as Trevor tugged me tight into his side. His hand gripped my hip possessively as if telling everyone around us who I belonged to.

When we got to the club doors the bouncers took one look at our group and let us through. It was moments like these when I was smug about knowing Trevor and the guys. It was better than standing out in the cold, waiting to get in.

The moment we entered, the deafening music slammed into me, the bass pulsing through my body as we navigated through the club toward the booths. Strobe lights flashed above, and the dance floor was a sea of people.

Somehow, we managed to snag an empty booth big enough for all of us right next to the dance floor. Sliding in after Trevor, I noticed Lydia and Landon walking in our direction.

The whole gang was here.

We were only seated for a second before a waitress appeared with a tray of shots. One of the guys must have flagged someone down. Who was I to complain?

"Cheers to the guys winning their game today." Mila lifted her shot as we all grabbed one.

"To kicking ass," Josie echoed. Everyone cheered, clinking glasses together before knocking the shots back.

The alcohol burned going down my throat as I tried not to cough. Fanning my mouth, I watched Trevor swallow his shot, not even flinching. *Show off.*

"One more then we are dancing!" Mila yelled over the music.

The memory of swaying with Trevor at the club in Australia made my body heat up. The last time we shared that moment, I was too tipsy to fully appreciate it. I wasn't going to make that mistake tonight. I was going to be with my boyfriend on the dance floor all night long.

Another tray of shots appeared and was quickly emptied. I didn't hesitate in knocking mine back with a wince. Breathing through the burn, I slid from the booth, putting my hands on the table and looking at Trevor. "Dance with me."

"Me?" Trevor acted confused as he pointed to himself, the corner of his lips twitching.

"No, Bryton." I deadpanned. "Come on." I made a grabbing motion with my hand. I gave him a little pout, knowing he wouldn't be able to resist. With a shake of his head, he slid out of the booth, grabbing my hand.

With a wide grin, I pulled him with me, the others following behind us. The music washed over my skin as we stepped onto the dance floor, the ground vibrating beneath us from the music and the crowd.

Trevor tugged on my hand, making me spin around to face him as his hands fell to my hips and mine landed on his chest.

The way Trevor stared down at me made my entire body light up. It might have been dark, but I could see a hungry look in his eyes. Could feel the intensity of them as he looked right at me as I danced against him.

I loved the way he looked at me, as if I were the most incredible thing he'd ever laid eyes on. With just one glance, I was a mess at his feet, especially when he gazed at me like he wanted to consume every part of me.

"You clean up well!" I yelled over the music. He may have only been wearing a simple white T-shirt with dark jeans, but he looked better than every other man in this place.

"So do you." His eyes roamed the dark blue dress I had on, the tips of his fingers toying with the string at the back that kept it in place. One little tug would have it pooling at my feet.

Meeting his hungry gaze, I ignored everyone around us and started shimmying my hips, going back and forth between dancing like a dork and grinding against him.

My skin was slick with sweat, and I was breathing heavily as I turned until my back was pressed against his chest. The bottom of my dress grazed the back of my thighs, the silky fabric making it easy to grind my ass back against Trevor.

Trevor's grip on my hips was almost bruising, and he helped guide me backward. I could feel how much he enjoyed what I was doing as he ground his groin against me, pressing his hard length into my backside.

"You're doing that on purpose, Sunshine," Trevor whispered against my neck, his lips softly trailing along my shoulder and sending a shiver down my spine.

"Maybe I am." I twerked my ass in response, smirking at the low groan he made at the movement.

One of his hands left my hips to press against my stomach, keeping my lower half pressed tightly against him. My back arched as my hands moved over my head to wrap around his neck. I was fairly certain our current position wasn't appropriate but not a single part of me cared.

"Do that again and I won't be responsible for what I do next." Trevor nipped at the skin on my neck, inducing a thrill that slipped down my spine and ended between my legs.

I moved my hips just slightly, feeling him harden even more.

"Behave."

Fuck. I loved when he talked like that. His voice got so dominating and deep. I could tell he was trying to control himself, but my bratty side was having none of that. Not caring about the consequences, I moved my hips down and in a circle, grinding even harder against his crotch.

"Shit"

I got the exact response I wanted. I did it again, getting more turned on by the second. I was basically dry humping him right there on the dance floor.

After the third time, Trevor stepped away from me. I opened my mouth to say something, only to close it when he grabbed my hand and yanked me after him. I stumbled in my heels but didn't say a word as Trevor shoved his way through the crowd of dancers.

My mind was in a fog and all I could think about was Trevor inside of me. Whether that be his cock, his fingers, or his mouth.

The way Trevor gripped my hand and marched through the club told me I had pushed him too far. A thrill of excitement shot through me.

Biting my lip, I stumbled after him as he headed for the

bathrooms. Luck was on our side as one of the doors opened right as we got there. Completely ignoring the line of people waiting, Trevor shoved past them and stepped into the restroom. Behind me, people protested but the door slammed shut a second later.

I was shoved against the door as he flipped the lock. A hand immediately encased my throat as Trevor kept me pinned against the bathroom door. Thankfully, it was a single bathroom.

"You little fucking tease," Trevor said through clenched teeth. The look he gave me made me groan under my breath. "Like I told you in Australia, if you want to be touched, all you have to do is ask."

"I want to be touched." My voice came out cheeky, making Trevor tighten his hand around my throat just a little bit more. I couldn't help myself, especially when he was towering over me, hand around my throat, a look on his face that said he was going to fuck me regardless of where we were.

"Couldn't have waited until we got home. Just an impatient little thing, you are." His thumb brushed the underside of my jaw.

I was not a fan of a man talking down to me, but when Trevor did it, I became putty in his hands.

"Hope you know your actions are what led to this. We could be out there dancing with our friends, but instead you're a greedy little thing who just can't handle not having my cock."

I pressed my thighs together, attempting to relieve the pressure between them.

"Maybe I'll just tease you and make you go back out there all wet and needy."

I shook my head as much as I could with his hand around my neck.

"No," I whimpered. I didn't want that. I wanted him. Right then and there.

Trevor brought his face close to mine. His lips barely grazed mine as he spoke. "Since you're so needy, tell me what you want."

"You," I breathed. I reached out to touch him, but in one swift move, he had both my wrists in his other hand, pinned above my head.

"Not good enough." His lips once again found my shoulder. "If you don't want to leave this room unsatisfied then you better tell me exactly what you want."

Not a single part of me cared that we were currently in the bathroom of a club with a line of people waiting outside.

"I want you to fuck me so hard I can barely walk out of here." The words left my lips without hesitation. I was too far gone to be embarrassed at how needy I sounded.

"See, it wasn't that hard, was it, baby?" Trevor's teeth nipped my ear, making my back arch as I groaned. "Don't you dare move these. Understand?" He squeezed my wrists. Once I nodded, he let them go, but I kept them held above my head like he asked.

I kept still as his hand left my throat and trailed across my collarbone, between my breasts, and down my stomach until he reached the hem of my dress.

"I bet you're soaking wet for me, baby." Before I could even mutter a sound, his hand slipped under my dress, fingertips finding my soaked thong. He groaned low in his throat. "I haven't even touched you yet."

I loved how vocal Trevor was. I'd never had a guy who turned me on just by words alone. At first, I was a bit embarrassed talking dirty with Trevor, but I came to enjoy it. Plus, who didn't love a man telling them what he was going to do with you naked beneath him.

"Spread those legs for me, Sunshine." I didn't need to be told twice.

I slid my feet apart, only for Trevor to nudge them even farther. The fabric of my dress hitched up around my hips.

"I'd love to take my time ravishing you but someone is bound to come kick us out of here, so this is gonna have to be quick."

"Yes, please." The urge to have him inside of me grew by the second. If I didn't have him filling me pronto I was going to lose it.

I was panting as Trevor unbuckled his pants. I wanted to reach out and touch him, but I kept my hands in place, knowing better than to move. did that before and it resulted in him edging me for half an hour.

Clasping one leg, he lifted it up around his hip to gain better access. His other hand gripped my ass, tugging me even closer to him as he moved my thong to the side. The moment I felt the tip of him touch me I let out a moan, eyes falling shut.

"Look at me," Trevor demanded, his grip on my ass tight-ening enough to make me snap my eyes open. "Good girl."

He teased my entrance with his tip, his eyes glued to mine as if daring me to look away from him. Right as I was going to snap at him to stop teasing me, he thrusted, slamming all the way to the hilt. My mouth fell open in a silent plea as I stretched around him almost painfully.

Trevor held still for just a moment as I adjusted before he started moving in and out slowly. I tried to contain the noises that wanted to break free from my mouth. The club may have been loud but the people right outside could prob-ably hear us. Surprisingly, the thought didn't disgust me as much as it probably should have.

Trevor's slow pace only lasted a moment before he clenched his jaw and slammed into me harder. He fucked me against the bathroom door, each thrust punishing as he gripped me tightly.

I pressed my lips together to hold back my moans but with each stroke it got harder and harder. My back rocked against the door before Trevor yanked me forward to meet him, thrust for thrust.

I lost the battle of keeping my hands above my head and dropped them onto his shoulders, trying to steady myself on my one foot.

I could feel him pulse inside of me as the two of us got closer to coming. His grunts and moans made my pussy clench around him.

Using the door as leverage, I moved my hips to meet his, trying to get him even deeper. I meant what I said earlier. I wanted to stumble out of here when we were done.

"Fuck, fuck, fuck." The words left my mouth as my legs started to shake. With Trevor busy keeping me upright, I slipped a hand down between my legs and rubbed my clit.

"Come for me," Trevor said through clenched teeth. Somehow, his thrusts got even faster and harder. He swelled inside of me.

I only lasted another minute before I came. My entire body shaking, the loudest moan ripping from my throat. No doubt the people outside the door heard it. I held onto Trevor as my eyes rolled back and my pussy clamped down around him.

Not even a second later, Trevor groaned as he came as well. He buried his head in my neck and slid his length inside of me a few more times before going still. Grateful for the door, I slumped back against it, breathing heavily. My mind was a jumbled mess.

It took us another minute before Trevor slowly shifted. He moved back just enough to look down at me, an odd expression on his face. Before I could blink, it disappeared as a smile grew on his face. My own tugged up as he bent down and softly kissed my lips.

"Guess we better get out of here," he mumbled against my mouth. Despite wanting to stay in this moment forever I knew we needed to leave. Everyone was probably wondering where we were.

I groaned as he slid out of me, instantly feeling empty. The two of us quickly got cleaned up and readjusted our outfits. There was no way the people outside didn't know what we just did. We'd been in here too long to be considered normal.

Biting my lip, I looked at the door in hesitation. I wasn't sure I wanted to go out there yet.

"Keep your head down and I'll lead us out." Trevor grabbed my hand and gave it a squeeze. "Just remember, they're all jealous they don't have a hot girlfriend to fuck." He gave me a cheeky smile that made me laugh. Placing a kiss at the top of my head, he reached for the door handle.

I kept my chin dipped as Trevor opened the door. I wasn't going to be embarrassed about what we just did, though. I had the best orgasm of my life from my sexy as fuck boyfriend. Everyone else could be jealous all they wanted.

Trevor was quick in yanking us out of the bathroom and down the hall before a single word was uttered. When we turned the corner, he slowed down and sent me a wink over his shoulder.

I was falling in love with his man so fucking hard.

29

TASHA

"We're going to have a sleepover," Lily, the same patient I saw before I left for Australia, said with a wide grin. It was crazy how much she had grown into herself in the last few weeks. Before I left for vacation, she was just starting to make friends and now they were planning a sleepover.

"That's fantastic, Lily. I'm so glad you're branching out and making friends."

"Hannah loves to read like I do." Lily went on to tell me all about them. I sat there watching as she smiled more than I'd ever seen. The difference between where she was when we first started seeing each other and how far she's come was truly remarkable.

With a promise to tell me all about it at our next session our session drew to a close. I made a note to sit down with Lily and her parents to discuss cutting her sessions down altogether.

Walking her to the door she paused for a second.

"Thank you, Ms. Davis." With a bright smile, she lunged forward, wrapping me in a hug. I hugged her back. She pulled back and gave me a small wave before heading out the door.

With a light feeling in my chest I grabbed my notepad and headed for my desk. Mr. Waltham was scheduled to arrive soon. He was my last patient of the day before I needed to leave to make it to Trevor's game tonight. I'd make it there, but it was going to be tight.

A knock sounded on my door ten minutes later, signaling Mr. Waltham's arrival. Yelling for him to come in, I grabbed my notebook I had just for him and moved away from my desk.

"Good afternoon, dear."

I grinned at him as he stepped into my office. "Good afternoon, Henry."

"Did you know you have a very tall, attractive man in your waiting room?"

My eyebrows shot up. "I do?"

He gave me a nod as I moved around him in efforts to go look. "Just give me a moment."

I knew exactly who it was. With a grin fighting to break free on my face, I stepped out of my office. Standing there, leaning against my receptionist's desk, was Trevor. My poor receptionist, Sofie, was staring at him with red, flustered cheeks. Trevor had the ability to do that to a woman.

"Hey." At the sound of my voice, Trevor straightened, turning to me with a smile that made my chest ache. I looked him up and down, sucking my bottom lip between my teeth at the sight of him.

My eyes raked over muscular thighs clad in a pair of dark gray slacks and up to the black button-up shirt with the sleeves rolled up to his elbows, his tattoos on display. His hair was perfectly styled back, my fingers itching to run through it. Not to mention the sexy scruff on his face he started growing out because he knew I liked it.

God, he looked mouthwatering.

Whoever made it mandatory for professional athletes to dress up before a game deserved a medal of honor. Because, damn.

"Hey, beautiful."

He stopped inches away from me.

"What are you doing here? You have a game in two hours." It was clear he was on his way to the arena with his appearance.

"I wanted to come see you before the game. You snuck out early this morning." His hands came to rest on my hips.

"Josie wanted to go over some things for the wedding before work, and I didn't have the heart to wake you up."

I knew he had a game today, and he needed the rest. Plus, he was an adorable sleeper, although clingy. I had to slide my pillow in between his arms in order to escape this morning. Every time we got in bed Trevor had to have his arms around me or his legs intertwined with mine. I never would have guessed him to be the type.

"I would have gotten up." I tried not to grin at the way he sulked.

"I know." I placed my hands on his chest as I looked up at him. I knew it was wildly inappropriate standing in the waiting room at work, flirting with my boyfriend with my assistant and patient waiting for me. But I couldn't bring myself to step out of his hold quite yet.

"I know you have work, but I just wanted to drop by and say hi." My heart skipped a beat. No one showed up the way Trevor did. Certainly not any past boyfriends. He made me feel seen every single day.

After feeling invisible by my parents, I never realized just how much I longed for affection. For years, I tried to gain their attention, seeking their approval. I craved any sort of affection they'd give me.

Subconsciously, I knew I projected feeling unwanted onto people I was with, letting myself accept the littlest bit of attention given. When past boyfriends wouldn't call me for days then ask me to come over late at night, I accepted it. I figured any was better than none.

The bar was so low that I let men treat me like a second option without saying anything about it. I accepted the love I thought I deserved. It wasn't until Trevor that I learned I deserved more than just the bare minimum.

"Once I'm done here, I'll be there front and center." I promised.

"You're my good luck charm."

"Of course I am." I beamed. "I bring good luck in waves."

"That you do."

The way he looked at me made my cheeks heat. Before Trevor, I rarely blushed but for some reason, he could get me flustered in less than a second.

Knowing he needed to get going, and I needed to get to Mr. Waltham, I rose onto my toes.

"You better leave so you're not late for your game." I pressed a quick kiss to his lips before pulling back. "I'll be there soon."

Before I could fully pull away, he pecked my lips once then twice. With a soft groan, he pulled himself away and stepped back, his hands leaving my hips.

"I'll be the one on the ice." He sent me a wink as he walked backward toward the door.

"Better make a goal for me."

"Always."

With one last smile, Trevor left my office, my eyes following him until he disappeared from view. Even the back of him looked great in his outfit. I bit my bottom lip at the way his dress pants hugged his ass.

"You two are so cute," Sofie gushed, making me glance

away from the doors. "He's even hotter in person." My lips twitched as she sighed, resting her chin on her hands. I found it comical how people lusted over my boyfriend.

I totally got it. Even when I was denying what I felt for him, I knew he was beyond attractive. The fact that he was *my* boyfriend was still a bit surreal. Like, yes, I snagged that!

"Oh, he left this for you." Sofie shook herself out of her daydream. She pulled a single lily flower from her desk, holding it out for me.

Right when I thought I couldn't fall for Trevor anymore, he went and did something like this. I didn't need a giant bouquet of flowers. The fact that he remembered that I loved lilies more than roses was more than enough.

I held the flower between my fingers as I brought it to my nose. He was too good for me.

Remembering Mr. Waltham was waiting for me, I snapped myself out of it. Ignoring the smirk on Sofie's face, I quickly walked back into my office.

"Sorry about that, Henry," I apologized as I closed my door behind me. Glancing over, I found him seated in his usual seat, a content smile gracing his face.

He kept grinning at me as I gently placed the flower on my desk and grabbed my notepad. When he didn't stop by the time I sat down, I sent him a look.

"Why are you looking at me like that?"

"You and Trevor Hall." He remarked.

"You know who he is?"

"Dear, I may be old, but I don't live under a rock. Everyone knows who Trevor Hall is."

"Oh."

"You two make a good-looking couple." It became clear he was watching us from my office the entire time. It was a bit embarrassing having a patient know about my love life, but it was bound to happen when my name was posted everywhere.

"These old eyes can spot true love a mile away," Mr. Waltham continued. My eyes widened at his words. True love? I liked him a lot but that didn't mean love...right? The growing feeling in my chest hinted at something else, but I couldn't think about it right now.

Clearing my throat, I veered our conversation back on track.

"Enough about me. How are things?" He was quiet for a moment as I waited for him to talk. I wasn't the kind of person to push someone to talk when they don't want to. I had plenty of patients who sat in front of me and barely said two words. Sometimes, it was more about having someone there than them listening.

"I talked to Rosette," he finally spoke after a minute. The last time he was here he didn't want to meet his new neighbor, fearing it would mean he was over his late wife's passing.

"How did it go?" I took note of him fiddling with his wedding ring.

"Good." He shrugged, the motion making me raise an eyebrow.

"Good?" I gently pried.

"I took your advice and went over to say hi. She invited me to a BBQ the neighbors were having."

"Oh, that sounds fun."

"It was...nice." Over the last six months, I had learned to read him and his tales, so I knew he had a good time at this BBQ, whether he wanted to admit it or not. He was definitely holding information back.

"I'm glad you had a good time. And I'm proud of you for finally talking to Rosette."

I could tell he was struggling to continue as he sat there quietly.

"Henry," I spoke softly. "Is everything okay?"

"Rosette is even better than I thought." He heaved a sigh like it was the worst thing to ever happen. "She's so nice and beautiful. She was a nurse in the military. That's where she met her late husband. He also passed away three years ago."

Mr. Waltham started rambling as he told me about Rosette. I leaned back in my seat, smiling softly at the way he talked. It was really cute seeing his eyes light up for the first time since he started seeing me.

He told me about how they had coffee on their front porches every morning this week. From the sound of it, Rosette and him had a lot in common. Both had military experience, both were widowed, and they loved the same genre of books and movies.

"I want to invite her over for dinner tomorrow night, but I don't want to look like a goon." Aw, he was nervous about asking a woman out.

"Well, do you have a plan on what you'd want to make?" I asked.

"She told me she loves seafood. So, I was thinking of making salmon."

"Once you know what you want to make, go over to her house, and just ask if she'd like to spend the evening with you. She'll say yes, I promise."

"Are flowers too much?"

"Not at all." I smiled, shaking my head. I imagined Henry all dressed up, walking over to Rosette's with flowers in his hands. Too cute.

The way he fiddled with his ring and then his coat sleeves I could tell he was nervous. This would be his first time since Carol's passing that he put himself out there. He was married for so long that dating wasn't an option. It was going to take some time, but I had no doubt that he would find someone who could make him happy again. Rosette seemed like the right person for that.

"You will have a fantastic time. Don't overthink it." I sent him an encouraging smile. He could do this. He sent me a small smile back along with a nod.

"Do you think I'm ready for this?" His question was probably one of the most vulnerable ones he ever asked. The hopefulness in his eyes made my heart ache.

"The only person who can answer that is you."

A lot of people thought therapists could solve all your problems. That they'd tell you all the answers and make you better. We didn't do that. Yes, we gave advice and listened to the person. But it was up to *them* to do the work. To make the change inside themselves. We just gave them a little nudge and the resources to make that possible.

The only person who could answer if Henry was ready, was Henry. I couldn't decide that for him.

"But I don't think it's a bad thing to be open-minded going forward. You never know where something can lead you."

"Thank you, Doc," Henry said after a few moments.

"Anytime."

TASHA

"They're just about to hit the ice," Terry, the usual security guard, called after me as he let me through to the lower-level seats.

"Thank you!" I yelled over my shoulder as I practically ran toward my section. I was running late.

After Mr. Waltham left, I was almost ready to leave but my work phone rang. It ended up being a patient in crisis. There was no way I couldn't answer. After making sure they were okay, I had less than twenty minutes to get home, change, and make it to the arena.

I looked like shit, not having had time to touch up my makeup, and threw on the first pair of jeans I found, along with Trevor's jersey.

Weaving around people, I jogged down the stairs and caught sight of Josie. She glanced over at me as I approached. I scooted in front of a few people to get to her.

"Hey." I greeted, slightly out of breath.

"You made it!" she yelled over the roaring crowd.

"Hey, babycakes." Mateo, Wyatt's younger brother, peered around Josie with a grin.

"Babycakes?" I raised an eyebrow at the nickname. "Please tell me you don't say that to girls."

"Nope, just reserved for you." He winked. I shook my head but my lips twitched in amusement.

"Is Mila here?" I leaned close to Josie so I wouldn't have to yell as loud.

"Yeah, she's grabbing us drinks. Lydia was going to come but she had to work."

I took in the ice rink, seeing both teams skating around and warming up. I missed Trevor's entrance. I searched for his number, grinning widely when I found him next to Wyatt and Bryton.

"Yay, you made it," Mila said. I turned just in time to see her walking toward us with her hands full of drinks. Reaching out, I grabbed two beers from her.

I ended up giving her my seat and moved around to Josie's other side with Mateo. With two beers in my hands, Mateo reached out to grab one, but I jerked them away.

"Nope."

"Babycakes."

"Your brothers would kill me." I shook my head.

"Mila said I could!"

I looked at Mila, who just shrugged.

"He's drinking at uni anyway."

I mean, she wasn't wrong. He's drinking at school and at parties so it really wasn't that much different. Mateo gave me puppy dog eyes, going as far as to make his bottom lip quiver.

"Fine, but if your brother finds out, it was all Mila." I handed him the beer with a look.

"Thanks, babycakes." He grinned, taking a big chug of it.

"Didn't know you were coming tonight," I said to Mateo just as the referees blew their whistles to start the game.

"Haven't been to a game in a while, and I have finals

coming up." Mateo shrugged. "That and the chance to be around three of my girlfriends."

"Your girlfriends?" Josie and Mila leaned around me to look at Mateo.

"Yep. We can have our own ménage à trois."

"A ménage à trois is three people. Not four," I pointed out.

"Four is an orgy," Mila said.

"An orgy," he breathed. His eyes widened, and I just knew he was imagining that scenario. Mateo leaned back in his seat, staring straight ahead, but he was lost inside his head.

"You broke him," I said to Mila.

"It'll keep him busy for a little bit." I snorted.

I finally turned my attention back to the ice as the game began. It only took me a second to find Trevor as he skated beside Wyatt, who had the puck.

I swear, every time I watched him skate, he got even more attractive. And knowing what was beneath all that gear certainly didn't help. I bit my lip knowing he was all mine and everyone here knew it too. I couldn't help but be a bit smug about that. I really was becoming a possessive girlfriend.

I loved watching him play. There was something so fascinating about watching him fly down the ice. It was intoxicating how powerful and in his element he was. You could just tell hockey was how he was meant to spend his life. I couldn't see Trevor sitting behind a desk pushing paper. He was supposed to be right there next to Wyatt and Bryton.

As Trevor skated by, I cheered loudly, drawing his attention. Even under his helmet, I could see the grin he sent my way. I tapped my lips twice, a cute signal we came up with a few days ago.

"You two are adorable." Josie nudged my arm with a wide grin.

"He's pretty great."

"Can't tell you how happy we all are that you are *finally* together," Mila gushed.

"Took you long enough," Mateo chimed in.

"I still can't believe you guys bet on us." I shook my head at my friends.

Mila raised an eyebrow. "How else are we supposed to be entertained?"

"The Bang Bet Club group chat is the best." Mateo sighed.

"About this group chat…" I looked at all three of them with narrowed eyes.

"We needed a place to talk about you guys and place bets without you knowing," Mila tried to justify it.

"We placed the bets on you guys back when we had game night all those months ago." Josie supplied, making me realize just how long it was going on for. So much has changed since then.

"We have a separate one going for Landon and Lydia that you can join now," Mila added. Well, at least I can join in on the fun for that one.

"Fine."

"Don't worry, babycakes, we can partner up." Mateo threw an arm around my shoulder. "Beat everyone's asses." I liked the sound of that. "Welcome to the Bang Bet Club."

***

"WHAT THE HELL WAS THAT?" Josie screamed, slamming her hand against the plexiglass.

Someone from the opposing team tripped Wyatt by swiping his skates out from under him. A move that should have gotten the guy put in the penalty box, but somehow, the referee didn't see it. If looks could kill, the guy would have dropped dead from the glare in Josie's eyes.

The game was tough. Both sides played defense so well The Knights only scored twice and the other team once. With each passing second, they played rougher, the hits getting harder.

"Pummel him!" Mila yelled beside her.

My hand shot out to grip Mateo's arm as Trevor chased after the puck, two guys on his tail. The timer ticked down the seconds until the final buzzer sounded.

The entire game I had to watch Trevor get slammed into the plexiglass, cringing after each one. Poor Mateo. His arm was probably going to bruise from how hard I squeezed it.

"Jesus, woman." Mateo groaned, trying to pull his arm back without success.

Trevor skirted around players, expertly moving the puck. He turned on a dime, making the two players on his ass almost collide.

"Go, go, go," I chanted.

"Babycakes, I need my arm." Mateo used his other hand to pry my fingers from him.

"Sorry," I muttered, barely paying him any attention. Not when Trevor sent the puck toward Wyatt, who skated a bit farther before sending it back to Trevor.

The two of them moved like a perfectly synchronized team. They didn't need to exchange a single glance before passing the puck to each other.

Trevor neared the net but just as he went to hit the puck, a body slammed directly into his side. Somehow, he managed to stay upright but the guy got right up in his face. Before I could even register what was happening, the guy threw a fist at Trevor's face.

My hand shot out to grip Mateo's arm again as I watched Trevor's helmet fly off. Almost immediately, Wyatt and

Bryton were there, as well as the rest of the players on the ice. Someone shoved the guy who hit Trevor, small fights starting to break out all over.

The players separated enough for me to see Trevor standing there, circled by Wyatt and Bryton. They had a hand on his shoulder, but it was clear he wasn't going to engage in any fights. A gasp left my lips, seeing the blood running down his face from his eyebrow. It wasn't a small amount either. My heart pounded in my chest, and my vision narrowed.

"Jo. Help," Mateo wheezed beside me as I crushed his wrist.

I completely ignored him as I kept my eyes on Trevor. He glared at the guy who punched him as the referee yanked a couple of players apart. I didn't like the sight of the blood running down his face. It was a cheap shot.

Josie and Mila yelled along with the crowd, the boos from the stands echoing in my ears. When the referee pointed to the opposing player and gestured toward their team's box, the booing turned to cheering. Pretty sure the guy was getting kicked out of the game for a stunt like that.

Trevor looked absolutely livid as he touched the cut on his eyebrow. Wyatt and Bryton were shouting something back at the other team, their faces filled with just as much anger.

When Trevor skated toward the team's box, I found myself standing up. I wasn't sure if I could go after him or if he'd want me to, but the sight of him hurt was making my heart pound. And not in a good way. I needed to make sure he was okay.

He'd been hit plenty of times over the course of his career, and I was certain this wasn't his first time being punched, but it was *my* first time seeing it happen. The overwhelming urge to see him grew.

"Go." Josie touched my arm, drawing my attention to her. "He'll want to see you." Mila nodded, agreeing with Josie. Even Mateo gave me the go ahead, although he probably only did it so I wouldn't squeeze his arm anymore.

Without needing to be told twice, I slipped past them to get to the exit. I marched up the stairs, side stepping a few people. They were barely a blimp on my radar as I headed for my hurt boyfriend.

With long strides, I made it back to where Terry, the security guard, was. He gestured toward the hallway that led to the team's locker room without me having said a word. Sending him an appreciative smile, I took off down the hallway. It took everything I had not to run toward the locker room.

My shoes slapped against the concrete as I nearly sprinted. I may have been down a few levels, but I could still pick up the roaring of the fans. Reaching the locker room door, I didn't hesitate in flinging it open and stepping inside.

It was my first time inside the Knights locker room, but I didn't let myself pause to look at everything. There was someone more important that needed my attention.

"Trevor?" I called out when I didn't see him at first glance.

"Tasha?" Following the sound of my name, I walked around a corner just as Trevor appeared. He was still clad in his hockey uniform, even his skates, as he held a cloth to his eye. As soon as he saw me, his hand dropped in surprise. "What are you doing here?"

"You're hurt," was all I said as I stepped closer to him. With his skates on, he was even taller, making me crane my neck up to look at him.

"Just a small cut."

"What if you need stitches?"

I didn't know why, but my hands started to shake. My mind going a million miles an hour. What if he was really

318

hurt? What if he had a concussion? Where's their damn team doctor?!

The rational part of my brain was telling me it wasn't anything serious. It was just a small cut, but it felt like something inside of me switched. I knew hockey players got hurt a lot, hell most of the guys on the team had fake teeth, but seeing the blood on Trevor's face evoked a foreign emotion in me.

"Babe, I'm okay." Bringing his free hand up, he softly cupped the side of my face, drawing my focus back to him.

I leaned my cheek into his hand as I swallowed the sudden lump in my throat. It wasn't a big deal, yet here I was, wanting to cry. What the hell was wrong with me?

"Can I…" I wasn't even sure what I was trying to say, but Trevor gave me a small nod like he knew.

Grabbing my hand, he led us toward a room near the back. Once we stepped inside, I noticed it looked like a doctor's office.

"Take a seat." I pointed to the chair off to the side as I went over to the cabinets to try and find something to clean his face with. I had no problem finding a first aid kit. The cabinets were stocked full of anything you could possibly need. Grabbing some alcohol wipes, I walked over to Trevor, who was sitting like I asked.

"Let's see it," I whispered. When he pulled the rag away, I winced at the cut above his eyebrow. While it looked like it hurt, it didn't look deep enough for stitches, but that didn't mean I wasn't getting the doctor in here to check later.

Standing between his legs, I ripped open an alcohol pad.

"This might hurt," I warned. Trevor didn't say a word as I started wiping at the cut. His hands landed on my hips as I cleaned his face. Every once in a while, he would squeeze if I got too close to the cut, but he didn't make a sound, keeping those eyes on me the entire time.

With gentle swipes, I cleaned the blood on his cheek. My free hand gently held the side of his face to keep it still as I worked.

Neither of us said a word, but I didn't mind. I had this unfamiliar swirling in my chest, and I wasn't sure what to make of it. When I looked into his eyes, that feeling grew until I was almost consumed by it.

"What are you thinking about?" Trevor whispered. His fingers slid under my shirt to softly rub my bare skin. The wipe in my hand fell to the ground as I brought both my hands up to tangle themselves in his hair.

I should have been grossed out by how sweaty he was, but as I gazed down into those eyes that became more and more familiar to me, I didn't care. A million thoughts were running through my head as I pushed his hair back, but one thing stood out the most.

It was right then I realized what it was.

Love.

Somehow, in a matter of weeks, I fell in love with Trevor Hall.

From every small action.

From every smile meant just for me.

From every time he showed up for me the last few weeks.

Trevor came in and completely obliterated the walls I had built around myself. For the first time in my life, I felt seen. Not just the good parts of myself, but the deep, ugly, broken parts. Somehow, Trevor saw that and stayed.

I expected to freak out at the realization but standing there, staring down at Trevor, I wasn't scared. How could I be? The man looked at me like I was the best thing to ever happen to him.

Mr. Waltham's words echoed in my head. Even he knew I was in love with Trevor before I could admit it to myself.

"Trevor." My voice came out shaky.

"Sunshine."

I had to tell him. It might not have been the right setting, and maybe I should have waited until we were home, but I had to say the words. Had to let him know how I felt about him.

"I love you."

I think I've loved Trevor for a while now, I just didn't want to admit it to myself. Didn't want to let myself believe it was possible.

Trevor went quiet, his hands frozen at my sides as he stared. When he had yet to say anything, nerves poked their way through. Maybe I shouldn't have said it. *Shit.* I should have waited.

"I-I—" I stuttered trying to think of a way to take it back.

"You love me?" His voice was thick as his eyes roamed my face.

I nodded, the lump in my throat making it hard to swallow. I was trying my best not to freak out that he had yet to say anything to my declaration. Telling someone you loved them was like jumping off a cliff and hoping they'd be at the bottom to catch you.

"I fell in love with you the moment I met you, Tasha."

Trevor's hands left my sides, lifting to cup the sides of my neck. He used his thumbs to tilt my chin up so we were eye to eye.

"You stole my heart the second you started arguing with me about fries and ice cream. I was just waiting for you to feel the same."

My legs threatened to give out from under me at his words. Trevor Hall loved me. *Me.* I wanted to cry and cheer at the same time. My heart skipped, and for a moment, the world seemed to pause, as if time itself was acknowledging the weight of Trevor's words.

"You love me?" I needed him to say it again.

"I love you, Tasha Davis."

Never did I imagine that the two of us would be here, confessing our love for each other. If someone had told me a year ago this would happen, I would have flipped them the bird.

It didn't matter that we were in the Knights locker room and that Trevor was sweaty and bleeding. Because this right here was the only thing that mattered.

"I love you too, Trevor Hall."

TASHA

"**W**hat are you going to say to your parents tonight?"

I sighed through the phone at Josie's question. I had absolutely no clue what I was going to tell them when I saw them. I'd been ignoring all their calls the past two weeks since the pictures of Trevor and I came out.

So far, they had called me every other day, more than ever before, but I didn't pick up. The thing was, I knew exactly what they were going to say when I saw them. And I knew they'd somehow try and guilt me into doing what they wanted, but they were going to be surprised tonight. I wasn't going to be a pawn in a game for them to use to help their firm. They'd gone too far this time.

"I honestly don't know," I replied. I still had a few hours to figure that out.

"Don't let them get to you. You owe them nothing," Josie said fiercely through the phone. *"Want me to come? I can be ready in an hour."*

Even though she couldn't see me, I smiled. If I said yes, she would drop everything and come to the gala with me. And as much as I would love her company tonight, I wasn't going to make her go. Not after how rude my parents were the last time.

"I'll be okay. Trevor will be there."

The only reason I was okay with going tonight was because I knew I'd have Trevor by my side. When I finally got the nerve to ask him if he wanted to come with me last week, he didn't even hesitate. I did try to tell him he didn't have to, but he wouldn't hear a word of it.

While him coming to the gala meant he'd have to meet my parents, and the world I grew up in, I was relieved he was coming. Having him there would help me get through the night with most of my sanity still intact.

"He's going to make it in time, right?"

"I hope so." I worried my lip between my teeth. The team was flying home, currently in the air as we spoke, but he was going to be cutting it close. He was gone for over a week for away games.

"Don't worry, he'll be there," Josie assured me.

I wasn't going to lie, I was a bit nervous that he wouldn't make it tonight and I'd have to endure the night alone. Being in a room full of people who would stab you in the back at any chance was not all that fun. Neither was knowing that the second you turned around they were talking about you behind your back.

I did warn Trevor about tonight. Warned him of the type of people he was going to have to interact with. I also had to caution him about the type of person I'd be tonight. I learned over the years I had to act a certain way around my parents' friends or else they'd pick me apart.

I just wanted him to be prepared, even if he assured me none of it would drive him away.

"I still can't believe two of my best friends are in love," Josie swooned. *"I knew the moment you two met this would happen."*

"No, you didn't." I laughed, entering my bathroom to get

324

started on my makeup. *"Uh, yes, I did. I even told Wyatt when we first met that you and Trevor would be good together."*

When I first met Trevor, I never once thought I'd be in love with the cocky hockey player who did everything in his power to annoy me. Obviously, there was an attraction there, but I hadn't allowed myself to even think of anything more. And now here we were, spending almost every waking second together and in love.

Crazy how things turned out.

"Taking credit for my relationship."

"Obviously. Without me, you wouldn't have met." I mean, she wasn't wrong. If she hadn't been stuck in that elevator with Wyatt none of us would be here right now.

"Also, I was thinking next week we could go check out some wedding venues." Her voice echoed around my bathroom as I put her on speakerphone.

"Aren't you supposed to look at venues with your fiancé?"

"Wyatt said he's fine with anything. He'd be okay if we went to Vegas and eloped."

Ever since we first met back in uni, the two of us talked about our dream weddings—a beautiful venue, big cake with the cute figurines on the top, and wearing a gorgeous gown and a veil with the perfect guy next to us.

"You are not eloping. I won't have it. You two are going to have the prettiest wedding, and I'll make sure of it."

"That's why you and I are going venue shopping." Josie laughed.

"I better be there for the cake tasting as well." The best part of weddings was trying tons of cakes for free.

"Oh, hell yeah. We will have to do multiple tastings just to be sure."

"See, this is why I love you."

The two of us talked on the phone for a bit longer as I got ready, helping to keep my mind off of tonight. As much as I wanted to stay on the phone and postpone the night, the clock ticked closer to the time I had to leave.

With words of encouragement and a plan to hang out in two days, Josie and I said our goodbyes. While I hated knowing that I had to go, I was looking forward to the gorgeous gown I picked out.

Last week, I convinced all my girls to go shopping with me—took five stores and many, *many* dresses to find the perfect one— but if I was going to be forced into going to an event I didn't want to attend, then I was going to go all out and turn heads.

Heading to my closet, I reached for the long black bag holding my gown. The thing was heavier than I would've ever expected, and so I struggled to pull it out. Maybe it was a good thing that I was working out with Trevor the last few weeks. It gave me the muscle I needed to carry this damn dress.

Laying it out on my bed, I slowly unzipped it, once again wonderstruck by its beauty. It was *stunning.*

Stripping out of the PJ's I'd been sitting around in all day, I grabbed my other new purchase. The burgundy thong had a matching bra but with the strapless dress I didn't need it tonight. I wanted to give Trevor something fun to slip off later, and this one left little to the imagination.

I grabbed the heavy fabric and stepped into it before tugging it on. It took a lot of maneuvering and twisting to get the thing zipped on my own, but once it was on, the dress fit me like a glove.

Grabbing the sides, I walked over to my floor length mirror, the fabric of the dress swishing on the floor.

The gorgeous deep red color made my tan skin glow. I loved the off-the-shoulder style of it and the cinching at the waist before it flared down to the floor. It showed just enough cleavage to not be too revealing. No one wanted to get me started on the high slit on one side either, exposing my leg with each step.

It was honestly one of the prettiest gowns I'd ever worn.

Time flew by as I touched up my makeup and before I knew it, I was slipping on my heels, ready for the gala, the car my parents sent minutes away from pulling up downstairs.

Smoothing my hands down my dress, I looked at my reflection one last time. Even with the added height from my heels, my dress brushed along the ground, but in a way, it almost looked like I was floating. I felt powerful in this dress.

My blonde hair was curled, hanging around my shoulders with a few pieces pulled up. I matched my eyeshadow to the dress, going for a smokey appearance. I paired it with a dark red lipstick. Not to toot my own horn, but I looked pretty damn good.

"Don't let them affect you, Tasha," I told my reflection. I wasn't about to let my parents or any of the people there get to me. I could play the game just as well as they could.

Pushing my shoulders back, I flashed myself a smirk before turning on my heel and grabbing the clutch I packed with my keys, phone, lipstick, and gum. It was time to get this thing over with.

THE RIDE to the fancy hotel where my parents held the gala wasn't bad. The car was nice and big, so I didn't have a hard time getting in with my gown. The driver was quiet and left me alone as I sent texts in the girl's chat. Josie, Lydia, and Mila sent encouraging messages and memes.

I did send Trevor a few texts, even though he was in the

air and wouldn't see them until he landed. I wished he was next to me, but at least he would be here soon.

When the car pulled up to the hotel, the first thing I noticed was the paparazzi lining the black carpet that led to the front doors. Of course there was a carpet to walk on and pose for pictures. The socialites were nothing but vain when it comes to cameras. Always wanting their pictures taken and shared for everyone to see.

I planned it so I would arrive late but not late enough to be considered rude. The last thing I wanted was to show up early and be stuck here any longer than I had to be. I wouldn't be surprised if my parents were already looking for me.

"Ready, Miss?" the driver asked, looking at me through the rearview mirror. With no other choice, I gave him a nod.

While he got out and came around to open my door, I took a deep breath. *You can do this, Tasha. It's just a few hours.*

As soon as my door opened, I was met with the sound of people yelling and the clicking of cameras. Swinging my leg out, I slowly slipped out of the car, making sure to move at a pace that got everyone's attention. With a steel spine, I stepped onto the pavement, my dress falling to my feet.

Plastering on a fake smile, I prepared myself to pose for pictures. Lifting the sides of my gown so I could walk, I headed for the black carpet ahead of me. An odd choice.

As I walked, flashes blurred my vision. Photographers yelled, finally catching onto who I was. Most of the questions thrown at me were about the relationship I had with Trevor Hall. Even with Josie and Wyatt's engagement announcement, we were still a hot topic.

Having done this before, I knew to stop and pose a few times, giving a few smiles and smirks over my shoulder as I went. These pictures would be all over the internet in a matter of minutes.

Leaving the photographers behind me, I stepped into the hotel, following the trail of people to the ballroom. As soon as I stepped through the doorway, I swore I felt every head turn in my direction. Squaring my shoulders, I walked farther into the lion's den, keeping my eyes open for my parents. I had yet to see them but knew they were here somewhere.

The giant chandelier hung from above was beautiful. Casting a warm glow over everyone standing in the ball-room. I only made it halfway through the room, weaving between tables, when I was stopped by someone calling my name.

"Tasha, dear!"

I tried not to groan at the sound of the voice. Mrs. Hans was the biggest gossip and every word out of my mouth would be repeated to everyone. Of course, she'd be the first one to come talk to me.

"Hello, Mrs. Hans." I turned around to face her, a fake smile on full blast. "Nice to see you."

"You look wonderful, dear." The expression on her face was just as fake as the rest of her. Coming up behind her was her husband.

Mr. Hans was your typical older white man in his late sixties. He made his money by investing in small companies then flipped them for millions. He wasn't the worst man I'd ever met, but he rarely kept his eyes to himself. They dropped to my breasts and then jumped back to my face. He was harmless for the most part.

"Thank you. You look beautiful as well." Like everyone else around, her dress was probably worth a fortune. No one would be caught dead showing up in a gown less than a few thousand dollars.

"You are too kind." Mrs. Hans touched my arm. "So happy to see you tonight. We weren't sure you were going to show."

"Wouldn't miss it."

"We saw that you are with that hockey player." *Ahh there it was.*

"Hall is a fantastic athlete," Mr. Hans chimed in. "Hopefully they bring home another championship."

"Is he coming tonight?" I didn't miss the glint in her eyes. She was dying to share something with the grapevine.

"He is. He's on his way, actually." This time the smile on my face wasn't fake. It never was when it came to Trevor.

"We would *love* to meet him." *Oh, I bet you would.*

"Hopefully, he gets here soon," I said politely. "I better go find my parents. It was nice to see you guys." I quickly made my exit, wanting to get away before she could try and get more information out of me.

Another thing I learned over the years was that you could talk to someone for a few minutes but then you had to make your leave. If not, you'd be roped into business discussions and gossip all night long.

Weaving between people, occasionally waving or flashing a smile to someone who said my name, I made my way toward the bar. If I was going to get through this night, I needed a drink. And I needed it ASAP.

Ordering a glass of wine, I grabbed my phone, hoping to see a text from Trevor saying he was on his way. I tried not to let my heart sink when there was no notification, my last message left on delivered.

He was most likely on his way and hadn't had time to text me back yet.

After a few minutes of wasting time by the bar, drinking half my wine, I knew it was time to face the crowd again. And my parents. With one last glance at my phone, I put it back in my bag. The bartender sent me a sympathetic smile as I grabbed my drink.

For the next thirty minutes, I bounced around from

person to person. As soon as I was done talking to someone, another was right there to take their spot.

I shouldn't have been surprised when every conversation steered toward Trevor and I's relationship. Although, I doubted half the people in attendance ever saw a hockey game.

I knew our relationship had been the talk of the town these last few weeks. I'd ignored a lot of what was being said about us, but I guessed it was big enough news for everyone here to know. News travels fast in socialite circles.

I politely answered some questions but easily switched the topic to business, which helped get the attention off of me. I long since mastered getting people to talk about themselves, something everyone in this room *loved* to do.

I politely excused myself from the conversation and made my way to the bar, needing a break. The entire time, I felt the weight of eyes on me. I caught a few comments about my dress, which just made me smirk. A lot were from old hags who didn't appreciate me showing so much skin. Not my fault their pervy husbands couldn't keep their eyes to themselves.

Having a second to myself, I pulled my phone out yet again. There was still no word from Trevor. He should have been here by now. My stomach twisted at the thought that something happened.

With a knot in my stomach, I sent him another text. I'd wait a little longer before texting Josie to see what was going on. Even if Trevor couldn't make it, I just wanted to make sure he landed safely.

I had to refrain from biting my lip in worry, not wanting to ruin my lipstick or get it on my teeth. As I was standing there looking at my phone, someone slid up beside me. A quick glance from the corner of my eye had me silently groaning. God, not her.

331

Of course, it was Alexa Blackwood, daughter of millionaire Patrick Blackwood, who owned the hotel we were currently standing in. As well as thirty others across the world.

"There you are, Tasha. Hiding out by the bar, I see." Her fake, nasally voice made it hard not to cringe when it hit my ears.

"Just taking care of work things." I turned to lean my arm against the bar, not bothering to put on a fake smile as I looked over at my ex-best friend. "You do know what a job is, right?"

The glare she sent me had me smirking. She didn't work a day in her life, her daddy having paid for everything she desired. While others were out working, she was jetting off to different countries doing whatever she pleased.

"Still being a disappointment?" The cruel smile she sent me made my jaw clench.

Back in the day, we were best friends. At one point, we were so close that I would spend almost every day at her house. We told each other everything. At eighteen, I considered her my truest friend. Obviously, that was not the case.

"If I'm not mistaken, didn't you have a big scandal a year ago and your parents almost cut you off?" I acted like I didn't see the headlines about her getting caught snorting coke in Italy a year ago. The thunderous look on her face had my lips curling up.

As Alexa glared at me, I looked her over. She wasn't wearing her usual style. Typically, her dress threatened splitting open with her cleavage. Instead, she was wearing a black gown that was...plain. Interesting. Her parents probably forced her into a simple dress to show off her new good girl act.

Alexa Blackwood was pretty, even with her natural brown hair dyed blonde. Years ago, she got her nose redone, and it was clear she had a bit of lip filler. But she wasn't ugly by any means, which was a shame since her personality was shit.

"I've heard a lot about your newest boy toy." She completely ignored my earlier question, switching the topic back to me. I didn't say a word at her implying Trevor was my boy toy. He was anything but that.

"Where is he? You've been telling everyone he's coming." She looked around trying to spot him, knowing full well he wasn't here.

"He's running late."

"Mmhmm." The way she said it had me narrowing my eyes at her. Alexa was a snake and anyone with eyes could see it. She might've pretended to be a good girl to get her image back, but she was as vindictive as they came. She was someone who would stab you in the back and not bat an eye.

"Who's husband are you going to sleep with tonight?" I asked, nonchalantly taking a sip of my wine. The cruel part of me revelled in the way she blanch at my words, head snapping in my direction.

Alexa stared at me as if asking how I knew that little bit of information. Little did she know, I knew *a lot* more than I let on. I may not have been active in social circles, but I knew what went on.

"Have a good rest of the night." I sent her a fake smile that said, *"Fuck with me, I dare you."* Letting her freak out on her own, I pushed off the bar and walked away.

Okay, maybe the night wasn't all that bad.

Ignoring people, I headed for the tables lined on one side of the ballroom. The reason why we were all here. The table was filled with different items to bid on for different charities. This was my favorite part about coming to this event.

Every year, I would go through the charities listed and pick one to donate to. I'd sign the sheet as if to bid for the item, but I never put enough to win, not wanting to claim the prizes that went along with the bid. Instead, the next day, I would find the charity and donate anonymously every year choosing a different one to donate to.

What no one but Josie knew was that I had a huge chunk of money in a separate account. Money my parents set aside for me when I turned twenty-one. It was…a lot of money. More than I knew what to do with. I've never wanted any of my parents' money and every time I saw the amount, it was like a slap to the face. So, instead of using it for myself, I used it for charities. What was the point of having it just sit there?

Walking down the line, I came to a pause when a specific one caught my eye. *Toronto's Women Clinic.* With a tight chest, I didn't even hesitate in writing a number down, making the biggest bid so far.

"Tasha." Once more, my name was called, but this one made my back straighten. My luck ran out as I turned around to face my parents.

It had been a bit since I last saw them, close to six months since we sat awkwardly at a dinner table together while barely talking, and when we did, it was all about my parents' law firm.

I kept the surprise off my face as my mother stepped forward and hugged me, followed by my father. I could count on one hand how many times they hugged me over the years. I knew their affection was only because there were thousands of eyes on us. Wouldn't look good on them if they didn't greet their daughter.

"Well, you look…lovely." My mother, Jennifer, looked me up and down, clearly scrutinizing my choice in gowns.

"You do too."

I had always been told I looked like my mother, which was a compliment. Jennifer Davis might've almost been fifty, but she could easily pass off as being in her late thirties. Her blonde hair was cut short and pulled into a tight bun, her cheekbones high and sharp. There was an air of regalness about her that almost made you feel like you were meeting the Queen.

"I see you've been making your rounds," my father, Robert Davis, added. I took note that his dark brown hair had more gray in it than I remembered, as well as his beard. Even with it, my father was the most intimidating man in the room alongside my mother. While I had my mother's blonde hair and face structure, I inherited my father's eyes. Cold, crisp, and gray.

One look from them was enough to get me to behave when I was a kid. And it wasn't just me that shrunk under his gaze. I saw how my parents' employees worked their asses off so they didn't get that look directed at them. My mother was no better.

"I have. I got stuck with the Pattersons for a while."

No sooner had the words left my mouth did silence settle on top of us. It was awkward as hell. On a good day, we didn't know how to speak to one another but everything that happened in the last month made things even worse.

"So, where is this *boyfriend* of yours?" I didn't miss the tone my mother had. The same tone she always inflicted on me when she disapproved of one of my choices.

"He's on his way. He had a game today." I forced myself not to look away from their gaze. When it came to my parents, I always caved. In everyday life, I was the last person to let others walk all over me but when it came to them it was like all my willpower disappeared and I became a little girl again, trying to gain her parents' approval and attention.

I always knew my parents resented me to some degree. They had me at such a young age while trying to balance law school. I was a baby they didn't really want yet kept. They managed, of course, and grew to be successful in their careers, but once they had enough money to hire someone to take care of me, I became someone else's problem.

"So, he plays sports."

I clenched my jaw at the way my father said it. Like playing hockey was the worst profession to have. If you didn't own a successful business or law firm, you were nobody in his eyes.

"He's one of the star players for the Toronto Knights. You know, the biggest hockey team in the league." I defended Trevor. To my dad, he was the biggest scum on the earth because he didn't wear a suit everyday for work.

Trevor might've played hockey, but he was a better man than my father would ever be. A better man than any in this room.

"Showing up an hour late says a lot about a person." My mother sniffed, looking around the room. The grip on my wine glass was so tight I was afraid I'd shatter the thing.

I wasn't going to let it show that Trevor being late hurt. It had been well over an hour since the gala started. With no text or phone call, it was safe to assume he wasn't going to show. My chest squeezed tightly at him not coming to the one thing I truly needed him to be at.

"He's a busy man and is making time to be here for me," I answered through my teeth.

"Hmm."

The three of us stood there in tense silence, letting everyone glimpse the *happy* family together. How wrong that was. Every part of me wanted to turn and hightail it out of there.

As a few more minutes passed, I opened my mouth to make up an excuse to get away, even for just a moment. I was on edge, dreading when they would bring up the topic of the arranged marriage—a conversation I had no intention of having with them, especially not here.

Just as I was about to walk away, I heard the faint sound of whispering. Even my parents stopped, turning to see what the murmurs were about. I watched as heads turned, but I couldn't tell what they were looking at.

Slowly, the crowd seemed to part. Everyone moved to the side just enough for me to finally catch sight of what that had their attention. Well, more like *who* had it. Standing between my parents, I watched with wide eyes as the one person I loved most on this earth appeared.

TREVOR

"Dude, you're going to burn a hole in the plane," Bryton said next to me, watching my knee bounce up and down.

"We'll get there in time, don't worry." Wyatt tried to soothe my nerves but it wasn't helping.

"I'm already going to be ten minutes late." I promised Tasha I would be there for her at her parents' gala, so I had to be there.

"Trust me, she'll be happy you're there, whether you're late or not." Wyatt said.

"I know it's just..." I ran a hand down my face. "This will be the first time I'll meet her parents, and they already want her to marry someone else. What if they convince her to be with this other guy?" Who would have thought me, Trevor Hall, would be so insecure when it came to a girl?

Tasha Davis made me feel emotions I had never imagined. I thought I knew what love was before, but it was nothing compared to the intensity of what I felt for her. With Tasha, it was deeper, more consuming—like she had unlocked a part of me I didn't even know existed. Every glance, every touch, stirred something in me that I couldn't ignore, and it left me wondering how I ever mistook anything else for love.

Every time I was with Tasha, I felt...alive. Like there was a part inside of me I didn't know was missing until I met her. Don't get me wrong, I was happy before I met Tasha. I loved my life. Playing hockey every other day, sleeping around with no commitment, hanging out with my boys—it was a life I was happy with.

The only thing that changed was instead of going out to the bar after a game and hitting on women, I went home with the only girl I had eyes for. There was nothing better than being wrapped around Tasha. I understood why Wyatt and Bryton loved to go home with their girlfriends after a game. I wasn't even ashamed at how obsessed I was with Tasha.

"Are you blind?" Bryton sent me a look like I was crazy. "That girl is so in love with you. Her parents aren't going to get her to change her mind."

I knew he was right. Hell, Tasha flat out said she was never going to do what her parents wanted her to, so I shouldn't have worried. It didn't stop the pit in my stomach, though.

"Who would've guessed Trevor Hall would be all twisted up over a girl?" Fitz, one of my teammates, gave me a shove from behind.

"First Bryton and Wyatt, now our man Trevor. Sad day," another chimed in.

I clenched my jaw as a few others added their own thoughts.

Next to me, Bryton rolled his eyes. When he first got together with Mila, the guys gave him a lot of shit about being tied down with one woman. Same went with Wyatt but he was quick to threaten anyone who said a bad word about Josie.

"The man is pussy whipped." The words barely left Fitz's mouth before I was up and out of my seat. My fist wrapped in his shirt within seconds, yanking him toward me.

"You say another word about my girl, and we are going to have a problem, Fitz. Are we clear?" No one around us dared to get up and separate us. I wasn't going to do anything to him, but if he spoke another word about Tasha, I wouldn't hesitate in kicking his ass. Teammate or not.

"We're good. We're good." Fitz quickly nodded his head, putting his hands out. I kept my grip on him for another moment before letting him go.

Wyatt and Bryton gave me a knowing look. They would have done the same thing if it was Josie or Mila. Most of the men on the team only thought with their dicks. There were a few that had serious girlfriends or wives, but a good chunk only chased puck bunnies. They'd learn that it gets old quickly.

"How are the girls doing?" Coach Barnum asked out of the blue from his spot in front of us. Wyatt shot Bryton and I a confused look before answering.

"Good. Josie is busy planning stuff for the wedding," was Wyatt's reply.

"She already invited me," Coach said, making the three of us raise our eyebrows.

I didn't know what it was about Josie and Mila, but the two wiggled their way onto Coach's soft side. To everyone on the team, he could be a total jackass but as soon as either of them appeared, he would smile and ask them how their days were. I didn't think I'd ever been asked that from him.

Hell, even Tasha somehow got on his good side even though she only met him a few times. I wouldn't say he had a soft spot for all women, though. Sometimes when the puck bunnies sat outside the locker room, Coach would storm outside and demand they move their asses. But our girls were somehow his favorite.

While Wyatt and Coach kept talking about the wedding, I zoned back out. I wished my phone worked this high up in the air so I could text her. Last thing I wanted was for her to think I wasn't going to show.

Trying not to let my nerves get the best of me, I settled back in my seat and waited impatiently for the plane to land.

"WHAT DO you mean we can't get off?" I asked the stewardess in front of me.

"The runway has debris that needs to be cleared before we can pull in and disembark," the stewardess explained.

"Can't you just open the doors now and let us off?" This was a private jet for crying out loud. We shouldn't have even had to wait to get off.

"It's unsafe to get off where we are at. We can't let anyone off until we get to the designated spot." The stewardess was being as nice as she could, but it was not helping my mood.

Instead of being ten minutes late to Tasha's gala, I was now looking at half an hour if I got off right now. Didn't help that the plane took off late. But from what the lady said in front of me, it could take another hour just to get off.

Breathing through my nose, I tried not to blow my shit. This wasn't happening.

"Thank you," Wyatt said politely to the stewardess as she walked back to the front of the plane. "Have you texted Tasha yet?"

"I have, but for some reason, it won't go through. I'll try

again." As soon as the plane had landed, I was up and out of my seat, ready to go. All I could think about was getting off this damn thing and getting to that gala. Even if I had to wear the suit I packed for away games.

Grabbing my phone, I tapped the screen only for it to stay black. I hit the power button, but the only thing that flashed was the dead battery icon.

"You've got to be fucking kidding me." I squeezed my phone in my fist. "Dead battery. Can I try your phones?" I asked Wyatt and Bryton.

They both held up their phones and said, "No signal."

It's okay, Trevor. Doesn't matter if you're late as long as you get there.

"Just think about it. You can make a grand entrance when you do get there," Bryton joked. "Everyone loves a grand entrance."

"Get someone to play a song as you walk in," Wyatt added, causing my lips to twitch. I knew they were trying to make me feel better about the situation, which I appreciated, but it did little to help the growing tension in my body.

For the next twenty minutes, we sat there on the plane. Every minute that passed made me more late and made the pit in my stomach double in size. Tasha was probably thinking I wasn't coming at all and ignoring her.

I never wanted to be someone that Tasha felt she couldn't rely on. She had enough people in her life like that, so I wanted to be the person she could always count on. Be the person she'd always go to when she needed something and knew that, no matter what, I would be there.

I was staring out the plane window when I noticed we were starting to finally move. The pilot's voice came overhead, saying we would be able to get off in the next ten minutes. With that, I had a little bit of hope that I would get to that damn gala before the night was over.

As soon as the plane came to a halt and the stewardess came out to put the door down, I was up and out of my seat.

"Trev." Wyatt got my attention as I reached for my bag overhead. I glanced at him over my shoulder as he held up his phone. "Josie is already here with your suit. I'll get your bag and take it back to your place."

"Josie's here?" was all that left my mouth.

"I texted her a little bit ago when I got a signal. You can change here and head over."

"She brought my suit?" I was repeating what he just said, but Josie being here, waiting for me, threw me off.

"Changing on the tarmac of an airport probably isn't the greatest but it will work." Bryton shrugged. "Mila brought stuff for you to clean up a bit too."

The fact that they both went out of their way to help me get to this event reminded me why they were my best friends. We may not have been blood-related, but they were more of brothers to me than anything.

"We know." Wyatt read my expression as he hit my shoulder and gestured toward the front of the plane. "Josie and Mila are waiting."

With a wide grin, I tapped Wyatt and Bryton's shoulders before hightailing it toward the door of the plane. Thankfully, the rest of my team had enough sense to stay seated. With the plane door finally open, I all but ran off the plane, shouting a quick apology over my shoulder.

I barely stepped off the stairs when I saw Josie and Mila standing off to the side of the tarmac, waiting for me. They waved their arms as I jogged toward them.

"Got your suit right here." The words were out of Josie's mouth before I even reached them. She held up the bag with a bright grin.

"And I got some makeup wipes to clean your face with." Mila added.

I was glad I took a shower before getting on the plane earlier, so I was perfectly fine not going home to take one.

"Thank you." I breathed.

"Let's get you to that gala." Josie declared.

Behind me, I could hear my teammates getting off the plane, but I didn't even care as I stripped out of my sweats and sweatshirt. A few of the guys whistled as I stood there on the tarmac in just my underwear. I flipped the bird over my shoulder as I tugged on my slacks.

When Tasha asked me to be her date last week, I instantly went out the next day to get a new suit. I had a bunch, thanks to hockey, but this wasn't just any party. From what Tasha has told me, it was an event with the richest people in Toronto. A suit I'd worn multiple times wouldn't cut it.

"Tasha is going to kill me for being late," I told the girls as I quickly buttoned up my black dress shirt.

"Maybe not kill you but threaten to chop your balls off, yes." Josie said.

"That doesn't help Jo."

"Hey, you asked." She shrugged.

"And you couldn't have replied with, 'She's just going to be happy you are there?'" I shot her a look.

"That, too."

"Gee, thanks." Josie just shot me a grin.

Shrugging on my suit jacket, I straightened the sleeve as Josie and Mila looked me over.

"How does it look?"

"Here." Mila stepped forward, bending over slightly so she could reach me. She ran her fingers through my hair for a minute before stepping back. "Perfect." I shot her a smile in thanks. These two were really saving my ass.

"Trevor." Josie came forward, reaching up to fix my collar. Despite hearing how fancy this thing was, I left the tie off. Didn't need something strangling me the entire night.

344

"Yeah?"

Josie peered up at me as I towered over her. The smile she wore slipped off her face, and her eyes narrowed.

"If you hurt my best friend. If you do anything to make her unhappy. I won't hesitate in making your life a living hell." As she spoke, her grip on my collar tightened. For such a small person, she could be scary as hell.

"Do you understand?"

I nodded with wide eyes.

"I wouldn't dream of hurting Tasha." The thought of hurting her made me sick to my stomach. Josie stared at me for another moment before she pulled back, her easygoing smile back on her face.

"Good." Using her hands, she wiped at my suit jacket. "Now, you better get going." She acted like she didn't just threaten me two seconds ago. I didn't think she was kidding either.

"Uh, yeah. Okay." Shaking off Josie's threat, I sent them both a thankful smile. "Thank you, guys."

"Anytime. Now go get your girl." Mila gestured over her shoulder to the car parked behind her. Mila and Bryton's Mercedes. Seeing my skepticism, Mila shook her head at me. "Don't worry, we'll get a ride with Wyatt and Jo. Get going." She all but shoved the keys in my hand.

With another thankful smile, I jogged toward the car and slid in. I had a gala to get to.

THE RIDE to the hotel where the event was being held took me longer than I thought. It was like everyone suddenly had somewhere to be, so the traffic was insane. Of course.

By the time I parked in front, I was a good hour and a half late.

Despite my tardiness, the steps to the hotel were lined with reporters. Seeing the car pull up, they all turned and lifted their cameras to see who it was. I was about to enter a room full of people I didn't even know for the woman I loved. Just knowing I was about to see Tasha had me unbuckling my seatbelt and stepping out of the car.

Straightening my suit, I walked around the front as reporters recognized who I was. The flash of cameras instantly surrounded me, along with my name being yelled.

"Trevor Hall!"

"Are you here to support your girlfriend?"

"Are you and Tasha Davis serious?!"

With one hand pressed to the front of my suit, I lifted my other one in half a wave. I politely nodded to the reporters as they snapped picture after picture. This was definitely going to make headlines tomorrow.

I only stopped for a few seconds, letting them all get their pictures, before heading for the doors. I had a girl to get to.

As I made my way into the hotel, I felt the unmistakable sensation of being watched. I was used to the attention, though. Being in the spotlight for hockey, you had to get used to people taking your picture and staring at you as you passed. Plus, none of it mattered when Tasha was so close.

I hadn't seen her in a week. A whole ass week. Yes, we texted, called, and Facetimed but it wasn't the same as actually seeing her. Touching her.

I paused right outside the ballroom to gather myself. I knew just beyond those doors was Tasha. And, of course, her parents. The same parents that wanted to put her in an arranged marriage. Just the thought of it had me clenching my jaw.

I wasn't sure how I was going to be able to control myself

around her parents. Hearing about Tasha's childhood and how they treated her made my blood boil. They treated her like shit, and then expected her to show up acting like the perfect family. Like they weren't using her as some pawn in a game to further their company's success.

There was a lot I wanted to say to them, but I knew Tasha wouldn't appreciate it if I snapped at her parents. Because despite all of that, she still loved them, and I completely understood. Even after everything my own parents did, there was still a part of me that loved them.

If biting my tongue made Tasha happy, then I'd try my hardest not to say something to her parents. But if the *man* they were trying to marry her off to showed his face, I wasn't sure I'd be able to hold back.

Ready to see my girl, I took a deep breath and stepped into the ballroom.

Almost immediately, eyes snapped in my direction. All around me stood well-dressed men and women. Their gazes assessed me, but I paid them no attention, my eyes already searching the crowd looking for the only person I cared about.

Chatter rose around me as people moved to the side and I walked farther into the room. As the crowd parted for me, my eyes finally fell on the girl I was looking for.

My attention flickered to the people standing on either side of Tasha, but they became nonexistent the moment my eyes met Tasha's. My heart stopped and restarted at the sight of her.

She was wearing the most gorgeous dress I'd ever seen. The red dress hugged her waist before flaring down to the floor, a high slit up on side showing her long, toned legs. Legs that I wanted wrapped around my waist.

She was the most beautiful woman in the room. And she was all mine.

33

TASHA

Trevor looked insanely attractive in an all-black suit. I'd never seen him in that style before, but it fit him perfectly. I swear the suit was glued to his body. The jacket fit his upper body so well, hugging his muscular arms. He left the collar open, a tiny bit of his tattoo peeking out. The black slacks showed off those powerful legs.

It had been the longest week of my life. I knew it was healthy for us to have time apart and not spend every waking moment together, but that didn't mean I didn't hate it. Waking up beside Trevor was one of my favorite things.

I had to force myself to stay where I was so I didn't run to him. But with each step toward me, all I wanted to do was launch myself at my boyfriend. Claim him in front of everyone in this room. My parents included.

When he was only a foot away, I lost the little bit of control I had. Not giving a rat's ass about who was watching, I ate the distance between us and grabbed the front of his suit, yanking him down to my level. Even in my six-inch heels, he had to bend over some.

The moment my lips landed on his, all my doubts and worries vanished. When he wasn't answering my texts, my first thought was that something bad happened. But seeing him here in one piece eased all those fears.

The amount of intensity that Trevor kissed me back with let me know he missed me just as much as I did. No matter how bad I wanted to make out with him, it probably wasn't the best time. Pulling back, Trevor softly cupped my cheeks, tilting my head back a little so I could look at him.

"You're here."

"I'm sorry I'm late. I'll explain later, but I'm sorry," Trevor spoke softly.

"I'm just glad you're here." For some reason, tears pricked the corners of my eyes as his thumbs brushed along my cheeks.

"You look absolutely breathtaking, Sunshine." The way his eyes roamed over my face made my body light up. "Can't wait to peel you out of this dress later."

"I look forward to it." The look that passed over his face had my lower belly tightening. Maybe we could leave right now. That thought flew out the window when I heard my mother say my name from behind me.

Trevor sent me an encouraging smile as he grabbed my hand. *It won't be that bad, Tasha.* With a deep breath, I turned and squeezed Trevor's hand, facing my parents.

"Mom, Dad. This is Trevor Hall. Trevor, these are my parents—Robert and Jennifer Davis."

"Nice to meet you." Trevor reached out to shake my parents' hands. The way they hesitated had me gritting my teeth. Trevor didn't seem fazed, though.

"Nice to meet you as well." My father shook his hand, at least looking somewhat friendly. Unlike my mother, who shook his hand like he was going to give her rabies.

"My daughter hasn't told us much about you." My mother noted.

"We've kept our relationship pretty private," Trevor swooped in to say before I could open my mouth. "Neither of us like outside forces trying to get in the way."

I had to fight my hardest to keep the proud smile off my face. His comment might've come off as innocent, but it was clearly a jab at my parents. A jab my mother definitely heard as her eyes narrowed at him.

"Tasha tells us you had a hockey game today, and you still made it here," my father butted in. For the first time, I wanted to reach out and hug my dad for changing the subject.

"I did. We've had games all week in the US, and we just landed a little bit ago."

"I hear your team is fairly good."

"They are the reigning Cup champions. I don't think 'good' is the right word," I interjected.

"Is that all you do? Play hockey?" my mother asked, using the same tone she did with me when she talked about my job. If it wasn't for Trevor's grip on my hand, I was pretty sure I would have snapped out a reply.

"I've also invested in some companies outside of hockey." Along with my parents, my eyebrows raised in surprise. I didn't know that.

"Oh. What companies?" Of course, that got my father's attention.

"Techscape, Medical Platinum, and NonProfits Secure," Trevor listed off. Growing up with parents like mine, I knew exactly what those companies were, and they weren't no small companies, either.

The fact that Trevor was invested in them was impressive. And just showed his net worth rivaled most of the people in this room. I never, and would never, ask Trevor how much money he had, but I knew his hockey contract was one of the biggest in the league. Add in three of the biggest companies in the world... Yeah, he had some money.

I watched him converse with my dad like a pro. Trevor had always been a people person, and watching him talk to my dad while exuding confidence, was attractive as hell. If he was nervous meeting my parents I couldn't tell.

After they talked for a good ten minutes, I finally inter-rupted them. Lacing my arm through his, I shot my parents a polite smile.

"I'm going to take him to get a drink." I wanted a moment away from my parents to talk to Trevor. Before either could say anything, I was tugging Trevor away toward the bar, bypassing the tables all around us.

Eyes followed us as we crossed the floor, the same eyes that hadn't left the two of us since Trevor arrived. I felt smug as hell at the fact that Trevor was hanging off my arm. No one here had a date that rivaled mine.

"If you were a peacock, your feathers would be out."

Peacocks were known for puffing out their feathers when they strutted by for attention. I felt no shame walking past people.

"Sometimes, you have to give the people a little show." I shrugged with a smirk.

"Mhm," Trevor replied with his own smirk.

After we ordered a drink, I turned to face Trevor, still keeping a hand on him. Like I had to keep making sure he was really here.

"I'm glad you made it," I spoke softly.

"I'm incredibly sorry I'm late. The plane took forever to take off, then we couldn't get off the plane because of stuff on the runway. And then my phone died," Trevor rattled off, almost like he thought I would be angry.

"I'm not mad." I stepped closer to him, my hand coming

up to his cheek. "I'm just glad you're okay." My thumb brushed against the spot on his jaw that was smooth to the touch. I had to admit, I already missed the slight stubble. He was definitely going to grow that back.

"You didn't have to come, you know." I would have been hurt, but I would have understood.

"Of course I did. I'll always be here." He leaned his face into my palm. "Couldn't leave you alone with these people. Did you see the lady in the snakeskin dress?" I laughed at the way his eyes widened.

"You haven't seen the lady dressed in the black leather yet."

"What did you drag me into?" He joked.

"You haven't seen anything yet. We don't have to be here too much longer, though. My parents have to make some speeches and then see about the bids."

"Well," Trevor grabbed his beer with one hand and extended his other one to me, "Let's go be the hottest couple in the room."

With a wide grin, I placed my hand in his.

"Lets."

"Save me," Trevor mouthed from across the ballroom. I grinned, completely ignoring the conversation going on around me.

A little bit ago, Trevor got snatched up by Mrs. Hans and dragged around to talk to different people. When I went to try and help, he waved me off, saying he was fine. That was half an hour ago and clearly he was wishing he had taken me up on it. Now, he was stuck talking to strangers about business.

I nodded along to whatever someone was saying beside me, but I kept my eyes on Trevor. I wasn't going to drop him headfirst into the wolves. Although, I found it a bit comical watching him shift on his feet in discomfort. Payback for being late.

After the fifth pleading look he sent my way, I finally relented. Poor guy had been on his own long enough. Opening my mouth to excuse myself, I noticed a figure heading toward my boyfriend.

I stilled, noticing exactly who it was. I watched as Alexa Blackwood walked up to Trevor, smiling. The grip on my glass tightened.

I trusted Trevor. I just didn't trust Alexa. Knowing her, she'd do something that gave the rumor mill something to talk about. Have everyone believe I was just using Trevor for his money, or that I cheated on him, or that he cheated on me with her. Whatever it was, it'd be so far from the truth.

Every part of me screamed to go over there, but I stayed where I was. Trevor could handle himself. But the moment she tried something, you could bet your ass I would be right there.

People were talking all around, but I didn't hear a single word. My eyes were glued to the girl who was now introducing herself to my boyfriend. I watched as she smiled up at him with her 'fake good girl' smile and touched his arm.

I could see Trevor's polite smile as he greeted her back, but I could tell he was only saying hello to be nice. Alexa kept talking, keeping that annoying ass smile on her face as she did. I wanted nothing more than to walk over there and slap it off her face.

When Trevor said something, Alexa threw her head back, laughing loudly and making a few heads turn to look at the pair. I clenched my wine glass tighter as my eyes narrowed. I doubted whatever he said was that funny.

Red was clouding my vision the longer the two spoke. I didn't want to cause a scene, but if the bitch put another hand on my man, I was going to lose my shit. When I saw Alexa step closer to Trevor, gripping his bicep, the control I had on myself snapped.

On the outside, I was calm as I excused myself from the group around me. I quickly drank the rest of my wine and handed it to a waiter as I slowly walked toward Trevor and Alexa.

My heels clicked on the marble as jealousy flared in my chest. Trevor was *mine.* Mine to touch, to kiss, to have. Apparently, someone didn't get the message earlier but they would now.

I'd never felt this kind of jealousy before, especially not with a guy. Yes, seeing someone flirt with a past boyfriend didn't sit well. Or seeing them after we broke up with someone else. But it was never like this. Like molten rage under my skin.

As I neared the pair, Trevor's eyes landed on me over Alexa's head. I didn't miss the look of relief on his face. It did little to calm the hurricane brewing inside of me. I wanted to walk up to Alexa and shove her, but I suppressed the urge.

"There you are," I spoke as I walked around Alexa, going straight to Trevor's side and lacing my arm through his. I looked up at his face, but from the corner of my eye, I caught Alexa's smile vanish, her eyes narrowed at me.

"Oh, I see you two have met." I looked at Alexa with the fakest smile I could muster. I hoped she could see the snarl resting underneath.

"Alexa was just telling me how you two are friends," Trevor supplied.

"Oh really?"

354

"'Tasha and I go way back." Alexa grinned at Trevor. "We were thick as thieves back in the day."

I didn't like the way she was looking at Trevor. Like she was picturing what he looked like underneath his suit. Unfortunately for her, she'd never know. What I was about to say was a bitch move, but I couldn't stand being next to Alexa any longer.

"We were. Right before you snuck into my phone and shared half naked pictures of myself to the entire school." I said it so casually, like I was talking about the weather. "Oh, and before you slept with my boyfriend." The first boy I ever truly liked.

Alexa slept over at my house that night. When I went to go shower, she grabbed my phone and went through my private pictures. Pictures I took in the safety of my bedroom. Some for my boyfriend at the time, and some just because I felt sexy in them. Somehow, she managed to send them to herself and cover up that she did so.

It wasn't until a week later when I walked into school, every single person whispering while staring at me, that I learned Alexa paid someone to send my pictures to everyone, and I mean *everyone*, along with photos of her with my boyfriend, the two sneaking around behind my back for months.

I had to walk the halls of school with everyone laughing, whispering, and judging me while Alexa stood there grinning with her arm around my boyfriend. Acting like she won some huge prize.

There was almost nothing worse than having someone who you thought was your best friend ruin your life. Someone you trusted who went behind your back and did something so disgusting.

All I wanted to do was run home and cry as everything in my life had been turned upside down. I lost my boyfriend, who I really thought loved me, and lost someone who I thought was my best friend.

Instead of giving Alexa what she wanted all those years ago, seeing me cry right there in the middle of the hallway, I did the exact opposite. I did exactly what my mother had taught me for years. I straightened my back, ignored everyone around me, and walked to class like nothing was wrong. Like I wasn't breaking on the inside. In the end, my indifference to it pissed Alexa off even more. I gained new friends out of which, though, which was probably the only blessing in the entire situation.

"Such close friends." My voice dripped with honey. I could feel Trevor's eyes on me as I narrowed mine at Alexa. I took a tiny step toward her as she stumbled back one. "Don't even think about touching what's mine. I have no problem ruining your life like you did mine all those years ago. Just a simple click of a button would have everyone in here knowing about your affairs."

Once more, Alexa's face paled at my words. There really was something wrong with me as I soaked up the expression on her face. It would be so easy to let everyone here know that she was sleeping with half of these women's husbands. And it probably would feel just as great.

Giving her one last warning look, I tugged on Trevor's arm, leading us away from Alexa Blackwood. If she was smart she'd leave Trevor and me the hell alone.

"Well, that was..." Trevor trailed off as we walked across the marble floor, going over to stand near a wall away from everyone.

"She's lucky I didn't do anything more for touching you," I muttered.

"Jealousy looks stunning on you, Sunshine," Trevor leaned down and whispered in my ear.

Tilting my head back slightly, I looked up at him.

"No one touches what's mine. Especially not her." I bared my teeth.

Trevor's hand came up and grabbed the side of my neck, thumb resting below my chin. Bending slightly, his lips hovered over mine. "I'm all yours, baby. Forever."

Forever wasn't long enough to be with Trevor Hall.

34

TASHA

"Thank you all for coming to our annual charity gala," my father spoke through the microphone from his spot on the makeshift stage.

Everyone was seated at their tables as my parents finally got the gala started. After my father's speech, hopefully they'd get on with the items people bid on so Trevor and I could leave. It was like we'd already been there for a hundred years.

A gentle squeeze on my knee had me looking over at Trevor. He sent me a soft smile that had my insides melting. I swear, every time I looked at him, I fell even more in love. How could I not when he was sitting next to me, looking like a Greek god in that suit?

While my father was busy talking on stage, I was busy staring at my boyfriend. From the moment I met Trevor, I knew he was incredibly attractive. I'd have been blind not to notice how good-looking he was—there was a reason he was named one of the hottest hockey players. But getting to know him on a deeper level, he became even more irresistible.

No one else saw the sides that I did. Saw the caring, affectionate, goofy guy who I fell head over heels for. Trevor was the guy that would be there for someone he loved no matter what. Just like tonight.

"What?" Trevor whispered, catching my eyes.

"Just looking." My chin was propped up on my palm as I stared at him, completely unashamed. He was mine to look at as long as I wanted.

The corner of his lip curled up as he ran his fingertips up and down my bare thigh. I heard nothing of my father's speech but it didn't matter. It was always the same one, the same people he thanked for coming. I was just here to look pretty and be silent.

For the next ten minutes, we sat there listening to the boring ass speech. The only thing keeping my attention was Trevor's fingers on my leg. He wasn't touching me in any sexual way but just a simple touch from him was enough to spread heat through my body.

"Now, onto the lucky bidders of the night!" my father announced, taking a step back so my mother could take the microphone.

"Bid on anything tonight?" Trevor leaned in to whisper, his breath fanning against my neck.

"Maybe." I sent him a teasing grin. I wasn't sure I'd win, but I didn't bid for the prize. I just wanted the money to go somewhere needed.

My mother started listing off the items and the highest bidders, polite claps echoed around the ballroom. Some of the bids were close to one hundred thousand dollars. To most people in attendance that was pocket change. Something they could write off at the end of the year.

"Now the trip to Ireland," my mother spoke with fake enthusiasm. "The money for this prize will be given to the Toronto's Women Clinic. The highest bid went to..." Her eyebrows seemed to scrunch before reading off the name. "My daughter, Tasha Davis."

I froze in my seat. I wasn't expecting to be the highest bidder. I typically bid just low enough that someone else would've wanted to bid higher than me. When it came to people's egos, they always wanted to be the top bidder. I had always been outbid before.

Everyone around me clapped, even my own parents who looked at me with weird expressions. Beside me, Trevor also clapped, sending me a wide smile. Awkwardly, I smiled and dipped my head.

"So you did bid on something." Trevor smirked once my mother started talking again.

"I wasn't expecting to win," I muttered. I was more than happy to fly under the radar when it came to donating. I didn't want the recognition.

"It's really sweet of you to donate, though," Trevor said softly. I met his gaze as he gently squeezed my thigh. "I'm proud of you."

His words made my chest tighten. Leaning forward, he placed a soft kiss on my forehead. Closing my eyes, I leaned into him.

"Thank you," I whispered so softly I wasn't sure he even heard me.

"I do hope you plan on taking me to Ireland with you."

"I was thinking of taking my other boyfriend. Sorry."

"Other boyfriend, huh?" Trevor pulled back, raising an eyebrow.

"Yep. He's tall, dark, and handsome."

"More handsome than me?"

I tilted my head to the side as I looked him over. "I mean...." The hand on my knee squeezed, making me jerk forward with a gasp. He leaned forward so his mouth was right next to my ear.

"Does he make you scream like I can?" Those fingers started moving up my leg, teasing ever so slightly.

"I... I..." All thoughts flew from my mind as his breath tickled my neck and his fingers neared the high slit on my dress. He was inches away from the lacey thong I was wearing.

"Does he make your pussy wet just by touching you?"

Trevor's fingers teased the skin on my thighs, goose-bumps following in their wake. This was the last place he should be teasing me. Our table was right near the front, surrounded by people my parents knew. Thank God our table was empty, just the two of us sitting there. If anyone were to look closely, they would notice his hand was up higher on my thigh than socially acceptable.

But the thought of Trevor touching me here just made my thong wetter. The dirty thoughts swirling in my head were not helping one bit. Damn Trevor for turning me on so easily.

"Sunshine." He prompted me to say something, but when the tips of his fingers dipped between my thighs, almost touching my thong, I lost my train of thought. "Uh-huh, that's what I thought."

He withdrew his fingers, bringing his hand back to my knee. With a smirk on his face, he turned back to the stage, leaving me sitting there severely turned on. He was such a fucking tease. I both hated and loved it.

Calming myself down, I tried to pay attention but it didn't help that all I could think about was getting Trevor back home and showing him just how much I missed him. Almost like Trevor could tell what I was thinking, he squeezed my thigh and whispered under his breath.

"Later, baby."

Later was too long. But I sighed, knowing nothing could

happen while we were here. We just had to make it through a few more hours.

About twenty minutes later, everyone who bid was announced as my parents thanked everyone for coming again. There would be dinner and more talking before Trevor and I could leave. As my parents walked off the stage and headed back to our table, I straightened my posture.

After they met Trevor, I'd done my best to avoid them. They had yet to bring up the arranged marriage, and I just knew they were waiting for the right time to do so. No doubt bringing it up in front of Trevor and being absolute assholes about it.

"Didn't know you placed a bid, Tasha," my father said the moment he sat down. I couldn't stop the slice of pain at the fact they never noticed my bidding before. That's how little they noticed me.

"I bid every year," I said, forcing myself to meet my parents' gaze.

"Hmm," was all my father said in response.

The catering staff came out then, placing plates in front of us. My parents didn't skimp on anything, especially the food. Like what Josie told Mila, the catering at the gala was top-notch. One year they hired a Michelin Star chef.

"So, Trevor," my mother spoke after a few minutes of silence. The way she said his name had my head snapping my gaze in her direction. I didn't like the way she was looking at him, like she was about to interrogate him. "What was your childhood like?"

I narrowed my eyes at her question. What the hell was she getting at?

"It was a bit rough, but I don't let the past define me," Trevor answered. This time, it was me putting my hand on his thigh and squeezing softly.

"Your parents had drug problems, didn't they?" My mother said it so casually as she took a bite of her food.

"Mom!" I hissed. How the hell did she even know that? But also, no matter where she pulled that information from, it also wasn't in her place to ask.

"What? A mother can't ask her daughter's boyfriend about his life?"

"You can't ask something so personal!" I was beyond appalled.

"It's okay." Trevor placed his hand on mine. "Yes, they did." He met my mother's gaze head-on. The look on his face dared my mother to say more on the subject. Something in my stomach told me this was going to go south. My mother hated being challenged. It brought out her lawyer side. A side that never lost if she could help it.

"And you supply their drug habit?"

"No, I do not," Trevor replied through clenched teeth. "My parents are no longer in my life."

"Hmm, interesting."

I glared at my mother. "What are you trying to accomplish?" I spoke before Trevor could. I could feel the tension radiating off him as Trevor sat beside me. His shoulders were tensed, back stiff as a board.

"I'm not trying to accomplish anything. I just find it interesting that a man who grew up penniless with drug addicts as parents is suddenly dating my daughter, who is here at our gala where very influential people are in attendance."

Did she think Trevor is some lowlife who's trying to worm his way into my life and *their* money? My mother definitely saw Trevor as nothing more than a pest. Unsuitable. My vision went red. My hands left Trevor's leg to grab the side of the table.

"Are you implying Trevor is using me to get *your* money?" I spat.

363

"Why else would he be here with you?" Her words were a blow to my stomach. I looked over at my father to see his reaction, but he just sat there stoned-faced waiting for my response.

Neither of them could even fathom that Trevor wanted to be with me because he loved me, not because he wanted my money or my status. They believed that was the only reason he was here. That I was only useful because of who my parents were.

"You can't possibly believe that he's here just because he loves me?" My voice came out higher pitched as I tried to hide the hurt at what they were implying.

"Honey, be reasonable." The condescending tone she had was enough to send me over the edge.

"Trevor has more money than you two combined," I hissed. I watched as my father glanced over at something, his attention focused elsewhere. Like he couldn't be bothered.

"Hon, look, they're finally here." My mouth snapped shut as my mother also stood up, plastering on a fake smile while looking at someone off to the side of us. Our conversation was discarded. Like it was a simple conversation about the weather that could easily be brushed aside.

It took everything inside of me not to stand up and tell them exactly how I felt. To yell at them, regardless of who was watching. To ask why they treated me the way they did. All of that was at the tip of my tongue but as soon as the three people my parents were waiting for came into view, I froze.

All the fire inside of me died right then and there. My entire body froze and my mind went into lockdown. I barely felt Trevor touching my arm and whispering to me, too focused on the one person standing in front of me.

Standing there in a tailored suit, his blond hair neatly styled and his face clean-shaven, I watched as he smiled and

364

shook my parents' hands without a care in the world. I already knew what the color of those eyes would be when he finally turned to face me.

All the air left my body as I came face to face with the guy who assaulted me.

The ground fell out from under me. That night in the club it was dark, but I would never forget the face of the man who pulled me into a dark corner and touched me without my consent. The face of the person who gave me nightmares and made it so I didn't feel comfortable alone out in public.

It was him.

"Victoria and Chaplin, this is my daughter Tasha. Tasha, this is Mr. and Mrs. Brown's son, Daniel," my father introduced the three. "We were telling you about them the other day."

It took a second for his words to sink in, but when they did, I felt like I was going to throw up. Daniel Brown. Finally a name to the face that haunted me for the last year. But that wasn't the part that made stomach acid slide up the back of my throat.

The guy who assaulted me was also the guy my parents wanted me to marry.

This couldn't be happening. I stood up, the chair scraping harshly against the floor, but the ringing in my ears drowned out everything else. My vision tunneled as I watched Daniel step toward me. The smile on his face seemed easygoing. Like he had no clue it was me. Was I just a faceless girl to him in that club? Just some piece of meat to grab and fondle and then forget about? Was I one of the many?

All those thoughts made bile rise up in my throat. I didn't think he remembered what he did to me. Yet there I was, still messed up and broken up about it.

As Daniel reached his hand out for me to shake, I took a step back. I didn't make it far as my back crashed into something hard. Hands landed on my hips but all I could see in that moment was *that* night.

The hands on my hips were Daniel's. The chest pressed against my back was his as he pushed me into the corner. I was vaguely aware of my body trembling and my head shaking.

Daniel looked at me, confused, as his hand hovered between us. I looked at it like it was going to attack me. It already had once.

"Sunshine," a voice whispered in my ear. I shook my head again. "Tasha." This time, it came out firmer. The hands on my waist gripped me tighter before turning me around.

Slowly, like I was stuck underwater, I moved my eyes up the dark suit to the face of the person holding me. My brain lagged behind and made it take longer for me to recognize Trevor.

"Sunshine." The nickname met my ears, working through the fog surrounding me. Trevor brought his hands up and cradled my cheeks. "What's wrong?"

From the anxious expression on his face, my reaction scared him.

"I… I…" I tried to form words, but nothing seemed to want to come out. Again, my head shook, trying to process everything.

Behind me, I could hear my parents saying something. Probably making up some excuse as to why I was freaking out, having no clue the real reason and probably not caring, either.

When Trevor squeezed my cheeks, I brought my attention back to him.

"Baby, I need you to tell me what's wrong." His green eyes went back and forth between mine, worry filling them. "Can you do that for me?"

I nodded, trying to shut everything and everyone else out. It was just Trevor and me. Nothing was going to happen.

Remembering Daniel was standing behind me, I stepped closer to Trevor.

"I…" I wetted my lips as I tried again. "He did it." The words came out so soft, but I knew Trevor heard me as his eyebrows curved down. I had to say the words before the courage left me.

"He's the one who touched me." I couldn't stop my voice from coming out shaky and in a whimper. I never thought I'd see the guy again. Toronto was huge, so there was a good chance I'd never come face to face with my attacker again. Yet, here he was.

He was the son of the man who wanted to merge with my parents. The son they all wanted me to marry regardless of how I felt about the situation. I couldn't even begin to process it all.

Of course my parents didn't know about what happened. I couldn't tell them. I did try. Once. Right before I went to the beach house in Florida. But as soon as I started to say something, my parents hung up for some work emergency. I knew then I couldn't ever tell them. *Wouldn't* ever tell them.

I never once imagined this would be happening.

Trevor's eyes flashed, like a fire had just woken inside of him. I could feel the tension steadily building in his body, every muscle tightening with each passing second. His hands were still cupping my cheeks gently, but I could see the hurricane building inside of him.

I knew then that my words were about to set off a storm that couldn't be contained. I was about to see a side of Trevor I'd never seen before.

"You did so good, baby." His words were soft as he pressed a kiss to my forehead. I leaned into him, hands fisted in his shirt.

"Can we... I want..." I knew I wasn't making any sense. "Can we go home?" I whispered.

"Of course." He spoke against my forehead. "But I need to do one thing first, okay?"

I knew what he was about to do. What it would cause, yet I found myself nodding, completely understanding and supporting what was about to happen.

With another kiss to the forehead, Trevor let me go, gently moving me off to the side. My arms came around my middle as if I could hold in all the emotions running through my body. In front of me, Trevor rolled his neck and shoulders before stepping up to Daniel.

Trevor moving caught everyone's attention. My parents, Mr. and Mrs. Brown, and Daniel's, all looked at Trevor, and their conversation halted.

"Hey, man. You're Trevor Hall, right?" Daniel greeted as Trevor stopped inches from him.

Trevor didn't say a single word. I could tell his silence unnerved Daniel as he went to take a step backward. Before he could, Trevor's arm snapped out and hit him square in the cheek. The sound rang out across the ballroom as Daniel's head whipped to the side.

Trevor gave him enough time to right himself and face him before he launched himself at Daniel.

With one hand gripping the front of Daniel's suit, Trevor kept him upright as he punched him over and over again. Shouts erupted around us as my father and Daniel's ran forward to help, trying to pry Trevor off of him. They didn't realize Trevor was pure muscle. They also didn't realize he knew how to fight.

Along with Mr. Brown and my father, a few security guards headed in our direction. The whole time I stood there watching silently, not moving an inch. Daniel's mother,

Victoria, was off to the side with my mother, hand pressed to her mouth. My own mother looked at the situation with wide eyes and a pale face. Yet, through it all, I said nothing.

Trevor landed one more punch on Daniel before stepping back. I could tell he was saying something, but I couldn't hear it over the roaring in my ears. When Trevor glanced at me over his shoulder, I saw the wild look on his face.

Noticed the way he was breathing heavily, hands clenched at his sides, eyes blazing. He looked like an avenging god. *My* avenging god.

A couple of security guards went to grab Trevor, but he shrugged their hands off, glaring at them with such intensity they stepped back. Ignoring everyone else, he stalked toward me until his chest was inches from mine, hands coming back up to cup my cheeks.

"You okay?"

The intensity in his eyes had my blood igniting. His knuckles were cracked and bleeding, but he didn't seem to care as he made sure I was okay.

At that moment, I was more than fine. The man in front of me just did what no one else ever had. *He defended me. He protected me. He loved me.*

"I'm okay."

Trevor kissed my nose before stepping to the side.

"You attacked my son!" Mr. Brown yelled, coming at us. He halted when Trevor took a threatening step toward him.

"Your *son,*" Trevor spat, "deserves more than he got."

"I will have you arrested!" Mr. Brown's face turned an ugly shade of purple.

The idea of Trevor in handcuffs had me stepping forward, finally finding my voice. I glared at Mr. Brown as his son laid on the ground groaning, his mother kneeling next to him.

"*I* should have your son arrested." The voice that came out of my mouth didn't belong to me. It came out cold and clear. I sounded like my mother at that moment. It was like seeing Trevor defend me ignited a fire in me. "Your *son* sexually assaulted me a year ago."

I couldn't believe I was saying this in front of everyone. In front of my parents.

"He touched me without my consent, and I'd be more than happy to throw his ass in jail."

Feeling all my anger, hurt, and disgust well inside of me, I sneered at the pathetic people in front of me. My parents just stood there staring at me, like I hadn't just said I was sexually assaulted. It was like the words didn't even register in their heads.

"If you even think about going after my boyfriend, I won't hesitate in making sure your son spends the rest of his life behind bars. I am my parent's daughter, after all." The only thing my parents ever taught me was to hold my cards close to my chest until I needed to show them. None of them, my parents included, knew just what I'd do to protect Trevor.

Mr. Brown stayed silent, finally learning to shut his mouth, as he continued glaring at me but I felt nothing, the fire inside of me extinguishing with each passing second.

I wanted to go home. Wanted to leave this godforsaken gala. Like he could read my mind, Trevor wrapped his arm around my waist and tugged me close.

Neither of us said another word as we turned to leave, the ballroom silent. I dared a glance over my shoulder at my parents one last time. I wasn't sure what I was expecting. Maybe some sort of remorse or shame. Something. But I should have known better because all I got in return were blank faces.

That was all it took. I knew with clarity that I was done.

Done trying to be the daughter they wanted. Done

begging for their love and acceptance. Done being their daughter.

Feeling like my heart was being ripped into pieces, I held onto Trevor as we left.

35

TASHA

"Are you okay?" Trevor asked once we were in his car. The moment we stepped out of the hotel we were swarmed with paparazzi, the cameras clicking, people yelling our names and throwing questions at us. Trevor shielded me from most of them and quickly ushered us into the car.

"Honestly, no." I didn't have it in me to lie.

I just felt...tired. So much happened that I was having a hard time processing it. My parents, the guy who assaulted me, Trevor protecting my honor. It was all a bit much.

I could feel myself wanting to shut down. To block everything and everyone out, just like I did when Daniel touched me in that club. But the hand on my knee kept me grounded. Just having Trevor close was calming the wave of emotions that threatened to drown me.

"It's going to be okay."

I barely noticed that Trevor was driving in the direction of his place instead of mine. In my head, all I could replay was seeing the set of eyes that had haunted me for a good year. Seeing the lack of emotions on my parents' faces. There had been nothing there when I accused Daniel.

I think that was the worst part. The two people who were supposed to love me no matter what didn't care that their daughter was assaulted. Didn't care enough to speak up.

As soon as Trevor parked in front of his house, I felt my shoulders relax a little. His place was exactly where I wanted to be. It took me a minute to get out of the car with my dress. I was in such a daze getting in, I wasn't even sure how I managed to fit in the front seat with it.

Trevor gently took my hand and led me up to the door, unlocking it with a quick flip, the comforting smell of citrus and woods wrapping around me. I wanted to bottle up that smell and take it with me everywhere.

Catching sight of Trevor's bags near the door, I remembered he hadn't even been home since he landed. Felt like a lifetime since I first saw him at the gala.

"You need to unpack. You can't leave this here." Reaching down, I grabbed one bag, grunting from the weight of it.

I started toward his bedroom, practically dragging it alongside me. He needed to put his stuff away. It wasn't fair he hadn't been home in a week and had to immediately come to my rescue. These bags need to be emptied.

"Sunshine."

I ignored him and kept walking. I knew what I was doing. I was deflecting. I was putting all my emotions into something else. Something that didn't involve myself and my traumas.

"It can wait till tomorrow," Trevor said, following behind me.

"No, it needs to be done now. You can also start your laundry." Not caring that it was almost eleven o'clock at night, I kept walking.

If I distracted myself enough, it would be like nothing happened. I could shove it all down and forget it ever happened. Yep, that was what I was going to do. Just pretend it didn't happen.

I could feel myself starting to breathe heavily. The sides of my vision darkened as I tried to heave Trevor's bag onto the bed. When it wouldn't move an inch, I gritted my teeth and tried again. Tears pricked the corners of my eyes as I tried one last time before letting out a yell.

"Stupid fucking bag." All the emotions I'd been trying to hold back came crashing down. Tears blurred my vision as I kicked Trevor's bag.

"Tasha."

Trevor came up behind me as a loud sob escaped my lips.

"Baby." Trevor's voice was tender as he gently spun me around to face him, wrapping his arms around my shoulders and tugging me into his chest. I clung to his shirt as I sobbed.

Trevor held me the entire time, softly rubbing my back. He didn't bother whispering that it would be okay because that was the last thing I wanted to hear right now.

For the first time in a long time, I let myself cry. I'd bottled up so much, never fully letting myself feel it all. Even as a kid, I shoved it all down. Everything my parents said and did. What other kids at school said to me. Even after what happened at the club, I just convinced myself I was okay.

I was far from it. I'd always just been good at hiding it.

"They didn't care." My voice came out muffled against his shirt. Saying those words out loud made it feel like my heart was going to crumble. "They just stood there." I wasn't sure what I was expecting, but I guessed a part of me wanted my parents to say something. To ask if I was okay.

"I know," Trevor whispered above me.

We stood there for who knew how long before my sobs subsided. I still clung to Trevor, seeking the comfort only he could give.

"I didn't expect to see him either." I whispered.

374

Daniel, being my assaulter, was the last thing I expected. I always thought I wouldn't be able to put a name to the face, but then there he was wearing a smirk, clearly uncaring of what he did and unknowing of who I was. Of course he'd be the type my parents wanted me to marry. Not caring to know who he was as a person, yet looked down at Trevor.

Trevor, who was ten times the man anyone in that room was. The type of man who beat the shit out of Daniel regardless of what could happen. Who was standing here holding me in the middle of his bedroom while I broke down. He was the man I wanted. The man I always dreamed of having but never believed I could.

"I'm not sorry for beating the shit out of him," Trevor spoke into my hair.

"Never be sorry." I lifted my head off his chest, meeting his eyes. "I will never be mad at you for defending me."

"Should have hit him harder." His words forced a rough laugh out of me.

"Pretty sure his nose is broken." A sick part of me found pleasure in that. I hoped Trevor broke his nose and bruised his face so badly it wouldn't heal for months. While it wouldn't make up for what he did to me, at least he'd be in pain.

Remembering that Trevor's knuckles were bleeding, I untangled myself from his hold. Grabbing his arm, I gently led him toward the bathroom to get him cleaned up. Pushing him to sit on the toilet, I went to search for the first aid kit.

The two of us were quiet as I pulled out hydrogen peroxide. My dress swished along the ground and around my ankles, my heels clicking loudly on the bathroom tile. I bet we were a sight to see. Still dressed to the nines, my face streaked with mascara, Trevor's hands bloody and swollen.

Trevor's eyes stayed on me as I grabbed one of his hands, getting to work on cleaning up the blood.

"Do you want to talk about it?" he spoke after a moment. I caught my bottom lip between my teeth as I worked. I knew it wasn't healthy keeping everything in. Hell, I was a therapist and here I was doing the exact thing I told my patients not to.

The only person I'd ever let myself be real around was Josie. She knew all the sides of me, the good and the bad. She was always that one person I could go to with everything. There had never been anyone else.

But here was Trevor, looking up at me with such love and patience. He wouldn't ever judge me and if I decided not to talk about it, he wouldn't be mad. I knew I could share every-thing going on inside me but not tonight. Tonight, I wanted to forget.

"No, not right now," I murmured, finishing up his hands. Putting the dirty cotton balls on the counter, Trevor cupped the back of my thighs.

"Just know that if you ever do want to talk about it, I'm here." The look in those eyes made my knees weak. "I will *always* be here."

Bringing my hands up, I ran them through his hair, softly tugging at the strands. His hands tightened around my thighs over my dress.

"Thank you. I love you."

Never thought I'd come to have such strong feelings for the man sitting in front of me. Falling in love was not the plan yet I fell headfirst.

"I love you too." Leaning forward, Trevor pressed his forehead into my stomach, holding me to him. My heart felt like it was going to burst, thundering in my chest as we stood there, the intensity of the moment nearly overwhelming.

"Take me to bed," I whispered.

Trevor pulled back to look up at me, eyebrows creased.

"Sunshine—" he started, but I shook my head.

"I want to. I need... I need you."

I needed Trevor to wash away tonight. To replace the memory of *that* night. I needed it more than I needed anything else.

"Please."

Trevor hesitated, looking into my eyes as if to be sure. Upon finding it, Trevor slowly stood up to this full height, his jaw clenching and those gorgeous green eyes locked onto mine. When his hands moved to grip my ass tightly, I bit my bottom lip.

"I did say I was going to peel you out of this dress."

"Can't back out of your promises."

He dipped his head to brush his lips against mine. "Never."

Needing out of this dress immediately, I forced myself out of his hold. With a curl of my finger, I beckoned Trevor to follow me as I stepped into the bedroom. Trevor prowled after me, eyes raking over my dress as if picturing me out of it. Little did he know there wasn't much underneath.

Excitement and anticipation grew in my belly as he advanced on me. This was *exactly* what I needed. Trevor only made it right outside the bathroom before crossing his arms across his chest and leaning against the door frame. He made no move to come take my dress off like he said he would.

"I thought *you* were going to take it off of me."

Trevor shook his head. "Not tonight. Tonight, you are going to take control."

My eyebrows raised at his words. *Me* take control?

"If you want anything, you're going to take it. I won't do anything unless you tell me to."

I knew what he was doing. He was giving me back control after what happened tonight. Showing me that everything would always be on my terms. I hadn't realized that was exactly what I needed. I needed to take back control.

I loved dominant Trevor. I preferred it, but tonight, he was right. Straightening my spine, I leveled a look at Trevor, hoping I looked more intimidating than I felt.

"Take my dress off." While it was a command, it came out more as a question. Trevor's lip quirked up, but he came forward to do as I said.

His hands landed on my hips and slowly trailed upward, fingers searching for the zipper. I held my breath as his fingertips barely brushed against the bare skin of my back. His eyes never once left mine as he gently tugged the zipper down, loosening the dress to the point that I had to hold the front or it would fall.

As soon as the zipper was down, Trevor stepped back, hands falling to his sides. Feeling a sense of power, I dropped my dress. The fabric pooled around my feet, leaving me bare aside from my red lace thong. Trevor's gaze moved from my breasts down to my panties in one long sweep. His jaw clenched, and I could tell he was trying his best to control the urge to touch me.

Knowing he couldn't touch me until I said, I smirked.

"Take off my heels." I pointed to the ground in front of me. Trevor didn't hesitate in moving to his knees. He peered up at me, a devilish look on his face. The sight of him on his knees, looking up at me, made my knees wobble.

A man as powerful and dominating purposely on his knees just for me was erotic as hell. *Fuck, he was sexy.*

I lifted up one foot and placed my hands on his shoulders. I watched as Trevor cupped my ankle, those skilled fingers unclasping the strap on my heels. A shiver ran up my spine at the feel of him stroking the sensitive skin.

He pulled the heel off before leaning forward and placing a soft kiss on my thigh. Tapping the back of my calf, he signaled for me to lift my other leg. Once more, he cupped my ankle and got to work.

Never in my life had I seen something so captivating. I'd never had anyone remove my heels for me before, but the way it felt, I certainly wouldn't mind if it became a regular thing.

Trevor gazed up at me, hands now on the back of my thighs, fingertips barely grazing the bottom of my ass. My hands had a mind of their own as they moved up his shoulders to run through his hair. The strands were so silky, I was jealous. What conditioner did he use?

Trevor kneeled there patiently, waiting for me to tell him what to do next. I was half tempted to tease him by lying on the bed, not letting him touch me while I touched myself, but I was too impatient.

"Take off my thong, please." I didn't mean to add the please at the end, trying to be dominating, but I was slowly losing my grasp on it. Trevor chuckled at my attempt as he grabbed the sides of my underwear and pulled them down in one motion.

"You'll be wearing these again," he whispered, flinging the pair off to the side.

With his head inches from my core, I gripped his head tighter and brought his face toward the place where I needed attention. My legs separated as my hips tilted forward.

"Tell me what you want me to do," Trevor spoke, stopping right above where I wanted him.

"Trevor," I groaned.

"Words, Sunshine."

"Lick my pussy."

"Your wish is my command." The moment his tongue touched my core, I was done. My head fell back onto my shoulders as a small moan left my lips. Using his hands, Trevor grabbed my ass and brought me even closer to his mouth.

All it took was a few swipes of his tongue to turn me into

a puddle. I gripped his hair in tight fists, and each time I tugged, Trevor moaned against me.

He ate me like a starved man. His tongue speared me and then moved up to my clit in a circle. Each moan from his mouth vibrated against me, making it that more intense. I couldn't stop my hips from grinding down on his tongue.

If it wasn't for his grip on my ass, I would have fallen back on the bed as I got closer to coming undone. Each swipe of his tongue brought me that much closer. I knew it wouldn't take me long to finish. I'd gone a week without him. It was crazy how fast you got used to waking up to someone between your legs.

"Right there," I moaned loudly, riding his face. I looked down at Trevor, our eyes clashing. He looked up at me with a gleam in his eyes. The sight of his head buried between my legs while fully clothed was enough to make me come.

I came with a shout, legs shaking, eyes rolling back. Trevor moaned, picking up his pace, prolonging my climax. Right when I thought I was going to collapse back onto the bed, Trevor pulled back, his face slick and shiny. The sight should have embarrassed me but all it did was turn me on even more.

"I could listen to you come for the rest of my life." His praise kicked my heart into overdrive.

"I need you." That was all I could get out, my mind a jumbled mess.

Trevor slowly stood up, towering over me as his hands came up to pluck my hardened nipples.

"Where do you need me, baby?"

"I… I…" My brain wasn't working properly, the growing need deep in my belly almost becoming too much. I needed him inside of me.

"Yes?"

"Trevvvv," I groaned already over being in control. I just needed him to take what he wanted.

"I need to hear you say what you want from me." His voice was so husky and filled with need.

"I need you to fuck me. I need you to take control." I didn't care how needy the words sounded coming from my lips.

"Are you sure?" I could see Trevor's control close to snapping.

"Please," I begged. His fingers rolled over my nipples, making my breath hitch in my throat. My core pulsed between my legs.

"I'm going to touch every part of you and erase every bad memory you have." Trevor's green eyes glared into mine, not letting me look away. "You'll only ever think of me when I'm done with you."

I knew he meant every word.

"Is that clear?" Those fingers tightened just a tad bit more, making me go up onto my toes with a hiss.

"Yes."

"Good girl."

He grabbed me behind my thighs and lifted me up. One second, I was in his arms, and the next, I was lying on the bed. Moving up onto my elbows, I watched with rapt attention as he unbuttoned his dress shirt, slowly revealing tan skin and tattoos. My mouth watered as he tossed his shirt on the ground, his abs on full display.

I wanted what was under those slacks, the slacks he was sliding off his muscular legs. One of my hands moved to grab my breast, but a shake of Trevor's head stopped me. Fisting the comforter, I tried my hardest not to touch as Trevor undressed in front of me.

I was full-on panting by the time he was done. Every inch

of his body was on full display for me. All of *that* was mine. *All mine.*

The dark look on his face had my stomach fluttering. My thighs fell open as he crawled onto the bed and in between my legs. As he kissed up my stomach, in between my breasts, and up to my lips, I was done waiting.

"No foreplay, please," I groaned against his lips.

I felt his hardness in between my legs, my hips tilting up to grind against it.

"Keep those beautiful eyes on me, baby," Trevor instructed. Tugging my bottom lip between my teeth, I did as he asked.

Eyes glued to his, Trevor reached down and grabbed himself, nudging at my entrance. He waited all of a second before sliding himself completely inside of me in one motion.

My eyes threatened to roll back in my head, but Trevor's eyes dared me not to. I clamped around his length, groaning at the fullness. Trevor's own moan followed. God, it felt so good.

My legs hooked around his waist, hips up so he sunk even deeper in me. I grabbed onto his biceps as he slowly started to move.

Trevor's thrusts were slow and loving. Every one molded all my broken pieces back together. I stared into his eyes, connected in a way that was so much deeper than I could have ever imagined.

Never in my wildest dreams did I ever think I would have someone like Trevor in my life. Someone who loved me enough to give me courage to love them right back. Before Trevor, I had been hell bent on believing that I was better off alone. That keeping myself closed off was the best thing to do.

I spent years wanting the type of love others had. Years

wanting my parents to finally see me as more than just a pawn. And for the first time, I was learning that I deserved more than I let myself have.

I may not have had a great family growing up, but I had one now, composed of my favorite people. And I found the love I finally deserved.

Being with Trevor gave me the courage to love. To love him and to love myself. To accept all the broken pieces. Lying here while Trevor whispered how much he loved me made me realize that I no longer feared intimacy.

I knew I had work to do on myself, but for the first time in forever, I felt like my future wasn't as unattainable as I once thought.

36

TASHA

"Josie, help me!" Mateo yelled.

"Sorry, you're on your own." Josie called out.

"Tasha. Babe." Mateo tried again.

I looked over at Mateo as he sent me a pleading look. His dirty blond hair was darkened from sweat and stuck to his forehead.

"You asked to be included," I reminded him.

"I didn't ask to be mauled by little children!"

Beside me, Josie snorted. "You weren't mauled." She shook her head at Mateo's dramatic tone.

"They knocked my feet out from under me and then tackled me on the ice," Mateo deadpanned, looking at the two of us with narrowed eyes.

"Looked like you just tripped." I shrugged. My lips tugged up at the appalled look that took over Mateo's face.

A week ago, when we were all over at Wyatt's mom's place talking about the charity event hosted at Landon's ice rink, Mateo practically begged to be a part of it, claiming he wanted to help and be around the kids. Now it seemed he was regretting that decision.

"Guys, I can't go back out there," he whined. "I'm too young to die and too pretty."

Josie and I shared a look at the puppy dog eyes Mateo gave the two of us. Obviously, it worked as Josie sighed.

"Fine." Mateo went to cheer but Jo held up her hand. "*But*, if you have to promise to take a picture later with the guys. Multiple pictures." She sent him a look daring him to argue.

"Anything!" Leaning over the sideboard, Mateo planted a kiss on Josie's cheek before quickly skating off. The movement caught the attention of a few kids who seemed attached to Mateo.

I watched with a grin as they skated after him, yelling his name as he tried to get off the ice.

"That kid." Josie shook her head in a loving way. Even though he's in uni now he still acts like a little kid. You can't help but love him.

"Oh, by the way!" Josie turned to face me, her camera still in her hand. "We found a venue."

"Please tell me it's the Graydon Hall one." I crossed my fingers. Out of the thirty venues we'd been to—yes, thirty—Graydon Hall was my favorite. The manor slash castle exterior with brick walls and huge windows was gorgeous. The beautiful garden where the altar would be only added to those vibes. And the entire wedding party could stay there.

"It is." Josie beamed.

A little squeal left my lips.

"Thank God." Aside from loving that venue, I was tired of looking at them with Josie and Wyatt. There were only so many places you could see before they all started looking the same.

"It's really happening." The excited smile on Josie's face made my own appear. The venue had the availability they needed too. Three months to go and they'd be married.

"Still can't believe my best friend is getting married."

"Me either."

The sound of laughter drew our attention back to the ice rink filled with little kids and players from the Toronto Knights. Every year the team did a huge charity event hosted at Hockey Haven, Wyatt's older brother's rink.

The entire team came out and taught the kids how to skate and play, doing five on five games. The look on the kids' faces when they stepped inside and saw the team was adorable.

Josie was here partly for work, covering the event for Fusion magazine, but also to see her man. Just like Mila and I were. Even Lydia came, although she was claiming she was only here to make sure the magazine got what it needed. Her stopping to stare at Landon told a different story.

When my eyes landed on my own boyfriend, I smiled. Trevor was squatted down in front of a little girl, only two showed up out of the thirty that signed up. When the girl stared up at Trevor with wide eyes, I was pretty sure she was developing a crush on him. The sight was enough to make my ovaries explode.

I nudged Josie and pointed at Trevor and the girl so she could get a picture. Seeing Trevor be so cute with the kids had me picturing how he'd be with our kids. Although, that was *way* too early to start thinking about.

"How's it going, by the way, with Dr. Hauss?" Josie asked, drawing my attention away from Trevor.

"Good, actually." And I meant that.

Two months ago, after everything happened at my parent's gala, I realized I needed to stop bottling everything up. It was Trevor who suggested seeing a counselor to talk about things. At first, I was leery. A counselor seeing a counselor wasn't a good look. But one night, after Trevor had to shake me awake because I was having a nightmare, I knew I had to do something.

The next morning, I called a fellow counselor I knew that worked in the same building and made an appointment. Trevor dropped me off with an encouraging smile and a promise he'd be right here to pick me up afterward.

I learned how my own patients felt coming to me. The awkwardness at first. Not knowing what to say and how deep to go. But Dr. Hauss was amazing. She was nice and let me talk in my own time, never pushing me on a topic I didn't want to discuss.

It took about three sessions before I opened up about the assault and meeting Daniel for the first time at my parents' gala. I told her everything. Even the parts I'd never told Josie or Trevor. Told her about my parents and growing up.

It was an exhausting session, and that night I cried while Trevor held me, but I felt a sense of relief afterward. Getting it all off my chest felt freeing, like sharing it with someone eased the weight on my shoulders. Honestly, I felt better than I had in a long time.

"Have I told you how proud I am of you?"

"Yes, but I don't mind hearing it again." I shot Josie a grin as I looped my arm through hers.

I knew Jo was referring to the fact that I'd cut my parents off. They tried calling me about a month ago, but I didn't answer, and I haven't answered their texts either. Aside from what happened that night, going to my counselor really opened my eyes to how they treated me all my life.

I had always come up with excuses for how they acted. That they were just busy with work. That I needed to work harder. That I needed to do this and that to gain their approval.

I realized I shouldn't have had to do anything extra than just be myself to earn my parent's love. They were my parents, and I still loved them, but for now, distance was the best option. I needed to feel better mentally and emotionally before I talked with them. It was hard but having Trevor by my side made it easier. My girls were there for me too.

The sound of Josie's name being yelled across the ice had her squeezing my arm and heading out onto the rink. I looked around at all the kids having the time of their lives. It was so cute seeing all these big hockey players guiding and teaching them, fake falling onto the ice all dramatically.

It was so sweet they all came out to be with the kids and supported Landon's rink. Landon specifically opened this place to help the youth, to offer a safe and uplifting place for them. From what I'd heard from Josie, he was doing really well and was able to hire more people to help out and coach teams.

"Don't want to go out onto the ice?" Wyatt came up beside me, leaning his forearms against the railing as he glanced over at me.

"And show up all the guys? Nah."

"Their egos are weak anyway." We shared a grin.

"You know, I've never seen Josie this happy. She's even happier than when you first started dating," I commented, leaning against the railing beside him. The two of us were looking straight ahead at Josie as she snapped pictures of the players, grinning widely.

"She's incredible." The adoration was clear on Wyatt's face. "You and Trevor seem really happy as well." This time, my eyes moved to Trevor.

"We are."

"Do I need to have the best friend speech with you?" Asked a second later.

"Best friend speech?" I turned to him.

"The whole 'I will cut your balls off if you ever hurt my best friend' speech you gave me when I first started seeing Josie."

"That was a pretty good speech." I remarked.

"My balls say otherwise," Wyatt joked.

"But yeah, go ahead with it. See if you can top mine."

Wyatt straightened up and cleared his throat. He towered over me in his skates as I turned to lean my back against the railing, waiting.

"Trevor is my best friend, basically my brother. I see how happy you make him and how happy he makes you, but," Wyatt tried to look threatening, but I could see the smile trying to peek through, "if you hurt my best friend in any way, I will punch you in the boob."

My eyebrows raised at the last part.

"You'll punch me in my boob?"

"Yes." The two of us fought hard to keep from grinning. I knew he was trying to come close to my 'cutting off your balls' comment but punching me in the boob was a new one.

I had no plans of ever hurting Trevor, so I wasn't afraid of Wyatt's threat.

"I will keep that in mind."

"Good." He nodded like he did a good job.

"Feel better?" Wyatt mirrored my grin.

"Just had to get that out of the way. Glad we are on the same page."

"That was a good speech. I'll make sure to tell Jo you did a good job." I mean, at least he tried. It was cute.

Before he replied, Josie called out his name. With a soft shove of my shoulder, Wyatt left to go back onto the ice to see his fiancée.

For the next little bit, I stood there watching as the kids had the time of their lives on the ice. The guys started a game, passing the puck back and forth. Of course they let the kids make every shot, lifting them in the air and making them laugh.

I didn't think I could be more attracted to Trevor but watching him instruct these kids was definitely doing something to me. One night, a while back, the two of us were lying in bed when he admitted that he was scared to be a dad.

He didn't want to bring up his kids the way he had been raised. Scared that history would repeat itself. I told him then that he would be the best dad ever, and watching him right now, I knew with all my heart he would be the type of dad that put others to shame. Trevor always went above and beyond for those he loved And that would continue once he had children of his own.

"Sunshine!"

I jerked out of my thoughts as Trevor called out for me. The damn nickname still made my heart flutter.

Trevor stood out on the ice, waving me over. I was so in my head that I didn't notice the kids were slowly leaving the ice as their parents packed up to leave. Stepping out into the rink, I made my way toward my entire friend group. I should have put skates on because I stumbled a few times before Trevor grabbed my hand and tugged me into his side, our fingers laced.

"That went off without a hitch." Mila grinned, leaning against Bryton. It really did. The kids were great, and we made it through without anyone crying so I'd call that a win.

"The readers are going to love the article," Lydia agreed, looking over at Landon as she said it.

"We should go out and celebrate," Wyatt suggested.

"Oh, let's go to Rick's!" Josie added, everyone agreeing.

"And afterward, you two ladies," Mateo came up, throwing an arm around me and Josie, "can come back to my place."

"Your place?" I questioned.

"Yeah, show you what a real man is like." Mateo smirked.

"Am I not included?" Mila butted in.

"All you beautiful ladies are welcome." He winked at

everyone, including Lydia. Biting my lip, I tried my hardest not to laugh.

I loved Mateo's confidence. Plus, we all knew he was doing it to get on the guys' nerves. Judging from the look every guy was sending his way, I would say it was working.

"Mmm, think you can handle four women at once?" I leaned into Mateo's side, looking up at him from under my lashes.

"We can be a handful." Josie played along, leaning into his other side. From the corner of my eye, I saw Mila step forward, but Bryton yanked her back with a glare.

"Y-yes," Mateo stammered, looking down at us with wide eyes. Sharing a look with Josie, I peeled my hand out of Trevor's, much to his dismay.

Reaching up, I placed my hand on Mateo's chest. "Then let's go."

Before Mateo could reply, I was being grabbed around the waist and yanked backward, my back hitting Trevor's front.

"You took my woman!"

"I thought I was your woman?"Josie replied before Wyatt grabbed her as well, pulling her away from his younger brother.

"Mila," Mateo tried.

Bryton shook his head at Mateo, daring him to try and claim his girlfriend. From my spot in Trevor's arms, I watched as Mateo turned to Lydia only to find Landon standing there, arms crossed. "Not a chance, baby brother."

"Everyone knows I could steal *all* your women like that." Mateo snapped his fingers. "I have tons waiting back at uni."

"Yeah, right." Landon snorted, making Mateo narrow his eyes at him.

"Well, at least I get laid," Mateo shot back. "How long has

it been, Lan? A year? Two? Never?" He fake gasped. "Don't worry, we'll find someone to pluck your cherry."

I watched with fascination as Landon stepped toward his brother in his ice skates. Back in the day, Landon was taller than Mateo, but over the last year or so, Mateo had really grown and filled out, easily rivaling his brothers.

"What did you just say?" Landon narrowed his eyes. The taunting grin on Mateo's face showed he knew exactly what he was doing.

"No need to be ashamed that I've had sex before you." Mateo slowly started to skate backward. "Maybe I can get Ms. Howard, the librarian, to take you out."

Every word that left Mateo's mouth had Landon glaring harder, jaw clenched.

"Lydia, honey, come be with a real man." With that, the control Landon had snapped. With a powerful push off the ice, he lunged for his brother. Surprisingly, Mateo was quick on his feet and quickly skated away.

"Get back here, you little shit!" Cackling, Mateo skated away from his brother. Wyatt stared after his brothers, shaking his head.

"I give Mateo three minutes before Landon tackles him to the ice," Bryton said.

"I give it two." Wyatt commented.

As the others started going back and forth about Landon and Mateo, I felt Trevor backing up. Turning me in his hold, Trevor grabbed me from behind my thighs and hoisted me up. My legs wrapped around his waist, my arms around his neck.

Behind us, Mateo yelled something at Wyatt, followed by, "You are asking for it." Without looking, I already knew Wyatt was also chasing Mateo around the ice.

Ignoring the chaos behind us, Trevor started skating with me in his arms. I grinned down at him, my fingers playing with his dark hair. I felt like I was floating as he effortlessly carried me across the ice. Of course he didn't seem fazed at the extra weight in his arms.

"What?" I questioned, at the weird look on his face.

"Move in with me."

My eyes widened. Move in with him? We'd only been dating for four months. Wasn't that too soon? As soon as that thought popped into my head, it disappeared. Yes, we'd only been dating a few months but this was it. Trevor was my person.

I couldn't see myself with anyone else. He had become ingrained in my soul. I was always at his place anyway. In the last two months, we stayed at mine only a handful of times. His entire bathroom was littered with my belongings, and I even had clothes there. It really wouldn't be all that different.

Trevor remained silent, a crease appearing between his eyebrows, worry filling his eyes. How could I say no to waking up with this man every morning?

Bringing my hand up, I cupped the side of his face. "I'd love to move in with you."

His grin almost split his face in two. Those green eyes sparkled with nothing but love. I dipped my head and captured his lips with mine as the two of us moved across the ice.

Trevor was my home. He was the person I'd been searching for my whole life and now that he was mine, I wasn't ever letting go.

37

TREVOR

God, she was perfect. That was all that came to mind as I laid there watching Tasha sleep. Her blonde hair slipped out of the bun she put it in earlier, strands falling across her face. She was curled up against my chest, legs draped around my waist.

When Tasha slept, she turned into a koala bear. She literally became so clingy it was adorable. If I so much as tried to move, she would cling to me tighter and would groan deep in her sleep. Which was why I was currently still lying here, arm numb from her lying on it.

It was still a bit surreal that Tasha was all mine. Sometimes, I couldn't help but think I'd imagined it all, and that I'd wake up and find Tasha gone. She may have only moved in a week ago, but it was as if she always lived with me. While it may have been a little bit soon to move in together, it felt right.

Everything felt right with her here in my bed where she belonged. Even her stuffed turtle from Australia fit on the bedside table.

With the urge to get as close to her as humanly possible, I

slowly lifted her leg off of me and gently twisted her to lie on her back. With her off of me, I was able to sit up and admire her from a different angle. The tempting thoughts racing through my mind brought a smirk to my face.

Peeling back the covers, I slid down the bed. I kept my eyes on Tasha to see if she'd wake up before I got into position. She didn't so much as stir as I moved to my favorite place in the world—in between her thighs.

She was still naked from last night, which made this even easier for me. I needed to taste her more than I needed oxygen.

Without wasting another second, I grabbed her thighs and spread her open. The sight before me was more glorious than anything I'd ever seen, and that included holding the Cup Championship trophy. I could've died a happy man right then. My grip tightened as I trailed my nose along her inner thighs.

I felt Tasha start to move under me and smirked. She wasn't awake yet but she was about to be. Unable to hold back anymore, I ran my tongue along her slit, groaning low in my throat at the taste of her.

Flattening my tongue, I licked the entire length of her pussy, my cock already hard in my boxers. The taste of her was the most addictive thing on the entire planet.

With each swipe of my tongue, I could feel Tasha starting to wake up. Her hips moved slightly and her breathing got heavier. When a moan escaped her lips, I smiled against her sensitive flesh. The noises she made went straight to cock, making it even harder.

Looking up, I met the eyes of a sleepy Tasha. Bringing my arms up, I hooked them around her thighs and hips, keeping her in place. With my eyes locked on her, I picked up pace, watching as she started to squirm in my hold.

Fingers threaded through my hair as Tasha's moans filled

the room. If only I could record that sound and play it every day. Moving a hand, I brought it up to play with one of her nipples. With just enough pressure, I pinched it between my two fingers, earning a low groan from Tasha. Her fingers in my hair tightened.

When she laid her head back, those beautiful eyes leaving mine, I pulled my mouth away and lightly tapped her pussy. I smirked as she jolted up. Now she was definitely awake. Tasha tried to bring her legs together, but I easily kept them open with one hand.

"Eyes on me."

When she didn't say anything in response, I did it again. The sadistic part of me loved the sound that left her lips. I knew it didn't hurt as she was practically dripping. The way she was looking at me made me want to slide myself deep inside of her, but I had other plans.

"Touch yourself for me."

Tasha's eyes widened at my words.

"I... Um.." I could see the hesitation on her face. One thing about Tasha was she had a hard time letting go. Of letting herself be vulnerable in front of people, especially during sex. She was slowly opening up, but I didn't want her hesitating when it came to me.

Reaching forward, I gently ran the tips of my fingers down her slit, feeling her wetness. Moving so I was leaning over her slightly, I peered down at her.

"Do you trust me?" I tried to keep my voice light, but it was impossible with how turned on I was.

"Yes," she instantly replied. My fingers softly circled her clit, resulting in a gasp that made my cock throb.

"Then touch yourself for me." Her eyes darted from mine down to what my fingers were doing between her thighs. With each breath, her nipples brushed across my bare chest.

Keeping her eyes glued to mine, Tasha brought a hand

down between our bodies and touched mine. Knowing she was still a bit nervous, I hooked my finger against hers and slowly moved it.

She could feel the difference in our fingers as we both rubbed her. Mine were more rough and calloused, while hers were softer. Using my knees, I kept her spread open as I hovered above her. I would wait until she was more comfortable before I sat back and watched.

Still seeing her shoulders tensed, I dipped my head down and placed kisses along her collarbone, the skin beneath my lips soft and smooth. I felt the sudden urge to mark her, littering her skin with bite marks and hickeys. I couldn't even remember the last time I gave a woman one of those.

With both my mouth and our fingers, Tasha relaxed back into the bed. The wetness dripping over my fingers showed me she was more than turned on. Pulling away, I let her touch herself.

I kissed all over her chest, taking her nipple into my mouth, swirling my tongue around the tight bud before moving to the next one. Giving them enough attention, I moved back onto my heels, watching her.

There was something so erotic about sitting there at the end of the bed, still clad in my boxers, while Tasha was completely naked, squirming against the bed with her hand between her thighs. Her face was flushed, and her eyes clouded over. Fuck, she was gorgeous. *And all mine.*

"That's it, baby," I praised.

My eyes were glued to her fingers as my own rubbed my hard-on through my underwear, groaning low in my throat. I had to physically stop myself from touching her. Watching her touch herself was going to be my undoing.

Tasha's eyes flicked from my face down to my crotch. The outline of my hard length was clear as day.

"Take them off, please," Tasha begged. I didn't need to be

asked twice. I wasn't exactly graceful as I tugged them off and threw them onto the floor. The only reason I had them on in the first place was so I could sleep against Tasha without my dick begging to be inside of her. I needed a little bit of a barrier if we were going to get any sleep.

With her eyes on me, I grabbed myself and stroked from base to tip. She bit her lip as she watched me touch myself. I never actually did something like this before. I always made sure the girl was having a good time, giving me at least two orgasms, before finding my own pleasure. But sitting here stroking myself in front of someone was a level of vulnerability I rarely showed. Something Tasha and I were learning to be with each other.

"Do you like watching me, baby?"

"Yes," she moaned, matching the same pace as me.

My moans seemed to give her confidence. Spreading her legs even wider, Tasha dipped her fingers inside herself. I was now regretting making her touch herself instead of doing it myself.

With hooded eyes and a smirk on her face, Tasha fingered her pussy, knowing exactly what she was doing. The tables turned. Not that I minded. While I did like being in charge and bending Tasha to my will, it was incredibly sexy seeing her take what she wanted.

I was fully hers. She could have whatever she pleased.

I let her have a few minutes of control, stroking myself to the same rhythm and pace she set. Every second that passed, my control got closer to snapping. I could tell Tasha was about to come as a beautiful red blush crept across her chest and neck. Her legs started to shake, and her moans were getting louder and louder.

I squeezed myself tightly with my fist so I wouldn't come. Not yet. I needed to be inside her when I did that.

"Trevor!" My name on her lips was music to my ears. As

Tasha came right before my eyes, the leash I had on myself unclipped. I slid back between her legs.

Grabbing the back of her thighs, I yanked her hips upward so only her upper body was still on the bed. A second later, I slammed my length inside of her. Tasha cried out, hands moving to grip the bedsheets.

I didn't give her a second of reprieve as I slammed into her like a madman. The sound of our skin slapping echoed around the room. The feel of her wrapped around me was enough to almost make me explode.

The two of us were like animals as Tasha wrapped her legs around my waist, pulling me impossibly closer. With one hand on her hips, keeping her up on an angle, I brought my other hand down to wrap around her throat.

The look on her face as I added a little bit of pressure had me groaning. She really was made for me.

"Look how beautiful you are taking all of me." I felt her clench around me. *Fuck.*

Using her legs, she moved her hips up and down on me. She was so fucking wet and tight.

"I... I need..." Tasha couldn't get the words out. Grinning, I leaned forward, getting closer to her face as I gripped her throat.

"Beg me."

"I..."

"You can do it, baby. Beg."

"Trevor," she whined. Not hearing what I wanted, I slammed forward and stopped. Her eyes pleaded with mine.

"Say what I want to hear." She was grinding her hips down, trying to find friction, but it wasn't enough to finish her off. "Tasha," I warned, my voice deep.

"Let me come. Please, Trevor. I need to come," she begged.

That was my girl.

"Good girl."

I made her wait another second before I pulled back and thrusted forward. Gritting my teeth, I fucked her as hard and as deep as I could. I could tell Tasha was so close as she quivered underneath me. Needing to see her come, I brought my hand down and thumbed her clit.

Not even a minute later, Tasha let out a loud yell as she came. She clenched so tight around me I had no other choice than to come as well. My own moans mixed with hers as my entire body tensed and released.

Tasha collapsed onto the bed, breathing heavily with her eyes closed. I eased myself down onto her, doing my best not to press too hard, but somehow, she still had the strength to pull me all the way down with her legs.

We were both slick with sweat, but after what we just did, neither of us cared. Not when I was still seated inside of her.

I panted against her neck as I came down from my high. Goddamn. Once I had my breathing under control, I gently pulled out of her and laid on my side.

"Well, that's a way to be woken up," she murmured a minute later. I chuckled as she laid there spread out.

"You okay?" I ran a finger across her stomach.

"More than okay." She turned her head to face me, a content grin on her face. I felt my own grow.

Man, I loved this woman.

"Want to take a shower?" I asked.

Tasha licked her lips and made a show of looking me up and down, pausing on my cock before coming back up to my face.

"Wash me, and I'll wash you?" she said with a wicked gleam in her eyes. Who was I to say no to this beautiful woman?

In one motion, I jumped off the bed, reached down, and yanked Tasha up and over my shoulder. She let out a squeal as I walked us quickly to the bathroom. I landed a smack on her ass with a grin. In return, she cracked my own ass before squeezing it.

"Nice and squishy."

A smirk grew on my face as I shook my head. Oh, she was going to pay for that comment.

38

TASHA

"**Y**ou made us late." I scolded Trevor.

"No, I didn't. You weren't even dressed." Trevor said.

"Because you kept trying to take my clothes off!

I sent him a look to which he shrugged. "It's not my fault you look good in everything."

I rolled my eyes at Trevor's comment, but a smile tugged at my lips. He really was the reason we were late for our date night but comments like that made it hard for me to be upset. Not that I could be when I had two earth-shattering orgasms before we left.

"You're insatiable."

"And you love it." Leaning down, Trevor kissed the top of my head. The action made my heart skip a beat. We'd been together for four months, and every time he did something like that, it filled my stomach with butterflies. There wasn't a day that went by that I didn't fall more in love with this man.

"Yeah, yeah." I shoved him as he opened the door for me to Landon's rink, Hockey Haven. "You're a chronic flirt."

"Only with you." Trevor smacked my ass as I walked in front of him. I couldn't fight the grin any longer.

"There you are," Josie called out as we came out by the ice rink. "We thought you two weren't going to show."

As Trevor went to greet Wyatt, Bryton, and Landon, I made my way over to my girls. Josie, Mila, and Lydia were sharing a grin as I approached. Over the last couple of months, Trevor and I had been known for showing up late because of...reasons. Something our friends teased us about endlessly.

"Blame Trevor," was all I said.

"Uh-huh." Josie just smirked.

"Are you guys ready to lose?" Bryton called out to us as the guys moved toward the benches.

"We are so going to kick their asses," Josie muttered, glaring over at her fiancé.

A week ago, while we were all having dinner together, the guys made a comment about how us girls couldn't win a hockey game against them. Not the smartest thing to say in front of four very independent women. Next thing I knew, we were agreeing to play a small game against the guys. Now here we are about to play a game.

I wasn't hopeful that we would win. I mean, hello, we weren't the best skaters. Lydia could barely stand up on skates, so going against four professional hockey players... We didn't stand a chance. Even though Landon wasn't in the NHL like the others, he played at university and owned a rink for crying out loud.

So yeah, I wasn't that hopeful we'd win, but I wasn't going to say that out loud. Not with the determined looks on Josie and Mila's faces. Lydia sent me a wide-eyed look. She tried to get out of doing this, but without her, we'd be down a person. There may have been other motives involved as well.

We all saw how she acted around Landon. We weren't sure if something happened in Australia, but they'd been keeping their distance ever since. So, Jo has made it her mission to force them together at every opportunity. This being one of them. Didn't help the bets in Bang Bet Club group chat were getting closer to the timeline people had.

"We got this," I whispered, linking my arm with hers. The look she sent me said otherwise.

When we approached the benches, where Landon already had the skates and sticks ready, I let Lydia take the spot next to Landon. He could help her with the skates. With a smirk in her direction, I went to sit next to my boyfriend.

By the time I sat down and took off my shoes, Trevor already had his skates on and was ready to go. I leaned down to grab my own skate, but before I could, it was yanked out of my reach. I bit my lip as Trevor squatted down in front of me.

My mind flashed back to our first real date when he did the same thing for me. I knew how to lace up my skate, but if he wanted to do it, who was I to say no? Plus, he looked hot kneeling in front of me.

"I'll try and take it easy on you," Trevor said as he lifted my ankle to slide the ice skate on.

"You don't need to take it easy on me." I peered down at him. "If I remember correctly, I out-skated you last time."

"You're cute thinking that." Trevor looked up at me with a smirk. His fingertips stroked the skin of my ankle, trying to distract me.

"Well, when we win, I expect a lot of groveling." I stuck my chin up.

"Hmm." Trevor moved onto my next foot, making quick work of gearing me up. "When we win," he lowered his voice to a whisper, "you'll be the one on their knees." That gleam in his eyes said he fully expected me to lose.

I tried my hardest not to show that his words affected me. Damn him and his sexy ass voice. He knew how to play me like a fiddle. But despite not minding that consequence, I wasn't planning on letting him win. No, he was going to be the one on his knees.

With more determination to succeed, I leaned forward, my hand reaching out to grab his chin. The scruff on his face tickled my fingers. I stopped inches from his lips.

"You're going to look so good on your knees later," I whispered. My lips barely grazed his before pulling back. With a smirk of my own, I twisted on the bench and stood up, leaving Trevor squatting there, staring up at me.

"Good luck, babe." Sending him a wink, I walked off as best as I could in skates. Behind me, I heard him mutter something, making me feel even more smug.

I made my way to the ice, needing a few laps to get used to the skates again. If we had any chance of winning, I was definitely going to need these few minutes on the ice. I was a little shaky at first as I got my footing, but in no time, I was doing a lap around the rink.

By the time I came back around, Josie was also on the ice. Wyatt teaching her to skate has definitely paid off. She looked like a natural. Maybe we had a chance.

"We have to beat them," she said the moment she skated to my side. I was in full agreement. We weren't going to let the guys win and hold it over us.

"We may have to play a bit dirty."

"How dirty?" Mila came up from behind us. Her skating wasn't the worst, but she wasn't that good either. I grinned at her eager tone.

"We're going up against four huge guys that will easily overpower us." My mind came up with some ideas. "We just need to distract them or play on their love for us."

"I like where you're going with this." Mila smirked, rubbing her hands together.

"I have some good ideas." Josie grinned mischievously. My eyes found Lydia as she stumbled onto the ice, holding on to the side of the rink with a death grip. We were going to need all the help we could get.

Not even a second later, all four guys skated onto the ice flawlessly.

Yep, we were royally fucked.

AFTER GOING over the rules on what we could and couldn't do, we were ready to play. The guys were definitely taking it easy on us. There would be no shoving or pushing against the boards. In Trevor's words, "We'll gently take the puck from you guys." His words only added fuel to the fire between us girls.

"Don't hurt yourself, blondie." Landon smirked over at Lydia as she wobbled on her skates. She finally made it out onto the ice without falling, although that was bound to change.

"You worry about yourself over there." Lydia's words held no bite to them, though, not as she struggled to stay upright. The only reason she was on the ice right now was to prove Landon wrong. His taunting about her sitting on the side- lines to watch only made her want to play that much more. I was pretty sure Landon did it on purpose.

"Okay, line up," Bryton called out.

I moved to stand in front of Trevor. He easily towered over me in his skates, but at least he wasn't wearing his hockey gear. He'd be even more intimidating if he was. Hell, he was already intimidating dressed in a pair of jeans and a Toronto Knights long-sleeve shirt. It matched the Knights sweatshirt I was currently wearing, courtesy of Trevor's closet.

As I stared him down, the others got in position around us. Josie against Wyatt. Mila against Bryton. And Lydia against Landon. The puck was right in front of Josie and Wyatt as we all squared off.

"That cute ass is mine." Trevor grinned.

"That's if you can catch me." I grinned back.

"Oh, I will," he promised.

Determined to beat Trevor, I leaned forward into my stick as Wyatt counted down. As soon as he hit one, everyone lunged forward. I looked away from Trevor, trying to find the puck. Somehow, Josie got it and was skating away from Wyatt.

I pushed off the ice toward her as her fiancé got right on her ass.

"Jo." I gestured for her to pass me the puck. The pass wasn't pretty and it slid right past me, but I managed to snag it before any of the guys could.

While I wasn't the worst skater, I was nowhere near on the same level as the guys. That was made very clear as Bryton skated in front of me, cutting me off. To avoid running into him, I skidded to a stop, sending ice everywhere. In turn, the puck slid right into Bryton's waiting hockey stick.

With ease only he and the others had, he skated toward the net and easily made a goal. Mila and Lydia weren't close enough to help. Well, shit.

Since the guys scored, it was now our puck. I remembered what Trevor taught me about keeping the puck close so I didn't lose control of it. It was surprisingly hard to keep an eye on the puck and yet look ahead so I didn't run into anyone. Damn, the guys really made this look easy.

I was skating the best I could as Trevor came up beside me. From the corner of my eye, I noticed he was barely pushing off the ice, just casually skating while I was trying my hardest to keep the puck in front of me.

"You good?" I didn't miss the taunting tone in his voice.

"Don't you even start." I pushed off the ice a little harder, hoping to get to the net. It didn't go unnoticed that Trevor was the only one guarding me, the others somewhere behind me. The net was wide open, but it was clear Trevor thought he could easily take the puck from me without much effort.

Well, I was going to show him.

"I'm not doing anything." I didn't have to look at him to know he was smirking.

As I closed in on the net, Trevor got closer, his stick slowly moving in front of mine. *Not gonna happen.* Before he could take the puck, I slammed to a stop, using my toe pick to move around him. A move I'd seen him do during games.

My move took him by surprise and gave me enough time to bring my hockey stick back and slap the puck into the net. A yell left my lips as I threw my hands up. I made a goal! The girls cheered.

Turning to face Trevor, I sent him a smug grin. "Suck it."

I skated away feeling like a complete badass. It was only one goal, but I managed to score on The Beast aka Trevor Hall.

My goal seemed to hype the girls up as we all lined up together. We'd only been playing for five minutes, but we all were starting to have a little hope we could win.

WE HAD no chance of winning.

Twenty minutes later, the guys made ten goals and we only made three. It was Josie and I leading our team at this point. Mila was too busy holding onto Lydia or trying to distract her boyfriend. Not that it helped much.

Lydia spent more time falling on the ice or clinging to the nearest person. Half the time, it was Landon she kept clutched close to her. So in a way, it helped get Landon out of the way but that left three other professional hockey players to keep up with.

So, the last five minutes Josie and I resorted to extreme measures.

"Tasha."

"Hmm," I hummed against Trevor's back, my arms wrapped tightly around his waist.

"What are you doing?"

Honestly, I wasn't even sure at this point. My idea of trying to hold Trevor back as he skated wasn't working out so well. He was twice my size and skated forward like my hold on him did nothing. I was trying to dig my skates into the ice but it made no difference.

"Stopping you."

Looking to the side, I saw Josie clinging to Wyatt's back as he skated. Her tactic was not working either.

Trevor's stomach flexed under my fingers as he chuckled. "Well, it's working like a charm."

"Come on. You have to let us score," I pleaded.

"Come take the puck from me then." He taunted.

"You're too big."

"We aren't talking about my dick, Sunshine."

I snorted at his comment. "It's not fair. What happened to taking it easy on us?" I whined.

"We are."

That's how awful we were at hockey.

As I clung to Trevor, he sent the puck to Wyatt, who was also unfazed with Josie on his back. I could do nothing but watch as he sent it into the net once more. 11-3.

"You guys are the worst," I muttered against his back.

"You guys can always call it." His words had me letting him go.

"Never." I shook my head. It wasn't gonna happen.

"We won't hold it against you." The twinkle in his eye said otherwise. No, the guys would hold this over our heads until the end of time.

"Team meeting!" I called out, narrowing my eyes at my boyfriend. "Just you wait and see."

With another chuckle and a shake of his head, Trevor went over to the guys as I got together with the girls.

"This is going great," Lydia said sarcastically.

Beside me, Josie pulled out her phone, rapidly typing on it.

"What are you doing?" I asked, raising an eyebrow.

"I'm calling in reinforcements." Jo looked at the three of us with a smirk. "Do you two mind sitting out the rest of the game?" she asked Mila and Lydia.

"God, no," Lydia answered immediately.

"My legs are exhausted," Mila added. The two were more than eager to get off the ice.

I looked at my best friend, wondering what she had planned. She sent me a look as her phone pinged with a text. She flashed me what it said. Seeing what was on the screen, I felt my own smirk growing. My best friend was an evil genius.

"We need a bathroom break!" Josie yelled out.

"Calling it quits?" Wyatt yelled back.

"In your dreams!" She shot back.

Mila and Lydia made their way off the ice, clinging to one

another. We really didn't think it through having them two on our team, but at least they tried.

As the two of us skated past the guys to get off the ice, they looked at us with smug expressions. They really thought we were done. I couldn't wait to see their faces in a few minutes.

39

TASHA

"**Y**ou sure you girls want to keep playing? It's okay if you want to quit." Wyatt said, leaning on his hockey stick.

"We're fine if you want to stop. No shame." Trevor added.

Josie and I shared an eye roll.

"We want to keep playing," I answered.

"Lydia and Mila aren't playing?" Landon looked at the two who were sitting on the bench next to us, happily munching on some snacks. Snacks I had no clue where they got.

"They're gonna sit this round out." Josie shrugged like it was no big deal. All four guys stared at us with surprised looks.

"Um, are you sure about that?" Bryton looked skeptical.

"Yep." Jo and I were stalling, waiting for our reinforcement to get here.

"Maybe we should—" Wyatt was cut off by a new voice.

"The help is here!" yelled our backup.

Mateo.

Mateo came up and wrapped his arms around Josie and I's shoulders. The two of us smirked up at the guys, enjoying the surprised looks on their faces.

"What are you doing here?" Wyatt asked his younger brother.

"My girls called, so I came."

It worked in our favor that Mateo was just around the corner and seemed more than happy to assist us.

"You can't have five players," Landon pointed out.

"We aren't. Mateo is taking Mila and Lydia's spots." He was better than them both combined. He was set to follow in his brother's footsteps of playing hockey before settling on football instead, so he was exactly what we needed.

"Is that a problem?" I asked, tilting my head to the side. The four guys in front of us looked at one another, having a silent conversation but shrugging.

"That's fine with us. We're still going to win." Wyatt looked at his brother with a confident grin.

"Skates are over by the counter." Landon gestured. When Mateo walked off to change into his skates, the guys turned to us.

"This is cheating." Trevor crossed his arms over his chest.

"You guys never said it had to only be us girls," Josie shot back, crossing her arms as well.

"Mateo practically is one of the girls." My lips twitched at my words. And he was... He just happened to grow a beard and have a dick. "Plus, it's three against four, so it's an advantage for you guys."

They shrugged. Professional hockey players and their egos. Trevor shot me a grin before they all turned and headed back to the ice. At least with Mateo we actually stood a chance.

Mateo came up behind us. "Okay, what's the plan, babes?"

"So, it's eleven to three." Josie said.

"Okay, not horrible."

"Lydia and Mila were no help," I supplied.

"Hey!" the two called out, having heard us.

"It's true," Josie shot back. "So, we need you to help us come back."

"We aren't horrible," I added. Josie and I weren't the worst, but not the best.

"Don't worry, I'll defend your honor." Mateo flexed his arms.

"Good. We need to win." Josie patted his chest. "Then we can hold it over their heads until the end of time."

"I like the sound of that." Mateo nodded. "Let's kick some ass, then afterward, we can go on that date." With a wink at Josie and me, he went for the ice. We shared a head shake. Mateo was never going to stop asking for a date. But hey, if he helped us win, I would consider it.

Grabbing our sticks, the two of us stepped onto the ice. With our little 'break,' I was ready to play again. Although, my legs were going to be so sore tomorrow.

As I passed by Trevor, I felt something hit my ass, making me whirl to face him. He held his hockey stick with a smug look. *Don't fall for it, Tasha. Don't do it.* My boyfriend might've been sexy as hell, but we were currently enemies.

Without saying a word, I skated over to Mateo and Josie. Exchanging determined looks, we lined up with the puck in front of us. I was more than happy to wipe the smug looks off the guys' faces.

As soon as Wyatt counted down to one, we were off.

Mateo was good. Like really good. He easily slid up to Bryton and Landon, skating between them with grace. I was curious as to why he chose football over hockey when he clearly was great at it.

"Tash." I barely had time to look over in his direction before he passed me the puck. He sent it with such speed all I could do was put my stick out and hope it didn't slide right by into Trevor's.

Somehow, the puck hit my stick and came to a stop in

414

front of me. My body reacted automatically by bringing my arm back and hitting it. The puck flew into the net.

"Hell yes!" Mateo yelled, pumping his fist in the air.

I finally understood why the guys celebrated when they scored a goal. I wasn't even playing in a real game or with tons of people watching, but damn, I felt like I was on top of the world.

Smacking hands with Mateo, I grinned widely, turning to face my boyfriend once again. He was trying to hide his smile, but I saw the way his lips twitched. I sent him a wink before the guys were in motion again.

We really weren't playing hockey the right way. After each goal, we'd get repositioned, but if we let the guys immediately take the puck, we'd get annihilated.

Deciding to use another tactic to make sure Trevor didn't get the puck, I came up to his side. Using my shoulder, I rammed into him, hoping he'd stumble to the side. Of course, that backfired. The guy was built like a freight train. It was like hitting a brick wall.

"Did you just shoulder check me?" He skated to a stop and looked down at me with a raised eyebrow.

"Yes. And?" I crossed my arms, trying my hardest to look threatening. From the amused look on his face, it wasn't working.

"I thought we said no physical contact."

"What are you gonna do about it?" I should have known better than to provoke him. I never learned. One second, I was standing there, and the next, I was hauled over Trevor's shoulder. It dug into my stomach as my hockey stick fell to the ice.

"Trevor!" I gripped the back of his shirt as he started skating. How the hell he could skate with me over his shoulder, I'd never know. He acted like I weighed nothing.

"Bry!" he called out. I lifted up slightly to see Bryton

glance over and hit the puck to Trevor, who easily grabbed it and skated toward the net.

"You can't score!"

"What are you gonna do about it?" he shot my words back at me. All I could do was glare. I couldn't exactly stop him while he carried me over his shoulder like a sack of potatoes.

Reaching down, I grabbed his ass as he shot the puck into the net.

"Grab all you want, Sunshine. It's not going to help."

Grunting, I rolled my eyes. Yeah, yeah, whatever.

"Tasha!" Josie yelled my name.

"He started it!" I yelled back.

"Trevor put her down!"

"Damn, there's her mom voice," Trevor muttered but did as she asked, carefully setting me back on my feet.

"Never mess with Josie's mom voice." Trust me, I'd been on the receiving end of it multiple times.

"She's scary," he whispered, moving past me. I one hundred percent agreed.

"We're only down by a couple. We got this, guys," Mateo cheered us on.

"Where's my trophy?"

"I want a medal."

"Oh, yes, I like that idea."

I smirked from where I was sitting at our table as my friends listed off things they wanted. Somehow, I wasn't sure how the girls—and Mateo—won. We beat Wyatt, Trevor, Bryton, and Landon by three.

The said four were currently glaring at the rest of us with

416

their arms crossed. They really didn't think we'd win, yet we did. What made it all the more hilarious was Lydia and Mila including themselves in the win even though they did nothing to help. They were our sideline cheerleaders so it counted.

The fact that me, Josie, and Mateo managed to beat three professional hockey players and Landon was mind blowing. I came into today thinking we had no chance. Before Mateo we didn't. But now here we were.

I was going to love bringing this up every other day. From the way Josie grinned at her fiancé, I knew she was never going to let him live it down. I mean, who could say they beat NHL players? They did this for a *living*.

To celebrate, we all went out to eat and to brag about our win.

"I'll be cashing in my prize later," I spoke softly so only Trevor could hear me. His hand on my thigh tightened as he leaned in, his breath tickling the shell of my ear.

"Love the thought of me on my knees, don't you?"

"Maybe." I smirked. The others down the table were too busy talking to care what Trevor and I were whispering about.

"You cheated so I don't think it counts." Trevor trailed his lips against my ear, sending shivers down my spine.

"We won fair and square." My breath hitched in my throat. "But if you ask nicely."

"Ask nicely for what?" His hand inched slowly upward. The tablecloth hid what he was doing, but I couldn't help but glance over at our friends to make sure they weren't looking at us.

"I..." I trailed off when his fingers grazed the sensitive skin at the top of my thigh. "I'll get on my knees," I finished.

"Hmm," he hummed. "You know, if losing means I get to have your legs on my shoulders, I don't think I mind."

Fuck.

I was more than tempted to call it a night and head home but our food hadn't even arrived yet. Trevor and his damn teasing. Of all places to whisper dirty things in my ear.

"I'll take my loss if..." He trailed off, those damn fingertips grazing the seam of my leggings.

"If?" My hips shifted down to try and get more pressure between my thighs.

"If you wear my jersey while I fuck you."

I couldn't stop the gasp from escaping my lips. Thank God it was loud in here and no one seemed to hear it. I nodded eagerly.

"Good girl."

Before he could say more, the waitress came by with everyone's food. A soft whine left my mouth when he pulled his hand away, which just made him chuckle.

"But know," Trevor whispered one last time, "you'll pay for cheating."

With that, he turned to his plate, casually striking up a conversation with Wyatt. My lips curled slightly as I picked up my fork, my fingers lingering on the cool metal a moment longer than necessary. A sense of warmth and contentment filled me as I thought about the future, the promise of what was to come igniting a quiet excitement within me. I couldn't wait to see what was in store.

BOOK THREE

Follow Lydia and Landon's Story
Coming late 2025

ACKNOWLEDGMENTS

Firstly, thank you every person who has supported my writing. Thank you for taking a chance on this little indie author. Every kind word, every kind review, has meant more than you'll ever know. So thank you from the bottom of my heart.

Thank you to Tasha. Thank you for letting me send you hours of voice notes talking about this book. Giving me advice and helping me just rant about the plot and the characters.

Thank you to Lauren. You've had to put up with me for years now and you are now stuck. Thank you for letting me talk your ear off every day about everything and nothing. Love ya.

Thank you to my girl group chat. Lauren, Jordan, SJ, and Jessica. You guys are the greatest. It's not everyday you meet a group of women that can uplift each other the way we do. And thank you for your endless support, help, and love.

HUGE thank you to Sara. Without you this book wouldn't be possible. You took this manuscript on without single hesitation when I needed help and you've made this book 100x better than I could have dreamed. So thank you so much.

Thank you to my mom. Thank you for letting me live my dream of being an author. For always being there to support me whenever I need it.

Love you all!

ABOUT THE AUTHOR

Kenadee Bryant is a new adult author of steamy romance, and currently lives in Nevada with her two dogs and cat. When not writing, you can find her reading, playing board games, or eating peanut butter cups. Alongside writing, Kenadee would love to one day open an animal sanctuary.

𝕏 ⓘ ⓢ 🄶

31124068R00256